# PAINTED
# LADIES

Previous novel by James Neal Harvey:
*By Reason of Insanity*

# PAINTED LADIES

## JAMES NEAL HARVEY

ST. MARTIN'S PRESS   NEW YORK

This book is for my mother,
Eunice Neal Harvey,
with much love.

This novel is a work of fiction. All of the events, characters, names and places depicted in this novel are entirely fictitious or are used fictitiously. No representation that any statement made in this novel is true or that any incident depicted in this novel actually occurred is intended or should be inferred by the reader.

PAINTED LADIES. Copyright © 1992 by James Neal Harvey. All rights reserved. Printed in the United States of America. No part of this book may be used or reproduced in any manner whatsoever without written permission except in the case of brief quotations embodied in critical articles or reviews. For information, address St. Martin's Press, 175 Fifth Avenue, New York, N.Y. 10010.

Design by Glen M. Edelstein

Library of Congress Cataloging-in-Publication Data

Harvey, James Neal.
    Painted ladies / James Neal Harvey.
        p.   cm.
    "A Thomas Dunne book."
    ISBN 0-312-07056-X
    I. Title.
PS3558.A7183P35   1992
813'.54—dc20                                                                91-37230
                                                                           CIP

First Edition: March 1992

10 9 8 7 6 5 4 3 2 1

# 1

Caroline Henderson left her apartment at 7:15 P.M., wearing a new blue dress, her best pearls, and her gray coat with the mink collar. A black felt hat was tilted at just the right angle over her blond hair, giving a casual, jaunty look. She carried a Saks Fifth Avenue shopping bag and a black alligator purse. Excitement coursed through her like an electric current.

She walked west two blocks, crossing Park and going on to the corner of Fifth and Seventy-third, where she caught a taxi. She told the driver to take her to the Plaza, then settled back on the seat, thinking about what the evening would bring.

His name was John Burton and he was from Los Angeles, Martha had said. In a suite at the Plaza, so he had to be loaded. Martha hadn't spoken with him; his assistant had made the date. Which was a new one for Caroline, but it seemed rather sophisticated. She could picture a handsome executive sitting in some vast office in Beverly Hills, telling the assistant to book him to New York on the morning United or American and to put him in the usual suite.

Or maybe he had his own jet. A Lear, or even a Gulfstream. Tell the pilots to be ready for takeoff by nine, he'd say. Also he'd want a table at La Grenouille that evening. And oh, yes—call Panache and tell them to send over one of their best girls, a blonde, of course. Someone really special.

In her mind's eye, he was tall and dark-haired, with a quiet, confident manner, sort of a Harrison Ford type but a little older.

He'd be wearing an oxford gray pinstripe with a red Mizrahi tie. Or maybe not so formal, since he was from L.A. Maybe a cashmere jacket and a pale blue shirt, to set off his tan. Everybody from California had a tan.

He'd be smitten from the moment he looked at her, seeing at once that she was not only beautiful but a real lady. They'd chat for a bit over a drink, getting to know each other, and when they went to dinner, he'd relish the way men—and women, too—stared at her in the restaurant.

They'd talk about a wide range of subjects, and he'd be surprised and pleased that there was almost nothing she couldn't discuss. Politics, theater, art, and especially travel: why the Plaza Athénée was the best hotel in Paris, how Marbella was much too crowded in August, why you went to Gstaad in March for great skiing. They'd drink Dom Perignon and she'd laugh delightedly at his jokes and be intensely interested in everything he had to say. At some point, their hands would touch, and her knee would brush his, and by the time they got back to the hotel, he'd be so hungry for her that he'd be practically panting.

Then he'd watch as she undressed, his eyes locked on her as she removed her clothes slowly and gracefully, not knowing she'd turned that simple procedure into an art form. He'd love the peach-colored lingerie trimmed with white lace, and the garter belt with real stockings and not panty hose. She didn't know why, but there was something about a garter belt that really turned men on. Sometimes they even wanted her to leave it on when everything else was off.

Jesus, just thinking about it was making her hot; she could feel the heat and the dampness between her legs. Take it *easy,* she said to herself, you've got a whole lovely evening ahead of you. And besides, maybe he's seventy years old and bald and you'll have to spend all evening helping him try to get it up. It'd serve you right, you idiot.

The taxi drew up to the east entrance, just opposite Grand Army Plaza, from which the hotel got its name. Caroline paid the fare and tipped the driver extra, for luck. When she got out, she looked over at the shimmering spray of water rising from the Pulitzer Fountain, and at the gilded statue of General Sherman. Couples were strolling on the sidewalk, enjoying the mild October evening.

Autumn in New York. Sinatra knew what he was singing about, didn't he? Caroline took a deep breath, again experiencing a surge of excitement, and walked up the steps and into the hotel.

As usual, the place was bustling. Early diners occupied tables in the Palm Court and the Edwardian Room, and the lobby was thronged with good-looking, well-dressed people. The women all wore expensive jewelry and most of the men were smartly tailored. She recognized silks and handbags and luggage and shoes and suits by their makers' names: Hermès, Jourdan, Gucci, Caraceni, Armani. Even the air was redolent with lush fragrances. She detected Joy and Chanel; and was that one Giorgio?

At the elevators, a security man studied her; but to her amusement, he was interested mostly in her legs. She stepped past him haughtily and entered a car along with other guests. The elevator whisked them upward and she was the only one to get off on the fourteenth floor.

Her pulse was racing now, and she stopped in the corridor and forced herself to quiet down. It was always like this when she knew it was going to be a special evening. Not that she ever had dull ones, but sometimes the men were not so appealing. Rich, yes. But occasionally homely, even ugly. Arabs, for example, could be particularly distasteful, with swarthy skin and hair all over their bodies. Ugh.

Tonight, on the other hand, would be wonderful. She could *feel* it.

There was a mirror in a rococo frame hanging on the wall beside the entrance to the suite. She looked at her reflection and was pleased by what she saw.

*Caroline, you are dynamite.*

She adjusted her hat and pressed the buzzer.

To her surprise, a woman opened the door. She was slim and attractive, with dark hair that came to just above her shoulders, wearing a sharkskin business suit. Horn-rimmed glasses added an additional note of seriousness to her appearance.

For an instant, Caroline thought she'd gone to the wrong suite. But then the woman's face lit up in a friendly smile. "Hi. I'm Bobbie, Mr. Burton's assistant. You must be Caroline. Come on in."

Caroline stepped past her and the woman closed the door. From the foyer, Caroline looked into the living room: The drapes were open, and through the windows she could see lights twinkling in the park, and in the hotels and apartment houses lining Fifth Avenue. To the right, the General Motors building loomed.

"Here, let me have your things." The assistant took her coat and hat and hung them in a closet. The Saks shopping bag, containing Caroline's working gear—hair dryer, makeup kit, fresh panties, and so on—she put on the shelf. As she did, she kept up a running chatter: "Mr. Burton will be out to meet you in just a few minutes; he's getting dressed. We've had quite a day. The company keeps its airplanes at Burbank and there was the usual jam-up on the freeway, so we were late getting out of L.A. Then when we got here, the limo was stuck in another mess trying to go over the Triborough. Please go on in and sit down. Can I get you a drink while we're waiting?"

"No, thank you." The last thing she wanted was the smell of liquor on her breath when she met him. She went into the living room and sat in a chair near the windows, taking in her surroundings. The room was furnished in antiques, mostly French provincial, and there were two breathtaking bouquets of yellow and white chrysanthemums, one on a coffee table in front of a sofa, the other on the mantel over the marble fireplace.

Bobbie crossed to a sideboard, where bottles and glasses and an ice bucket were standing. She picked up a glass. "Sure you won't join me?"

Caroline shook her head. "Thanks, no."

Using tongs, Bobbie put one ice cube into the glass, then poured Glenfiddich over it. She added a splash of water from a crystal pitcher. "I just love coming to New York, especially at this time of year. You don't get much theater in California, you know. I have tickets to the new David Mamet play. Have you seen it?"

"Yes, it's excellent."

"Good, I can't wait." She sat down on the sofa and sipped her drink. "I like his work. The dialogue is always rough and raw, but he has such a marvelous ear. You really believe the characters, don't you think?"

"Absolutely. I thought *Glengarry Glen Ross* was a very important play, but this one is even better."

"Oh, great. My tickets are for tomorrow night. Tonight I'm going to dinner with a friend. And maybe to Renata or Nell's later on. Speaking of dinner, I made reservations for Mr. Burton at Lutece. It's one of his favorites. I hope you like it?"

"Yes, I do. It's a favorite of mine, too."

Bobbie crossed her legs. Caroline noted that they were as long as her own and almost as good. If Burton had this to travel with him, why did he bother to call a place like Panache?

"Tomorrow's for shopping," Bobbie said. "Another great reason to come to New York. Where did you get that dress, by the way?"

"Saks."

"It's lovely. Do you shop there often?"

"Thank you. Yes, now and then. Although to tell you the truth, I usually have the best luck at Bloomingdale's."

"Ah, Bloomie's. That's another must for me. They're always at least six months ahead of L.A."

Caroline tried a small probe. "Are you staying here also?"

"Yes, I'm on the tenth floor." She smiled. "In a single that isn't

4

nearly as nice as this. But it's still the Plaza, right? We used to stay at the Regency, but about a year ago it seemed to slip a little."

"Have you been with Mr. Burton long?" Another probe.

"It seems like forever. I do everything for him. All his personal business, that is. Absolutely everything." She smiled again. "Even engaging you."

"How did you hear about us, by the way?"

"Oh, Martha's very well known in Los Angeles. She has a great reputation. You have a number of clients from there, don't you?"

"A few."

"We've used other services in New York, but I kept hearing Panache was outstanding, so I called. I told Martha Mr. Burton wanted her best, and here you are."

It was bald flattery, but Caroline didn't mind a bit. She ate it up, in fact.

Bobbie finished her drink and put the glass down on the coffee table. "Now there's some business we have to attend to." She rose and stepped to the desk, opening the center drawer. She took out a thick white envelope and returned to the sofa. When she was again seated, she opened the envelope and withdrew a sheaf of bills. "I believe your fee is twelve hundred, is that right?"

"Yes, but it isn't necessary to go into that now. We're one of the few places that doesn't expect payment until the end of the evening. It's nicer that way, just part of how we do things."

"Oh, I know that. Everything about Panache is class, right?"

"We think so. At least, that's what we try for."

Bobbie was counting bills, all hundreds. "But we have our own way of doing things, too, you see. You may think it's a bit quirky, but please bear with us." She placed a stack of money on the coffee table. "There now. That's twelve hundred."

She paused for a moment, then peeled off five more bills. "And . . . this is something extra, for you." She added them to the pile on the table.

Caroline looked at the money. A five-hundred-dollar tip? Not bad. In fact, excellent. So if this was what Mr. Burton and his Miss Superefficient considered "a bit quirky," who was she to argue?

"Go ahead," Bobbie said. "Take it. And tuck it away, please, out of sight. I have to tell you, Mr. Burton's sort of a romantic. He likes the idea of you two falling in love. But only for the evening, of course. And while you're together, he wants it to be a real love affair. So naturally, if money was to change hands, that would spoil it. Do you see?"

"Yes, I think so." What Caroline saw was that Mr. Burton was

5

getting better by the minute. Harrison Ford indeed. With a touch of gray at the temples, and the heart of an adolescent. And pockets bulging with cash. She just might fall in love herself. But only for the evening, of course. She picked up the money and slipped it into her purse.

"And now," Bobbie said, "if you'll just bear with us, there's a little routine I have to put you through."

"A routine?"

The assistant smiled disarmingly. "Oh, it's all part of the romance I was telling you about. The fantasy. It has to be perfect, for Mr. Burton to really enjoy it. So there's something a little unusual I have to ask you to do."

Uh-oh. Was Burton into something freaky? If he was, the evening would be over before it even got started. Just the thought of that stuff made Caroline nervous. Something a little unusual? Like what? S&M, maybe? Or bondage? Well, forget it. She'd return the money and get the hell out of here. A few months back, she'd walked out on a boorish official from OPEC, and more recently, a guy from the French delegation to the UN had wanted to beat her with a whip. That time, Caroline had forgotten she was a lady; she'd told the Frenchman to go fuck his hat and had run for the door. When Martha heard what had happened, she put the guy on her PSL: permanent shit list.

But Bobbie seemed anxious to dispel any notion that something strange might be in the offing. She raised a hand. "Now don't get nervous. Nobody's asking you to do anything kinky. It's just that I have to check you out. You know, look you over to be sure there are no blemishes, nothing to destroy the romantic illusion."

Caroline remained tense. "What do you mean by looking me over?"

"You just take off your clothes and let me see you." The assistant indicated the closed door that Caroline presumed led into the bedroom. "He's probably still in the shower. And anyway, he won't come in until I call him to be introduced."

Caroline still wasn't convinced. "That's all? Just undress, you look, and then I get dressed again?"

"That's all. And to show you we don't want to put you to any trouble for nothing, here's another three hundred." More bills were peeled off, and this time Bobbie handed them to her. "That makes a nice round figure, doesn't it?"

It certainly did. Of the basic $1,200 fee, Caroline would turn over $500 to Panache, the service's standard split. The remaining seven hundred, plus a tip that now amounted to eight hundred, was hers to keep. Fifteen hundred dollars. For having dinner at what many people considered the best restaurant in New York, and then getting what hopefully would be a good lay? She added the bills to the ones already in her purse.

Bobbie put the sheaf back into the envelope. "Okay?"

"Yes, I suppose so."

"Good." The assistant got up and went back to the desk, returning the envelope to the drawer and closing it. She turned back to Caroline and leaned against the desk. "All right, you can get undressed."

Caroline took off her pearls and put them into her purse, then placed the purse on a nearby lamp table. Rising from her chair, she slipped her dress over her head. The material was crepe de chine, as light as gossamer. She draped the dress over the back of the chair and then unhooked her bra. Ordinarily when she undressed on a working date, she did it slowly, almost as a striptease. But this, as Bobbie had made clear, was different.

She laid the bra over her dress and stood up straight, facing the assistant and arching her back a little. It was hard to tell with the business suit, but it didn't look as if Bobbie had too much on top. So let her see what a real pair looked like. Caroline was a perfect 34C, and thanks to a solid hour of calesthenics each morning, in addition to what nature had so generously given her, she had a bust that invariably caused guys to slaver. And that women looked at with undisguised envy—as Bobbie was looking now.

"Beautiful," Bobbie said. "Really beautiful. Please go on."

Caroline slipped her panties down over her hips and stepped out of them. She added the panties to the other things on the chair and again stood up straight. Now wearing only her garter belt, stockings, and her black pumps, she could tell from the way Bobbie's gaze was fastened on her that she was making a great impression. Naturally. And just to rub it in a little, she did a leisurely 360.

Bobbie's voice was a whisper. "My god, you certainly are spectacular."

A dyke, maybe? Was that the answer to all this? Bobbie handles everything but Burton's dick, because she's a lesbian? That could be it, Caroline thought. It was plausible enough. And if that was what Bobbie was about, it was fine with Caroline, so long as the assistant wanted nothing more than to see the goods her boss was paying for. Okay, Bobbie, you can look, but don't touch.

"The rest of it, too," Bobbie said. "If you don't mind."

Obediently, Caroline sat down on a chair and unfastened her stockings. She took them off, then removed the belt, as well. When she stood up this time, she was wearing nothing but her sapphire ring and the tiny Patek Philippe watch her father had given her as a college graduation present.

The assistant's eyes were wide with admiration. "Wonderful," she said. "Just wonderful." She stood there for a moment, obviously enthralled, and then opened a side drawer in the desk, taking from it a folded bit of red cloth. She passed the cloth to Caroline. "Here, take this, please. Go ahead, open it up."

Caroline shook it out, and found herself holding a filmy length of scarlet chiffon.

Bobbie continued to watch her intently. "Have you ever done any dancing? You know, ballet or modern dance, or anything like that?"

"I studied ballet, yes. When I was in school."

"Okay, so here's the idea. Mr. Burton simply adores seeing a pretty girl dance after making love. Nothing formal, you understand, but sort of as if she's just exuberant. You know, happy because it was so good. And if she kind of twirls a red scarf while she's dancing, it makes him ecstatic. Don't ask me why, it just does." She grinned disarmingly. "Maybe he thinks he's a bull, and you're the matador. I don't know."

Caroline laughed. The request was a little nutty, but so what? She'd done things that were more peculiar than this. In fact had even done them enthusiastically, at times. As long as they hadn't been spooky. So what the hell—if a guy was shucking out two thousand dollars for a few hours of entertainment, he had a right to expect his money's worth. She glanced at the scarf. "Will there be music?"

"Probably not. It would be better if you sang a little and danced to that. You know, not fancy. Sort of as if you were just humming to yourself. Do you get the idea?"

"I think so."

"Try it. Go ahead, give it a whirl."

Okay, Caroline thought. Here goes nothing. She began by humming the first melody that came into her head, a Strauss waltz. Remembering her training, she did a series of balancés, following them with a glissade.

"Ah," Bobbie said. "That's lovely. But if I can make a suggestion, slow it down a little. Yes, that's it. Terrific."

Caroline made another turn, a pas de chat, and after that performed a number of arabesques that were languid and graceful, if she did say so herself, holding the scarf so that it fluttered behind her.

"That's perfect," Bobbie said. "You're really great."

She was getting into it now, actually enjoying it. And even though this was only a preview—an undress rehearsal, as it were—the danc-

8

ing was making her excited. She could imagine the handsome and sophisticated Mr. Burton lying back on the bed, watching and admiring her as Bobbie was doing now, only more so.

She'd be doing the slow turns, letting the red scarf drift, and after a time he'd tell her to come back to bed. His voice would be low and thick the way a man's became when he was fully aroused. Then maybe she'd tease him a little, not returning immediately but continuing to dance and sing. She didn't have a great voice, but it wasn't bad, either.

She turned and dipped, dipped and turned, humming softly, the scarf floating in the air like a wisp of red smoke.

"Higher," Bobbie said. "Hold the scarf higher. Here, let me show you."

The assistant stepped behind her and lifted Caroline's wrist until it was over her head. "That's it. Much better."

Caroline stretched her arm up and back a little, and as she did, the scarf was suddenly ripped from her hand and wrapped tightly around her throat, the move as fierce and quick as that of a striking snake. The cloth bit into her flesh like a length of wire.

Caroline gagged, clawing at her neck. "What—wha—"

The woman's foot hooked around Caroline's shin, tripping her. She fell heavily to the floor, facedown, both hands struggling to relieve the awful pressure at her throat. She tried to rise, getting to her knees and elbows, but now she felt Bobbie sitting astride her, legs clamping her sides.

*Jesus Christ—this can't be happening.*

She twisted and turned desperately, but the grip of the woman's thighs was like a vise. Caroline's face was burning hot, and brilliant pinpoints of light were jabbing her eyes. Her fingers tore at her throat, nails digging into her flesh, but as hard as she tried, she couldn't tear the scarf loose. It was so tight it was buried in her neck.

She heaved convulsively, her torso jerking as her lungs demanded oxygen. The pain was much worse now, terrible pain in her throat and her chest and her head. She heard a roaring in her ears, and was dimly aware of another sound above that—the sound of a woman chuckling.

Caroline lurched and bucked, but her strength was draining rapidly. The pinpoints of light grew larger, until they became explosions—brilliant, incandescent bursts that were like fireworks going off in her head.

Then the roaring in her ears grew louder still, and she was no longer able to control her body, no longer had the energy to fight. She slumped to the floor.

The pain was overwhelming, but she didn't care. She gave herself up to it, and her efforts grew feeble, and stopped.

And then there was nothing.

# 2

The bell burbled. It didn't ring the way an honest telephone would, but instead made a liquid sound, like a bubbly fart. Ben pulled a pillow over his head to shut it out. Who would be calling Patty at this hour of the morning?

The burbling continued, until she stirred beside him and mumbled something unintelligible. He heard her fumble for the phone, lifting the receiver from its cradle on the bedside table and pulling it under the covers with her. Her voice was a croak. "Hello?"

She listened for a moment, then nudged him and shoved the phone at him.

Feeling a twinge of guilt, he took it. "Tolliver."

"Lieutenant, it's Ed Flynn. There was a homicide last night, in the Plaza Hotel. A woman was strangled. Brennan just called. He wants you on it."

"The Plaza? That's in the Midtown North. What's it got to do with me? Or with Brennan?"

"Beats me, Ben. He said for you to go to the hotel right away. He'll meet you there."

Ben groaned. He had to reach across Patty to hang up the phone, and when he did, she muttered an obscenity. Jesus, what a way to start what was supposed to be a day off. He got out of bed, feeling angry and groggy at the same time, and stumbled over a heap of clothing as he made his way to the bathroom. The clothing, he realized, was his. Lying where he'd left it a couple of hours earlier. He turned on the light and closed the bathroom door behind him.

As he stood over the toilet, a string of thoughts ran through his mind. The first was that he'd promised to spend the day with Patty— take her for a drive in the country to see the fall colors, stop somewhere for lunch. Maybe up toward Millerton. There were some nice old inns up there he knew she'd like.

But he could forget that now. If Brennan was on his way to the crime scene himself, something big was going down. Maybe the victim was a celebrity—a movie actress, or a rock star.

And yet, why was Brennan involved? As a zone commander, Brennan's areas of responsibility were the detective squads in the Sixth, Ninth, and Tenth Precincts. A homicide in the Plaza was outside his jurisdiction.

And of all the detectives in Brennan's command, why had Tolliver been singled out for this? Ben's job was to run the detective squad in the Sixth, the Greenwich Village precinct that had plenty of problems of its own. At the moment they were overrun with cases ranging from robbery to rape, plus a number of open homicides. Did he really need another one, in some fancy uptown hotel? Or more to the point, did it need him?

Maybe Brennan had been stuck with the assignment for some reason or other and wanted to jam it to Tolliver in a fit of pique. The captain could be a prick at times.

But the thing to do was to stop guessing and haul himself up to the Plaza. Whatever this was about, he'd find out soon enough.

He poked through the medicine cabinet, getting out a toothbrush and Patty's razor and a can of shaving cream. The razor would be dull, he knew, and there were no fresh blades. Women didn't seem to worry about such things.

Her shaving cream was something else that puzzled him. The stuff was like the whipped cream that came in a can. Back in his own apartment, he had a mug of soap, a badger brush, and a straight razor so sharp you could split a hair with it. The apartment might be a dump, small and dingy and filled with crapped-out furniture, but the important things, like his shaving gear and the coffee maker and the stereo, were all first-class.

The toothbrush was new, encased in a plastic sleeve. He took it out and squirted toothpaste onto it, anxious to get rid of the awful staleness in his mouth. It was strange the way booze could taste so good the night before and then turn to shit by morning.

At least he wasn't using her toothbrush; this one apparently had been bought for a guest. For him? Or had it been intended for some other guy? No matter, it did the job. He scrubbed away the crud, and when he rinsed out his mouth, he could again run his tongue over his teeth without scratching it.

He shaved next, and he'd been right: The razor was dull as hell. He dragged it back and forth across his jaw, cursing when he nicked himself. After that, he stepped into the tub and turned on the shower.

The hot water was a blessing. As it pounded down onto his face

11

and his shoulders, he could feel the heat restoring him as he soaped his body. By the time he rinsed off the suds, he actually was feeling pretty good. He turned off the water and got out of the tub, rubbing himself down with a thick towel.

Among the bottles of cosmetics on a shelf was a tiny radio. He wished he could turn it on to hear the news, but he'd made enough noise as it was. Again rummaging around in the cabinet, he came up with a comb. As he worked on the tangles, he noted that when his hair was wet it was jet black. Later, when it dried, the flecks of gray would reappear and he would look his age once more.

Maybe he ought to get some of that stuff you saw on TV that promised to cover gray so well it would make you look thirty forever. Shangri-la in a bottle. Which was so much bullshit. He was what he was, so why kid anybody, least of all himself?

Continuing to peer into the mirror, he was amazed that the pale blue eyes staring back at him were reasonably clear. There was almost no red in the whites, which was a small miracle, considering the amount of alcohol he'd put away the night before. The mustache could stand a trim, however. But he didn't have time to mess around with it now. He returned the razor and shaving cream to the cabinet and stuck the toothbrush into the ceramic holder, beside hers. At least he could be tidy.

When he emerged from the bathroom, he was surprised to see the bed empty. Surprised and disappointed, because he loved a morning quickie when he'd spent the night with her. She'd be all warm and sleepy and yet she'd be ready almost immediately. That was one thing he'd always make time for.

But this morning she was already up, even though she'd had a very short sleep, and the smell of coffee brewing and bacon frying was floating in from the kitchen. He picked up his clothing from the floor and tossed it onto the bed, then pulled on his shorts, wishing he had a fresh pair. His corduroys came next, as soft and well-worn as an old pair of gloves, followed by a blue oxford-cloth button-down, slightly frayed.

Sitting down on the bed, he strapped the ankle holster onto his left shin. The pistol was a snub-nosed .38 caliber S&W Airweight. It was made of alloy, half as heavy as a Colt, and not as accurate. Which wasn't important; what you needed a piece like this for was work in close, and it served that purpose well enough.

Some detectives no longer carried revolvers, but instead had gone to the 9mm automatics, having decided that if the bad guys were armed with cannons, they could at least give themselves an even break. But Ben stayed with the Smith, partly because it was like the corduroys: comfortable. He did keep a Beretta in his car, however. He pulled on his socks and shoes and followed the tantalizing trail of breakfast smells.

Patty was standing at the stove, wearing a white terry-cloth robe and a pair of mules, her dark hair pulled back and held by an elastic band. He patted her rear end, and she turned and gave him a cheek to kiss, seemingly without much enthusiasm.

"Sorry," he said. "I don't even know what this is all about. But I have to go."

Her tone was dry. "Duty calls."

"Yeah. Maybe I can get back before long." He knew it was a lie, even as the words came out of his mouth, but he wanted to offer something.

"You can eat, though, before you go?"

"Uh, sure. Of course." He sensed that he'd better, if he didn't want to make this any worse than it was. And besides, he was hungry as hell. He sat down at the small table and she put a plate of fried eggs, bacon, and toast in front of him. At her own place, she set out a smaller plate, with one piece of dry toast on it. Then she also sat, facing him, and poured mugs of coffee from the electric pot.

The eggs were as he liked them, once over, and the bacon was just right, crisp and delicious. He smeared his toast with butter and blueberry jam and ate ravenously. In only a few minutes, his plate was empty.

Patty took one bite of toast as she watched him eat, sipping her coffee and saying nothing until he finished. "Like some more?"

He sipped his coffee and raised his free hand. "No, thanks. That was just great."

"Glad you enjoyed it."

So she was pissed, and who could blame her? She had to be wondering why she wasted time on this asshole cop when there were about a million guys in New York who'd give their left nut to spend the night with her. An exotic dancer in a Village club called The Casbah, she had a body Ben had thought existed only in his imagination, until he met her. Most of the time, they got along very well, out of bed as well as in it. But it was his crazy schedule—or non-schedule—that imposed a strain on the relationship, making him less dependable than the weather.

She looked at him. "When do you get another day off?"

"Sunday, I think." That was almost surely another lie; whatever the circumstances that required him to go to the Plaza this morning, he knew damn well they wouldn't just go away that quickly. He was

13

getting into something; he could feel it. So why wouldn't he tell her the truth—that he didn't know when he might see her again?

Because that would be piling one problem on top of another. Better to let a day or so go by, let her simmer down. He'd call her when he got a chance, might even be able to get over here tonight after she finished at the club. For now, the best thing to do was to apologize and make some vague promises, and then get out as gracefully as he could.

But she surprised him. "That's just wishful thinking, isn't it?"

"What is?"

"That you'll get Sunday off."

"I told you, I don't even know what this is all about. I'm as disappointed as you are. I was looking forward to spending the day with you."

She finished her coffee and set the cup down. "Look, Ben, the last thing I want to sound like is some kind of nagging wife, or something. But you can't just work all the time, you know. I mean, I know how much the job means to you, I really do. But there's more to life than being a cop, even though you don't seem to think so. Sooner or later you're going to say, Hey—what am I doing? Where's the time I ought to have for myself, and for someone I want to share it with?"

"Yeah, I suppose that's true." Why did women always pick a time like this to try to get you into a deep discussion?

She was holding him in a cool, steady gaze. "Nobody wants to wait forever, you know."

This was getting too heavy. He drained his coffee and put the mug down. "I'll call you, when I know what's going on."

"All right."

He rose from the table, and stepping around to where she was sitting, he pulled her up into his arms. Her body was warm against his, and as she put her arms around his neck, he was aware that she smelled good, a faint scent of soap and a fragrance he couldn't identify.

His mouth was close to hers. "That's better."

"What is?"

"Holding you like this."

A faint smile was playing at the corners of her lips, and that was a good sign. "You mean it's the best you can do?"

"Of course not. They don't call me a dick for nothing, you know."

"Couldn't prove it by me, Lieutenant."

He cupped her buttocks in his hands and she pressed herself tightly against him, beginning a slow, grinding motion.

14

"If you're not careful," he said, "you could make me late for work."

Her tongue flickered against his lips. "So who wants to be careful?"

She had a point; you had to decide what things in life took priority. He scooped her up in his arms and carried her into the bedroom.

# 3

On his way out of the apartment, Ben retrieved his windbreaker from the front-hall closet and put it on. He shut the door behind him and trotted down the stairs.

Patty's place was on Bleecker Street, in a better neighborhood than his own. The rattrap he lived in was on the third floor of a drab building on Bank Street that should have been torn down years ago. In sharp contrast, this part of Greenwich Village was charming, with small, quaint apartment houses and boutiques and restaurants, and there were trees lining the sidewalks. People were hurrying by on their way to work, and shopkeepers were setting out merchandise for sale—everything from freshly made bread to flowers and paintings. The air was cool and fresh and overhead the sky was a high, hard blue. Patty was right: This was going to be a nice day.

His car was parked in front of her building, a battered gray Ford sedan with a plate lying on the dashboard that read, POLICE OFFICIAL BUSINESS. He unlocked the car and climbed in behind the wheel, dropping the plate onto the floor.

As he started the engine, the discussion they'd had came back into his mind. If he had a choice, how would he spend this day? Would he drive through the countryside with her, admiring the red and gold autumn leaves, and then have lunch someplace upstate, get a chance to relax and talk about things? Or would he be on his way to Central Park South, to one of the fanciest hotels in New York, called into a homicide investigation that was miles from his own Sixth Precinct?

The answer was obvious.

He put the Ford in gear and pulled away from the curb, feeling a jolt of adrenaline as he headed uptown.

Except for a number of patrol cars and two Crime Scene Unit vans parked in Grand Army Plaza, it didn't look as if anything unusual had taken place. There were no police barricades, and only two uniformed cops were standing near the side entrance of the hotel. Ben knew why: The management would be doing everything in its power to low-key the fact that a murder had been committed here. He nosed the Ford in among the blue-and-whites and put the police plate back on the dash before getting out of the car.

The steps leading up to the entrance were covered with red carpet. A maintenance man was polishing the brass handles on the doors, and a doorman in an elaborate maroon and gold getup touched his cap as Ben walked up the steps and entered the lobby. The two cops paid no attention to him.

Seeing how he was dressed, he wondered why the doorman was deferential, but then he reflected that nowadays you couldn't always judge people by their clothing. Not that any of the male guests were wearing zippered jackets as he was; most of them were in business suits. Still, the hotel probably had a rule about not taking a chance on offending anyone. He turned right, and at the end of the corridor made another right, heading for the main part of the lobby that faced onto Central Park.

The area was full of people, and there were lines at the counter in front of the reception and cashier's stations. Ben hadn't been here for several years, and the opulence was something to see. The counters were clad in veined white marble, as were the elevator wall and a table with a large bouquet of flowers on it. There was also gilt trim everywhere he looked, and descending from the high, vaulted ceiling was an enormous crystal chandelier.

One of the elevators had been closed off, and a hotel security guard and a uniformed cop were standing in front of it. That was the only visible sign that a crime had occurred, and if you weren't overly curious, even that would escape your attention. Ben stepped to the elevator and pulled his wallet out of the back pocket of his corduroys, showing his shield and ID to the guard and the cop. "Lieutenant Tolliver," he said. "Sixth Precinct."

The policeman was a young guy with a row of ribbons on his chest, holding a notebook. "Morning, Lieutenant. It's on the fourteenth floor." He wrote Ben's name in the notebook, the crime-scene log.

The security guard was older, red-faced and thick in the middle, wearing a navy blue blazer with a crest on it. Probably a retired cop. Whatever, he wasn't happy about what was going on. His territory had been not only invaded but violated. He nodded to Ben and pressed a button for the elevator.

As Ben waited, a TV crew arrived, one guy carrying a camera, another with equipment cases, two more who probably were reporters. They approached the guard, who told them they weren't allowed upstairs, and an argument ensued. It grew louder when the elevator doors opened and Ben stepped into the car. He pressed the button for 14 and the doors closed, cutting off the TV crew's complaints.

The elevator was as decorous as everything else in the hotel, with mirrors and paneling trimmed in gilt. As it rose, he clipped the wallet to the collar of his jacket, letting it hang open so the shield and his ID would be in plain sight.

The situation on the fourteenth floor was very different from that in the lobby. Cops were everywhere, both in uniform and in civilian clothes. The guests would have been evacuated from their rooms, Ben knew, and the hotel would have found accommodations for them on other floors. A door was standing open just down the hall, and men were going in and out. As he made his way toward it, he recognized a detective from the Midtown North squad, Joe Spadone, talking to a uniformed cop.

Ben raised a hand. "Hey, Joe."

The detective looked around. He was about the same age as Ben and apparently in good shape, but there the resemblance ended. Spadone was wearing a three-piece gray suit and a red and white striped tie, and except for the gold shield clipped to his jacket, he easily could have been mistaken for a guest. He smiled broadly. "Hey, Ben. First we get Brennan, and now you. Department must be running out of detectives."

"Headquarters told us there was a homicide and we should investigate," Ben said. "They were afraid you guys would fuck it up."

"They got that right. Now that you're on it, I might as well go back to the station house."

"Or to Gallagher's."

"Even better." Gallagher's was a saloon on Fifty-second Street where midtown cops often hung out.

Ben inclined his head toward the nearby open door. "What's the story?"

"Hooker came to work, somebody iced her."

"The guy who rented the room?"

"Could be. Registered on an AmEx card as John Burton, from Los Angeles. We already ran it down; the card was stolen."

"You get a description of him?"

"No. A woman checked him in."

"A woman?"

"Yeah. Said she was his assistant."

"You get her name?"

"No, but we got a description of her from the clerk and a bell-man."

"And?"

"Early thirties, dark hair, glasses, well dressed in a gray business suit. Carrying a raincoat."

"Luggage?"

"One piece. A man's suitcase she said belonged to her boss."

"But nobody saw him?"

"Nobody we could find so far."

"She check herself in, too?"

"The desk says no."

"What about the victim—what time did she show up?"

"We don't know. And we won't have the time of death until the post."

Ben hooked his thumbs into his belt loops. "You find out who she was?"

"I thought you'd never ask. She was carrying two sets of ID. One said her name was Caroline Clark, but that was her working name. Her real name was Patterson. Caroline Patterson."

"So?"

"So her father is Spencer Patterson. You heard of him?"

"Wait a minute. He involved in real estate? And politics?"

"That's the guy. A very big developer. And a major power behind the scenes in the Democratic party."

"Power meaning contributor."

Spadone grinned. "The party don't run on goodwill alone. But for him it's an investment."

"And his daughter was a hooker?"

"Can you believe it? With his money? He could buy this joint."

"You sure, about the ID?"

"Yeah, it checked out. She had a driver's license and credit cards on her. We called Patterson, and he said from the address of her apartment and the description, it was her. Also she was wearing a watch he gave her. He agreed to go to the morgue later on."

"How about the hooker part?"

"Not positive, but it sure looks like it. The phony name, and she had a kit with her. Extra panties, hair dryer, K-Y jelly, spermacide, all the usual shit they carry."

"You find anything else on her?"

"Only the decoration."

"The what?"

Spadone jerked a thumb toward the open door. "Take a look."

Ben went past him into the living room of the suite. A trio of CSU

18

men were in the room, dusting for fingerprints, gathering fiber samples. Liquor bottles and glasses were standing on a sideboard, and the detectives were paying particular attention to these. There was also activity in the bedroom, and Ben walked on in.

More cops were working in here, one of them taking pictures with a flash camera. Art Weisskopf, who was Joe Spadone's partner on the Midtown North squad, stood talking with Captain Michael Brennan and the medical examiner. Weisskopf was another sharp dresser, thin-faced and with quick, darting eyes that reminded Ben of a ferret. Two ambulance attendants were unstrapping a portable gurney. Looking past the crowd, Ben saw a figure on the bed. He stepped closer.

The woman was naked, lying on her back and propped up by a mound of pillows. Although he had seen scores of murdered women, the appearance of this one gave him a jolt.

Her mouth, eyes, and cheeks had been painted with red and blue makeup, the features exaggerated so that she looked more like a huge doll than a human female. The cosmetics had turned her lips into a monstrous parody of a Cupid's bow, and each cheek wore a red circle the size of a silver dollar. Her blue eyes were bulging from their sockets, dollops of mascara outlining them. She had blond hair, standing straight up from her head and held in place by a red silk scarf wound tightly around it.

Her nipples also had been rouged, making them appear to be about three inches across. Her legs were spread, the knees raised, and the hair on her pubis had been made up in purple tones, the labial folds of her vagina in red.

Ben stood staring down at the grotesquely adorned body, so startled by her appearance that at first he hardly noticed the angry furrow girdling her throat. Apparently a strong, thin cord had been used to strangle her. As was typical in a case of death by asphyxia, many of the blood vessels in her eyes had burst, and there were shadows of cyanosis around her neck. There would be others near her eyes, but the bizarre makeup obscured them. From between the scarlet lips, her tongue protruded like a thick blue worm, and he realized the tip of the tongue also had been painted.

"So the guy's an artist," someone said.

Ben glanced up. Michael Brennan had stepped beside him and was looking at the body.

"Hello, Cap," Ben said.

"Good morning, Lieutenant. What took you so long?"

"My day off, supposedly. I was hung over." Which was true, even if it was only half the reason he'd been late getting up here.

"Uh-huh. Happens to all of us."

Ben wondered whether he meant the hangover or losing the day off, and decided it didn't matter.

Brennan continued to gaze at the corpse. As always, the captain put Ben in mind of an old heavyweight boxer, the kind who in his youth would have fought in neighborhood clubs in the Bronx or Queens. He would have been in six-rounders on Friday nights, going in against spades and Ricans and getting his face pounded into hamburger, the crowd loving it, a slope-shouldered stone Irish street brawler who never took a backward step.

This morning Brennan had on a rumpled blue serge suit, probably the only one he owned, and a black tie worked into a small greasy knot. Even with the short-cropped gray hair, it was easy to imagine him wearing boxing trunks instead.

"What we have got here," Brennan said, "is somebody from a prominent family."

Ben nodded. "Joe Spadone filled me in."

"Yeah." The captain looked around. "Maybe we better talk outside."

Ben followed him back through the living room and out into the corridor. They walked down the hallway until they were out of earshot of any of the other cops. When Brennan was satisfied they wouldn't be overheard, he leaned against the wall and folded his arms. "Spadone tell you about her father?"

"Spencer Patterson, he said."

"And you know who Patterson is." It was a statement, not a question.

"Yes."

Brennan rubbed his nose, a blob of gristle in the middle of his face. "Sometimes in this business, you run into what you might call a delicate situation. You understand what I mean?"

"Yeah, I think so."

"Good. Because that's what this is. See, we got a homicide we have to investigate, but at the same time, we don't want to cause the victim's family any more pain than they already got."

"Or embarrassment." He wished Brennan would stop pussyfooting around.

The captain cocked his head, studying him. "That's correct, Lieutenant. So we proceed with tact. Certain things don't have to be made public. They stay confidential, because officially that helps our efforts to apprehend the perpetrator. Caroline Patterson died in the Plaza Hotel. It was a homicide; she was strangled. We're investigating. And that's it. See?"

"Yes. I understand."

"Now, we're gonna get a lot of heat from the media. They'll go apeshit over who she was and how she died. They'll think she was shacked up with some guy and he killed her. Which is true, up to a point. The other things they don't have to know about. So they'll write a lot of stories about how maybe she had a married lover, or maybe a couple of lovers and one was jealous, and whatever else they can dream up. It'll be tough on the family, but not as bad as it could be. Naturally, the chief and the PC will back us up. We give out only what I just told you and nothing else. Any questions?"

"Yes. What am I doing here?"

"I was coming to that. The reason you're here is that you got a reputation."

"I've got *what?*"

"I'll spell it out for you, Lieutenant. Just listen to me, and pay close attention. You're here because Galupo asked for you."

Anthony Galupo was the Manhattan Borough Chief of Detectives. This was getting stranger by the minute.

"And the reason he did that," Brennan went on, "is that you're very well known for your work on the so-called Greenwich Village murders."

Ben got it then. The murders had been a sensation, the work of a maniac who preyed on young women, luring them to his studio on the pretense he was a photographer. Ben had not only cracked the case but had killed the perpetrator, nearly losing his own life in the process. As a consequence, the media had given him a big play, thereby destroying forever his prized anonymity. Like it or not, as a New York cop he'd become almost as famous as Popeye Doyle.

"So what the chief is doing," Brennan said, "is setting up a special task force on this case, with you in charge. And even though he didn't tell me this next part, it wasn't hard to figure out. I'm sure you can see the logic just as quick. What he'll say to the world is, Look—I got one of our best detectives on it. The same detective who ran down the terrible killer that terrorized the city, the one who murdered those girls. Even the media will be impressed. But more important, so will the DA's office. Because they'll be able to say the same thing. Not just to the media but to Mr. Patterson. Okay?"

Ben knew he should keep his mouth shut. But he didn't. "I didn't join the department so I could play politics."

The captain fixed him with a blank stare. "You were in the service, weren't you? Marine Corps?"

You know goddamn well I was, Ben thought. "Yes."

"What was your rank?"

"Sergeant." He waited, anticipating what he would hear next.

"So when your platoon leader told you to take out a patrol, what did you say?"

Sometimes I told him he was out of his fucking mind, Ben thought. But Brennan wouldn't understand that. The captain had fought in Korea. Another time, another world.

"Well?"

"I told him yes sir," Ben said.

"Uh-huh. That's what I thought. You still remember the words, right?"

"Yes, sir."

"Good, that's the proper response. Chief Galupo wants to see the both of us, later on. Right now let's take another look at Miss Patterson. I'll tell the other guys how this is gonna go."

Maybe the reference to the marines wasn't so far off the mark at that. In any outfit, you had to put up with a certain amount of chickenshit.

Brennan spoke over his shoulder as he started back up the hall. "You coming, Lieutenant?"

Ben followed him back to the suite.

# 4

The captain made it brief and to the point, announcing to the others what he'd already told Ben. Chief Galupo had directed that a task force be formed, headed by Tolliver. Because Spadone had caught the case, he would stay on it, along with his partner, Weisskopf. The zone commander responsible for Midtown North had been informed by the chief, and Brennan had spoken with Phil Monahan, the lieutenant who headed the detective squad in that precinct. Until the case was closed or they were notified otherwise, Spadone and Weisskopf would report to Tolliver.

As Brennan spoke, the two detectives glanced briefly in Ben's direction. Their faces were expressionless, but he knew what had to be going through their minds. The NYPD was as political as any other big-city organization, with more factions than you could count. Some of those factions ran along ethnic lines, particularly Irish, Italian, and black. Others were territorial, involving rivalries among the boroughs. Still others were based on allegiances to various high-ranking officials. Together they were like a cauldron that never stopped bubbling. Neither Spadone nor Weisskopf would say it, but they—and plenty of others—would be pissed that the case had been given to the commander of another detective squad.

Which was just too fucking bad. Tolliver hadn't asked for this. If anything, he was more uneasy at being hung with it than these two were at having to take orders from him.

When he finished, Brennan asked whether there were any questions. There weren't. Good, the captain said. They would then hear what the ME could tell them.

The assistant medical examiner's name was Robert Kurtz. He was young, but fatigue circles under his eyes made him look older. He was also gaunt, another sign of overwork, and as he spoke he gestured nervously with his hands. "Time of death is a tough one in a case like this," he said.

"Why is that?" Ben asked.

"Asphyxia. It's different."

"You mean because of the slower cooling rate?"

"That's right." The ME looked at Ben. "I take it you've worked on strangulation homicides before, Lieutenant?"

"Some." In fact, he'd worked on many of them. But he wanted to hear Kurtz's explanation. It might give them something they could otherwise overlook. "Run through it for us, will you, Doc?"

The ME waved a hand toward the body on the bed. "Normal rate of temperature loss for a nude adult is four to five degrees an hour for the first few hours after death. Then it slows down to maybe one or two degrees an hour after that. After eight hours or so, the skin gets cold to the touch."

"I felt her arm," Spadone said. "It was still a little warm."

Kurtz's head bobbed. "Yes, because she was strangled. That produces a lot of vascular congestion, so the body heat is retained for a much longer period of time. She's still limber, too. No rigor mortis yet."

"So the point is," Brennan said, "you can't pin it down."

"Not until we do the post. Once we open her up, we can get a much better idea."

"How about a guess?" Weisskopf asked.

The ME shrugged. "Don't hold me to it, but I'd say earlier than you'd think. I mean, if she'd been killed by a gunshot or a knife wound, the temperature of the body now would indicate she died maybe four or five hours ago, tops. But because she was strangled,

23

I'd go so far as to say early yesterday evening. Maybe around eight o'clock."

Ben glanced at the dead woman. The paint had turned her features into an obscene caricature of what she must have looked like alive. Even with the garish makeup, you could see that she'd been beautiful. And that she'd had a great body, with superb muscle tone. Inevitably, he thought of Patty, unable to keep himself from making a comparison.

He turned to Kurtz. "Did she have intercourse?"

"I don't think so. The vulva had to be dry before the makeup was applied."

"Maybe he cleaned her up with a towel or something before he put it on," Ben said. "Maybe he had sex with her and killed her, then dried her off and put on the makeup."

Kurtz considered it. "Yes, I suppose it could have happened that way."

"A sex killer usually murders his victim during the act," Ben went on. "Or just after."

"Or just before," Brennan interposed. "We've had a few of those, too. Guys who get off with a dead body."

"Necrophiliacs," Kurtz said.

"So maybe that's what this guy was," Brennan said.

Kurtz shrugged. "Anything's possible. But that's another thing we'll look for in the autopsy. Fluids in the vaginal tract might tell us something."

Ben shook his head. "I don't think it happened that way. I mean, that's some paint job, isn't it? He must have taken his time."

"Yeah, but it could also be what turns him on," Brennan said. "First he pays the girl to let him paint her, or else he pays her to do it herself. She's a pro; she's used to guys with nutball ideas. So she goes along. Then he surprises her. Kills her and humps her after."

Again Ben shook his head. "I still don't buy it. If that was the way it went, the makeup would have been smeared when he had sex with her. And if not then, it sure would have been when he strangled her."

"I agree with that," Kurtz said.

Ben turned to the other two detectives. "What shape was the bathroom in?"

"A mess," Weisskopf said. "Wet towels all over the place."

"Anything else in there?"

"No, that was it."

"You find prints anywhere?"

"Forget about it," Spadone said. "He not only wiped everything down, he used something like alcohol to do it with."

"Probably booze from the bottles in the living room," Weisskopf said. "The CSU couldn't even get latents."

"What about her stuff?"

"All bagged and tagged. You want to see it?"

"Yeah, let's take a look."

They went back into the living room, where one of the forensics people, a detective named Frank Muller whom Ben knew from other cases, obliged them. Wearing rubber gloves, Muller took the victim's clothing and personal articles out of plastic bags, holding them up for inspection before carefully putting them away again.

Ben noted the quality of the clothes, all new, all very expensive. The purse alone must have cost well over a thousand dollars; it was black alligator, and the label said it came from Nardello, in Rome. He had Muller lay out its contents on the desk.

There was a wallet, also of black alligator and matching the purse, a comb, a small package of Kleenex, a mirror, a roll of mints, charge slips from Saks and Bloomingdale's, and a pile of change that included twelve quarters. The wallet contained the two sets of ID Spadone had told him about—driver's licenses and credit cards—plus a number of business cards from boutiques and department stores, and ninety-six dollars in small bills.

Ben looked up from the array on the desk. "What else?"

The CSU detective produced a large shopping bag, glossy black with the red Saks logo on it. He emptied it carefully onto the desk, spilling out the standard call girl's working gear. Ben noted that the spare panties were silk, pale peach and trimmed with white lace. The other things were ordinary, lubricants and deodorants and spermicide, stuff you could find in any drugstore. The hair dryer was a cheap one, made in Hong Kong.

Spadone was looking at him. "You see what I mean? She had all the equipment, right?"

"Yeah, that she did." He poked through the business cards. All of them were from stores that sold elegant women's clothing and accessories.

Except one. It was a stiff piece of parchment paper, bearing the name PANACHE in engraved letters, plus a telephone number. Ben picked it up and studied it. He memorized the number, then put the card back with the others.

"Where's her makeup?" he asked.

Muller raised his hands, palms up. "Except for what she's wearing, there wasn't any."

"No containers, no applicators?"

"Nothing. Not even a lipstick."

25

"So the guy took it all with him," Spadone said.

"Looks that way."

Ben was quiet for a moment. He glanced back into the bedroom and saw that the ambulance attendants were putting the still form into a body bag. Somehow the streaks of red and blue and black cosmetics seemed to confirm the young woman's vulnerability. She'd been used badly, turned into human graffiti by a psychopath.

Brennan was shrugging into a raincoat. He looked over at Ben. "I'm going back downtown. You coming, Lieutenant?"

"Not yet," Ben said. "I want to stay with this for a while."

"Okay, but remember, the chief wants to see us. He'll be holding a press conference on this and he's gonna want you there."

"I won't be long," Ben said.

The captain nodded and walked out the door.

Ben turned and looked at the items on the desk once more. It made no sense. Caroline Patterson had grown up in a rich, powerful family. People like her attended the best schools, vacationed in places like Newport and Palm Beach, traveled in Europe. She'd have had money, friends, connections around the world—everything a girl could ask for. But she'd wanted more.

More *what?*

Thrills, perhaps. Excitement. Living on the edge. Maybe that was what she'd been after.

What she'd found was something else: a whore's worst nightmare.

The ambulance attendants wheeled the gurney with the trussed-up body bag on it through the living room and out the door of the suite. Ben watched them go.

"Maybe the guy made some mistakes," Spadone said.

"Such as?"

The detective waved a hand. "Leaving all this shit behind. So we got a quick ID, a lot to go on."

Ben wasn't so sure. "Maybe."

Weisskopf approached them with a uniformed cop in tow. "They found the guy in room service who took an order from this room last night. Also the waiter who brought it up. They're outside in the hall."

"Good going," Spadone said. He turned to Tolliver. "The desk told us there was only one order from here."

"Let's go," Ben said. They left the suite.

Standing just outside the door with another cop were two men wearing beige and brown uniforms with gold trim, one much older than the other.

The older man spoke with an Hispanic accent. He said his name was Roberto Curzon. He had taken the order: one fifth of Glenfiddich, one of Stolichnaya, various mixers, ice and glasses. The time on the ticket said 7:15 P.M. The younger man was the waiter. His name was Alberto Ruiz.

"You remember the call?" Weisskopf asked Curzon.

"No, sir. We get so many. I just wrote it down and we filled the order."

Ben addressed Ruiz. "You delivered it?"

"Yes, sir." His accent was heavier.

"Who let you in?"

"A woman."

"Can you describe her?"

"She was kind of thin, with dark hair. She wore glasses."

"What about her clothes—what was she wearing?"

Ruiz raised his shoulders and dropped them again. "A gray dress, maybe?"

"Was she alone?"

"No, sir."

"Who was with her?"

The waiter's gaze darted nervously from one detective to another. "I don't know. See, when I push the buzzer, a man inside say who is it and I tell him room service. He don't open the door. I hear him tell somebody to let me in. Then I hear a door slam inside. The woman, she open the door and I roll the cart into the room."

"So you never saw him?"

"No, sir."

"Did she sign the check?"

"No, she give me cash."

"You remember anything else?"

"No, sir."

"Okay," Ben said. "Thanks. You can go back to work. We'll want to talk to both of you later on. Be sure you're available."

A cop escorted the pair to the elevator, and the detectives went back into the suite. Ben took another look around in the living room, and then in the bedroom and the bath. As Spadone had said, the bathroom was a mess, with soaking-wet towels on the floor and in the tub. When he returned to the living room, he asked Muller whether the CSU intended to take the towels, and was told they did.

There were telephones in here, but Ben wanted privacy. He told Spadone and Weisskopf to go on questioning members of the hotel staff, saying he'd check back with them later, and left the suite. He took the elevator down to the mezzanine, getting off there and returning the leather case containing his shield and ID to his back

27

pocket. Then he caught another down elevator, this one crowded with hotel guests. When the car disgorged its passengers in the lobby, Ben moved along with the others. He noted that the cluster of reporters had grown larger, and louder in their protests at being denied access to the fourteenth floor.

There was a bank of telephones on a lower level. He went down the steps and picked up a phone, dropping a quarter into the slot and calling a number.

"Vice squad. Warneke."

"Lieutenant Tolliver, Sixth Precinct," Ben said. "Sergeant Paretti there?"

"Yeah, just a minute."

A moment later Paretti's Brooklyn accent came through the receiver. "Hey, Ben. I figured maybe you retired."

"I did, but nobody knows it except you. How's it going, Al?"

"Same shit. What can I do for you?"

"I'm on a homicide," Ben said. "Young woman, in the Plaza Hotel."

"That makes her a classy young woman, right?"

"I guess. You know an escort service called Panache?"

"Sure. Very exclusive, very expensive. Run by an ex-show girl named Martha Bellamy. They got a rep for the best-looking broads in New York."

"If you know so much, how come she's still operating?"

"You kidding me? What we chase is street whores. We don't bother those services. Even though everybody knows what business they're really in, the courts say they got a right to operate. On top of that, Bellamy has got friends in high places. If I ever touched that one, I'd be walking the Lincoln Tunnel."

"Like that, huh?"

"Believe it. Your young lady work for them?"

"She might have. Where they located, do you know?"

"Uptown someplace. Wait a minute." There was a pause, and then Paretti came back on. "It's on East Sixty-third. You want the phone number?"

"I have it. Thanks, Al."

What he would do next was clear enough, but his cop's instincts were putting up signals. One of them was that this was no ordinary homicide—not that he'd ever thought it was. Captain Brennan's remark that they were faced with a delicate situation was the understatement of the year.

Hunt down the man who killed Caroline Patterson? Ben would do his level best. But he'd better watch his own ass while he made the attempt.

The other signal was just as strong. It was that Joe Spadone was wrong. The perpetrator hadn't made mistakes; he'd only wanted the cops to think he had.

Ben picked up the telephone once more, and dropped another quarter into the slot.

# 5

Monica Darrin had been on since 4:00 P.M., Panache's regular opening time. Now it was 5:30 A.M., and she was exhausted. She poured her fourth cup of coffee since coming to work and turned on the TV, switching channels until she found a movie.

Apparently the film was some kind of horror story involving teen-aged kids. The kids were in a cabin in the woods, and judging from the ominous music, they were being stalked by an evil force. Monica couldn't tell yet what the evil force would turn out to be, but she knew it would be horrible and that it probably would scare the shit out of her.

She certainly hoped so.

Otherwise she'd fall asleep, coffee or no coffee. She'd flipped through every magazine in the Panache office—*Vogue, Glamour, Cosmopolitan, Town & Country, People,* even *Reader's Digest,* for God's sake. She'd also cleaned out half the box of Godiva chocolates that lay open on her desk. Out of boredom, she told herself. So a scary flick was welcome, and the grosser the better.

An actress who was between engagements, Monica had taken this job only to have something to do until she got her next part. Actu-ally, it would be her *first* part, and without the salary she earned here, she'd most likely be on her way back to Youngstown, Ohio, where her prick of a father would shake his head and tell her he'd known all along she had no talent.

So although the job wasn't really acting and sometimes like to-night it kept her up until all hours, she was fortunate to have it. Then, too, Martha *appreciated* her. Said she had a beautiful voice, cultured and well modulated, perfect for the telephone. Martha often told her she was bright, too—something her parents had never done.

At first, Monica had been disappointed that Martha hadn't considered her quite right to go on dates, sensing that she was about to experience another failure in a long line of them. What she'd been hoping for, when she applied to Panache, was that she'd be launched into the glamorous life of a New York call girl, making tons of money and getting laid by charming, sophisticated men. When she was turned down, it was crushing. But then Martha had convinced her that with her quick mind, and her instinctive tactfulness, and especially her lovely voice, she'd be *perfect* as one of the phone girls.

Nobody had ever told Monica she was perfect before. Certainly not anyone in her family, not her teachers, not her high school drama coach. Not even the boys she'd given blowjobs starting when she was fourteen and wanted somebody—*anybody*—to like her for her own dear self.

Once she'd become used to handling the phone, she'd found it was actually better than going on dates, in many ways. Of course, she didn't make as much money as the girls who did, but she enjoyed many advantages they didn't. For one thing, it wasn't necessary to spend a fortune on clothes. She could be as comfortable as she was tonight, wearing a pair of jeans and a sweater.

And if she put on a few pounds, as indeed she had, that was okay, too. Whereas Martha would be furious with the escort girls if they gained an ounce. And Martha furious was something Monica would not want to contend with.

When it came right down to it, the money was pretty good. Monica was paid a base salary and a percentage on top of that, and most weeks she made at least six hundred dollars. Once or twice, she'd made over a thousand. But that was unusual.

The thing that really made the job worthwhile, however, was that she got to play a part every night, and that helped to keep her skills sharp. A call would come in, and Monica would answer in warm, rich tones, and she could sense the guy reacting as soon as he heard her voice. She'd banter a little, exchanging pleasantries, always friendly, obviously cultivated, never using a curse word or even letting an off-color remark enter the conversation. She'd find out who he was and where he was, and while she chatted and held the phone with one hand, the other would flick over the keyboard on the IBM 230 and call up information on him if he was a client they'd served before. If he wasn't, she'd be entering data as they spoke.

As did any performer, Monica lived for applause. And while callers didn't beat their palms together after speaking with her, what they often did do was ask her, beg her, sometimes plead with her to go out with them. Never mind any of the others, Monica, they'd say, the girl I want is *you.* It was more than heartwarming; it was thrilling. In fact, there were times, after a long chat with a witty, sexy guy, when Monica would be so excited she could hardly stand it. But she never broke the house rules, never went out with a client, never so much as met one face-to-face. Not that she didn't want to, but Martha would kill her if she did.

That aspect aside, working the phones was something Monica was not only good at but that she loved. When the telephone rang, she was *on.* So skilled was she, in fact, that in recognition of her talent and her dedication, Martha had given her a raise and bestowed on her the title of assistant. Thus in almost every respect, the outlook here was up.

The downside was that the hours were terrible. Five nights a week, she worked from four in the afternoon until two or three the next morning—which cut into her own sex life, of course. Fortunately, her boyfriend was also an unemployed actor, temporarily engaged as a ticket taker in a theater on Broadway. He thought Monica was with a telephone-answering service—which was true, in a way.

So the hours sucked. And sometimes, to her disgust, they were even worse. That was because she wasn't permitted to leave the office until the last girl called in to say her assignment had been completed and she was safely home. The rule was that the call had to be made within two hours after the girl left her date, no matter what. Only after Monica had received that last call could she pack it in and return to her studio apartment on East Ninety-sixth Street. The one exception was when the date was an overnight, in which case the girl didn't have to check in with Panache until the following morning.

The trouble was, occasionally a girl would forget. She might be an airhead; Panache had several of those. She also might be a little tipsy, which could further impair her memory. So she'd go home and not call in and Monica would be stuck here as she was tonight, falling asleep over some shitty movie, dreaming of the revenge she'd exact when Miss Dimwit finally made contact. It didn't happen often, because Martha would raise holy hell with the girl, warning her that if she did it again, Panache would drop her. In this ball game, it was two strikes and you're *out.*

Monica looked at her watch. God, it was 5:40. She picked a chocolate out of the box and ate it, then sipped her coffee and found it cold. When she slammed the cup down onto her desk, some of its contents slopped out and she had to mop up the mess with a Kleenex.

Tonight was hard to understand. Panache had sent out fourteen girls, which was about average for a weeknight, and all but one had been accounted for.

Caroline Clark was on a dinner date. Allowing two or three hours in the restaurant and a couple of hours in bed after that, she should have telephoned Monica long ago. Even if the guy had found her so alluring that he wanted to run up the tab by keeping her overnight, she was required to call in with that information, as well. There were no exceptions.

What made tonight perplexing was that Caroline was one of their best people—maybe *the* best. God knows she had the looks, and the style. Like many of the other girls, Monica was in awe of Caroline. She genuinely was what many of them could only pretend to be, not just stunningly beautiful but with an impeccable background: rich, well educated, socially connected. So much so, in fact, that Panache had to be careful about sending her out, not wanting to pair her off inadvertently with somebody she just might know from the New York Yacht Club, or the Westchester Country Club, in both of which her family held memberships, or even with somebody she might have dated for free. For that reason, nobody but Martha was permitted to book Caroline, and even then Panache's owner always checked with Caroline first before sending her on a date.

Therefore, because she was intelligent as well as a knockout, Caroline was regarded as totally dependable. For her to forget about calling in was unheard-of. For a moment, Monica weighed telephoning Martha at her home, which was only a few blocks from here, but then she dismissed the idea. Being awakened early in the morning was another thing that could cause Martha to throw a shit fit. Better to give Caroline more time.

Settling back in her chair, Monica returned her attention to the movie. The Panavision on her desk had only a seven-inch screen, smaller than the one on the IBM monitor, which made watching it difficult. Especially when she was so fucking tired that she was ready to fall down. But she'd stay awake no matter what. Caroline would come to her senses sooner or later. Maybe the guy was such a stud, he'd turned *her* on.

In the movie, the evil force turned out to be a blob, whose color and consistency reminded Monica of what she'd coughed up when she had the flu. An enormous flood of the stuff was slowly rolling up against the outside wall of the cabin. The kids were inside, and the blob was trying to get at them by oozing its way through the crack under the door.

The girl who had the lead was one-dimensional, in Monica's professional opinion. All she could do was gape at the yellow shit that was threatening to engulf them and scream. She did have great jugs, though, which probably explained how she'd won the part. To become more comfortable while she watched, Monica undid her belt buckle and put her feet up on the desk. Despite her resolve, her head drooped forward and her eyelids grew heavier.

*Jesus Christ.* She must have fallen asleep. Her back was stiff and her mouth was cottony. Swinging her feet to the floor, Monica stood up and rubbed her eyes. Her watch said 8:30. Despite the babbling TV, she'd been out for almost three hours. Maybe Caroline had called and she'd slept right through it. No—the ringing of the telephone would have awakened her; she was sure of it. But there would be no further diddling around. She'd call Martha and let her know Caroline hadn't been heard from.

Monica reached across the desk to turn off the TV. As she did, she saw that a female commentator was on the tube, delivering a local newsbreak. As the woman's words registered, Monica froze.

". . . in the Plaza Hotel, the newscaster said. "A maid found the young woman dead a short time ago, and hotel security guards called the police. As yet she has not been identified, but our sources tell us she was the victim of a homicide. We have reporters on the way to the Plaza now, and will report further as soon as we get additional information. Meantime, two suspects have been arrested in connection with the murder of a crack dealer on East One Hundred Seventeenth—"

Monica turned off the set, feeling as if she'd been punched in the belly. The *Plaza?* And a young woman was *dead?* It couldn't be. It was someone else, of course. And yet, that was where Caroline had been sent to meet her date. Over twelve hours ago. And they hadn't heard a word from her since.

Hands trembling, Monica picked up the telephone and called Martha Bellamy's number.

# 6

Whatever can go wrong will go wrong. Murphy's Law.

Martha Bellamy lived by it, constantly striving to anticipate any contingency. The way she saw it, if you were smart you stayed out of trouble by preventing it from happening. Which was why she regularly made cash gifts to the right people, and could always be counted on for a favor. She maintained her political contacts religiously, burnishing her reputation for dependability and discretion.

She was also known to be scrupulously honest. If she gave you her word, you could depend on it, no matter what. She was shrewd, loyal, and resolute. As a result, in all the years she'd been operating Panache and building a tidy fortune from the proceeds, she'd never had a problem she couldn't handle.

A girl became pregnant? Or fell in love? Or got drunk and made a fool of herself? Or even worse, ran off at the mouth? Nothing to it. At the snap of Martha's fingers, the offender would be gone from Panache forever. Moreover, Martha would let her know there was a dossier on her, which would induce instant amnesia—at least on anything to do with Panache, its clients, or its owner.

Or perhaps an overzealous politician was off on a clean up–New York crusade? Wonderful. Martha wholeheartedly supported the concept of a vice-free city. After all, Panache wasn't involved in vice; the service it provided was strictly social, and on a very high level at that. If anyone was to challenge that premise, Martha knew whom to call for a quiet chat. Whereupon the irritant would simply disappear. She might even get an apology. It had happened, once or twice.

Of course, money wasn't her only form of currency. From time to time, she'd send one of her girls to someone in power purely as a gesture of goodwill, and he'd be as delighted as a small boy with an unexpected present. Naturally, records of all such transactions went straight into the computer. To know instantly just who owed her what favors, she had only to call up a document showing the names of various individuals, cross-referenced by corporation, law firm, or political office, as the case might be. Many were clients as well as beneficiaries of her largesse. It was a terrific system; IBM had provided her with the means to maintain a computerized bank of markers.

This morning, however, was another thing entirely. When the call came in from Monica, Martha was dumbstruck. Of all the desperate situations she'd tried to foresee, this was one that had never occurred to her.

A *homicide?* A *murder?* In the Plaza Hotel, where Caroline had been sent last evening to entertain the well-connected, moneyed John Burton from Los Angeles? And Caroline hadn't been heard from since?

For Christ's sake slow down, Martha, she told herself. You're acting as silly as that bubblebrain Monica. Homicide is something that happens to street tramps. Or to cheats whose lovers are driven mad by jealousy. Or to bimbos mixed up in drug deals. Not to young ladies. Especially not to young ladies of Caroline's class. So keep your drawers dry.

Nevertheless, she'd better get out of bed and hurry down to the office. Even though it was only 8:40 A.M., practically the middle of the fucking night. She'd also phone Patrick, just in case. Two heads were always better than one in times of crisis.

If there was a crisis.

She called his number, becoming annoyed when the telephone rang nine times before she got an answer. Even then it wasn't Patrick who offered a sleepy hello, but one of his little boyfriends.

At last he came to the phone himself, his tone cool and collected, as always. "Good morning, Martha."

"Patrick, there was a murder last night in the Plaza . . . a young woman. Monica just called me; she said it was on TV. Caroline never called in and that's where we sent her. Maybe I should—"

"Hey, not so fast, okay? Have you tried her apartment?"

Jesus, how could she be so stupid? Ordinarily, it would be the first thing she'd do. But this morning, she wasn't thinking straight. It was Monica's fault, the dumb little shit. Blowing her out of bed with that hysterical phone call.

"Have you?"

Her reply was sheepish. "No."

"Like me to try it?"

"No, I'll do it. Sorry to bother you so early. It's probably nothing."

"No problem, I was about to get up, anyway. It's a beautiful day."

She hung up. That was Patrick for you. Totally unflappable, one person she could always count on. Martha opened the leather-bound book on her bedside table and found Caroline's number. Her slim forefinger touched the buttons on the phone.

This time she counted up to twenty rings before putting the instrument down. Now what? Certainly she didn't want to make a fool of herself again with Patrick. Nevertheless, her anxiety was rising once more. She called him back, taking care to keep her voice calm as she told him there had been no answer from Caroline.

"Probably had a big night and turned her phone off," he said. "Tell you what. I'll just nip over there and check on her, okay? I'll call you after I've found out what's going on."

"Thanks, Patrick. You're a darling. But I'm going down to the office, anyway. I have some things to catch up on, and Monica must be pretty bleary. You can reach me there."

Martha put the phone down and pressed the button on her bedside table. Moments later, there was a knock on the door.

"Come in, Chang."

The little houseboy entered, taking two steps into the room before he bowed to her, a broad smile on his round yellow face. "Good morning, Missy."

She noted with approval his freshly laundered, starched white jacket. Getting out of bed, she stretched, and then took off her green silk pajamas, letting them flutter to the floor.

Stepping toward the bank of mirrors on the wall opposite the door, she inspected her body, as she did every morning. It had served her well, and she treated it with care and respect. Not quite six feet tall, with red hair and green eyes that made a startling contrast with her milky white skin, Martha's appearance was striking, whether she was dressed in her usual chic or naked, as now.

She turned sideways, checking her boobs and her belly. Good. Very little droop, and no flab. Nor was there a sag in her ass. Well, maybe a tiny one, but for someone her age—which was nobody's business but her own—she was in downright phenomenal shape, if she did say so herself.

Glancing at Chang's reflection in the mirror, she could see him watching her with admiration. Which was all it was, of course: admiration, not lust. Chang was as gay as Patrick, and that was about as gay as anybody could get.

It was also the way Martha wanted it. There were no men in her personal life, and no women, either. She had friends, of course, droves of them. But not a single one in an intimate, let alone sexual, relationship. The only people she trusted were homosexuals, and even with them she was watchful. As often as her clients implored her, she never slept with any of them—nor with anyone else for that matter, male or female. As far as she was concerned, the only thing fucking would accomplish was to fuck up your life. For sex, she relied on herself, assisted by suitable devices and props.

"Open the drapes, Chang, will you please? And draw me a bath."

As he went about carrying out her orders, she dropped to the deeply carpeted floor and began her daily calisthenic routine: push-ups, back bows, bicycles, knee bends, toe touches, in sets of one hundred each. The routine took twenty minutes, long enough for her to break a good sweat.

After that, she went into her bath and slipped into the sunken tub, luxuriating in the Chanel-scented suds. Usually she would spend at least an hour in here, constantly replenishing the hot water, but this morning she was in a hurry. Speaking with Patrick had been reassuring, but she still had no definite word on Caroline. She stepped out of the tub, and, grabbing a towel from the heated rack, hastily rubbed herself dry.

Back in her bedroom, she turned on the TV, keeping one eye on it as she dressed in a blouse and slacks. Flipping channels, she found only one newsbreak, but it was about yet another crisis in the Mideast, and she turned off the set. As she drew on a cashmere sports jacket, she glanced out the window. Far below and to her left across Park Avenue, she could see flags undulating on the marquee of the Regency Hotel. Sunlight flooded the street. Patrick was right; this would be a beautiful day.

But she couldn't stop worrying. John Burton, from Los Angeles. A new client, but he'd been recommended by Lew Brodnitz. Well, not exactly, come to think of it. Actually, it had been the other way around. Burton's assistant said Panache had been recommended by Brodnitz. Martha had been pleased by that; Lew was an excellent client, a favorite of the girls who called from the Sherry Netherland whenever he was in New York.

That was another thing. Martha had never spoken with Burton, but only with his secretary, who was Bobbie something. Lamson, Lambert? Whatever, the name would be in the computer—which was another reason to get to her office quickly.

Breakfast was a small glass of freshly squeezed grapefruit juice and a cup of black coffee. She gulped both, telling Chang she didn't know when she'd return. Then she slung the strap of her cordovan bag over her shoulder and hurried out the door. The doorman flagged a taxi for her, and less than ten minutes later, she arrived at the apartment Panache used as an office.

# 7

When Martha walked in, Monica was standing beside her desk, a stricken expression on her bovine face.

"I'm so glad you're here," Monica said. "Patrick just called."

"And?"

"He said to tell you he was on his way."

"Did he say anything about Caroline?"

"No. Just that he'd get here as soon as he could."

Monica's eyes were red-rimmed; apparently, she'd been crying.

Martha studied her. The kid was peering back at her, on the verge of coming apart. Obviously what Monica needed was reassurance. And if there was one thing Martha prided herself on, it was that deep down, under the gloss and the smooth manners and the impeccable grooming, she was one tough broad. All her life, she'd been at her absolute best when the pressure was on. But she was also aware that such strength was unusual.

Her tone softened. "Take it easy, Monica. Go wash your face, and then make fresh coffee. Lots of it. After that, I want you to go home and get some sleep, okay?"

"Okay, but—"

"Yes?"

"Would it be all right if I stayed here? You know, just until—"

"Of course it would. Now get busy."

Martha went through the room she'd converted into a lounge for the girls and into her private office, closing the door behind her. She put her bag on the credenza behind the desk and took off her jacket, tossing it over a chair. Sitting down at her desk, she turned on the TV, then switched on the IBM and inserted a diskette into the machine.

Her fingers hit the keys, calling up the document containing the names of Panache clients. And there it was.

*Burton, John. Executive, Genflight Corporation, Los Angeles. Tel. 213–457–1200. 1st contact 10/13 by assistant, Bobbie Lambert. Rec. by Lew Brodnitz. Arriving NY 10/14 Plaza Hotel. Requests best we have. Must be blond. 10/14 Caroline Clark booked for dinner 7:30, Plaza suite 1404.*

Martha sat staring at the screen, her mind racing. It was too early to call the number in California; offices there wouldn't be opening for several more hours. But there'd be a security force. She picked up the telephone and called the number that was on the screen.

After several rings, a voice said, "Genflight. Security."

"Good morning," Martha said. "This is the Beverly Hills Florist. We have an order for one of your executives, to be delivered first thing this morning. I think the name is John Burton. Could you please check to see if the name is right? The order was called in by his assistant, Bobbie Lambert."

The voice sounded bored. But at least it wasn't snotty, which was what you could expect in New York. And it was also polite. "Yes, ma'am. Just a minute, please."

As she waited, Martha tapped her fingertips on the surface of her desk. She wasn't quite sure what this would prove, if anything. Except that she'd been stupid not to double-check the reference. Lew wouldn't have minded a bit if she'd given him a ring, probably would have been glad to hear from her. He was another one who—

"Ma'am?" The security guard was back.

"Yes?"

"We have a John Burton, but no Bobbie Lambert. There's nobody here by that name."

A cold lump formed in the pit of Martha's stomach. "Thank you. We'll check back later." She hung up.

No Bobbie Lambert? Then who was the woman who called yesterday, sounding bright and chatty? The lump grew heavier.

There was a knock on the door. It opened, and Patrick Wickersham walked into her office. He was wearing a typical outfit, this one all black—Sulka shirt, gabardine trousers, wool blazer, Gucci loafers—the only touch of color a red ascot at his throat. His nails gleamed with clear polish, and his short black hair appeared to have been recently trimmed. Even when dressed casually, he looked elegant.

Patrick came directly to the point. "She's not home. There was no answer from the lobby, and the night doorman had been on since two. He hadn't seen her. Of course, she might have gotten home before he went on, but I don't think so. She would have heard all the noise, with the phone ringing and then the doorman buzzing her apartment."

With Patrick, Martha didn't have to pretend. "Jesus, I'm worried. Really worried."

"Yes, of course. No sense letting it get to you, though. Monica's just made fresh coffee. Care for some?"

Martha sighed. "I could certainly use it."

He left her office, returning a few moments later with coffee for both of them. He placed the cups and saucers on the desk and sat down in a chair opposite her, seeming as coolly insouciant as ever.

Martha toyed with a pencil on the desk. "The news was on ABC, Monica said. We have a client there, Hank Sherrill. Maybe I could call him and ask."

Patrick pursed his lips. "I wouldn't do that. You'd shake him up, and then if it turned out to be nothing—"

"Yes, you're right, of course. It's just wanting to do something, other than sitting around waiting to hear."

"I know how you feel, but don't jump to conclusions. It could very well be that she simply went off somewhere, and for once forget to call in."

"I suppose so, but there's something funny here. The guy I sent her to see didn't make the date; his assistant did. I just checked the company in California he works for."

"What did they tell you?"

"That he was with them but there was nobody by the name of the assistant."

"Um, that's odd. But there may be a perfectly reasonable explanation."

"I hope so."

He sipped his coffee. "That's a lovely blouse."

"Thank you. I got it at Bergdorf's. Their fall collection is one of—"

The telephone rang. They both looked at it, watching the lighted button that told them Monica had answered the call on line 1. This had to be Caroline—Panache didn't open for business until 4:00 P.M. No client would be calling at this hour.

The lighted button began blinking, indicating the call had been put on hold. At the buzz of the intercom, Martha picked up the telephone. "Who is it, Monica?"

She sounded out of breath. "It's the police. A Lieutenant Tolliver. He asked for you."

Martha tensed. A *cop?* And he asked for *me?*

She kept her voice steady. "I'll speak with him."

Inhaling deeply, she punched the button. "Martha Bellamy."

"Miss Bellamy, this is Detective Lieutenant Tolliver speaking. I'm investigating a homicide that took place last night. The victim is a young lady named Caroline Clark. I believe she was working for your company. Is that correct?"

It felt as if the lump in her stomach had turned to ice. "I . . . know a Caroline Clark, yes."

"She was found dead in the Plaza Hotel a few hours ago."

"Are you sure? I mean—"

"Yes, I'm sure. I want to come and talk to you. Please stay where you are. I'll be at your office inside of twenty minutes."

"No," Martha said. "That's not possible. I—"

But he'd already hung up. She put the phone down.

Patrick was watching her. "Yes?"

Her mouth was dry. "Caroline is dead. That was a detective and he wants to come here to talk to me. Christ, Patrick—"

His bland features showed no hint of anxiety. "So? Let him come. You're running a legitimate business, aren't you?"

"Yes, of course." She shook her head. "My God, poor Caroline."

The door burst open and Monica came into the office, sobbing.

Apparently, she'd been listening in on the call. She ran to Martha, who stood up and put her arms around her.

The girl's shoulders shook uncontrollably. Martha patted her back and spoke softly to her. "There, there. Go ahead and cry. I know how you feel."

As she held Monica, Martha looked up and saw Patrick making a circling motion with his forefinger, the show-biz sign to speed up your act.

Gently, she pushed Monica away, continuing to hold her by her arms. "Listen to me, Monica. I want you to go home and get some sleep. Take a long hot bath, and then put some whiskey in warm milk and drink it. After that, go to bed. Do you understand?"

Monica nodded, shuddering. Martha reached into a desk drawer and pulled a handful of tissues from a box, handing them to her.

As the girl blew her nose, Martha opened her purse and took a hundred-dollar bill out of her wallet, handing that to her as well. "Here's some money for a cab. You're on this evening, aren't you?"

Monica wiped her face. "Yes."

"Okay, be back here by three-thirty. And Monica?"

"Yes?"

"Stay off the phone when you get home. Don't discuss this with anyone, including your boyfriend. You know nothing about anything. Is that clear?"

She bobbed her head.

"Good. Now run along."

When the girl had left the room, Martha turned to Patrick. "Jesus—a *murder*. Do you know what the media will do with this? It could be the end of Panache. If there is one thing we positively cannot survive, it's publicity."

"We don't have any publicity," he said. "Not yet, anyway. Right how, let's hurry and tuck a few things away. Before our visitor arrives."

"Yes, of course." She stepped over to the fireplace and touched the underside of the mantel. A double course of bricks swung away, revealing a deep compartment. Returning to her desk, she ejected the diskette from the computer and turned the machine off.

In the next few minutes, she and Patrick swept up all the diskettes from her desk, as well as the contents of her file drawer and the book of telephone numbers, and deposited them in the compartment. Patrick then went into the outer office and returned with a load of similar materials, which he placed with the others. That done, Martha swung the brick panel back into place. It closed with a click.

41

Moments later, the doorman's voice crackled from the speaker box on her desk. "Miss Bellamy?"

She touched the switch on the box. "Yes, Tony?"

"There's a police officer here to see you. Lieutenant Tolliver."

Her tone was calm. "Send him up."

# 8

The building seemed typical of the ones that had sprung up on the east side of Manhattan in the fifties and sixties, yellow brick with a canopy out front and a uniformed doorman. It was clean and well kept but had none of the feeling of solidity and permanence you found in the older structures on Park and Fifth and upper Madison, as if they were real and this was only a pretender.

Ben showed the doorman his shield and told him who he was and what he wanted, and then waited while the man spoke into a house phone just inside the glass doors.

The doorman hung up and turned back to him. "Seven C. Turn right off the elevator."

The lobby was done in green, with thick carpeting and a pair of upholstered benches. An elevator door opened and two people emerged. The first was a gray-haired woman leading a small ugly dog on a leash. The other was a pudgy girl wearing a sweater and jeans. Her eyes were red and swollen, as if she'd been crying.

Ben stepped back to let them pass and then entered the car, which took him up to the seventh floor. When he found the apartment, he pressed the buzzer and a man opened the door.

Tolliver knew at a glance the guy was gay. He had on a swishy black outfit with a red scarf around his neck, but Ben would make him for a homosexual no matter what he was wearing.

"Yes?"

He held up the wallet so that both his shield and ID were visible. "Lieutenant Tolliver. Miss Bellamy is expecting me."

The man in black stepped back, and when Ben had entered, he closed the door.

"Who are you?" Ben asked him.

"My name is Patrick Wickersham. I work for Miss Bellamy. If you'll come this way, please."

He followed the guy, taking in his surroundings. The room was set up like an office, with three desks and a number of straight-backed chairs. On each desk was an IBM computer and two telephones.

From there, they went into a larger room, this one furnished with sofas and lounge chairs covered in flowered chintz. Pictures of landscapes hung on the walls, and there were stacks of magazines on the tables: *Vogue, Cosmopolitan, Elle,* all women's reading material. To the left, an open door revealed the kitchen, white with blue curtains. A stack of dirty dishes stood in the sink.

At the far end of this room was a closed door. Wickersham knocked on it and a woman's voice said to come in. He opened the door and stepped aside. Ben went past him into the room.

Martha Bellamy was a surprise. Ben wasn't sure what he'd been expecting, but it wasn't a willowy redhead who looked as if she could be a working girl herself. At least she did until you got close enough to see the hairline wrinkles at the edges of her eyes and around her mouth. She was sitting at a desk, studying him as he approached.

"Good morning, Lieutenant." She glanced at Wickersham, who was standing in the doorway.

"I want him to stay," Ben said. There were two chairs in front of the desk. He sat down in one of them. Bellamy nodded to Wickersham, who took the other.

Ben unzipped his windbreaker. "Sorry I had to give you that bad news."

She made no reply but continued to hold him in a steady gaze.

"Miss Bellamy, I understand what you're running here is an escort service and Caroline Clark was one of your girls. Is that right?"

"What is it you want to know?"

"The answer to my question."

Her lips compressed into a thin line.

Ben sat back in his chair. "Look, let's understand something. As I told you, I'm in charge of a homicide investigation. The victim was employed by you. My job is to find out who killed her, and apprehend the party or parties responsible. I have no connection with the vice squad, and anything you tell me will remain confidential. Okay?"

"Why did you refer to the vice squad? Was that some kind of threat?"

"No. I just wanted to put you at ease."

Her hands were like the rest of her—long, slim, and well cared for. She folded them on the desk before answering. "Lieutenant, I've been in business a long time. It's a legitimate business. Panache is a New York corporation, and I pay taxes to the city, the state, and the federal government. We are a social service, and that's all we are."

"Sure. And therefore it'll be fine with you if I question some of your other employees, right? Some of your other girls?"

She frowned. "I don't want you harassing my people."

"I'm not planning to harass anybody. But I am going to do my job, with or without your help."

She was silent for a few seconds. "What did you say your name was?"

"Tolliver. Ben Tolliver. I run the Sixth Precinct detective squad, but this is a special assignment." He knew she was wondering just who she had to call to get shed of this peckerhead.

She opened the center drawer of her desk and took out a package of cigarettes, putting one into her mouth and lighting it with a small gold lighter. She blew out a stream of smoke. "What happened, to Caroline?"

"She was strangled," Ben replied.

"*Strangled?* That's horrible. Poor, poor Caroline."

"Her body was taken to the morgue at Bellevue. Her father is going down there later to make a positive identification. It's the law a relative has to do that, if one is available."

Bellamy didn't look quite as confident now.

"Who was she seeing, in the Plaza?"

She hesitated.

"If you won't cooperate, I'll have to take you in for questioning."

The green eyes flashed. "And I'll be out again in less than an hour."

"That might be. But in the meantime, reporters will see you. They'll ask their own questions. And they'll also take pictures. Your customers read the newspapers, don't they? And watch TV?"

"Don't let him intimidate you," Wickersham said.

Ben looked at him. "Shut the fuck up."

Bellamy raised her hand. "Wait. Let me understand this. You said anything I told you would remain confidential. Does that mean that if I help you in your investigation, then my name and the name of this company would stay out of it?"

"Yes."

"But what if somebody finds out Caroline . . ." Her voice trailed off.

"If they do, they won't get it from the police."

She dragged on the cigarette, apparently thinking it over.

"We know her real name was Patterson," Ben said. "Clark was only her working name, right?"

"Yes."

"And her father is Spencer Patterson. Did you know that?"

Of course she knew it. But now the implications would begin to sink in. She'd realize this was no nickelshit issue she could brush off just by picking up the telephone. There was an almost imperceptible change in her expression as the muscles around her mouth sagged.

Ben led her a step further. "It wouldn't be in anybody's interest to embarrass her family. That's something the police department is aware of." Jesus, he sounded as bad as Brennan.

But Bellamy wasn't going to roll over that quickly. "How do I know I can trust you?"

"For one thing, you have my word on it." He glanced at Wickersham. "And that's as good as a legal contract, because I'm stating it in front of a witness." Which was bullshit, but it sounded good.

"You're saying nobody would know you were questioning me—or that Caroline was working for Panache?"

"That's correct. Otherwise we go to the station house. And while you're there and the reporters are asking you questions, I get a judge to sign a warrant so we can get your records. I'm sure you realize the district attorney's office will be extremely interested in this case."

Wickersham cleared his throat, as if sending her a signal not to give in.

But Bellamy paid no attention. She looked up at the ceiling for a moment, and then her gaze came back down to fasten on Ben. "All right, Lieutenant. What do you want to know?"

# 9

"Who was she with?" Ben asked.

"His name was John Burton," Bellamy said. "From Los Angeles."

"When did he call?"

"He didn't. His assistant did. From California, before they came to New York. Spoke to me. That was two days ago."

"She give you her name?"

"She said it was Bobbie Lambert. But then—"

"Yes?"

"This morning I called his company. Genflight Corporation, in L.A. I talked to security there and they said they had a John Burton, but nobody named Bobbie Lambert."

"Why did you call?"

"I was worried, about Caroline."

"We all were," Wickersham said.

"Had you done business with Burton before?" Ben knew Burton's AmEx card had been stolen, but he wanted to find out whether they knew him.

"No," Bellamy replied. "He was new."

"How'd this woman get your name, did she say?"

Bellamy hesitated. "No."

Ben let it pass. "Tell me exactly what she said to you."

"She said her boss had heard a lot about us from his friends, and so he told her to call us. She said they'd be coming to New York the next day and that he wanted the best girl we had. Had to be a blonde. They'd be staying at the Plaza, and would call to confirm after they'd checked in."

"They?"

Wickersham spoke up. "Assistants sometimes travel with their bosses." He made it sound as if he was explaining civilized customs to an aborigine.

"She told me to have the girl there at seven-thirty," Bellamy said, "and that Burton would be taking her to dinner."

"And then back to the Plaza?"

"Whatever."

"Was the girl to stay overnight?"

"No."

"So you picked Caroline."

"Yes."

"How many girls did you have working last night?"

Wickersham again broke in. "I don't see what that has to do—"

Bellamy silenced him with another flick of her long fingers, as if she was shooing a fly. Apparently she was resigned to opening up, having decided the alternative would be worse.

"We had fourteen," she said.

"Any all-nighters?"

"One."

Ben didn't know Panache's rates, but since this was one of the top call-girl outfits in New York, they had to be steep. With fourteen girls working on a weeknight, the gross would be sizable. What's more, much of it would be in cash, which meant it could be skimmed. Bellamy's operating expenses would be only the rent, the phones, and a couple of girls to answer them—plus some payoffs and her assistant. No wonder she was touchy. Many of America's corporate

46

.

bandits weren't doing as well as she had to be. To say nothing of the shit they had to take from boards of directors and unions.

"Did you know there was a problem," Ben asked, "before I called you?"

"Caroline hadn't called in afterward, and that's what had us worried."

"How long had she been working for you?"

"About six months."

"How did you first get together?"

Bellamy again hesitated. "Through her boyfriend."

"Her boyfriend?"

"He had been, at one time."

"What are you saying?"

"Caroline wanted a job . . . like this one. There was a guy she used to go out with, and she asked him. He told her about us, and then he called me. He introduced us."

Ben decided his theory that the Patterson girl had been a rich kid looking for kicks was probably correct. "You ask her why she wanted the job?"

"No. That was her business."

"Were you surprised when somebody with her background wanted to work for you?"

"Nothing surprises me, Lieutenant."

That had to be true. "But certainly she didn't need the money, right?"

"I don't know whether she did or not. I know she didn't get along with her father, so maybe she did need it."

"But with her looks and education, and her connections, she could have had a lot of jobs, wouldn't you say?"

Bellamy's green eyes were steady. "Our girls don't come to us just because it pays well. They also like the work."

Job satisfaction and money, Ben thought. The two things most people wanted from a career. Apparently whores were no exception. Although it was hard to equate somebody like Caroline Patterson with the hustlers who fed him street information. Or with the girls he'd known when he was in the Marine Corps, in places like Subic Bay and Panama City. But another thing he'd learned was that people were the same, everywhere.

"How did she get along here?"

"Very well. The girls adored her, because she was everything they wanted to be. That is, some of them are terrific, when it comes to looks. We have several models, for example. And a number of actresses. But Caroline wasn't only beautiful, she really had class. And

47

she knew people everywhere." For the first time since Ben had arrived here, Martha Bellamy smiled. "The only problem we had was that men kept falling in love with her."

"The ones who fell in love with her ever make any trouble? As a result of the infatuation, that is?"

"Oh no," Bellamy said. "Nothing we couldn't handle. Whenever someone starts getting possessive, we just switch him to someone else and tell him the girl has moved to Paris, or something."

"But nothing like that ever happened with her?"

"Sure it did. But it was never anything serious. A guy would call me and rave about her, saying he just had to see her again, nobody else would do. And I'd say, Yes, but you haven't met Melissa, have you? Or Ashley, or whoever. And right away he'd start fantasizing about the other girl, thinking she might be even better."

Patrick sniffed. "Men are like children. Always hoping for a sweeter lollipop."

That suggested an interesting mental picture. "Did you know her well personally?" Ben asked Bellamy.

"Quite well. That is, we got to be pretty good friends. There were a lot of things we had in common. Mutual acquaintances, for instance, especially people in show business. I used to be in the theater, you see."

Sure you were, Ben thought. Third from the end in the chorus line.

Bellamy brushed an errant hair back from her forehead. "So we were always exchanging notes on everything from where to buy clothes to the newest restaurants."

"She ever confide in you about her personal relationships? Either inside or outside the business?"

Bellamy thought about it. "No, not really. Except—"

"Yes?"

"Once she kind of let her hair down. Said her father was a real bastard. She hated him. But that's the only time I ever remember her saying anything like that about anyone. Even the clients she didn't much like."

"Who were they?"

"Oh, she didn't much care for Arabs, so I never sent her to one, after the first couple of experiences. No matter how much they were willing to pay. You wouldn't think it, but even as rich as they are, some of them can be grungy. But so can some of the others, for that matter. We had a French baron who actually stank. Can you imagine that? His family owns a château on the Côte de Beaune. Instead of taking a bath, he'd douse himself with cologne. The girls couldn't stand him. I finally suggested he call someone else."

48

"There are times," Patrick said, "when you simply have to act on principle."

"You say her boyfriend introduced you?"

"Former boyfriend," Bellamy corrected.

"Okay. Who is he?"

She stiffened.

"Relax. He won't know I spoke to you. I could have learned it from her family, or a friend."

"His name is Rodney Burnaford."

"He live in Manhattan?"

"Yes, he's a stockbroker."

"Which firm, do you know?"

"Prudential Bache. He's in their midtown office, on Fifty-first Street."

"I take it he's still a customer?"

"He calls us, from time to time."

"Did he ever ask to see Caroline?"

"No. I mean, he's not that kinky."

"Uh-huh. Ben got to his feet. "Thanks for your time, and your cooperation."

Bellamy rose from her chair. "I hope you meant it, Lieutenant, about keeping this confidential. I've been frank with you because you gave me your word."

"It works like everything else," he said. "As long as you play square with me, I'll play square with you."

"That's fair enough."

"I want to be sure I can reach you anytime I need to talk. When I call, I'll just use my last name. Okay?"

"Yes."

"What's your home number, by the way?"

She took a business card out of a drawer in her desk and scribbled the number on it, then handed him the card.

Patrick Wickersham stood up and smoothed the red ascot at his throat. "I'll show you out."

# 10

There was a public telephone on the corner, a semi-enclosed glass booth. Ben went to the booth and called information for the number of Pru-Bache's Fifty-first Street office. He called the number and asked for the man whose name Martha Bellamy had given him.

The voice was brisk and pleasant. "Rodney Burnaford speaking. How may I help you?"

Ben told him who he was, and that he was investigating a homicide. When he said the victim's name was Caroline Patterson, there was silence.

"You still there?" Ben asked.

". . . Yes. Yes, I'm still here. God, what a shock."

"I understand you knew Miss Patterson quite well."

"That's true, I did. God. What happened, Lieutenant?"

"She was found dead this morning in the Plaza Hotel. Look, it's important that we get together. There're some questions I want to ask you."

"I see. When?"

"As soon as possible. I'm not too far from your office."

"All right. But, uh—not here."

"Okay, where then?"

"We're right next door to 'Twenty-one.' Do you want to meet me in the bar? Say, in an hour or so?"

"Fine, see you there. I'll ask the bartender for you." He hung up.

It occurred to Ben that his old blue corduroys and his windbreaker wouldn't much resemble what the other patrons would be wearing. In fact, dressed as he was, they probably wouldn't even let him in. Unless he flashed the tin, which he didn't want to do.

He dropped another quarter into the slot and called the Midtown North station house. The desk answered, and Ben said he wanted to talk to Phil Monahan.

When he was put through to the lieutenant in charge of the detective squad, he said, "Phil? Ben Tolliver. Did I wake you up?"

"No. As a matter of fact, I was just getting packed to go live in the country, now that you and Brennan are running the police department. What can I do for you, Commander?"

Ben knew there was a cutting edge under the banter; Monahan would be pissed at having another detective put in charge of a case in his territory, especially a homicide with the dimensions this one had. In the era of TV, a lot of cops looked on publicity as the fastest route to promotion. And to a guy like Monahan, with a wife and a bunch of kids and a mortgage, a promotion was something you'd go to war over.

"I need a favor," Ben said. He could imagine the reaction that would generate.

It did. "We are your humble servants, Mr. Tolliver. Sir."

"Yeah. I'm across town, and I need to borrow a jacket and a tie."

"You going formal, now that you're a big fucking deal? Don't tell me—you're gonna be on 'Donahue,' right?"

"Or maybe 'Sesame Street.' How about it?"

"Yeah, I guess maybe we could work something out. Come on in. Our tailor will give you a fitting."

"Thanks, Phil." He hung up and walked back to where he'd left the Ford. From there, he drove down to Forty-second Street and turned right, heading for Midtown North's headquarters.

As he nudged the car through the bumper-to-bumper traffic, he thought of his discussion with Martha Bellamy. The key question was whether the Patterson woman had been killed at random, as it seemed on the surface, or had been a carefully chosen target. There was only one way he knew to find the answer.

It took what seemed forever to get to his destination, which was between Tenth and Eleventh avenues. He parked in the lot beside the station house, among a number of patrol cars and detectives' personal vehicles.

When he walked in, there was a commotion in front of the desk. Two cops were wrestling with a young black woman while the sergeant on the desk watched, looking bored. The woman's hair had been braided into cornrows, and she was wearing bright blue spandex shorts. She was trying to knee one cop in the balls while twisting her head to bite the second cop's hand, which was clutching her throat.

"Bitch!" one of the cops hissed.

"Motherfucker!" the woman snarled. She sank her teeth into the cop's hand, and he slugged her in the eye with his other one.

Ben walked past and went up the stairs to where the detective squad was housed. Monahan shook hands when Ben entered his office. The squad leader was as broad in the shoulders as Ben, but not as tall. Freckles on his high forehead and on his short nose gave him a boyish appearance.

"I appreciate your help," Ben said.

Monahan gestured at his suit jacket, a tan glen plaid with wide

51

lapels. "I would've loaned you mine, but it probably wouldn't be good enough."

"Hey, cut the shit, Phil. You know I didn't ask for this assignment."

"Yeah, I guess so. Fucking department is all politics anyhow, you know that? Not just inside, but out. You got the mayor beating on the PC, and the PC beating on the cops, and the DA trying to screw all of us."

"So what else is new?"

"Nothing. My old man was on the job thirty-two years. Retired a captain. He used to say the politics were like a log floating down the East River with eight jillion piss ants on it, and every one of them thinks he's steering."

"So what's the answer?"

"Beats me. You in this NRA ruckus?"

"I'm trying not to be." It was an issue that had caused a deep schism between the administration and the police unions: on one side, liberal politicians and a faction among the cops favoring gun control; on the other side, many officers backing the National Rifle Association. Ben thought there was no clear answer; each group had a point, but they were equally intransigent.

"That's a good example of what I'm talking about," Monahan said. "Sit down, Ben. You want some coffee?"

"No thanks." He dropped into a chair.

The Midtown North squad commander sat on the edge of his desk. "You know, I heard that when the PC was just a cop, he was gung ho for the NRA. Now he's done a complete about-face, for Christ's sake."

"He's under pressure too, right?"

"Yeah, sure he is. But it's still hard to take. The bad guys are running around with Uzis and M-tens, and if a citizen carries a twenty-two, he can go to jail. You hear about that broad with the Mace?"

"The one who was attacked and squirted the guy?"

"Right. He beat her up and raped her, and then after she finally got the Mace out of her purse and zapped him, she was arrested. Now she's up on assault and weapons charges, and get this—the guy is suing her. Says she damaged his eyes."

Ben smiled. "As somebody once said, life is not fair. You probably didn't realize that."

"The fuck I didn't. How you doing with the case?"

"Just getting started."

"Joe Spadone told me the girl was working. That's wild, isn't it? Somebody like that?"

"Yeah, I thought so."

"You know, I'll be frank with you. I was a little bent when you were put on it. But I know that's just more of the same. Fucking politics. And when I thought it over, I decided I was better off not being involved."

Ben wasn't so sure that was true, but he was willing to give Monahan the benefit of the doubt.

"You want a reason?" Monahan went on. "I'll tell you. There won't only be the squeeze because it's a big case. This one'll have the DA's office all over it, and who do you think they'll take it out on? There'll be some busted balls, you wait and see."

"You're probably right."

"I know damn well I am. This guy Spencer Patterson is a power."

"So I understand."

"You think he knew what his daughter was doing?"

"I have no idea. I just hope the media doesn't get hold of that part."

"Shit, you think they won't?"

"I don't know that, either. Brennan told you they want to have Spadone and Weisskopf stay on it?"

"Yeah, that's okay with me. They're both good people. Brennan said the chief was appointing a task force?"

"That's the plan."

"Something, isn't it? You take the borough of Manhattan alone, there's at least one dead hooker a week, a lot of them homicides. And you know what? Nobody gives a shit. Now along comes Miss Rich-bitch with her big-shot father, and boom! All the city's forces rise up in righteous wrath."

"Yeah. Did Spadone come back here?"

"No, he's still at the scene. You want to call him? I got the Plaza's number right here." He picked up a pad from his desk and placed it next to the telephone.

Ben called the hotel and was put through to the suite on the fourteenth floor. When Spadone came onto the line, Ben told him the woman who'd checked John Burton into the hotel was using the name Bobbie Lambert, and to get out an APB on her right away. He said Spadone and Weisskopf should also contact the LAPD with that information, as well as NYSPIN, which was the New York State Police Information Network. Spadone told him they already had a police artist working with the room waiter on a composite sketch of the woman. Ben said he'd check back later and hung up.

"You ask Sex Crimes about the MO?" Monahan asked.

"Not yet," Ben said. "But I will. You get me a jacket and a tie?"

"Yeah, as a matter of fact, I did."

Monahan got to his feet and stepped to a table, where a tan sports jacket and a red and blue striped tie were lying. He brought them over. "How about these? Made to order, right?"

Ben took off his windbreaker and dropped it onto his chair. He put on the jacket, finding it a little snug under the arms, but altogether not a bad fit. "Hey, this is great."

"And your tie, sir." Monahan held it out to him.

He threaded the tie under the button-down collar of his shirt and knotted it. "How do I look?"

"Like a cop in a jacket and a tie."

"Thanks a lot. Where'd you get them?"

"Borrowed them off a uniform. He won't need them until after his tour."

"Good. I won't be long."

He left the precinct house and returned to his car, carrying his windbreaker.

# *11*

A double line of gleaming limousines was parked in front of '21.' There were Cadillacs, Lincolns, a Mercedes, and a Rolls, the chauffeurs slumped behind their steering wheels, waiting for their employers to finish lunch. The practice had caused a traffic jam on this block every day except Sunday for more than fifty years, but no cop in his right mind would tell one of the drivers to move.

Ben pulled in at the end of the line and tossed the police plate onto the dash before getting out of his car. As he reached the sidewalk, he looked back and was amused by the sight: the beat-up gray sedan sitting forlornly among the stately limos, a poor relative who'd shown up at the ball, unexpected and uninvited.

Walking to where the canopy extended over the sidewalk, he glanced up at the hitching-post jockeys standing on the steps and remembered the first time he'd seen them, coming by here as a kid on a rare foray to midtown from his home in the Bronx. The jockeys had all been painted as black boys then, wearing the racing colors of a number of the restaurant's clientele. Now their faces and hands were pink—a sign of the times.

He went down the steps to the entrance and through the brass doors. In his years on the force, he'd been in the place several times, always on business. He'd never been able to understand what all the fuss was about; it was only an ancient brownstone that had been a speakeasy during Prohibition.

Nevertheless, New Yorkers who'd made it, or hoped to, or wanted others to think they had, still congregated here, and the descendents of Jack and Charlie, the original bootleggers, had gotten rich. The families had sold out, and although some people thought the joint had become a kind of high-level tourist trap, it still had a certain cachet. As Sid Caesar once said of another institution, it was so far out, it started to be in again. But to a certain class of New Yorkers, it would always be '21,' no matter what.

The greeter at the door was welcoming patrons by name. Obviously, the key qualification for his job was to have a memory like a computer, and Ben envied him his skills. He oozed charm to the regulars, but when Ben walked in, he simply nodded coolly.

The bar was straight ahead; a sitting room was on the right. To the left were the stairs leading up to the formal dining rooms. Ben went past the cigar stand into the bar, with its toy airplanes and cars and trucks and other junk hanging from the ceiling, and with the upright posts and the tiny tables jammed together and bedecked with red and white checkered tablecloths. It could have been a saloon anywhere— not pretentious, as it was here, but the kind of dump that had just become stuffed with bits of nonsensical shit over time.

The room was crowded. People were talking loudly and looking to see whether they recognized anyone or were being recognized, and the ratio of waiters to customers seemed about one to one. Ben elbowed his way up to the bar, but before he could ask for the man he had come here to meet, a voice spoke into his ear.

"Lieutenant Tolliver?"

Christ, was he that obvious? "Yes?"

The guy was tall and slim, with slicked back brown hair and a toothy smile, wearing a gray flannel suit and a tab collar with a skinny red tie. He grabbed Ben's hand and pumped it. "I'm Rodney Burnaford. I thought that might be you."

"Uh-huh. Glad we could get together. It was important for me to talk to you."

"Sure, I understand. But I was really shaken up when you told me what it was about. Caroline Patterson dead? It just doesn't seem real."

"It's real," Ben said. "And it was a homicide."

Burnaford shook his head.

"You and Caroline Patterson were good friends, is that true?"

"Yes, we were. My God, I still can't believe it. Do you have a suspect?"

"Not yet."

"That poor kid. Who'd want to hurt Caroline?"

Ben didn't answer.

"Would you like a drink, Lieutenant?"

He noticed a glass in Burnaford's hand. The contents were dark, probably bourbon on the rocks. "Yeah, fine."

Burnaford signaled to a bartender, and Ben ordered vodka over ice. He would rather have had bourbon, but vodka didn't leave you with a breath, at least in theory. It was axiomatic: the better the booze, the easier to tell you'd been drinking it.

Burnaford leaned toward him, speaking close up, the only way he could make himself heard over the din. "Can you tell me any more about it? You said she was found dead?"

"She was strangled. That's about all we know, at this point."

"Jesus. Was her family notified?"

"Her father was. Who else is there?"

"One sister, Samantha. She's younger. Their mother died only about a year ago."

"How'd she get along with them?"

*"Comme ci, comme ça.* With her mother and Samantha, okay, as far as I know. But she and her father were like oil and water. No, that's too tame. More like fire and gasoline."

"Why was that?"

"Well, I'd say her first mistake with him was not to be born a boy."

"Anyone else in the family?"

"I think some cousins, aunts and uncles, but they were all distant."

The bartender set a glass in front of Ben. He raised it and said cheers. The vodka was cold from the ice and tasted fresh and clean. He took a long swallow and put the glass down carefully on the polished mahogany surface of the bar.

He looked at Burnaford. "Did you know her a long time?"

"Sure, we were in school together. At Taft. I was a couple of years ahead of her, so we weren't really friends then. She was kind of a gawk at the time. Then I went to Dartmouth and she went to Smith. One weekend when I was a senior—it was Green Key, which is a big deal at Dartmouth—one of my fraternity brothers had her up as his date. Talk about the worm turning into a butterfly—she was a knockout. That summer, I saw a lot of her. My family lived in New Canaan, and the Pattersons had a home in Rye, besides their apartment here in town. They still do."

"So what was your relationship with her after that?"

"Why, uh—we were just friends."

"Were you sleeping with her?"

He frowned. "That's pretty personal, isn't it?"

What did this asshole think was happening here—it was just two guys having a friendly drink at a bar? "Answer the question. Did you sleep with her or didn't you?"

"Look, Lieutenant—"

"No, you look. I ask you a question, you give me an answer. That way, we'll get along fine."

Burnaford set his jaw. "I'm here because I agreed to see you. I thought I might be able to help. That doesn't give you the right to go nosing around in people's private lives."

"Caroline Patterson doesn't have a private life. Or any other kind. You want, we'll make this discussion more formal. At Sixth Precinct headquarters. We can talk about *your* private life. Including the whores you use. Pru-Bache know about them?"

Burnaford reddened, and his tone became less confident. "I don't, uh—"

"This is a homicide investigation. You understand that?"

"But I'm not a, I mean—"

"A suspect? I don't know yet. Where were you last night?"

"What? I was home, in my apartment. I got there about seven-thirty. The doorman can tell you."

"We'll check."

He licked his lips. "Listen, I'll tell you anything I can. But will it, you know, be kept in confidence?"

It was a standard question. Ben gave him a standard answer. "Of course it will. Now what about you and Patterson?"

"I . . . yes."

"Uh-huh. So you were lovers."

Burnaford was very earnest now. "Not really. Look, I'll try to tell you just the way it was. You see, you'd have to know Caroline. She could just crook her finger and guys would come running. She had anybody she wanted. Yeah, I slept with her. But on her terms. When she'd let me."

"So she was seeing other people, as well?"

"Oh, all the time. And not just college guys, either. She had affairs all over the place, even with friends of her father. At least, that's what I heard."

"Did you keep on seeing her?"

"Whenever I could. Whenever she'd go out with me."

"How long did this go on?"

"A couple of years, off and on. After Smith, she did graduate work at Surval Mont-Fleuri, in Switzerland. Which was just one more thing for her to fight about with her father."

"Why was that?"

"He wanted her to go to Harvard, to the B school. Or if not there, to the London School of Economics. So she'd be prepared to go into his business, you see? But Caroline wasn't having any. It was another way to defy him."

"And that made him angry?"

"Furious. Instead of the son who'd carry on in the family firm, he had this wild daughter who'd tell him to go fuck himself, and in public. I saw her actually do that one night, at the Westchester Country Club. It was at the Sunday-night buffet and she yelled it out, right in front of all these people. I thought the old man would have apoplexy on the spot."

"What then, after Switzerland?"

"Oh, she knocked around here and there. Lived in Europe for a time, in Paris."

"If that was against her father's wishes, what was she doing for money? Did he give it to her?"

"No, her mother did. To tell you the truth, I don't think her mother was all that crazy about dear old Spencer, either. He totally dominated her, and why she put up with it, I'll never understand. But the one thing she wouldn't knuckle under on was Caroline. Whatever Caroline wanted, all she had to do was ask her mother. Of course it was all on the sly, but I imagine the old man knew what was going on."

"And then her mother died."

"Right. Lung cancer. It really broke Caroline up."

"You said that was a year ago?"

"Yes."

"Did that create money problems for Caroline?"

"Sure. Her father thought he could really put the crusher on her then."

"Didn't her mother leave her anything?"

"Oh yeah, but it was all tied up in trusts. You could see Spencer's Machiavellian hand at work there, too. She wouldn't have been able to touch any of it for years."

"Still, it would have been easy for her to get a job, wouldn't it?"

"Not one that would pay the kind of money she was used to."

"What about her men friends—wouldn't one of them have been willing to marry her? Or keep her?"

"There again, you didn't know Caroline. That was the last thing she'd do—let herself be beholden to anybody."

"So what did she do?"

Burnaford hesitated. It was obvious he wasn't sure just how much this cop knew. "I'm not sure."

"Yes you are. In fact, you knew all about it, didn't you?"

The stockbroker stared at him. Red was creeping upward again, from under his white shirt collar into his neck and cheeks.

"You still don't seem to get it, Mr. Burnaford. You may be a suspect in this case, or at least a material witness. Now tell me about what Caroline Patterson was doing for money. And how you were involved in helping her get started."

It had the desired effect. Burnaford squirmed, as if his underwear was too tight. "Jesus, Lieutenant, I swear to God I don't know anything about her death. But this other stuff you're asking me—I could lose my job, if anything like that got out. I mean, our clients are prominent people. Maybe I should . . . talk to my lawyer."

"If that's the way you want to play it, fine. But just so you know what'll happen, it goes like this. I'll arrest you on suspicion of murder. Then I'll read you your rights. After that, I'll take you downtown with me. You'll be allowed one phone call, which is when you get to have that conversation with your lawyer. Then we put you in a cell and the process takes over. You could also be facing vice charges. And of course, we'll make an announcement to the news media."

Burnaford looked as if he'd swallowed a mouthful of shit.

"Or would you rather stick with the original agreement? Which was, you cooperate and it stays confidential?"

He chewed his lower lip, then drank the remainder of his bourbon. "Listen, you know I'm not a suspect. I can prove I was home all evening. The doorman not only saw me come in but I made several phone calls. It'd be easy to check on that."

"It's your choice. Call it."

"You said there could also be vice charges."

"There could be, but there won't if you answer my questions."

"Can I depend on that?"

"Yes." Of course he could. A john had to be caught in the act, and even then was rarely arrested.

Burnaford seemed relieved. "All right, I'll tell you. It was Caroline's idea. We had lunch a few months back, right here in this room."

He looked at his empty glass, and then at Ben's. "You want another drink?"

"Yeah, okay."

Burnaford motioned to the bartender for another round. He turned back. "She wanted to know if I knew any call girls."

"And?"

"And I said sure. She asked me all about it. How they worked, how much they made, all that."

"And you gave her a complete rundown."

"Oh hell, a lot of guys use them. You know that. I told her everything she asked about."

"Including the names of the ones you do business with."

". . . Yes."

"Such as Panache."

Burnaford deflated, like a tire that had run over a nail. He had to be thinking that the cops knew everything, and were only trying to trip him up. "She wanted me to help her. Practically begged me. All I did was make a phone call for her."

The bartender set fresh drinks in front of them. Both men raised their glasses and drank.

"What phone call?" Ben asked.

"I spoke to the woman who runs Panache."

"Martha Bellamy."

"Yes. I told her there was this terrific girl I knew who, uh—wanted to meet her."

"You tell her about Patterson's background?"

"Some. I knew she'd want to interview her. But I also knew Caroline couldn't miss. She was what a guy dreams about getting when he calls for a girl. A stunning blonde with a great body. And on top of that, she was smart, educated, and hip. That's the kind of girl a place like Panache would die for."

"So what happened then?"

"Martha said to have Caroline call, and a couple of days later she was in business."

"You see her after that?"

"Oh sure. Just for lunch, though. Never, uh, professionally."

"When was the last time?"

"A few weeks ago. At Quilted Giraffe, and she took me."

"Was she happy with the job?"

"She loved it. Said she was making a pile of money and had a great apartment on Seventy-third Street."

"She go into any detail, about the work?"

Burnaford smiled. "As a matter of fact, she did. Told me stories that had both of us bent over laughing. Some of those guys must have been real birdbrains."

"She tell you who any of them were?"

"I . . . really don't remember."

Ben sighed.

"Hey, be reasonable, will you? I honestly don't recall. There was nobody I knew. Not personally, anyway."

"But the names were familiar?"

"One was. Barry Conklin."

"Who's he?"

"The head of Rockford Company. Investment bankers, on Wall Street."

"What about him?"

"Apparently he went nuts over her. You know, what's a nice girl like you, and all that stuff. He wanted to take her away, have her all to himself. Told her to name her terms, she had a blank check. But she brushed him off. I gather he was really pissed. Conklin's the kind of guy who doesn't like to be told no. She said he even badgered Martha about it. But Martha knows how to handle those things."

"Uh-huh. Any others?"

"Not that I recall."

"Okay. Now I want you to do something for me."

"What is it?"

"I want you to sit down, this afternoon or maybe tonight at home, and think of anybody else she may have mentioned to you. Either then or any other time, any person she was seeing or who might have had an interest in her. If you come up with anybody, you call me. You got that?"

"Yes."

Ben dug his wallet out of the back pocket of his corduroys and withdrew a card, handing it to him. "You can reach me at this number, at the Sixth Precinct. If I'm not there, leave word. All right?"

"Okay, Lieutenant." He was obviously glad the discussion was coming to a close.

Ben drained his glass and set it down on the bar. "Thanks for the drinks." He pushed his way through the crowd standing at the bar and left the restaurant, noticing the place seemed even louder and more crowded than when he'd come in.

Out on the street, two uniformed chauffeurs were leaning against the front fender of a Mercedes that was parked at the curb. They glanced at him as he came through the doors and walked up the steps to the sidewalk.

Ben looked to his left and spotted a street vendor's stand on the corner of Fifth Avenue. He walked down to the stand, which was doing a brisk business, and waited his turn. The vendor was roasting frankfurters and frying onions, and there was a pot of steaming sauerkraut on the grill.

Ben was hungry, and the smells were making him hungrier as he stood waiting. As always, he associated the aroma with Yankee Stadium, and the times he'd worked as a delivery boy to pay for a seat in the bleachers.

He ordered a dog with everything on it, paid for it, and bit off a mouthful as he walked back toward his car. When he passed the pair of chauffeurs, he saw them watching him, looking puzzled. He winked at them and took another bite as he walked by.

# 12

The apartment was more than a place to live; it was a work of art. Bobbie walked slowly through the rooms, experiencing deep pleasure as she looked at her precious possessions, at the colors that ranged from pale orchid and mauve to night violet.

The furnishings were a mixture of styles and textures. Some pieces were European; others were Oriental. A few were contemporary, but most were antique. Yet thanks to her faultless taste, all of it blended together in perfect harmony. The sofa was upholstered in a rich plum velvet, the flanking chairs in French gray. On the lacquered brass coffee table was a painted Chinese tray that held a pair of Louis XVI candlesticks. A Dufy over the sofa depicted a scene on the Riviera at Antibes, and to one side was an ancient Cantonese screen with a motif of golden serpents on a black field. Near the screen stood a bronze sculpture of a woman. The piano was a Steinway grand, on which rested a jade tree in muted tones of pearl, pink, and emerald.

Bobbie loved jade. There were vases and boxes and carvings of it in here, each one a breathtaking example. She left the room almost regretfully as she went on into her bath.

This area was also special to her, with a character of its own. She'd had it done in blond onyx, with a vaulted ceiling and walls of neo-classical beveled mirror panels. The huge tub was set into the floor, its gold-plated faucet and handles fashioned in the shape of a swan with wings extended. When you depressed the wings, water flowed from the swan's bill. The sink was a long oval whose fixtures were also in an avian motif, only these were smaller birds, one each for hot and cold. Light came from wall sconces she'd found in Rome. The toilet and bidet were in an enclosed alcove.

But perhaps the best feature of the room was the ceiling, a re-creation of one she'd seen in Florence. On its arched surface was a scene of the sky. Across the azure heavens, puffy white clouds drifted and cherubs flew. She especially liked the effect when she lay back in the tub and looked up at it.

The tub was filled now with hot water topped with mounds of suds; Bobbie had drawn a bath earlier. She slipped out of her silk robe and dropped it onto a bench, and then stepped into the steaming tub, descending the steps and settling into it. The suds came up to her chin and smelled deliciously of Joy.

There was a panel beside the tub, convenient to her right hand. One of the knobs controlled the temperature of the water, another the temperature of the room. She didn't touch these; both her bath and the atmosphere were fine. Instead, she turned a third knob, which brought music from hidden speakers: her favorite symphony, Beethoven's Sixth, the *Pastorale*. Finally, she turned down the lights, darkening the room until only the painted sky overhead was il-luminated.

Almost weightless in the hot, fragrant water, she stared up at the scene above her and allowed her thoughts to wander.

The incident in the Plaza had been intensely gratifying. Bobbie had gotten the little blond fool to go for her story with almost no effort. All she'd had to do was flash the money, and after that the bitch would have swung by her heels if Bobbie had asked her to.

Instead, Bobbie'd had something much more inventive in mind.

The staging was wonderful. Getting her to strip, and then go through that ballet routine, was ingenious. The girl had been so vain, so full of herself, doing her turns and arabesques, the red scarf fluttering behind her.

And then, *surprise!*

Bobbie stirred as she recalled the thrill of that moment, whipping the scarf around the girl's neck, so quickly she'd never had a chance to resist.

And then riding her, Bobbie feeling the power in her own arms and wrists, drawing the silk tighter and tighter, using all her strength, the girl choking and clawing at her throat, bucking and heaving, Bobbie laughing with excitement as she controlled her, forced her, domi-nated her, the silk cutting deeper into the slender neck.

63

Until at last the fight had gone out of her. Not abruptly, but gradually, like a long, tired sigh. And when the fight was gone, so was her life.

Painting her had been a brilliant idea. What Bobbie had done was to express, in precise terms, what she'd felt. And wasn't that the essence of all art? Of course it was. An *expression*.

The girl was a prostitute. A whore. Human excreta. Bobbie had needed to show that. But show it in a way that had artistic value. Which meant it had to be abstract, of course.

Picasso had said it best when he talked about his early love affair with Cubism: *a dance around life.*

Wonderful.

But what Bobbie had danced around was death.

Now, however, it was important to keep the affair in the Plaza in perspective. It was only a down payment. There was still so much more to do, before she'd be anywhere near satisfied. Bobbie's suffering had been too great, her humiliation too monstrous, for the blonde to represent anything more than a token. Instead, what had happened to the little slut was merely a taste of what was yet to come.

And besides, the experience had been so brief, had ended so abruptly, that afterward Bobbie had slid into a dark valley of gloom.

What was the term her therapist used to describe such a feeling? Ah, yes. *Postcoital depression.* The sadness following orgasm.

The French, of course, had a more poetic term for it: *la petite mort.* The little death. Leave it to the French when it came to anything to do with fucking.

Lying here dreaming about her plans was picking up Bobbie's spirits; she grew excited as she thought about what she would do *next time.* Lifting her foot, she touched one of the swan's wings, bringing a fresh stream of hot water into the tub. Then she lay back once more, and her hands sought the secret places of her body.

Looking up, she saw the drifting clouds and the smiling pink cherubs, heard Beethoven's immortal strains fill the room.

A wave of emotion swept over her.

# 13

Bellevue Hospital was the centerpiece of the huge complex of medical buildings that ran from Twenty-third Street to Thirty-fourth, on the East River. A sprawl of brick and stone, the old facility put Ben in mind of a fortress, defending its inhabitants against disease and wounds and suffering, and steadily losing the battle. On one hand, it had a reputation as one of the finest teaching hospitals in the United States. On the other, the place was considered a horror by both patients and staff. The word among residents was that after four years, you became either a good doctor or an inmate of the nut ward.

The morgue was in the basement. Ben parked the Ford in the space reserved for official vehicles and went down the steps into the cool, dank air, an atmosphere redolent of chemicals and decay, the smell of the dead. The borrowed jacket and tie had been returned to Monahan, and he was again wearing his windbreaker. He showed a white-coated attendant his shield, and the guy led him to where a small group of men was standing.

One of them was Dr. Kurtz, the assistant medical examiner who'd been at the Plaza earlier. Another was a tall, gray-haired man Ben assumed was Spencer Patterson, Caroline's father. A third was a uniformed cop. Kurtz introduced him to Patterson and to the cop, a young black patrolman named Wheeler who was on assignment to the morgue from Midtown South.

"I got here as soon as I could," Patterson said. "I was playing golf when word came to me."

Ben nodded. He'd expected someone coldly authoritarian, and the man certainly fit that description.

Although he had to be in his early sixties, Patterson was erect and robust, with no sign of excess weight, his skin deeply tanned. Most likely a onetime jock, Ben thought, the type who took pride in his athletic prowess and in staying in shape. There was a marked resemblance to Patterson's daughter in the blue eyes and the even features. He was wearing what was probably considered casual clothing in his circles, a tweed jacket and gray flannels, a white shirt and a blue figured tie.

The attendant showed them the way, through swinging doors and down a hallway, the sound of their footsteps echoing from the tiled

65

floors and the stainless-steel drawers that lined the walls. In the corridor, a number of bodies lay on trays, waiting consignment to the metal compartments. Some of them were covered with sheets, and some were not. A few of the corpses appeared unmarked, but others were misshapen, even mangled.

It had to be brutal for Patterson, Ben thought, coming face-to-face with death this way, all of it raw and with none of the pretense you'd find in a funeral home, the bullshit they gave you about slumber and peace and eternal rest. Here you got reality: the undisguised effects of stabbings and gunshot wounds, of heroin ODs and car accidents, of drownings and exposure.

The body of one man looked as if it had exploded, and Ben knew at a glance what had happened; the guy was a suicide who'd gone out a window in some tall Manhattan building and then had hit the pavement with such impact his body had burst.

Ben glanced at Patterson to see how he was taking it, but the patrician features revealed no clue. The tall man marched steadily down the corridor, head up, looking neither left nor right. When the attendant stopped before one of the doors in the wall, the group closed around him. Kurtz nodded, and the attendant opened the metal door and pulled out a drawer.

The body inside was covered by a sheet. When the cloth was drawn back, the men looked down at Caroline Patterson's face.

At least they cleaned her up, Ben thought, probably washed her down with alcohol when they brought her in. All traces of the garish makeup were gone, but in some ways this was worse, as if she'd been wearing a mask earlier that had hidden the horror, and now the mask was gone and you saw what she must have suffered before she died. The bulging, bloodshot eyes looked back at you as if in reproach, and the protruding tongue jeered silently. It was foolish to attribute emotions of the living to the expression on her dead face, but Ben couldn't help it. Even the angry red furrow encircling her throat was more vivid now, against the white flesh with its purpling cyanotic splotches.

The men stared silently for several seconds, the only sounds distant rattlings and rumblings and the murmur of voices as people went about their work in the hospital above them.

Kurtz's voice was gentle. "Is this your daughter Caroline, Mr. Patterson?"

There was no answer for a moment. Then the man's head, with its neatly trimmed gray hair, bowed a little. His tone was flat. "Yes. It's Caroline."

"Would you sign this, please?" Kurtz handed Patterson a clipboard and a pen.

There was a form on the clipboard. Patterson wrote his name at the bottom of the form with a flick of his wrist, then returned the clipboard and the pen to the ME.

Kurtz drew the sheet over the dead woman's face, and once more nodded to the attendant.

As the drawer slid back into place, Patterson said, "I'll have a funeral director take her out of here this afternoon."

The medical examiner cleared his throat. "I'm afraid that'll have to wait until some time late tomorrow, Mr. Patterson. After the autopsy."

"I don't want an autopsy," Patterson said.

Kurtz looked uncomfortable. "That's something we, uh—"

"It's the law," Ben said. "Whenever there's a homicide, New York State requires an autopsy."

The older man regarded Tolliver. A glint was visible now in the blue eyes, and Ben began to see where Patterson's reputation had come from.

"What is your responsibility in this?" Patterson asked.

"The police department has appointed a task force to investigate the case, Mr. Patterson. I'm the detective in charge."

"And you said your name was, what—Tolliver? Is that right?"

"Yes, sir. Lieutenant Ben Tolliver. Sixth Precinct."

"I think we should have a talk, Lieutenant." He turned to the others. "If you'll excuse us, gentlemen."

Patterson steered Ben away from the others to a place out of earshot farther down the corridor. When they were alone, the older man said, "Why is this case being given special attention?"

The question caught Ben off guard. "I suppose it's out of respect for you, Mr. Patterson."

"Who made that decision?"

"As far as I know, it was Chief Galupo."

"Would he have decided that on his own?"

"No, sir. I'm sure it was cleared with the police commissioner. Or maybe it was the other way around. The commissioner may have ordered it himself."

Patterson considered this. "Lieutenant, when I was informed of Caroline's death a few hours ago, a number of things went through my mind. The detective who called said it was a homicide, and naturally, I was stunned. So I began thinking about what could have happened. Do you have a suspect, by the way?"

"Not yet."

"Then you should know these things. My daughter was a very bright young woman, but she was also willful and irresponsible. No matter what my wishes, she did as she pleased. She had affairs, a number of them. Some of the people she became involved with were not the type I would have expected her to be seeing. Not the kind of men with whom someone of her background and education would find much in common. Some were even what I'd call unsavory."

"Are you saying you think one of them might have caused her death?"

"I think it's a strong possibility. Don't you?"

There was something about the conversation that was off center. Did this guy know what his daughter had been doing and was trying to cover it up, or pretend it wasn't so? Or could he be ignorant of the truth? "What do you think happened, Mr. Patterson?"

"I think she went to that hotel to meet someone. A man she was having an affair with. There was a fight, which could have been over any number of issues. Perhaps she wanted to break up, and he didn't. Or he learned she was seeing other men. Or he was some bum with an extortion scheme. There are many possibilities."

There certainly are, Ben thought. But none of them are what you're suggesting.

"Whatever it was," Patterson went on, "the man became enraged and killed her."

"Is there someone in particular you think we ought to question?"

"There may be. That's something I'll have to give careful thought. In the meantime, I'm chagrined by the way this is being handled. I believe the police department is giving undue attention to the fact that Caroline was my daughter."

"That may be," Ben said.

Patterson's tone was dry. "It may indeed. As it is, the newspapers and the television people will have a field day. You may not know much about how I conduct my business, but I assure you I'm not one of those nouveaux riches who'd do anything to get his name before the public."

"There's no way to prevent the media from blowing this up as much as they want to," Ben said. "You know what competition is like with them. They'd kill each other for a story."

"I'm quite aware of that. But at least it could be toned down on the police end. What the media don't know, they can't exploit."

And if they find out what your daughter was actually doing in that hotel suite, this'll be the story of the year, Ben thought. He heard himself say, "We'll do what we can to keep it as low-key as possible."

Patterson looked down at him. Ben was six two, and this guy had to be a couple of inches taller at least. He'd probably played football at Yale or someplace and never got over it. "You don't have to assure me of anything, Lieutenant. I'll see to it that this is handled properly."

That put things in perspective, didn't it? To the Pattersons of the world, it was all a matter of whom you knew and how you used the contacts. But whether the man liked it or not, Ben would go after this until he was ordered to do otherwise. At the same time, he'd do what he could to comply with Patterson's wishes. Not because he owed it to this officious prick, but because he'd already put in close to twenty years with the NYPD and was not about to fuck it up.

"There's one thing you could do that would be helpful," Ben said.

"And what is that?"

"I'd like you to tell me who these men were your daughter was seeing. The people you said you thought were . . . unsavory, as you put it. If there's anyone you think I should be talking to, I'd like to know who that is."

"As I said, I'll have to think about it."

"All right, but I'd appreciate any help you could give me."

"Very well. I'll also speak to the district attorney. He—"

"Yes?" Maybe you were about to say he owes you a favor, Ben thought.

"Nothing." Patterson reached into the inside pocket of his jacket and withdrew a billfold. He took a card out of it and passed it to Tolliver. "You can reach me at this number."

Ben put the card into his wallet, saying, "Let me give you one of mine."

Patterson raised an imperious hand. "That won't be necessary. I know who you are. Let's go back to the others. I have a lot to do today."

# 14

The press conference was held at NYPD headquarters, 1 Police Plaza. Chief of Detectives Anthony Galupo did the talking, facing a cluster of microphones and TV cameras while reporters yelled questions. Brennan and Tolliver stood just behind the chief, a gaggle of uniformed brass flanking them.

In years past when cops made statements to the media, such conferences were conducted on a catch-as-catch-can basis. And even today, when one was held at some remote precinct house, it would be more or less impromptu. But when the conference concerned a story like this one, the procedure was entirely different. Nowadays, the department had its own public-relations wing, whose staff was responsible not only for issuing information regarding cases the police were working on but also for juggling just this type of hot potato.

All an experienced cop had to do was look around, Ben thought, and he'd know what was going on. The homicide was a sensation, because of Spencer Patterson's prominence in New York business and social circles, and because his daughter had been the victim of a murder with sexual overtones. Which was why the conference was being held at headquarters and with Galupo as spokesman.

But it wasn't an emergency situation, involving such issues as public safety or racial tensions, so the commissioner was not present. If it had been, not only the PC but the mayor himself would be standing here, blinking at the TV lights and the flash cameras. The PR people would have seen to that.

Nevertheless, the case would generate an immense amount of interest, because of the personalities involved and the nature of the crime, both of which made it the kind of story the media lusted after. So the powers that ran the NYPD would handle it carefully, but not give it undue attention. If they did, the media would roast them for that as well, claiming that in New York the rich got better treatment than the poor. Which was the truth, of course, and had been ever since the Dutch screwed the Indians out of the island of Manhattan, but no official could afford to admit it.

". . . and therefore I have directed that a special task force be formed," Galupo was saying, "to investigate this brutal murder and to apprehend the perpetrator. The man I have put in charge of that task force is Detective Lieutenant Tolliver, one of the New York Police Department's ablest officers."

Sweet shit, Ben thought. For almost twenty years, I did everything I could to avoid publicity. Because there's only one reason for your sources to trust you. It isn't enough to pay them and do them jailhouse favors. Above all else, you have to protect them. Which means you never reveal their identities, never let anyone know they're talking to you. If you do, they're dead. They know it, and you know it. So the last thing in the world you want is for anybody to make you as the man.

That's why I never tried to attract attention, the way a lot of

ambitious cops do, why I never wanted to build a rep. All I wanted
was to do the job. So what happened? I got lucky and closed a big
case, and now I'm like a bug under a microscope—a personality, no
less. Joe Asshole, famous cop. What stupidity.

And why did it come about? Politics. Brennan may be a cement-
headed Irishman, but when he laid this one out, he knew what he was
talking about.

"Who are the suspects?" a reporter yelled.

"We have no suspects at this time," Galupo answered. "The investigation is in its early stages."

"What was she doing in the Plaza Hotel?" someone else shouted.

"That's one of the things we're trying to determine."

The questions became a barrage. "Who was she with?"

"Who rented the suite?"

"Who was she having an affair with?"

The chief let it go on for awhile, in order not only to give the
impression that the police were doing everything possible to solve
this reprehensible crime but also to make clear that the Manhattan
Chief of Detectives was a dedicated public servant who had to take
a lot of crap as he carried out his duties. He answered the questions
patiently, his replies merely revealing that so far the police had little
to go on.

None of the reporters so much as suggested that Caroline Patterson might have been a prostitute on assignment.

Galupo finally called a halt and stepped away from the microphones. The battery of lights was extinguished, and the babble of
questions trailed off to low-level grumbling. As the group of police
officers broke up, he told Brennan and Tolliver to follow him into his
office.

Once inside with the door shut, the two detectives sat on straight-
backed chairs in front of the chief's desk. As always when he was in
Galupo's presence, Ben felt something akin to awe.

For one thing, Galupo was Italian. He'd grown up on Mulberry
Street, in a neighborhood where there were people who were proud
of the fact that they spoke almost no English. Where there were
grandmothers who never wore anything but black. Where the kids'
heroes were named Gambino and Gotti and Gigante, and where the
citizens would have elected Joe DiMaggio president of the United
States if it had been possible.

Not that plenty of Italians hadn't made it big in America. Lee
Iacocca was chairman of Chrysler and Francis Coppola had won
Academy Awards and Frank Sinatra was the greatest pop singer in
the history of the world. And right here in the state of New York,

you had a governor who not only was a goombah but who had the balls to tell the Pope to go fuck himself, if the governor disagreed with an edict from the Church.

What was unusual was that Galupo was a high-ranking *cop*. Because in the NYPD, the Irish still ran the show. Sure, among the brass you could find bohunks and Germans, a couple of Hispanics, a few Jews, and a surprising number of blacks. But that was because the administration stood on its head to appeal to the voters of Harlem and Brownsville and the South Bronx, and also to show the citizens and the media how evenhanded it was.

But when push came to shove, as it sometimes did, the people who made the decisions were of the same origins as they had been since the NYPD was formed, back in the late nineteenth century. So for Anthony Galupo to have become Chief of Detectives in New York's most prestigious borough, he not only had to be very lucky and very tough, he also had to be very good.

Galupo was all of those.

Which didn't necessarily endear him to other cops. To most of the men under his command, he was a ballbuster. And to the Irish, he was also an upstart dago. Respected, but still a wop. It was something the three men who were together in his office today clearly understood.

The chief peered at Tolliver. He was sitting bolt upright in his chair, the way he always did, as if he had a poker up his ass. His hair might have been combed with black shoe polish. "You got any questions?"

"The task force," Ben said. "Where do I get the men?"

"You've already got them."

Ben was puzzled. "They've been assigned?"

"The two people from Midtown North who caught the case," Galupo said. "Spadone and Weisskopf."

"And that's it?"

"Department's shorthanded, Lieutenant. I'm sure you know that."

For Christ's sake. The bullshit at the press conference had been just that: bullshit. What the investigation would really boil down to was the work of three detectives, Tolliver and two guys borrowed from another precinct. It took an effort for him to keep his composure.

Galupo was watching him. "What else?"

"What about questions from the media?"

"Be as cooperative as you can. Anything you can't handle, refer them to the captain or to me."

Brennan spoke up. "Don't worry about the attention you're gonna get. This thing will be big news until tomorrow, and then something else'll shove it out of the way."

Balls, Ben thought. While it's true the public will probably forget it in a hurry, the bad guys won't. I don't want any attention coming my way, if I can avoid it. "What if I duck the reporters altogether? Just because I'm running the case, that doesn't mean I have to be a spokesman, does it?"

"You'll be helpful and courteous at all times," Galupo said. "We have enough problems trying to carry on the department's business without ruffling the media's feathers."

"I'll work out of my office in the Sixth," Ben said.

Galupo nodded. "Fine. But don't try to do both jobs at once. You got a pretty good sergeant in there with you, right?"

"Ed Flynn."

"Yeah. Let him run the squad until this thing gets cleaned up."

"All right."

"Did Patterson ID the girl's body?" Brennan asked.

"Yes. I was at the morgue when he did."

The chief's eyes narrowed. "And the captain here has explained to you how it's important not to give out anything that would upset the family, right?"

"Yes. I understand that."

"Did Patterson know what his daughter was doing in that hotel?"

"I don't know. He just said he thought she was having an affair and maybe they got into a fight or something."

Galupo expelled air from between thick lips. "That might have been just a signal to stay away from any other possibility. Which wouldn't be a bad idea."

"I talked to the people who run the escort service she worked for," Ben said.

"Who are they?"

"It's called Panache. The owner's name is Martha Bellamy."

"Go light on that," Galupo said. "It would be much better if Patterson's theory turned out to be the correct one."

Jesus Christ, Ben thought, what's more important, to close the case or to protect Patterson from negative publicity?

Brennan answered the question for him. "Whatever happens, we can't bring back the man's daughter for him. Better that the family don't have any more pain."

Tolliver clamped his jaws together.

"One other thing," Galupo said. "The district attorney is taking a personal interest in this case. He's already assigned an ADA to it."

The chief looked at a notepad on his desk. "The man's name is Brian Holland. You're to call Holland and work closely with him." He tore the sheet off the pad and handed it to Ben. "And that's another place to watch your step. Keep this guy informed, but be careful, if you understand what I'm saying."

"They know she was working?"

"Sure, but they want it kept quiet, too," Brennan said.

Ben looked at the zone commander, and then at the chief.

"I'm sure you understand the problem," Galupo said. "The DA is taking a lot of heat because the courts in Manhattan can't handle the caseload. Arresting whores is bullshit, because they're no sooner in than they're out again. Vice has to pick them up because it's the law and because there're pressure groups. But it's a waste of everybody's time, including the girls'. You know that, right?"

Of course he knew it. "Yes."

"So if a homicide investigation happened to tip over a call-girl ring that was doing business with some prominent citizens, everybody could lose. That kind of a case would get blown up by the media, but it'd be almost impossible to prosecute. The DA would look like an asshole, and there's enough strain between him and the commissioner as it is."

Ben looked down at his hands and folded them on his lap. Was this what he'd spent all those years in the department for? So he could get to cope with this shit?

Galupo seemed to sense what Tolliver was thinking. "You got a good future ahead of you, Lieutenant. No reason you can't keep on going right up the ranks. But there's one thing every cop who makes it has to learn on the way. The job isn't just police work. You follow me?"

"Yes, sir," Ben said.

"Good luck."

The meeting was over.

# 15

B rian Holland was furious. Standing in the shower at his Fifth
Avenue apartment, he shook his head as he thought about the
case. Of all the ridiculous, unexpected developments he could imagine, getting stuck with this shitbomb was about the worst. The victim
was Spencer Patterson's daughter? It was unthinkable.

It was also bad luck—dreadful luck—which was ironic, because
Holland didn't believe in luck at all. In fact, he was certain it could
be virtually eliminated by intelligent planning. And Holland's entire
life had been based on preparing for the next move, thoroughly,
rationally, meticulously. Beginning at Fieldston, when he first decided on a political career. And then later at Princeton and the UVA
law school. He had preferred Harvard, but when he knew he
wouldn't make it, he'd exhibited characteristic resourcefulness by
gaining admission to Virginia and then posting a brilliant record.

Yet here he was now in this stupid, awkward situation. He'd never
met Patterson—in fact had only seen him once, at a fund-raiser in the
Waldorf, but the man was well known as a behind-the-scenes power
in New York politics. The developer had unlimited connections, and
very deep pockets. Why had he also had an idiot bitch of a daughter
who'd gotten herself killed in the Plaza Hotel? And far worse, coming to the heart of the dilemma, why had Holland been assigned the
case?

Because the DA was a bumblehead. The man was too old, obviously on the verge of senility. He was the type who'd stayed on long
past his prime—if he'd ever had a prime—and was now capable only
of making dumb mistakes, such as this one. He'd actually thought he
was doing Holland a favor by putting him on the case. Instead, he'd
shoved his brightest young prosecutor into a no-win situation.

To begin with, the case was still under investigation. So it was in
the hands of the police, and Holland would have little influence
there. He'd know what was going on, but that was all. Breaking it
would be up to the cops, and he had only contempt for the NYPD's
ability to solve crimes. If a murder took place with police officers
looking on and the killer surrendered at once and made a detailed
confession in front of witnesses, the cops might close the case. Otherwise, they were in over their heads.

This wasn't merely an impression on his part; Holland knew that statistics bore him out. There had been over two thousand homicides in New York the previous year, and fewer than half of them had been solved.

So as the cops went about their fumbling, anyone associated with the case would also be tarred by their failure. Patterson would learn who the assistant DA handling it was, and that inevitably would lock in the wrong kind of association with Holland's name. Patterson might even blame him for a lack of progress.

And if Brian tried to wriggle out of the assignment, the DA would be angry and resentful. Shit, what a mess. But he'd think of something; he had to.

Meantime, there were other factors to deal with, such as this evening, which entailed another carefully planned part of his life. He'd reached the point that, in order to keep his career on track, he had to settle into marriage. With a proper bride, of course, one with background, money, and family connections. Brains were not a requisite. Fortunately, and as another example of his ability to plan ahead, he'd chosen an excellent candidate.

He turned off the shower, stepped out of the glass enclosure, and toweled down. He'd told Stephanie he'd pick her up at 7:30, which was an hour from now. There would be plenty of time to dress.

The suit he chose was a new one that had been tailored for him by Dunhill's. It was gray worsted, double-breasted, and with a Turnbull & Asser shirt and a blue Sulka tie, it was smashing. The suit also had a dash he took care not to exhibit during the day, when he wore stodgy Brooks Brothers outfits. It was important, he believed, to play the part of a conservative, no-nonsense plugger when he was in the office.

On the other hand, evenings were another thing entirely. With his slim good looks and his obvious flair for wearing clothes, he cut quite a figure. Looking at his reflection in the three-paneled wardrobe mirror in his bedroom, he couldn't have been more pleased.

Well, he could have, come to think of it. His hairline was receding, and that irritated him. His hair was still black and full on the sides, but it was definitely becoming sparse on top. In fact, his forehead was noticeably higher than it had been just a few months ago.

What was even more annoying was that there wasn't much he could do about it. It would continue to recede, of course; hair loss was hereditary. His father had been bald when he was quite young— even younger than Brian was now. And Brian couldn't buy a hairpiece, because he hadn't yet lost enough for one to work. Maybe he should get some of that stuff Upjohn was hawking in those awful commercials, where some boob stood in front of a mirror and talked to himself.

But the hell with it. He looked great, thinning hair notwithstanding. There was still a half hour to kill; Stephanie's apartment was only minutes away from his. He went into the living room and turned on the TV, then sat down in his favorite chair to watch the local news.

It was a stream of the usual drek: The Reverend Dan Marydale was addressing a rally in Harlem, protesting the way Oriental owners of grocery stores treated the brothers. With his long hair and a necklace, Marydale looked like a fat black hippie, a holdover from the sixties. Tonight was a switch for him, railing against Asians instead of his usual white targets. After that came a story about a rise in infant-mortality rates in city hospitals, which was equally boring.

But then there was coverage of a press conference on the Patterson case, and Holland was instantly alert.

The police spokesman was Manhattan Chief of Detectives Anthony Galupo. Holland didn't know Galupo except by his reputation, which was excellent. With the chief were a number of senior uniformed officers, and Holland was amused at how much they resembled one another. All of them seemed overweight, with gray hair and red faces, and with gold braid dripping from their hats and uniforms.

Along with the uniformed cops were several plainclothesmen. Galupo announced that one of them, a lieutenant named Tolliver, would be leading the task force assigned to the case. The chief made it sound as if Tolliver was the new Dick Tracy, but Brian had never heard of him. Obviously, the police were as given to hype as any other public figures.

While Galupo was answering questions from reporters, Holland studied the man the chief had extolled. Certainly there was nothing very distinguished about his appearance; he was tall, with craggy features and a mustache. His hair was black and might have had a little gray in it, but it was hard to tell. Even with cable, TV in a Manhattan apartment building left a lot to be desired.

The detective also seemed ill at ease. He looked at the sky, then down at his hands, anywhere but into the camera. It was as if he was uncomfortable or even embarrassed to be standing there among his superiors. His clothes were a letdown as well. He was wearing a zippered jacket and baggy pants, and Holland realized he was the only man on the platform without a tie.

So this was the detective he'd be expected to work with on the Patterson case? Good God. Maybe he ought to ask the DA to take him off the case after all, before this charade went any further. At least he'd be cutting his losses early on. And besides, in a week or two, the old man would probably forget whom he'd assigned, anyway. Still, Brian reminded himself, it wouldn't do to be rash. He'd have to handle this the way he did everything else that was important to him: carefully weighing every possible aspect.

He got to his feet and snapped off the TV. On the way out, he paused for one more admiring glance at himself in the hall mirror. Tonight would be a good time to test the waters with Stephanie, to get a sense of how she'd feel about becoming Mrs. Brian Holland.

The answer to that was obvious: She'd be thrilled.

He smiled at his reflection and left the apartment.

# *16*

Washington Square Park was thronged with people, as it was most evenings when the weather was pleasant. Tonight the air was a little cool, but it was still Indian summer, mild for October and with only a hint of the cold blasts that would rake the city a few weeks from now. Ben sat on a bench just up the walkway from the arch and watched the passersby.

They were of all ages and colors, young and old, black, white, Hispanic, Asian. Many were paired off, boys and girls with arms around each other, strolling more slowly than other pedestrians. Some of the couples were of one sex, both partners male or both female.

Younger kids sailed by on roller skates or skateboards, shrieking as they went. There were pigeons waddling along, paying little attention to the human activity as they searched for food. A brown youth with a gold chain around his neck strutted past, carrying a boom box. The blaster was huge, gleaming with chrome and covered with dials and knobs, its speakers pouring out a torrent of *muy bonita musica.* Salsa? Rumba? Ben wasn't sure.

He suddenly realized he was tired. It had been a long time since he'd been blown out of Patty's bed by that phone call.

So what can you expect? he asked himself. One thing you don't get much of on a big case is sleep. And this one is just beginning.

He'd brought a paper sack with him. Opening it, he took out a can

78

of Budweiser and popped the top. The beer was ice-cold and tasted wonderful. He swallowed a long draft and went on watching the parade. He'd been there about fifteen minutes when the girl came ambling up the walk.

She was easy to spot. Tall and shapely, with a spray of black hair that had been straightened and spiked, her skin was like burnished copper in the glow of the lights in the park. She had very long legs, encased in red spandex shorts that came to mid-thigh. And despite the cool air, she was wearing only a thin cotton singlet that showed off deep breasts with thumb-sized nipples. When she reached the bench, she dropped onto the seat alongside him.

He looked at her and smiled. "Hey, Shirley. How you doing, honey?"

"Doin' fine, Ben. How 'bout you?"

"Great. Want a beer?"

"Now that's my man."

He took another can out of the sack and opened the top before handing it to her.

She drank from the can and belched softly. " 'Scuse me."

"What've you got for me?"

Shirley swallowed more beer before answering. Her voice was warm and rich and still carried a trace of Georgia. "After you called me, I ask around. My fren' Louise? She works uptown. Early tonight she done a guy; he say he's a waiter in the Plaza Hotel. He told her that woman got killed there last night? He say she was a workin' girl."

"What else did Louise tell you?"

"That mostly it. 'Course, she don't know if it's bullshit. But if the guy told the truth, it's scary, you know? Anytime a girl works, she takin' a chance anyhow. But in a high-class hotel, you don't expect nothin' like that."

"No," Ben said. "You don't."

She drank again. "Thing is, a call girl ain't the same as on the street. She can make a lot of money, but without nobody lookin' out, she can get her ass in a jam."

"Nobody looking out?"

"No pimp," Shirley explained. "Call girl goes out there on her own. She got nobody to protect her. Turning tricks can be dangerous, man."

"Uh-huh." It was weird, the hookers' point of view on pimps. A guy would have a half dozen girls on the street, and they'd hand over every dollar they made in return for a place to sleep, a few bucks for spending money, and protection that amounted to little more than a fantasy. On top of that, if they threatened his authority or sassed him, they'd be rewarded with a beating.

And if they held out on him, punishment would be far worse. A few weeks ago, cops from the Sixth had pulled a floater out of the river, a black girl wearing shorts much like Shirley's, her belly ripped from crotch to sternum. There wasn't much question the knife wielder had been her pimp; other girls had been quick to pass the word. Detectives in Ben's squad had been tracking the guy for weeks, with no success. Yet hookers all believed they were better off with a pimp than without.

Shirley looked at him. "You think the waiter tellin' the truth? I mean, the TV say she a society girl. You believe it?"

"I don't know," Ben said. "But I appreciate hearing what your friend told you." He passed her a twenty-dollar bill, tightly folded.

She murmured thanks as she slipped the money into her shoe.

The story will go around, he thought. No matter how the cops might try to keep it quiet, there's no way the lid will stay on the reason Caroline Patterson went to that hotel. Sooner or later, it will go around. Hell, it already has.

Shirley sipped her beer. "Kinda cool tonight, ain't it?"

"Yeah, but nice. How's it going?"

"Okay, but I could be busier. Better when it's hot out."

"I like your shorts. I see a lot of the girls are wearing them now."

"Oh yeah, they popular."

"Pretty tight, though, aren't they? Good thing you don't have to take them off."

She laughed and slapped his thigh playfully. Her teeth were large and very white. "That's 'cause I got what they call a good head for business."

He smiled. "I'll bet."

Her voice became a purr. "Maybe I could give you a little demonstration?"

"Sort of like a test drive?"

She giggled. "Yeah, like that."

"Sometime, maybe. But tonight I've got too much work to do."

She drained the can and set it down on the bench, then stood up. Looking down at him, she cocked her head to one side. "Anytime, baby."

"Good night, Shirley. Be sure to call me if you hear anything else."

She slowly made her way back down the walk, hips swinging, long legs stretching the red shorts, hands at her sides with fingers extended.

80

Pretty girl, he thought. If it wasn't for her protection, she could be rich.

She'd also done him a service. As more people heard stories like the one she'd told him, a number of them would become nervous. They would be the johns who were Panache's customers, and they'd be worried about what the investigation might uncover. It was another angle to pursue.

He finished his beer and dropped the empties and the paper sack into a trash barrel as he left the park.

# 17

L e Cirque was crowded, but its owner was obviously delighted to see him. The restaurateur bowed. "Good evening, Mr. Holland. And welcome."

"Hello, Sirio. I think you know Miss Drake."

He bowed again. "Of course. How nice to have you here." He beckoned to a captain. "Arturo will show you to your table."

When they were seated, Holland called for the sommalier, telling him to bring a bottle of Bollinger. As the steward hurried off, Stephanie looked at Brian curiously. "Are we celebrating? And if so, what?"

He smiled. "That depends."

"Ah, a mystery. I like mysteries. Are you going to give me clues?"

"Possibly." He thought she was especially attractive tonight, with her sandy hair pulled back in a chignon, and wearing a low-cut black dress that showed off her figure, which was striking.

"Do I win a prize if I guess right?"

"Oh, yes. You'll win a prize."

"How will I know if I've won?"

"I'll give you the word, Stephanie."

"Promise?"

"Promise." So she wasn't bright; in fact was close to inane. But that was no handicap, as far as Brian was concerned. The last thing he'd want for a wife would be some twit who thought she was as clever as he. Or worse, one who might be bold enough to try to dominate him. As it was, Stephanie was invariably deferential. As well as decorative. Put those appeals together with her social position and family fortune, and she was just about perfect.

"How was your day?" she asked.

"Fine. Busy, as usual."

"I would think so. Must be exciting, to be the district attorney."

"I'm not, Stephanie. I'm only an assistant district attorney." And only one of more than two hundred in the Manhattan office, but he didn't add that. Actually, her obsequiousness pleased him.

"Well, practically," she said. "It's just a matter of time. Someone with your ability."

He smiled and patted her hand.

The sommalier returned and made a fuss of presenting the champagne to Brian, who favored him with an almost imperceptible nod. The man pried loose the cork and the bottle opened with a festive pop. He then poured a bit for Holland to taste, while a waiter brought a silver bucket on a stand. When their glasses had been filled and the steward was gone from their table, Brian and Stephanie toasted each other, the crystal flutes ringing musically as the rims touched.

Stephanie sipped her wine. "I love champagne. It always makes me feel the occasion is special. Although I'll admit I think any occasion is special when I'm with you."

"That's lovely, Steph."

"So what happened today? Are you working on some big, exciting case? I'll bet you are."

The corners of his mouth curled in amusement. "As a matter of fact, I am."

"Ooh, tell me about it."

He held up his glass, as if to downplay the importance of what he was saying. "Actually, I've been asked to take on the Patterson murder."

Now there was genuine awe in her tone. "You're going to be in charge of *that?* Brian, that's wonderful. I'm so proud of you."

"Oh, it's something of a plum, I suppose." The truth was that he'd been trying desperately to think of a way *not* to work on the case, but her reaction was gratifying. Maybe the visibility would be worth the risk, at that.

"I saw it on the news twice tonight. Once at six and again at seven."

Why anyone would want to watch the news twice was beyond him, but that was Stephanie for you.

She was wide-eyed. "It's some scandal, isn't it? I didn't know her, but Betsy Maxwell did. Imagine her being murdered like that. Strangled, in the Plaza Hotel. Isn't that ghastly?"

"Yes."

82

"And is it true? I bet you know, don't you?"

"Know what? Is what true?"

"What they're saying. About what she was doing there."

"Stephanie, what are you getting at?"

Her tone dropped to a conspiratorial level. "Betsy called me today at the office. Of course, everybody's talking about it. In fact, that's just about all we talked about the whole day."

Brian could believe that. Stephanie was with Pearson Brothers, an auction house. It was one of the few jobs her education, a major in art history at Pine Manor, would qualify her for. "And what did Betsy tell you?"

She dropped her voice lower still, until it was little more than a breathless whisper. "Betsy said Caroline Patterson was a call girl. She said she knew some guy who was a customer of hers. Caroline was using a different name, but the guy recognized her from a picture he'd seen in *Town & Country*. He went back and looked it up and he was positive that's who it was. Isn't that something?"

"Um."

"She was really wild, you know. I mean, she had a terrible reputation. So nobody was surprised at anything she did. But can you imagine how her family must feel about it? They'd have to know, wouldn't they? By now? Her father must be *furious*. But I'll bet you knew all that, didn't you?"

He felt a dull pain in the pit of his stomach.

She prattled on. "I don't envy you, having something like that to contend with. But at the same time, it's going to be the case of the year, isn't it? Brian, I'm so happy for you."

"Um."

"Well, aren't you thrilled? Pretty soon everyone in New York will know who you are. And when you, what do you call it, prosecute the case, you'll be famous."

"Uh-huh."

"God, you're always so cool. Even about something as big as that. That's one of the things I love about you."

Goddamn it, he thought.

She touched his arm with the tips of her fingers, and at the same time brought her leg into contact with his. "I'll bet that's what we're celebrating, right? So I guessed, didn't I?"

"Yes," he said, hoping that would shut her up. "You guessed."

"Do I get my prize now? Or do I have to wait till later?"

"Later, Stephanie. After dinner."

She pressed her leg tighter and rubbed it up and down. "I bet I know what it is."

# 18

When Ben got back to Sixth Precinct headquarters, he had trouble finding a parking place. There was a lot next to the station house, but as usual it was packed with police vehicles—RMPs, traffic scooters, vans. He finally located a spot for the Ford on Charles Street. When he'd squeezed into the space, he put the plate on the dash, locked the car, and walked back to the squat gray brick building.

It was early, but already the action was heating up. As he walked in, cops were trying to separate a well-dressed couple who were kicking and clawing at each other—apparently a lovers' quarrel. But then he was startled to hear the woman call the man a stinking cocksucker in a bass voice. As he went up the stairs, he decided it was still a lovers' quarrel.

When he reached the squad room, detectives were questioning a heavyset man with long greasy hair and a beard who was sitting beside Ed Flynn's desk. The guy had on a blue smock that was covered in multicolored smears of dried paint.

Flynn was leaning back in his chair, dressed in his customary style, sporting a navy chalkstripe that made him look more like a stockbroker than a detective sergeant. He was holding a pencil between his forefingers, which added to the impression.

Two other members of the squad were hovering over Ed's desk, and neither of them looked like cops, either. Frank Petrusky was bald and sweating in a lumpy brown suit; Carlos Rodriguez had on a tight-fitting yellow shirt and fawn-colored slacks. Rodriguez's head was capped with shiny black curls, and a gold chain gleamed at his throat. Another detective was busily typing on a beat-up Underwood a few feet away, paying no attention to the group clustered around Flynn.

Ben stopped to listen.

"So what happened, François?" Flynn asked.

The bearded man raised both hands and his shoulders, then let them drop. His eyes were wide. "I really don't know. I was painting, see, in my studio. Irma and me have separate rooms where we work. I was just about to take a break, go out and make a fresh pot of coffee, when boom! There's this noise. At first, I thought maybe it was the sculpture she was doing, and it accidentally fell over, you know? That can happen, sometimes. Specially when it's something big, like this impressionist thing she's doing of an American Indian."

"Come, on François," Petrusky said. "What happened?"

"I'm trying to tell you, for Christ's sake."

Flynn gestured with his pencil. "Just continue with your story."

The bearded man glared at Petrusky for a moment, then turned back to Flynn. "Just as I'm about to close the door, I notice something on the floor. I run over, and oh shit—it's Irma. Right away I see there's blood coming out her nose and the back of her head, and she's out of it. I realize what must've happened was, she was up on the ladder and it went over. See, sometimes Irma has a drink or two when she's working."

"And what did you do then?" Flynn asked.

"I ran down on the street to get help. I thought maybe I'd see a police car or something."

"Why didn't you call nine-one-one?"

"I guess I just panicked. When I was out on the sidewalk, I tried to get somebody to help me, but nobody would. So I finally did get the idea to call the cops or an ambulance or something, and I went into Shanahan's for the phone. But somebody was on it. So while I'm waiting, I hear sirens, and it's the cops, thank God."

"Hey, François," Petrusky said. "Do you really—"

Flynn cut him off. "Let the man finish."

"So I run out to tell the officers what happened, and then we go back up to the studio, and I can see Irma's hurt real bad. She didn't even move from when I left her. A couple minutes after that, the ambulance got there and I rode with her to St. Vincent's. We were still in the emergency room when these two come in and start making a lot of stupid accusations—saying I hit her. The dumb shits."

Petrusky brought a thick forefinger close to the tip of François's nose. "You watch your mouth, you fat fuck."

Flynn's tone was mild. "Gentlemen, please. I'm only trying to find out what actually happened."

"We talked to the neighbors," Petrusky said. "They told us her and François were having a knockdown dragout. They heard a lot of screaming, dishes smashing on the wall, Irma and him yelling curses. A real war."

"Hey," François said. "Everybody argues now and then. It was nothing."

Rodriguez spoke up. "Yeah? It was nothing? Then how come we saw broken glass and shit all over the floor in there?"

François's eyes narrowed, and a crafty expression flickered over his hairy face. "You went in my apartment? And you didn't have no warrant?"

Carlos smiled. "The door was standing open, asshole. We looked in from the hall."

"We pulled it closed for you," Petrusky said. "I heard the lock snap, so you don't have to worry about somebody robbing the place."

"Yeah," Rodriguez said. "You got other things to worry about."

"After the fight, you went down to Shanahan's all right," Petrusky said. "The bartender told us you were on your second vodka when the cops went to your building."

Petrusky glowered. "I told you, I was waiting to use the phone."

"What else did the neighbors say?" Flynn asked.

"They told us the two of them were always fighting," Petrusky replied. "They'd get drunk and François would beat her up."

François bared his teeth. They were yellow and one of the incisors was chipped. "That's a goddamn lie."

"The neighbors gave you statements?" Flynn asked the detectives.

"Sure," Petrusky replied. "We got 'em from six people."

"One lady lives right upstairs," Rodriguez said. "A couple times Irma told her she was scared he'd kill her."

"Oh, shit," François said. "That's ridiculous. I told you, we were together almost five years. Like man and wife."

Flynn spoke to him in an offhand tone. "You're under arrest for assault and attempted murder."

"Bullshit!" A spray of spittle burst from François's mouth. Some of the drops glistened in the tangled beard; others landed on Flynn's desk.

"Tell him," Flynn said to Petrusky. He got out a tissue and blotted the moisture on his desktop.

"You have the right to remain silent," Petrusky began.

Ben raised a hand. "Hey, Ed?"

Flynn looked around. "Hello, Lou. Didn't see you come in."

"You got a minute? When you're finished there?"

"Sure thing. Be right with you."

Ben went into his office and closed the door. He took off his jacket and sat down at his desk. The small room's cinder-block walls were painted green, and the light from the overhead fluorescent bars gave his hands an unhealthy cast. He took out his wallet and picked through it for the Panache card. When he found it, he called the number.

# 19

A feminine voice answered, sounding cultured and pleasant. "Good evening, this is Panache."

"Ben Tolliver calling," he said. "I want to speak with Martha Bellamy."

"One moment, please. Mr. Tolliver, did you say?"

"Right."

A minute later, Bellamy came onto the line. "Hello, Lieutenant. What can I do for you?"

"I wondered if you had a chance to think over the things we talked about. Maybe you have some ideas for me." It wasn't the actual reason for his call, but he wanted to see how she'd react.

"Oh yes, I thought about it. But I haven't been able to come up with anything that might help you."

"Uh-huh. That's too bad. There's one thing you can do, though."

"Oh? And what is that?"

"You can give me a list of your customers."

There was a pause, and then she laughed. "Give you a list . . . of our clients?"

"That's right."

"Lieutenant, I'm sorry, but we don't keep such a thing."

"You don't?"

"No, we don't. And now if you'll excuse me, I'm quite busy."

"When I was in your office," Ben said, "there was a computer on your desk."

"So?"

"You use it to keep records, don't you?"

"Of course. But only of transactions for accounting and tax purposes. And the company's expenses. Rent, telephone, all the normal costs of doing business."

"Plus information on your customers, right?"

"Wrong. I told you, we have nothing like that."

"Any of them pay by credit card?"

". . . Some do. Why?"

"Because the credit-card companies keep records. And so do the banks, when people use Mastercard. I can get the DA to subpoena those records."

Her voice took on a hard edge. "Then why don't you do that,

Lieutenant, if you think it's so important? But of course, there are a few things you should keep in mind."

"Like what?"

"Like some people might be highly upset if they were to find out a policeman was poking around in their private lives, sticking his nose in where it didn't belong. As I think I pointed out to you, Panache is a legitimate business. There is nothing whatever wrong or illegal about the service we provide. My attorney tells me we would have excellent grounds for a lawsuit against the city if our business was damaged or even threatened by some overzealous police officer."

So she'd talked to her lawyer. Ben had known that would happen. He also knew he was on thin ice. It might be wise to let this angle cool a little, until he had a chance to talk with the ADA who'd been assigned to the case.

"Are you still there, Lieutenant?"

"Yeah, I'm here."

"Well. It was nice speaking with you. Good night."

He heard a sharp click, and then the hum of the dial tone. He slammed the phone down. "Son of a *bitch!*"

There was a knock at the door, and Ed Flynn came into the office, a grin on his face. "Did you call me, Lou?"

Despite his anger and frustration, Ben had to smile. "Sit down, Ed."

"How about I get us some coffee first?"

"That sounds good."

As Flynn ducked out, Ben thought again of Bellamy. Jesus, what a set of balls on that woman. She'd come right out and laughed at him. But what had he expected?

Okay, so sometimes he made mistakes—everybody did. He'd had his best chance when he'd first confronted her and her assistant in Panache's offices. He should have demanded a list of her customers then. Bellamy would have pissed her pants, but he might have been able to bluff her into giving him the names.

No. He was kidding himself. Martha Bellamy wore elegant clothes and had nice manners and talked about her career in the theater, but that was a bunch of shit. She hadn't become a successful madam because she was a cream puff. Just under that polished surface was one tough broad. She was also clever and deceitful. And one of the first things a rookie cop learned was, never trust a hooker or a gambler. A whore is a whore.

Flynn returned with Styrofoam cups of black coffee. Ben sipped his and found it steaming hot, but he was grateful for the caffeine hit.

The sergeant sat down on one of the straight-backed chairs. "How's it going, Lou?"

As Ben considered the question, one corner of his mind marveled at the way Flynn always managed to look as if he'd just come from the barbershop, on his way to a heavy date. His chalkstriped suit was neatly pressed, with one inch of white shirt cuff showing, and the burgundy tie held a perfect knot. His dark wavy hair was trimmed, and his smooth jaw looked as if he'd shaved a short time ago. No wonder the guy was so successful at hunting pussy; he always was dressed for the kill.

"Lousy," Ben said at last. "Every time I turn over a rock, what crawls out is politics."

Flynn nodded sympathetically. "That figures. This guy Patterson's got better connections than the bishop."

"I believe it. Everybody from the top down gives me the same speech." He raised a clenched fist in mock righteousness. "The NYPD will do everything in its power to break this case." He dropped his hand back to the desk. "So long as we don't offend anybody."

"Brennan said the chief talked to you."

"Yeah, he sure did." Ben gave Flynn a rundown on what had taken place in Galupo's office, and also filled him in on what he'd done up to now in the investigation.

The sergeant listened intently until Ben finished. "And all you got to help you is Joe Spadone and this other guy, what's his name?"

"Art Weisskopf."

"I don't know him."

"I didn't, either. But Phil Monahan says they're both good."

"Yeah? Phil could give a shit whether you get anyplace on this."

"True enough." He drank some of his coffee, then hooked his thumb in the direction of the squad room. "You're gonna have trouble with that."

"With François? Oh, yeah. He called his lawyer and got the guy's answering machine. He had a fit. Said it shouldn't count as his phone call."

"Tough, François."

"So he'll be our guest, at least until tomorrow, when we send him down to the pens. But I know what you mean. Even if the lawyer's a scumbag, he'll tell him all he has to do is keep his mouth shut and we got no case."

"Too bad you don't have a witness."

"Isn't it? There is no doubt in the world that prick beat up his old lady and then left her unconscious on the floor while he went out to a bar. But if he sticks to his story, he's almost sure to beat the charge, if it goes to trial."

"If it goes," Ben said. "But even if the ADA gets the grand jury to indict, a conviction would be something else. First thing François's lawyer will do is produce a flock of witnesses who swear the woman's a drunk, and that's why she fell off the ladder."

"Was a drunk."

"Was?"

"We got a call from St. Vincent's. She died a little while ago."

"So it goes to murder two."

"Manslaughter," Flynn said. "If we're lucky."

"Now who's the fucking lawyer? You thinking about changing careers, Ed?"

"Wouldn't be a bad idea." Flynn yawned and got to his feet. "I'm gonna pack it in. There's a broad waiting for me on Broome Street."

"A new one?"

"Semi-new. I've seen her a couple times. Her husband's a musician. He's got a gig at the Blue Note."

Ben smiled. "No wonder you appreciate music."

"Yeah, I'm a real fan." He opened the door, then turned back. "Say, Lou?"

"Yes?"

"Brennan said I was supposed to run the squad while you're on this other thing and I should stay out of it."

Ben waited.

"Anyhow, I'm in it, you know that. Whatever you need me to do, just say the word."

"I will, Ed. Thanks."

When Flynn left the office, Ben's thoughts returned to Martha Bellamy once more. She may have slammed the door on him, but nevertheless he'd managed to get a few things out of her when he'd gone to her office.

Opening a drawer in his desk, he took out a pad and jotted down a list of names: Martha Bellamy, Patrick Wickersham, Spencer Patterson, Rodney Burnaford, Barry Conklin.

The coffee seemed to have picked him up a little; at least he didn't feel as tired as he had earlier. Nevertheless, he wished he could get out of here and go back to Patty's apartment. When she came home from the club, he'd have a couple of drinks with her and something to eat and then they'd go to bed.

But that was wishful thinking. She might not be overly pleased to see him, after he'd blown his promise to spend the day with her. Even though the way they'd said good-bye that morning had certainly left nothing to be desired. Maybe it'd be better to give her some breathing room for a day or so. And anyway, right now he had too much work to do.

He looked at the piles of paper on his desk. On top of one of them was a manila envelope that had been sent to him from the lab. He opened it and saw that it contained eight-by-ten glossies of the crime scene.

# 20

B en pulled out the photos and looked at them. There were long shots and close-ups, some of them focused in tight on Patterson's garishly made-up face and breasts and crotch. With its outlandish decoration, the woman's body seemed as startling in the photographs as it had when he first saw it.

Not that there was anything unusual about a killer desecrating the body of a victim. Ben had seen corpses chopped, flayed, and even cut apart and the pieces rearranged. Women sometimes had objects stuck into one orifice or another. Two years ago, the naked remains of a female had been found in an alley off Bleecker Street with a cigar in the vagina. The ME said the cigar had been lit when the killer inserted it. And a favorite gesture of Oriental murderers—and of some Italian mob guys as well—was to cut off the penis of a male and leave it stuffed in his mouth. But that was more likely to be a message to business associates than the work of a psycho. Nothing personal, as it were.

He'd also seen signatures. Initials and even whole phrases were sometimes found carved in the victim's skin, or burned in with a cigarette. Bite marks were also common. And to make identification difficult, professionals often cut off the victim's fingers and knocked out the teeth.

But he'd never run into anything like what had been done to Caroline Patterson's corpse. What kind of mind would conceive such an idea?

He thought about it for a time, and then he riffled through his Rolodex for the number of Dr. Alan Stein and called it, glancing at his watch as he waited for an answer. It was close to midnight, but as a psychiatrist who was a consultant to the NYPD, Stein was on call twenty-four hours.

91

Not that the department put many demands on him. Most cops regarded shrinks as phonies, and some thought they were flat-out frauds. But virtually all police looked at them with cynical suspicion. Witch doctors, Brennan called them. Nevertheless, Ben respected the man and often asked for his opinions.

When Stein came onto the line, Tolliver told him what had happened in the hotel and what he'd learned of the victim's background. Stein said he'd seen a newscast on the case and that it sounded interesting. Particularly in light of what Ben was telling him now—things about which the media knew nothing. Tolliver said he wanted to see the doctor as soon as possible, and Stein told him to come ahead. After letting Flynn know where he could be reached, Ben left the precinct house. He took the photographs of Patterson's body with him.

Stein's office was on the opposite side of Manhattan, on East Tenth Street near Tompkins Square Park. Ben drove the Ford, making it over there in less than fifteen minutes. The doctor lived where he worked, in one of the three-story row houses that had been built in the nineteenth century as middle-income housing and now went for a small fortune when you could find one for sale. Ben went up the steps and rang the buzzer.

The doctor squinted at him through a peephole in the massive front door, then swung the door open and told his visitor to come in. Once Ben was inside, Stein shut the door and double-locked it, dropping a steel bar into place. A red light in a wall panel indicated the alarm system was activated. Ben followed him down the hall to his office, at the rear of the house.

As always when he came here, Tolliver was curious that anyone could work in a room like this. There were no windows, and the air smelled stale and musty, like the back room in a pawnshop. The clutter was incredible. The walls were covered with bookcases jammed to overflowing, and more books were stacked haphazardly on the surfaces of tables and the doctor's desk and on the floor. Where there were no books, there were messy piles of paper. The requisite Freudian couch stood against the wall opposite the desk, and a sagging armchair was at right angles to the couch. Cones of light flowed from a couple of rickety lamps. Except for a computer on one of the tables, the office might have belonged to an earlier century.

Stein's personal appearance was just as sloppy. A heavy gut pushed out the front of his checked flannel shirt and hung over his khaki pants, and his gray-flecked beard was straggly. When he peered out from behind his black horn-rims, the thick lenses magnified his eyes, so that he looked like an owl in need of a shave.

An ice bucket and bottles stood on a table. Stein went over there. "You want a drink?"

"Vodka would go good," Ben said. He pushed some papers aside and sat down on the couch, watching as the psychiatrist packed two glasses with ice and poured the clear liquor into them. Stein handed a glass to Ben and said, "Cheers." Both men drank, and the doctor eased his bulk down into the armchair. Ben took the photos out of the envelope and passed them to him.

Stein studied the pictures for several minutes, examining each one with care before going on to the next. Once or twice, he grunted softly as he looked at them.

"So what about it, Doc?" Ben asked. "What do you think we've got here?"

Stein sipped his vodka, while the owlish eyes continued to stare at the pile of photos. He dropped them into his lap, and when he looked up, he said, "You know you may not be dealing with a psychopath at all."

"Yeah, I thought of that. Maybe just somebody who wants us to think we are."

"Correct."

"But on the other hand, if the killer really is a nut case, what do you make of this?"

"A number of things. The hostility is obvious, of course. And something as elaborate as this makeup job indicates not just rage but hatred. It took time, you see, as well as a steady hand. If he'd gone berserk, killed her in some sort of paroxysm, he would have cut or slashed or bludgeoned—as you'd expect. But he didn't. He did this with great care, which suggests he wasn't only venting hostile emotion, but that it was also intensely gratifying to him."

"Okay, so he hated her. What else?"

"I didn't say that."

"What? You just—"

"I said he was motivated by hatred. But he might not have hated her personally at all. Might not even have known her, for that matter."

"Ah. Which would mean that what he hates is women in general."

"Maybe."

"And the Kewpie doll makeup—that tell you anything?"

"Why that motif, you mean?"

"Yes."

Stein pursed his lips. He picked up one of the photos, a full-body

93

shot of the corpse, and held it close to his eyes. When he put it down, he said, "I would think it was meant to express contempt. To denigrate. But he might have chosen any number of designs, so to speak. Why this particular one, I couldn't say."

"Okay, here's another one for you. What do you make of the team—the man and woman working together?"

"Let me think about that, for a bit."

"Sure, go ahead."

Stein lifted his owlish gaze toward the ceiling. From time to time, he sipped vodka as he concentrated.

He was an odd character, Ben thought. Living here alone, seeing only his patients and the cleaning woman who came in each day and cooked his dinner before she left. Stein didn't even have a nurse or an assistant. And obviously, this was one room the cleaning woman wasn't allowed into. If you took a dust cloth to it, you'd probably choke to death.

Yet the man had a better understanding of the criminal mind than anyone Ben had ever met, not only in the NYPD but among the faculty of John Jay College of Criminal Justice, as well. Stein had spent eight years on the staff of Fairlawn Hospital in Virginia, an institution devoted to the treatment of violent psychopaths. He'd once told Ben that after the third year there, he realized the hospital's best hope was not for successful treatment of its patients, but to keep them from getting back outside. After the eighth year, he'd left the staff and come to New York to begin a private practice. It was either that, he said, or in time he would have become a Fairlawn inmate himself.

"There are a number of possibilities," the doctor said at last. "One is that the man is the killer and the woman procures for him, because he totally dominates her. She's his slave, relating to him the way the women in Charles Manson's so-called family did to him. Another is that they kill together, because they're both psychotic, and their personalities complement one another. The psychiatric term for that kind of relationship is a *folie à deux*. Perhaps the most famous example in the history of crime in America was Leopold and Loeb."

"They the teenagers who killed another kid just to impress each other?"

"Yes. In Chicago, back in the twenties. It caused a sensation at the time."

"What else?"

"Still another possibility is that there was no man—that she acted alone. I'm sure you thought of that."

"It crossed my mind. Nobody ever saw him, and it was a woman who called the service for a girl."

"Yes. But that's extremely unlikely. As you know, sex murderers are almost invariably male." He put the photos on the floor and stood up. "Here, let me freshen your drink."

Tolliver handed over his glass. "Thanks, Doc. But go easy this time."

Stein lumbered back to where the liquor was. As he made two more drinks, he said, "Which leads us to still another possibility."

"That there was no woman."

The doctor handed the glass back to him. It seemed to have just as much vodka in it as it had had the first time. Ben swallowed some of the drink, not tasting or feeling it.

Stein settled back into his chair. "Exactly. Whenever you have a homicide and there are symbols involved, the sexuality of the killer is a factor. He's a male, but his sexual identity is often badly confused. On the surface, he may seem to be an ordinary heterosexual. But he is never normal."

"So a nice-looking lady registered for the suite and ordered booze, and then called for a girl. But she might not have been a lady at all."

Stein nodded. "As I say, it's just one of several possibilities. You might be interested to learn that there are more transvestites in New York than there are people in Altoona."

"That's comforting to know."

"And I would also point out that all of us, male and female, carry in our personalities some tendencies of the opposite sex." He smiled. "Even you and I, Lieutenant."

"Uh-huh."

"You'll find an extreme example among penitentiary inmates. The most macho males are the first ones to take prison wives."

That was true enough. When he'd visited joints like Attica and Sing-Sing, Ben had observed that the toughest inmates all had punks and guarded them zealously. "Yeah, I've seen that. But what you're telling me is that the two likeliest scenarios here are that it was either a male-female team based on a sick relationship or a man masquerading as a woman. Is that right?"

"I would say so, yes."

"You laying odds one way or the other?"

"No, I'm not. But neither would surprise me."

"Anything else come to mind?"

"Not at the moment."

"Okay, Doc. I appreciate your seeing me."

"Always a pleasure, Lieutenant." Stein picked up the photos and gave them back. "I'll go on thinking about this, and if further ideas come to me, I'll call you. Meantime, be sure to keep me posted as to how you're doing."

Ben returned the photographs to the envelope. "One other thing."

"Yes?"

"Why would a girl like Caroline Patterson want to be a whore?"

"Aside from defying her father?"

"Yeah. What else was there?"

"The same element you find in all prostitutes, regardless of background. Deep down, the woman is convinced she's worthless."

Ben swallowed the last of his drink and stood up. "I wonder who gave her that idea?"

"Not hard to guess, is it?"

"No, it's not." He put his glass down on the table where the liquor was and made his way back down the hallway to the front door, Stein following.

When the psychiatrist opened the door, Ben turned to him. "One last question."

"Sure."

"You think he'll do it again?"

"Of course. Don't you?"

# 21

The law offices of Cohen, Dietrich and Rakoff were on Madison Avenue at Fifty-second St. Martha rarely visited the firm in person; most of her dealings with them were conducted by telephone, as was virtually all her business. But today's meeting was important. When she'd called Abe Rakoff, he insisted on two things: first, she was to say nothing more to the police, and second, she should come in for a conference as soon as possible.

Actually, Martha didn't mind making such a trip. In fact, she rather enjoyed it. Coming down here gave her an excuse to dress in some of her daytime best, and she got a kick out of playing the role of high-powered female executive.

Today she was wearing a black box-cut jacket and checked skirt from Saks, and over that a lightweight gray wool coat she'd bought at Bergdorf Goodman. With the outfit topped off by a vermilion hat that had been made for her by DeMauri, she looked terrific. When she got off the elevator and strode into the reception area, the girl at the desk regarded her with a mixture of envy and respect, and a man sitting in one of the visitors' chairs stared appreciatively.

Rakoff kept her waiting five minutes. She stood, because it would indicate she hadn't expected to be out here very long. And also because it showed off her height, which made her appearance even more impressive.

The reception room was more or less standard, richly paneled in wood and furnished with leather chairs and dark red carpeting. A number of old oil paintings hung on the walls. It occurred to her that what all lawyers wanted you to think was that they were sober and respectable and had been in business at least a hundred years.

Abe himself came out to greet her, a rumpled hulk of a man, extending his hands to take hers and giving her a perfunctory kiss on the cheek. "Martha, how are you? God, but you look wonderful."

"I'm fine, Abe. How are you?"

"Very busy, but delighted you could make it. Please come in."

He grasped her elbow and steered her through a door and down a hallway into his office, closing the door and indicating a chair. "Please have a seat. May I take your coat?"

She unbuttoned it as she sat down, saying she'd keep it on. Instead of sitting at his desk, he took another chair near hers. She glanced about, at the antique mahogany desk overflowing with stacks of papers, at the prints of English fox-hunting scenes on the paneled walls.

Martha was always amused by Rakoff, partly because she understood him so well. It was something akin to the way she'd felt about the first man she'd lived with, a cardplayer who took her to Atlantic City when she was sixteen and taught her the fundamentals of how you got along in the world. The cardplayer was a heavy drinker, but she'd admired his cleverness. Even after a dozen scotches, he could sit at a blackjack table and count cards with machinelike accuracy.

"Would you like some coffee or something?" Rakoff asked.

"No thanks. Let's get down to business."

"Okay. To tell you the truth, I was shocked when you called yesterday. I mean, here you have one of your girls murdered, and not only that but it turns out she's from a prominent family. Do you realize how important Spencer Patterson is?"

"I'm beginning to. TV has gone nuts over this."

He waved a hand deprecatingly. "They'd do that anyway. You get a pretty blonde killed in an uptown hotel and to the newspeople it's like a gift from heaven. But what's really amazing is that she was a Patterson and a hooker."

"At least they don't have that part. Yet."

"Yet is right. This cop. Tolliver, you said his name was?"

"That's it."

"He told you the police would do their best not to let anyone know she was working. Is that correct?"

"Yes. It sounded as if they were as anxious to keep it quiet as I was."

"Uh-huh. That I can understand. One thing Patterson's got a lot of besides money is power. Too many people owe him to make the mistake of crossing him. He's somebody you wouldn't want for an enemy, especially if you were in politics."

She shook her head. "Damn. All the months Caroline was with me, I didn't know that about her. I knew her family was rich, and I had a vague impression that her father was an important man. I also knew she hated him. So I just figured that had a lot to do with why she was working and let it go at that. I never guessed he was *that* big."

The telephone buzzed. He excused himself, getting up from his chair and going to his desk to answer the call and then speaking in low tones.

Martha watched him, again amused by his smooth manner. Despite his square suits and his carefully cultivated style, she knew Rakoff had spent his boyhood as a hustler on Delancey Street. He'd told her once, over drinks, about how he'd figured out when he was still young enough to do something about it that lawyering was the ultimate con.

Once he'd decided on it as a career, he never looked back. He went to City College, and then to Brooklyn Law School, graduating from both institutions with highest honors. Now, twenty-five years later, he was enjoying the fruits of his success—a partnership in a prestigious Manhattan firm, a luxurious home in Scarsdale and another in Boca Raton. Both his daughters were alumnae of Ivy League colleges, themselves married to successful men.

The only element that hadn't worked out to his satisfaction was his marriage. Sylvia was an incessant whiner, at age fifty all diamonds and tits.

Of course, Abe hadn't left it at that. He stayed with the marriage for a variety of reasons, his daughters chief among them, while he put up with Sylvia and her kvetching. But he was also one of Panache's steadiest clients. He needed the action, he said, to keep from going stale. Which was bullshit, of course, but nothing new to her.

Some middle-aged men who could afford it collected sports cars; others raced sailboats. But they all had their toys. Abe's were girls.

He finished the call and returned to his chair. "You were telling me about this cop questioning you. The thing I don't understand is how you could open up to him that way."

"Oh hell, Abe. I didn't really tell him that much. Besides, he already knew a lot, anyway. And like I told you, the cops must have their own reasons to shut it up. I suppose that comes back to her father, right?"

"Absolutely. Have they tried to contact you again?"

"Yes. The same guy called me last night. He wanted a list of our clients. Customers, he calls them."

"What'd you tell him?"

"That we don't have any list. I said we were a legitimate business and if he made trouble for us, I'd sue the city."

"Good. How'd he take that?"

"I don't know. I said it and hung up."

"Also good. Where do you keep your records, by the way?"

"In the office."

"In the *office?*"

"Relax, I've got a good system. Everything's on the computer, and I have backup diskettes."

"How's it set up, your computer?"

"I have an IBM Seventy on my desk. It's linked to three terminals outside, one for each of the phone girls. They can call up data or input it, but they can't copy the data and they can't erase it. Only I can do that. God forbid I ever have a raid, but if I did, I could wipe out everything in seconds."

"You say you have backups? Where are they?"

"Also in the office. But they're in a secret compartment I had built into the fireplace."

"Get them out. Right now, today."

"Why? They're safe there."

"That's what you think. There's always a chance some fool might get wind of all this and try to be a hero. Or who might think he saw a way to take Spencer Patterson down. With a warrant, the police could not only go through your place, they could pull that fireplace apart brick by brick."

"All right, I'll take them home."

"No, give them to me. That way, you'll know they're safe. This is one place where no court order could reach them. And another thing. How much does your assistant know about your business?"

"Patrick? He helps me run the place."

"But he shouldn't know everything. You don't let the phone girls know too much, do you? Then don't let him know, either."

"But hell, Abe—Patrick's reliable, and he's very smart."

"And I'm telling you it's better to keep him out of some things. Mainly your finances. If he asks why, say it's on advice of counsel. Who's your accountant, by the way?"

"Jules Berger. I think you've spoken with him in the past."

"Oh yes, sure. I'll call him."

"Don't worry, I'm careful about paying taxes, if that's what you're thinking. At least on all receipts except cash."

"Excellent. You can't be too careful with the IRS. Those bastards think they're a separate government and they can do anything they please."

As he spoke, several thoughts flashed through Martha's mind. So Rakoff wanted the computer diskettes to be stored with him? Okay, but she'd make another set for herself, just in case. And only she would know about them.

*Trust as few people as possible, Martha, and trust nobody completely.*

"I'll send one of our messengers up for the diskettes later today," he was saying. "Have them in a sealed package, ready to be picked up. Okay?"

"They'll be ready."

"Good." Abe scratched his jaw. He was heavy and moved slowly, his clumsy physique tending to give an impression of mental stodginess, as well. But that was deceptive. If you looked closely, you saw that his eyes were as bright as a hawk's. "I wonder what the real story is," he mused.

"What story?"

"With the Patterson girl. Was the guy who did it somebody who had it in for her? Somebody who knew she was working and then trapped her into going to the Plaza? Or maybe somebody who was looking for a way to get at her father?"

"Not a chance," Martha said. "The woman who called me to book the date asked for a blonde, the best we had. I was the one who picked Caroline."

"A *woman* called you?"

"Yes. Said she was with a company in Los Angeles, but that turned out to be phony."

"I see. You have to wonder about her, what her role was. Maybe she did it. Or maybe the guy she called for just wanted a beautiful girl so he could have the pleasure of killing her."

"I suppose that's possible."

"Or maybe they were both nuts. Got their kicks by killing her together."

"Also possible."

"You ever have to deal with crazies? Some spook trying to get you to send him a girl?"

"Oh, we get our share of creeps, even though we try to be careful about screening and references. But I see to it our girls are well trained. If there's any sign of danger, the girl is to leave, and fast. On the other hand, if the john wants something unusual and there's no harm in it, then it's up to her to decide if she wants to do it. If it doesn't bother her, fine. I just tell them to see they get paid for it."

He peered at her. "What do the men ask for? The unusual things, what are they?"

She shrugged. "There are guys who want to be hit, or maybe get stomped on. A few of them want a golden shower."

"Have her pee on them."

"Right. Some girls will accommodate them, others won't. Depends on the girl. Caroline was squeamish about stuff like that. There was one guy, a Frenchman, who wanted to whip her, and she ran out. I pretended to put the guy on my shit list, but I just sent him somebody else."

"You get other kinds?"

"Sure, we even have one who's a fetishist. But that's rare."

"What's he into?"

"He gets off by licking the girl's shoes, especially if they've got some shit on them."

"Is that right?"

"Yeah. He has her go in the bathroom and do them up, and then she comes out wearing only the shoes. He gets down and cleans them off for her, one at a time. At five hundred a shoe."

"Christ. I can't imagine some of your kids doing stuff like that. Pamela, for instance."

The girl he was referring to was one of his favorites. Martha decided to soften it a little. "No, of course not. I have only one or two people I'd send on that kind of date."

"What do some of the other clients want to do?"

"Mm, let's see. Cross-dressing. We've got a couple of those. One of them puts on this cutesy little dress and then has the girl rape him. At least, he pretends it's rape. He has a dildo he gives her to do it with."

"Fascinating. What else?"

Martha smoothed her skirt. "Fuck you, Abe. I'm not paying you three hundred an hour so I can tell you bedtime stories."

He laughed. "Fair enough."

"You have any more advice for me?"

"Yes. What we have to concentrate on now is damage control. So there's another thing I want you to do. From now on, until we're sure all this has blown over, I don't want you to take on any new clients."

"None? What if we're extra careful to check them out?"

"No. It won't hurt to turn away a little new business for a while. At least that way, you'll know who you're dealing with."

"All right. I'll go along, for a while."

"I suppose your girls all know?"

"About Caroline? Of course. It went around like wildfire."

"You caution them against talking about it?"

"You bet I did. But it almost wasn't necessary. They were all shit scared."

"Yeah, but caution them again, and put the fear of God into them."

"Okay, I will."

"Any of them quit?"

"Two did. Said they wanted to take long vacations. But most of them can't, even if they wanted to. They need the money."

"You get much turnover, normally?"

"A fair amount. Some girls burn out, or get married, or whatever. And some I have to let go. Those are the ones who don't follow my rules about dressing and manners, or get into booze or drugs, or whatever. But there's no shortage of candidates. I've got a waiting list as long as your arm of kids who want to work for me. We're the best service in New York, as you know very well. We've got the best girls and the best clients, and our girls make the most money. Or almost, anyway."

"Almost?"

"There are a few out there who work on their own, and specialize in taking on the real freaks. Those girls make astronomical amounts. But they take astronomical chances, too."

"You know any of them?"

"Sure. One or two used to work for me."

"And now they're competition?"

"Not at all. They handle stuff I wouldn't touch. In fact, once in a while I even steer them business. When somebody calls for something like that, I give him a couple of numbers and tell him to forget where he got them."

"I see."

"What else do you have to tell me, Abe?"

"That's it, for the moment. By the way, the Patterson girl didn't use her own name, did she?"

"No. She called herself Caroline Clark. But the other kids put it together, or it leaked out, or something. Whatever happened, they had the word within a few hours. I got calls all day yesterday, girls wanting to know if it was true. Some of them were really broken up."

"I'm sure they were. But then you were operating last night, weren't you?"

"Business is business, right?"

"It certainly is."

Martha rose. "Thanks, Abe. It was good to see you."

"Good to see you, too, Martha." He got to his feet. "I'll walk out with you."

When they reached the elevators, he glanced sideways at her. "Any new talent I should know about?"

"Yes, as a matter of fact, there is." She knew Rakoff liked petite blondes. "We've got a girl who just joined us. Comes from Omaha. She's small, with a great body and hair the color of straw."

He grinned, obviously intrigued. "Sounds interesting. I'll call you."

"You do that. Her name's Sharon."

"Got it."

The elevator arrived, and as the door opened, he said, "I wonder why he didn't call one of them."

Martha stepped into the car. "Who? One of what?"

Rakoff held the edge of the door to keep it from closing. "The man who killed her. Why didn't he call one of those people you were telling me about—the ones who specialize in rough stuff?"

"I don't know," Martha said. "I guess he wanted it to be a surprise."

# 22

Bobbie was trembling with excitement. Many times in her life she'd tried to imagine what it would feel like to destroy an enemy—to mete out the final punishment.

And now she knew, and it was better than her wildest fantasy.

Because dreaming about it was one thing, but actually experiencing it was a thousand times more satisfying. The emotional rewards would be locked away in her memory forever.

Even there, she'd outdone herself. With her creative talent, she'd found a way to turn the act into an art form—constructing vivid, powerful imagery she would remember and treasure always.

She'd once read a theory by the psychiatrist Emil Stacher, who claimed that the drive to achieve sexual conquest was fueled by a subconscious desire to kill. Bobbie could see that now, could understand what he meant.

Because at the climatic moment, she'd had a shuddering, draining orgasm.

Tonight she would take the next step, and anticipation was making her heart pound. She bathed, and then dressed carefully, keeping her eye on the clock. It was important that everything go off exactly as planned. She wanted to get there in plenty of time.

Stacher was right; this was like getting ready for a tryst with a lover—a secret meeting that would be illicit, daring, feverishly exhilarating. In achieving her purpose, she'd attain the ultimate sexual thrill.

Except that it wouldn't be a lover she'd be meeting, but a member of the lowest of all human subcultures: a filthy, drug-addled whore. Even worse, a whore who specialized in acts of degradation.

Before leaving the apartment, Bobbie took one last look around at her precious possessions, at the cool, soothing colors. Later she'd come back here and lie in a perfumed bath, and relive the climax over and over again.

She turned off the lights and closed the door behind her. The slut she was going to see had no idea what was about to happen to her. Bobbie smiled to herself, thinking about it.

# 23

Lisa Miller awakened at the usual time, a little after 4:00 P.M. She stretched, slowly becoming aware that she had a headache and her mouth tasted like shit. Beside her Beth stirred, and Lisa looked over at the tousled blond curls on the neighboring pillow. Despite the pulsing in her temples and the foul coating on her tongue, she felt an urge to reach out for the other girl. But she also felt a strong need to urinate. She got out of bed and made her way into the bathroom.

Sitting on the toilet, she rubbed her eyes and concentrated on feeling better. According to what little she knew about yoga, it was supposedly possible to improve your condition by doing that. She didn't know whether it was crap or not, but she often tried it. Today nothing changed; the headache continued to hammer away. She flushed the toilet and went to the sink, peering at her reflection in the mirror.

Her eyes were puffy, and her brown hair resembled a rat's nest. It was a good thing the date wasn't until a few hours from now. She'd hold ice cubes under her eyes until the puffiness disappeared. Lately that was something she had to deal with almost every day. She put on a robe and went into the kitchen.

There was a box of Cheerios in the fridge. Lisa kept the cereal there along with any other food that might be on hand, because if she didn't, the cockroaches would walk off with it. Sooner or later, the roaches would probably figure out a way to take the whole refrigerator.

This was supposed to be a luxury apartment, and the rent would certainly make you believe it, but to call this dump luxurious was a laugh. Besides the roach problem, there were cracks in the ceiling the super had promised to fix months ago and hadn't, and the windows didn't fit properly, so no matter how hard you tried to keep the place clean, it was a losing battle. Not that she tried that much—cleaning was Beth's responsibility. But there was a permanent layer of dust on everything—and not just ordinary dust, either. This stuff had black cinders in it.

So why didn't she move? West Sixty-eighth Street was a crappy neighborhood, and with the money she was making, she could afford a better apartment. Now was a good time, too. For not much more than she was paying here, she could get a nice place on the East Side. Maybe over toward the UN, or in one of those fancy buildings with a fountain out front near Bloomingdale's. She knew several girls who had apartments like that, people she'd worked with at Panache. So why didn't she do it?

Bills, that was why.

She filled a bowl with Cheerios and poured milk over the cereal, then sat down at the table. As if to remind her of her profligacy, a basket of mail rested on the table, jammed full of old letters and postcards and department-store flyers and bills, bills, bills. She looked at the basket and wished she could drop the whole fucking mess down the garbage chute.

Come on, Lisa, she said to herself. Admit it. The bills aren't the problem. They're the *result* of the problem. The problem is the white stuff. And the yellow jackets. And the 'ludes. Something for takeoff, something for flying, something for coming down. Fasten your seat belts, ladies and gentlemen—we're going right over the fucking moon. Jesus, even the thought of it was making her nose itch.

But that was the truth, wasn't it—where most of the money was going? Admitting it at least put things in focus. The question was, What was she going to do about it?

Quit, of course. It wouldn't be hard. For one thing, she didn't have a real dependency. Mostly, she just used for fun, or to relax. So getting off it would be easy.

She got up from the table and put water on for coffee. The pot still had stale brown liquid in it, left there by Beth, no doubt. What that young lady needed was a good kick in the ass. Lisa had told her not once but a hundred times that she was expected to keep the place clean, to vacuum and dust and tidy up.

But come to think of it, she shouldn't be all that hard on Beth. The girl was only seventeen, and her childhood had been as rough as Lisa's, if not rougher. So if she sat around watching soap operas and smoking grass, was that so bad? She'd been on the street when Lisa found her, turning tricks for a black pimp. What Lisa had done was to rescue her, actually. Maybe she'd even saved Beth's life.

The first time Lisa had seen her, it was a raw afternoon in late March. Beth was drifting along Lexington Avenue, pretending to window-shop but looking up whenever she saw a potential john and giving the guy an obscene flick of her tongue. A couple of the men hesitated, but then moved on. What seemed strange was that the girl was obviously young and had a great body, and yet she was getting no takers. But then she turned, and when Lisa got a good look at her face, she saw the reason.

Her right eye was wearing a mouse the size of a golf ball. It was shiny red in the center, so swollen that it was shut tight, and under that was a blue-black bruise that ran down her cheek. No wonder the guys weren't buying any; the girl looked as if somebody had tried to drive a fist through her face.

When Lisa came alongside, she said, "Hi, honey. How's it going?"

The kid glanced up with her good eye, her expression wary and frightened, like a mouse seeing a snake.

Lisa smiled. "It's okay, I'm working, too. Only not today. Things kind of slow?"

The girl nodded. "Kind of."

"Then how about having a cup of coffee with me? There's a place just up the street."

She still seemed uncertain. "I don't know."

Lisa detected a pronounced southern accent. Her smile widened, and when she spoke this time, it was in her own West Virginia drawl. "Hey, you talking to another country girl."

The kid relaxed on hearing it. Okay, she said, she could use some coffee. They went into the luncheonette and Lisa ordered a cheeseburger and a chocolate malted for her friend, a black coffee for herself.

While the kid ate, Lisa asked her, "Where'd you get the love tap?"

She hung her head.

"Your pimp, huh? The bastard ought to be in jail. Did he hurt you bad?"

It had the effect Lisa wanted; a fat tear rolled down the kid's left cheek. Her right eye apparently was too swollen to expel moisture. "It hurts."

Lisa reached over and patted her hand, pleased to have an excuse to touch her. "Course it does. Poor little face all swole up like that. What's your name, honey?"

"Beth." The cheeseburger was nearly gone.

"I'm Lisa. You been in New York long?"

"No, just a few weeks. I came from Charleston on the bus."

"That when you met him, when you got off the bus?"

She stopped chewing for an instant. "How'd you know that?"

"They hang around the terminal. Looking for fresh meat."

"Guess I was kind of dumb, huh? But I didn't know one soul here. Otherwise, I wouldn't go with no nigger."

"Of course not. There wasn't anything else you could do. You want another cheeseburger?"

"No, that's enough. Thank you." Beth drew on the straw. "But you don't go on the street, do you? I mean, you look so . . . nice."

"No. I did for a while," Lisa said, "But that sucks. We agree on that, don't we?"

The question produced a smile. "Yeah, we sure do. So then, where do you work—in a house?"

"Lord no. Only dogs work in houses. I'm a call girl."

Beth's good eye widened. "A call girl? Really? Wow."

Lisa was amused. It was as if she'd announced she was a rock star. To this kid, she'd clearly made the big time.

Beth leaned forward. "How'd you get into it?"

"I answered an ad."

"An *ad?*"

"Sure, in *Variety.* Escort services run ads in there all the time."

"Gee, I can see why they wanted you. You really look, you know, dynamite."

"Thanks." She felt a tiny thrill at hearing Beth express admiration for her appearance, at having the girl respond to her.

"I bet you just walked in and that was it," Beth went on.

"No, it wasn't that simple. I had to go through this long interview. See, a lot of people think the place is the best one in New York. It's called Panache."

"What'd you tell them?"

"A lot of shit."

Beth threw her head back and laughed, then wiped her mouth with a paper napkin. Her lips were lush and full and Lisa felt a sudden impulse to lean across the table and kiss them. But she didn't, of course. She'd be very cool, take her time. This chance was too good to mess up.

"Really," Beth asked, "what'd you say?"

"A bunch of lies about how I was studying modern dance, and that was why I needed the money. The lady who runs the place puts on airs, like she's in society. Talks about how she was in the theater and all, but after you've known her awhile, you figure out the theater was Minsky's."

"What's Minsky's?"

"A burlesque theater, but it's not there anymore. Now it's just something you say, when you mean burlesque."

"Oh."

"She wants everybody to think that what she's running is like a finishing school for young ladies, only the young ladies peddle their ass on the side. When I went there, I knew just how to play it. I even laid on my no-accent accent."

Beth giggled. "Wish I could do that. I try all the time, but I still sound like a mushmouth."

"Hey, don't worry about it. You listen to the way people in New York talk? Noo Yawk? Hey, buddy—where's da fuckin' subway to Brooklyn?"

This time they both laughed, and then Lisa reached out and touched the younger girl's arm once more. "Nice to meet somebody who's real down-home."

"She ask you anything else?" It was obvious what was going on in Beth's mind. She was wondering if a place like Panache might be her own ticket out of the trap she was in.

"That was about it." Lisa glanced through the window at the crowds on the sidewalk. "Your pimp around here now?"

"No. When I left the room, he was in there shooting up. Told me to come down here and make some money."

"And so far you haven't made any."

She shook her head.

"So when you go back, he's liable to bust your other eye."

Beth bit her lip, and another tear appeared.

"Hey," Lisa said, "I have an idea."

"What is it?"

"Why don't you cut out on him? You could stay at my place, while your face got better. I have a real nice apartment."

"Gee, I don't know."

"Later on, I could help you get a job where I work."

The good eye was wide open again. "No shit?"

"No shit," Lisa said. "Not only that, I'd break you in myself. Show you the ropes."

"Wow. That would be just fantastic." She pronounced it as if each syllable was a separate word.

"You like grass, Beth?"

"Sure."

"Okay, tell you what. We'll take a taxi home, and then we'll smoke a couple of joints, to celebrate."

Beth's lush mouth curved in a smile, and she reached across the table to shake hands. This was, Lisa decided, her lucky day.

After paying the check, she guided the girl out the door. Leaving her near the entrance, Lisa stepped off the curb to hail a cab, but it seemed that every damn one she saw was busy. She stood there with her arm in the air while the stream of traffic rushed by.

That was when she heard the scream. She turned back in time to see a black man knock Beth to the sidewalk. Blood streamed from the girl's nose, and she held up her hand to ward off further blows.

"Bitch!" the pimp spat. "No good motherfuckin' white *bitch!*"

He drew back his foot and kicked her in the belly. She retched, then vomited up a sour mixture of cheeseburger and chocolate milk shake.

Pedestrians recoiled in horror but did nothing to help. In this city, the rule was, Don't get involved. A few people stopped to watch, but most of them simply got out of the way.

The pimp had on a long black overcoat with a fur collar. He bent over the cowering girl and shook his fist. "I tell you to work, you *work*. You hear, bitch?"

Beth was slobbering, begging him not to hit her again. Blood and vomit dripped from her face onto her jacket.

Lisa's hand closed around the stag-horn handle of the switchblade. She carried the knife in her coat pocket, never in her purse, where getting it out would take longer. She took it out now, holding it close to her leg so it wouldn't show.

Stepping over to the black man, she tapped him on the shoulder with her left hand, while with her right, she thumbed the button on the handle of the knife and felt the blade snap out.

The pimp straightened up and turned to her. He was very dark, what they would call a blue, down home. His overcoat was hanging open, revealing a ruffled shirt. When he saw Lisa, the expression on his face showed surprise and then anger.

He snarled. "Who the fuck—"

Lisa slammed the blade into his chest with a quick upward thrust, driving six inches of steel all the way to the handle guards.

His mouth popped open. His eyes bulged. He looked down, and realized what had happened.

Realized that she'd killed him. And was astonished.

The eyes swung up again, and fixed on her. His lips moved. "You . . ."

Lisa pulled the knife out, and when she did, blood spurted in scarlet gouts from the wound.

He went down slowly, first to his knees, both hands clutching his chest, and from there over onto his face.

Lisa retracted the blade and stuffed the knife back into her coat pocket. Then she grabbed the girl's wrist and dragged her to her feet. Holding the thin arm in a tight grip, she ran back across the sidewalk and into the street, Beth stumbling behind her.

Lisa held up her hand and brakes screeched as a taxi skidded to a stop less than a foot from them. She saw the driver shaking his fist and swearing, but she also saw that the cab was not engaged. Pulling Beth around to the side of the vehicle, she opened the door and pushed her inside. Then she hopped in beside her and slammed the door.

The driver was still spitting invective, but Lisa ignored it. "Go down to Forty-second Street and turn right," she commanded. "I'll tell you where to go from there."

As the taxi pulled away, she turned and looked out the rear window. There was a larger crowd now on the sidewalk in front of the restaurant, but no one was paying any attention to the cab.

Beth pressed her face against Lisa's breast, shuddering.

As the taxi turned the corner and drove past the Grand Hyatt, Lisa put her arm around the girl.

This really is my lucky day, she thought. After all.

\* \* \*

110

She smiled now, thinking back to it, her anger at Beth gone. It *had* been her lucky day. And if the kid seemed a little lazy sometimes, that was nothing, compared to the good things about her. Which brought an idea to mind.

She peeked into the bedroom and saw that Beth was still sleeping. There was plenty of time before Lisa had to get dressed, so why not? It'd be fun, wouldn't it? Especially if first she treated herself to a little toot, just to make everything sharper. She turned and went back into the kitchen.

Her stash was on a top shelf in one of the cupboards, in a metal lockbox. Lisa had no objection to Beth using pot, and in fact even saw to it that she was well supplied. It was good insurance, in a way, because Beth would be less likely to get antsy, as long as she could spend her evenings staring at the tube with a good buzz on. Which was reassuring to Lisa, knowing that while she was out working, Beth would stay put.

But the hard stuff was another story.

Lisa twisted the combination lock and opened the box, poking among the vials of shiny capsules and taking out the plastic sack of white powder. As she did, she thought again of the bills crammed into the basket on the kitchen table. Everything was just so damned expensive. What she had right here in this box had cost a fortune.

And face it, that was the real reason she'd left Panache and gone out on her own. Even with all the money she'd been making with Martha, it had never been enough. Now she was working the weirdos, the S&Ms, the B&Ds, the whip and chain nuts, and bringing in twice as much.

And it still wasn't enough. The only one making real profits from her work was her dealer. But she'd quit soon. Kick it altogether. Or at least cut down. She laid out two lines of coke and snorted them through a straw.

Ah-h-h-h. God *damn*. A delicious warmth spread through her body, and a moment later she felt buoyant enough to spread her arms and float into the air.

*Look at me, everybody. The daring young lady on the flying trapeze.* And if high was good, higher was better. She went back into the box and came up with a tiny glass tube of amyl nitrite. She inhaled the contents of the tube as well, and the effect was startling. She was so sharp now, so much in control, she could do anything. And so hot that the mere thought of Beth's body was maddening to her. She put the junk away and returned to the bedroom, pulling off her robe and climbing into bed.

She put her arms around the girl and kissed her long and hungrily, full on the mouth.

Beth stirred, and then her lips opened. Lisa put her hand between the smooth thighs and inserted a finger into the moist warmth. She brought her mouth down to the small, firm breasts, kissing and licking the nipples while her finger probed, and then she began moving slowly downward, her heart pounding, so excited that she could barely breathe.

It lasted for what seemed like hours, her passion sweeping her along in a delirium of ecstasy. She caressed and kissed and sucked, her body trembling, orgasm after orgasm rolling over her in waves. Once Beth gave a small, choked cry of joy, and that added even more to the intensity of what Lisa was feeling.

But when it was over, she realized their lovemaking had consumed only a few minutes. Her body damp with perspiration, she rolled over and stared at the ceiling, depression already descending on her like a black cloud.

# 24

She couldn't let this happen. She'd been too happy just a short time ago, and she couldn't let Beth see her go into a funk. Then, too, there was her date. She had to keep it, even though it was suddenly disgusting to think about. There was no way she could turn her back on the money. She got out of bed and went back into the kitchen.

Her fingers were shaking and she couldn't make them work properly. Fumbling with the combination lock was frustrating, and it took her three tries to get the damn box open.

When at last she swung back the top, she ignored the bag of coke and instead checked the vials. The one containing yellow jackets she pushed aside. If there was anything she didn't need at this point, it was another depressant. What she wanted was a jump start, a big red. A rocket.

There, found them. She opened the vial and shook out a fat capsule of methamphetamine, its scarlet color and shiny surface reminding her of a drop of blood. Beautiful. And better take two, she was really down. Stepping to the sink, she gulped the capsules and chased them with water.

It took a few minutes for the meth to take effect, but then it began to spread its glow. The rush was much slower than what you got from sniffing, but that was good. What it gave you wasn't so much of a jolt, but more a wonderful sense of well-being that lasted much longer. A short time later, she was herself again—optimistic, strong, up.

She went into the bathroom and showered, then washed her hair. When she'd toweled herself off, she blew her hair dry, styling it so that it looked thick and fluffy and a little on the wild side. Next came liberal dashes of perfume, from a new bottle of Giorgio. The stuff smelled lovely, but she couldn't help reminding herself that the tiny vial had cost $150.

Well so what, for Christ's sake? She was making a pile of bread every time she went out, and now that she'd decided to cut down on what she was spending for junk, she'd have even more to spend. She went back into the bedroom.

What to wear? That was something else she wanted more money for—new clothes. The closet was jam-packed, and yet there wasn't anything in it she was crazy about. And in her business, you had to look terrific every time you went out.

She had to admit Martha had been right about that. The old bitch may have had a lot of goofy ideas on other subjects, but her notions of how a girl had to dress and act were on the money.

At least on the outside. The freaks Lisa was seeing now were turned on when you looked sophisticated, but when you took off your outer clothing, they wanted to see black lace with heart-shaped cutouts over your pussy, and cantilevered bras that pushed your jugs up until you looked like you were carrying a pair of melons around with you.

And heels. That was another departure from the Panache code. With Martha setting the ground rules, you wore sleek pumps from Saks or Charles Jourdan or someplace. But the S&M nutballs wanted spikes, four-inchers that made you think you were on stilts, afraid if you stumbled, you'd break your ass. God only knew what went on in some guys' heads.

But Lisa had sensed there was big money there, right from the beginning of her time at Panache. Most of the johns had been square, with the typical guy wanting you to have a drink or two with him or sometimes dinner while you listened to whatever bunch of shit he was handing out. All about how the world was a hard, competitive place that crushed ordinary men, but he was unique, according to him, because of his tremendous drive and his great intelligence and most of all his gigantic balls. Then finally he'd take you to bed, and after a few minutes of huffing and puffing, it'd be all over.

The freaks, on the other hand, were shy when you first met them. And instead of bragging about their money or their careers or their possessions, they wanted you to be their partner in acting out fantasies, some of them so weird, it made you wonder how they ever thought them up.

A lot of them got off by having you play toilet games with them. Mostly that type wanted you to shit, either while they watched or on them. One guy told her that Adolf Hitler had had the same obsession, that he liked to have his lady friends crap on his head. No wonder the Germans lost the fucking war.

Another frequent request was for a beating; the guy would want you to take a whip and whack his ass with it. But other times, you ran into men who had whole scenarios they expected you to go through with them. One of her regulars was a bond salesman who liked to put on a dress and plead with her not to hurt him, groveling on the floor while she kicked him.

Another guy wanted to pretend she'd caught him masturbating, and as punishment she was expected to slap him around and call him vile names while he went on beating his meat. Still others wanted to be handcuffed or tied with ropes while she abused them.

Not surprisingly, nearly all the other girls at Panache had been repelled by such weirdos, and refused to go near them. But Lisa had seen that what they wanted was relatively harmless, and the rewards were sensational. The first time Lisa pissed on a guy, he gave her five hundred dollars. At rates like that, she'd be happy to hose anybody down.

So Lisa had told Martha to keep them coming, she'd accommodate any spook who called. As a result, she'd become Panache's unofficial playmate for the offbeat types, as Martha delicately labeled them.

It had come to the point, finally, that Lisa had figured out she could make at least twice as much going on dates with creeps as she could with routine johns, and even more if she didn't have to cut Panache in for a share. And why should she be turning over part of what she made to Martha? Just because Panache had a telephone and somebody to answer it? What Martha was providing for her girls was little more than a sense of security, anyway. She was nothing but a fucking den mother.

So Lisa had gone out on her own. The first thing she'd done was to call a couple of the guys she'd dated through Panache. Then she'd engaged a telephone-answering service, and within a week, she was rolling. Now she had all the action she could handle.

She got dressed, putting on a racy green outfit Martha wouldn't have approved of, which suited Lisa just fine. Back at the mirror, she was pleased by what she saw. The dress fit beautifully, hugging her hips and setting off her boobs in a way that went with the loose hairstyle she'd achieved with the hair dryer. What a change in attitude a couple of red zappers could make.

Suddenly, she became aware that Beth was watching her. The girl's tone was sullen. "Where's the date?"

Lisa resumed studying her own image, running her hands lightly over her hips, enjoying the feel of the material. "I have to go across town. Fifty-seventh Street."

"Who's the guy?"

"I don't know; he's somebody new."

Beth was quiet for a moment. Then she said, "How about taking me along?"

Lisa shook her head. "I can't do that. This is a double as it is. Another girl and I are gonna do him."

"You said you'd break me in. You promised me."

"Course I did, honey. And I will."

"When?"

Lisa was exasperated. "Be patient, will you? There's things I have to coach you on first."

"How long would that take, ten minutes? It ain't as if I never worked before."

"Yeah, but this stuff is different—what these guys want."

"Maybe I'd do better if I started with that place where you used to work."

"I don't think so. Remember how I explained to you about how they want you to have an education and everything?"

Beth's tone grew sullen again. "You always got some kind of an excuse. You know what I think? It's a lot of shit. All you want is to keep me holed up here so you can go down on me whenever you feel like it."

Lisa went to her, sitting down beside her on the bed and grasping the thin arm. "Aw, honey, that's just not true. Sure it's great when we make love. But look what I've done for you. Now you got a nice place to live, good food, anything you want."

"What I want is to go out and have some fun. I want nice clothes and I want to go out to places where people dance and everything. If I was working, I could do all that. Maybe later on, I could even have my own place."

That sent a pang of fear into Lisa's chest. She squeezed Beth's arm. "Tell you what, honey. Next week, I'll fix us up with a couple guys; we'll go to a disco, or a fancy club. Maybe Regines, someplace like that. Okay?"

"Yeah, that'd be nice. Would we be working?"

"Maybe. I'll see what I can do. Now I have to go. See you later, hon." She bent over and kissed the lush lips, but Beth didn't respond.

Lisa stood up. Her voice brightened. "Hey, you hungry?"

"A little."

"Why don't you call Mah Sing and order up some Chinese? I'll leave money for you on the counter. Okay?"

"I guess so."

"And cheer up, will you? I hate to see you down. Have yourself a toke, hm? That'll make you feel better. You still got plenty of that good stuff I bought you last week, right?"

"Yeah."

"Okay, sweetie. Gotta run." She dug a pair of spike-heeled black shoes out of the closet and put them on. Then she left the room.

From the front-hall closet, she got out a raincoat and slipped into it. Circling back into the kitchen, she took a twenty-dollar bill out of her purse and placed it on the counter under the wall telephone.

Her bag was in the bedroom, a Louis Vuitton tote. She raced back in there and picked it up, tossing in a fresh pair of panties. Beth was watching again, the same sullen expression on her face. Lisa waved on the way out, but Beth made no response.

After stuffing her hair dryer and deodorants and toothbrush and a few other odds and ends into the bag, Lisa went into the living room. A cabinet with a TV on it stood against the wall opposite the sofa. She got out her keys and opened the cabinet.

Inside was an assortment of devices. She took out a coiled whip, several short lengths of white nylon rope, two pairs of handcuffs, a truncheon made of black rubber, and a slim chain with chromium links, dropping these into the tote bag as well. Then she locked the cabinet, and carrying the bag, she left the apartment, double-locking the door behind her.

# 25

The Pennywhistle was on Second Avenue, near the corner of Fifty-seventh Street. A bar with Tiffany lamps and small tables along the windows, it was the kind of place frequented by a hip crowd of Upper East Side singles. The taxi deposited Lisa at the front entrance, and when she'd paid the driver and turned to go inside, she saw that there was standing room only—which was to be expected. It was early evening, and this was a popular meeting place, as well as one where you could get picked up in a hurry, if that was what you were after.

Not that people were so much into that these days. The AIDS crisis had scared hell out of everybody, not just the gays. In particular, young unmarried professional women were reluctant to go any further than a drink with guys they didn't know. Nevertheless, the Pennywhistle was jumping.

Lisa had told the other girl what she'd be wearing, and to be on the lookout for the Vuitton tote. But with the crush at the bar, she wasn't sure they'd make contact so easily. She pushed her way into the mob, conscious that a number of the young men were looking her over. And then above the din, she heard someone call her name.

A young woman was standing at one of the small tables, smiling and waving. Lisa returned the wave. She slipped and slid past the drinkers to the table, inadvertently bumping people with the bag, which weighed a ton with all the crap she'd packed into it.

The woman stuck out her hand and smiled. "Hi. Welcome to the zoo."

Lisa shook hands and took the proffered chair, dropping the tote to the floor and shoving it against the wall with her foot. It was a relief to sit down, out of the mainstream of bar traffic.

"You're right on the button," the woman said. "But we can take time for a drink, if you want one." She pointed to a glass in front of her on the table. "I'm having a martini. What would you like?"

"That sounds fine." Lisa never drank them, in fact almost never drank alcohol in any form these days, but she wanted to be congenial.

A waiter came by and the young woman drained her glass, handing it to him and ordering two more.

She turned back to Lisa. "I hope you brought a derrick and a machete?"

Lisa smiled. "Of course. Also a jackhammer and an ax."

They both laughed, and Lisa sat back in her chair, unbuttoning her raincoat and brushing her hair away from her face while she surreptitiously looked the other girl over.

She seemed older than Lisa, but she was quite good-looking, with dark hair tumbling to her shoulders and eyes of an indeterminate color, which might have been gray green. Overall okay, but not quite a Panache type, even though she was wearing an obviously expensive gray suede coat with a stand-up collar. Too much makeup, for one thing. Martha wouldn't approve. It was funny, but Lisa was forever finding herself judging other women by Panache standards.

"You live far from here?" the girl asked.

"Sixty-eighth Street. On the West Side."

"Oh."

"Exactly. It's the pits. I want to find a place over in this area somewhere."

"There are plenty available, from what I hear. The real estate market is way down, so you can get a good deal. I'm on Eighty-second, off Madison."

"Sounds great."

"It is. I just lucked into it, too. Friend of mine moved to France and subbed it to me. Bless her heart."

"What if she comes back?"

"She won't. I put a contract out on her."

They laughed again, and at that point the waiter returned with their drinks. The martinis were on the rocks with twists of lemon, served in chunky glasses. Lisa raised hers and said, "Cheers." Her new friend followed suit.

The drink was icy cold and the gin gave it a distinctive flavor Lisa hadn't experienced in a long time—not since coming to New York, in fact. Back home, the boys she knew often drank gin, but straight out of the bottle. Up here, she ordered white wine, if anything, and then only to keep some guy company. And although the martini felt good going down, she was aware of a growing sense of edginess. She could have kicked herself for not having tucked a couple of reds into her purse before leaving her apartment.

She put the glass down. "Have you seen this guy before?"

"Oh, hell yes. Lots of times." The young woman grinned. "That may be why he wanted two of us. I think he's getting bored with me."

"Then why didn't he just get somebody else?"

"Probably doesn't know anybody. Or maybe he's afraid to. A lot of girls won't touch a guy like him, and sometimes the ones who will are snakes, you know? Once they get their hooks into a freak, they'll do anything from ripping him off to blackmailing him. But I talked to Martha, and she said you were okay."

"How do you know her?"

The girl held up a hand and waved it languidly. She spoke with a parody of a British accent. "My dear, I was one of Panache's little darlings. After I got my Ph.D. in poetry from Harvard, Miss Bellamy thought I might qualify." She put her hand down and her speech returned to normal. "I was with her for a year, and then I got smart."

"Same as me. I make a lot more now that I'm on my own."

"Of course. These guys may be a little strange, but that's where the money is."

"You were telling me about the one we're going to see."

"Oh, yeah. His name's Eddy, by the way. I think the real reason he wants a threesome is for the experience. He probably has this porno flick running around in his head, with two girls working him over instead of one. And as long as he can afford it, who are we to argue?"

"Sure. It's fine with me." Lisa was definitely uncomfortable. The gin was doing nothing for her; she was coming down fast. It was also hard to think clearly. Sitting here seemed unreal to her. Soon she'd begin to sweat, and that would be embarrassing. She could only hope they'd get started before it became a real problem. After that, nobody would notice. In the meantime, she'd just have to hold on. She sipped her drink.

"If you don't mind my asking, where are you from, originally?"

"West Virginia."

"I thought I heard just a trace."

Lisa smiled. "Most people don't pick up on it. This guy, Eddy you said his name was?"

"Right."

"What's he like to do? Or have done?"

"Mostly it's a play he stars in. First, he's the aggressor, the brute who's in charge. He ties you up or handcuffs you, and then he punishes you—only not really. He snarls and curses, calls you all kinds of lovely names. That's Act One. Then, to his amazement, you break free and chain *him* up. That's Act Two. Act Three is when you whip him. Or tonight when we both whip him, I suppose. I'm not sure just how we'll play it with two of us. Make it up as we go along, probably."

"Does he want to screw, after that?"

"Are you kidding? The only thing that gets him off is the whip. You snap that thing at his ass or his balls and he gets delirious. I've gotten so I can actually tickle his dick with it." She grinned. "And then, stand back."

Lisa managed a weak smile. She drained her glass and put it down on the table. As she did, a wave of heat came up from her chest and spread its way into her neck and her face. Then suddenly, it was gone and she felt cold. She hoped to hell she wouldn't get sick and ruin everything.

The girl opened her purse, took something out, and put it into her mouth. Raising her glass, she swallowed the last of her drink.

Lisa was watching. "What was that?"

"Hm? Oh, nothing. Just a little booster."

"Not meth, by any chance?"

"Yes, as a matter of fact. You want one?"

"Sure, I could use it." Jesus, could she use it. The understatement of the year.

The girl went back into her purse and came up with a brown capsule, handing it to Lisa. "Things go better with coke, and even better with speed."

Lisa had used methamphetamine in a variety of forms, including tablets she'd ground up and inhaled when she was in a hurry to get the effect. Capsules were handier in a situation like this, and also the high would be smoother and would last longer. The color of this one was new to her, but never look a gift horse and all that. She popped the capsule onto her tongue and washed it down with the melted ice remaining in her glass.

The young woman looked at her watch. "We'd better get moving." She signaled to the waiter to bring a check, waving Lisa off when she offered to pay it.

"Do we have far to go?" Lisa asked.

"No, he's right in the next block. Owns a town house, no less."

"That must be nice."

"It's fabulous—wait till you see it. Beautifully decorated, mostly antiques. And he's also got a lot of great modern art. It's funny, but here you have this lovely old furniture right alongside a bunch of abstract paintings, and yet somehow it all goes together. The result is wonderful. And to top it off, he even has some statues he bought in Greece and Italy, places like that."

The drug was beginning to do its work; Lisa no longer felt tense. The effect was different from what she'd expected, more soothing than she usually experienced with an upper. In fact, she was totally relaxed, almost to the point of feeling drowsy.

She refocused on the conversation. "What does he do? For a living, I mean?"

"He's a numismatist."

"A what?"

"He deals in rare coins. I didn't know what it meant, either, until he explained it to me."

The waiter returned with the check and the woman paid it in cash. She and Lisa then left the restaurant, pushing their way back through the boisterous crowd standing four and five deep at the bar.

The streetlights were on now, and as they walked, Lisa was vaguely aware of the contrast between this neighborhood and the one in which she lived. There were trees along here between the sidewalk and the street, and the area was much cleaner, the buildings neat and well cared for. It took them only a few minutes to reach their destination.

The house was tall and faced with gray stone. The front door and all the trim and the window munions were painted black. There were wrought-iron bars over the windows. The street number was inscribed on a brass plate beside the steps, but Lisa couldn't make it out. The houses on either side butted up against their neighbors and all were about the same height. Many had window boxes with beds of ivy, and geraniums bearing the last of their red and pink and white blossoms before the autumn frosts.

Lisa followed the other girl up the steps, and when she reached the small landing in front of the door, she suddenly felt dizzy. She put out a hand and grasped the railing to steady herself. In a moment, the feeling passed.

The young woman unlocked the door and swung it open. It was strange that she didn't knock and wait to be admitted, and that she had a key to the place, but Lisa gave it no further thought. For some reason, she didn't care. Another wave of dizziness swept over her, and then just as quickly as the first one, it left her.

The girl was standing beside the open door. "After you," she said.

Lisa stepped past, carrying her tote. The thing felt so heavy now, it was all she could do to lug it into the house. Once inside, she found herself standing in a dimly lighted circular entry hall. The other woman snapped a wall switch and more light came into the hallway. Lisa saw what looked like marble busts on stands against the walls, but she wasn't sure that's what they were. She tried to focus her eyes, and couldn't. She put her bag down, and as she did, the other woman closed the door and locked it.

Lisa unbuttoned her raincoat with an effort, her fingers stiff and clumsy.

The woman picked up the tote and linked her arm with Lisa's. "I'll carry this for you. Come on in."

It was hard to walk. She had to concentrate on putting one foot in front of the other. But somehow she didn't care about that, either.

"I think you're really going to enjoy this," the young woman said. "And by the way, my name's Bobbie."

# 26

The New York City Criminal Justice Building was at 100 Centre Street in lower Manhattan, a sooty hulk not far from City Hall. Tolliver entered through the South Entrance Hall lobby. The gloomy granite-walled area was swarming with people, their footsteps echoing from the olive green stone floors. In this vast structure was based an enormous bureaucratic machine: judges and prosecutors, prison guards and clerks, stenographers and police officers. Yet most of the cases that glutted it were relatively unimportant.

Sure, there were felons here who had committed crimes ranging from murder and rape to armed robbery. But the majority of defendants were nickel-and-dimers: prostitutes, fare beaters, drunks, exhibitionists, pimps, shoplifters, gamblers, and other small-time lowlifes, and the charges brought against them were often knocked down to a Dis Con—Disorderly Conduct.

But serious or otherwise, the volume was staggering. AR-1, the primary arraignment court in Manhattan, operated around the clock, with as many as five hundred of the newly arrested passing before haggard, overworked judges in each twenty-four-hour period. Even at 3:00 A.M. there were lawyers arguing over bail and plea bargains, while corrections officers escorted prisoners between the courtrooms and the pens.

Because most cases did not involve issues of life and death, many of the nearly three hundred assistant district attorneys handling them were themselves undistinguished. They were mostly young lawyers who looked upon the experience they would gain here as a stepping-stone to a more lucrative position, perhaps with a firm specializing in the practice of corporate law.

Only a few were heavy hitters. They were the senior ADAs who got the big juicy cases that could launch political careers. While the low-level ADAs routinely worked on as many as 250 active cases at a time, nearly all of them ratshit, each of the top prosecutors was involved in no more than a dozen. And those were choice.

Ben knew Brian Holland had to be a member of the elite. He would be a shock trooper. A star.

Approaching Holland's office, Ben reminded himself to be careful. He'd never met this guy, so he'd want to get a sense of what he was like before opening up too much. Most ADAs were okay; you could trust them, up to a point. But some were wimps who were so concerned with the rights of criminals, they might as well have been defense lawyers.

For that matter, *all* lawyers were people you had to be cautious around. It was questionable whether they were born that way or picked up their habits at whatever law school they'd gone to, but Ben had never met one who didn't think of himself first.

*What's in this for me?*

They didn't ask the question out loud, but you knew it was in the front of their heads. If the guy was in private practice, he looked at any situation as if it had a price tag on it, telling him what his fee was going to be. Or if he was on the DA's staff, a case was measured by what it could do to advance his career. And God help the poor schmuck who had to settle for a public defender.

Even Holland's office was far better than the average ADA's cubbyhole. It was more spacious, with windows and a vestibule, and an outer area where his trial preparation assistant, a dumpy woman with thick legs and a beehive hairdo, sat at a desk. Although you wouldn't call it plush, the office was a lot more comfortable than the green cinder-block cell in which Ben had to work.

When he arrived, Holland was on the phone. He waved Ben to a seat while he went on with his conversation. The ADA was young, but his manner seemed prissy, as if he'd already decided what he'd be like as an older man. He had on the Ivy League uniform: gray flannel suit, white button-down, striped tie. His dark hair was combed straight back and was thinning in front, which added to his serious look.

As Ben sat there, he thought there was something else he couldn't quite identify, but then he realized the guy seemed a little effeminate. Or was that because of what the psychiatrist had said about people having secondary sex characteristics? Lately Ben had found himself seeing female tendencies in men and male tendencies in women.

He glanced around the room. The furniture was standard issue, battered wood and gray metal, but there were a few personal touches, as well. Framed diplomas hung on one wall, and Ben could figure out the Latin well enough to see the guy had graduated from the University of Virginia Law School—the same one Teddy

Kennedy had attended after he was thrown out of Harvard for cheating.

There was also a silver frame on the desk with a picture of a girl in it. She wasn't bad-looking, but her face wore that haughty expression they handed out in private schools, as if she wouldn't say shit if she had a mouthful. Or if she did, it would be carefully enunciated.

Holland hung up and leaned over the desk to shake hands. When he spoke, his style made Ben think of Spencer Patterson. He wasn't as imperious, but that was because he was still young and hadn't yet proved to the world why he should be one of the people running it. He was sure he'd get there eventually, however. You could see he was banking on it.

"Well, Lieutenant. Don't believe we've met before, have we?"

As if it was up to Ben to keep track. "No."

"I was pleased to learn you're in charge of the investigation. I'm assured you have an excellent reputation. In fact, that was one of the reasons I agreed to handle the case. Suppose we begin with your bringing me up-to-date on what progress you've made. Start at the beginning, if you would."

Ben described what the police had been able to piece together on what had happened in the suite at the Plaza, including details of how the young woman's corpse had been smeared with makeup. He skipped over his visit to Panache, however, as well as his talk with Rodney Burnaford. And he made no mention of his discussion with Dr. Stein.

When Ben finished, Holland leaned forward, frowning. "Let me be sure I have this straight. You're saying that this woman rented a suite for her boss, and also engaged the Patterson girl for purposes of prostitution. Then when Patterson showed up, the boss killed her, perhaps with the woman's help. Is that correct?"

"Yes."

"Doesn't that sound like an execution? They wanted Patterson dead, for whatever reason, and then they painted the body to throw off the investigation?"

"I don't think so. They called an escort service for a girl, but they had no way of knowing the girl would turn out to be Caroline Patterson."

"Which in itself is mind-boggling. Imagine someone with that background working as a call girl."

"Yeah, it's hard to figure."

"And if it was a random killing, that makes painting her body all the more weird, doesn't it?"

"Not when it comes to what you run across in sex crimes."

"In other words, assuming this was the work of a sexual psychopath, his actions fit an established pattern?"

"One pattern, anyway. Sometimes the perpetrator is making a statement; other times, he might want to go on punishing her, after she's dead. What was in this guy's head, it's too early to tell. But you can be sure that inflicting pain was part of it."

"Even if he'd never seen the victim before?"

"Sure. What he was most likely doing was using her as a substitute." It occurred to Ben that he was even starting to talk like Stein. Dr. Tolliver, eminent shrink.

"Ah. A substitute for someone he harbored resentment toward, or hatred."

"Yes. Usually that person was someone who abused him, early in his life. Could have been a parent, or anybody who knocked him around a lot when he was a kid."

"You sound as if you've run into a number of them."

"Everybody has, if they've worked on homicide cases long enough. Couple of years ago, we had a guy who killed a string of women, and then after we got him, we found he'd been raised by an aunt who used to beat him. When he'd done something she considered really outrageous, like stealing money from her purse, she'd burn the head of his dick with an iron."

"Um. What did he, that is—"

"He'd strangle his victim and then ejaculate on her face."

"How peculiar."

Ben had never heard it described that way, but it certainly wasn't normal. Maybe Holland had a point.

"You say he wants to inflict pain. That's not always so, is it?"

"I don't know. But I never saw one that didn't."

"Yet from what I understand, this type of criminal doesn't necessarily kill his victim."

"No. Sometimes he stops at rape. But it's always violent. He's at least going to hurt her. A lot of it seems to be that he wants to degrade her. He's getting even—in his head, at least. So he rapes her, beats her up, might even mutilate her. And if he's crazy enough, he kills her."

Holland was clearly fascinated. "As strange as all of this is, the business of his assistant makes it even more so. Do you have a theory as to how she might have fit into it?"

"At this point, no. That part was new to me."

"You know, Lieutenant, I don't have your broad experience in homicide cases. The ones I've worked on have all been rather simple—in terms of motive, at least. And without the psychosexual aspects you've described. But tell me this—aren't many rapes committed simply because the man wants gratification?"

"Not usually."

"But in such circumstances, there would be no murder, true?"

"Hard to say. When I was a rookie cop, a guy in the Two-five raped a ten-year-old on the roof of a tenement. Afterward, he threw her off the roof so she couldn't tell her mother."

"Ah, but in that situation, the murder was one of expedience, wouldn't you say?"

"No, I wouldn't. I think he raped her to hurt her. And remember, that doesn't mean a guy like that doesn't enjoy it. He gets off on hurting because the hurting and the sex are all the same thing to him. When he threw her from the roof, he probably got off on that, too."

"There was another homicide case you were involved in that was quite famous, isn't that so? The Greenwich Village Murders?"

Ben had sensed this was coming. The story followed him around like Chinese crotch rot. Once you had it, you had it.

Holland was studying him. "You were involved in that, weren't you?"

"Yeah, I was."

"And those killings were sexual in nature also, weren't they?"

"Yes. The guy killed pretty girls and then mangled them with his teeth. After that, he took pictures of them and sent the pictures to a TV station, hoping they'd be shown over the air."

Holland shook his head. "A monster."

"History is full of them."

"That's quite true, isn't it? Bluebeard, Jack the Ripper, the Marquis de Sade—quite a rogue's gallery. Interesting from a legal standpoint, as well."

"I suppose."

"As far as this case is concerned, I'm sure you realize it's vital that we be meticulous in preparing it. Otherwise, we could lose it even before getting to trial. Assuming you apprehend the perpetrator, of course."

Ben thought of François, the artist who'd bashed in his girlfriend's head. "Yeah, I know that."

"Have you been writing memos to your superiors about it, by the way?"

"I've just started." What the ADA was referring to were the Uniform Force 49s, the confidential one-page reports that contained not only information but opinions, as well. UF-49s were intended for cops' eyes only. Ben had sent only one on this case, to Brennan.

126

"Then you should know we're now being pressured to provide copies of such material to the defense, under the *Rosario* rule."

"Is that so?"

"I'm afraid it is. I point it out because I think we both recognize the delicate aspects of this case. Which is all the more reason for us to work together as cooperatively as possible. Wouldn't you say?"

"Sure."

"Very well, then. Please keep me informed as you move along. I would hope that someone with your skills as an investigator would have this wrapped up soon."

Ben stared at him. "We're a little shorthanded, counselor."

"Shorthanded? But you're heading a task force."

"I have two detectives," Ben said. He saw surprise and then what might have been contempt flicker across the ADA's bland features.

Holland recovered quickly. "Well, sounds as if you have your work cut out for you."

"Uh-huh." The guy must have suddenly realized the case was a dog, something Ben had seen almost from the beginning. Now Holland would probably start figuring a way to get out of it.

The TPA came into the office, approaching Holland's desk and placing a thick file jacket on the surface. "It's time for you to leave," she said to him.

"Thank you, Marge," Holland said. He stood up. "Sorry to rush you, Lieutenant, but I'm due to take a case before the grand jury."

"Sure, I know you're busy." Ben got to his feet. "Be talking to you again soon."

Holland was busy leafing through the papers in the file jacket.

Ben turned and left the office.

# 27

"Ben, there's some broad on the phone," Flynn said. "She won't talk to anybody but you. Claims she's got something you'd be interested in."

Ben looked up from his desk. It was early afternoon and he hadn't had any sleep and his eyes burned. This could be one of his street girls, maybe Shirley. "I'll take it."

He reached for the telephone and punched the lighted button with a forefinger. "Tolliver."

"Lieutenant Ben Tolliver?" The voice sounded young and breathless. He didn't recognize it.

"Yeah, who's this?"

"My name is Monica Darrin. I work at Panache."

He sat up straight in his chair. "Yes?"

"I have some information for you, if this can be kept absolutely confidential."

"Of course."

"You must understand, I'm taking a terrible chance by contacting you. Even this call could put my life in danger."

The way she spoke sounded overly dramatic, as if this was an act. He wondered whether somebody was pulling his leg. "How'd you get my name?"

"When you came to see Martha Bellamy? I was on my way out. I asked the doorman and he told me who you were."

He still wasn't convinced, but neither could he turn away what might be a genuine source. "Okay, what've you got?"

"I can't talk over the phone."

"Look, Miss—"

"Darrin."

"Miss Darrin, what's the nature of the information?"

Her voice dropped in volume, so that it was barely audible. "I have a list for you."

"A list of what?"

"Our clients."

If this was on the level, he could have himself a hell of a break. "Where are you? I'll come get it."

"No. Better if we meet somewhere out of the way."

"How about in the Village—can you come down here?"

"I'd rather not. Could we make it in the Theater District?"

"Sure."

"How about Sardi's, then?"

"Fine. When?"

"As soon as possible. I have to be back at the office before four. That's when I go to work."

"Okay, I'll go straight up there now."

"Good. I'll recognize you—I know what you look like."

"See you there." He hung up.

On his way through the squad room, he told Flynn where he was going, and then he bounded down the stairs and out the Christopher Street door of the precinct house. As he headed for his car, he realized his fatigue was suddenly gone.

128

# 28

To a lot of people, Sardi's was an institution, almost as famous a Theater District landmark as Times Square itself. But like a lot of other popular places, it also had had its ups and downs. The restaurant still did a booming business, but these days its customers were more likely to be blue-haired ladies from Westchester than show-biz regulars. And the red leather banquettes and the paneling had been replaced with new ones.

The caricatures that covered the walls had been updated, too. Standing at the bar, Ben realized he didn't know who half the actors and actresses in the Hershfeld drawings were. The older ones, he could recognize—people like Barbra Streisand and Hume Cronyn and Liza Minnelli, but he knew that was because they had been around a long time.

It was midafternoon now; only a few tables were occupied, evidently by tourists or others who didn't have jobs to go back to. He ordered a beer and nursed it while he waited.

So far, he and Spadone and Weisskopf and Flynn had done nothing but spin wheels. Except for the room-service waiter, none of the employees of the Plaza remembered seeing Caroline Patterson in the hotel. The clerk who'd registered her had drawn a blank.

The CSU had gone over the suite with great care and had come up with zip. No stains, no fingerprints, no fibers, not so much as a hair, other than a couple the lab report said had belonged to the victim. The few microscopic bits of flesh found under her fingernails had come from her own neck. And there was no blood—not from Patterson or anyone else. The makeup that had been used to decorate the body had been ordinary brands off the shelf, and Ben assumed it had been Patterson's, part of the kit she'd brought with her to the hotel.

The autopsy report had been just as empty. She'd died of asphyxia, and the ME hadn't found anything much different from what he'd run across in other strangulation cases. Death was due to oxygen deprivation leading to cardiac arrest. The cervical vessels had ruptured, which invariably occurred in such circumstances, and the pressure of the rope or the wire or whatever had been used by the killer had crushed her larynx, which was also common when someone was choked to death.

To Ben, however, one aspect *had* seemed surprising: the report said that except for the deep red furrow girdling her neck, there were no other bruises or contusions on the body. Only a few scratches on her throat, caused by her fingernails when she'd tried to claw the thing loose from her neck. Usually in a strangulation, you got cuts and battered features, because it climaxed a violent struggle, with the loser coming up dead.

So why hadn't Patterson put up more of a fight? Was the guy someone she knew, after all?

The cops had questioned the room-service waiter at great length, inasmuch as he was the one witness who remembered seeing the woman who rented the suite. A police artist had worked up a sketch with the waiter's help, and what it showed was a skinny female with dark hair. On seeing it, Ben thought you probably wouldn't confuse it with more than a hundred thousand other young women in Manhattan.

A computer check on MOs had given them nothing worthwhile, nor was there a rap sheet on Patterson in the vast computer bank at NYSID, the New York State Identification System in Albany. Data in the National Crime Center in Washington was just as dry.

The detectives were now checking further on Caroline Patterson's personal contacts. The funeral had been held that morning, a small private service for the family only, at a chapel in Rye. Ben had made an appointment to call on Spencer Patterson this evening, which would be rough, coming on the same day, but he had no choice. With any homicide, the longer the investigation went, the less of a chance you had of closing the case.

The real problem, of course, was something else. Trying to work a case like this with a handful of cops was not merely difficult, it was ludicrous. Ironically, Brennan would be the first to tell you that the only way to break one of these—unless you got very lucky—was to grind it out. You sifted a thousand possibilities, checked out a million details. And yet Brennan had sat there as if carved from stone while Galupo had laid this dogshit assignment on Ben, giving him only two detectives to help him.

In his anger, he forgot about nursing his beer and drained it. The bartender drew him another—they served draft here, the heavy glass mugs kept frosted in a freezer under the bar—and it tasted much better than the stuff you got in cans. He drank half of this one, as well.

She came in, at long last, wearing dark glasses and a raincoat with the collar turned up. It was easy to guess who she was from the way she stood looking around, as if she was uncertain, and he spotted her before she saw him. When she recognized him, she hurried over to where he was standing.

"Monica?"

"Yes." Her tone dropped dramatically. "What should I call you?"

"Ben. You want a drink?"

"A glass of white wine?"

"Sure."

He asked the bartender to pour her one, and while the man did, Ben looked her over. Frizzy brown hair and plain features, body a little on the chubby side, from what he could see of it under the raincoat. Nothing you'd give a second glance, and definitely not your basic all-American call girl.

She raised her glass. *"A votre santé."*

"Luck." He drank more of his beer. "What have you got for me?"

She glanced over her shoulder and then back at him. "Computer diskettes. With all our clients' names and a lot of other information."

"Great. How'd you get them?"

She looked around again nervously. "Do we have to talk here? I'd rather be somewhere more private."

"Sure, come on." He led her over to a table. As they sat down on the red leather banquette, a waiter scurried over, and Ben told him they were just having drinks and didn't want to order food.

"So how'd you get the diskettes?" Ben asked her once more.

"I made copies when they were out of the office."

"They? You mean Bellamy and Wickersham?"

"Yes. It was early, and I slipped into her office and ran off a set. You can make copies only from her machine."

"Uh-huh. You mind taking off the glasses? It's hard to talk when you've got those on." What he actually wanted was to get a better look at her.

"Certainly, I'll be happy to." Her voice had a rich tone, and she had a way of carefully enunciating every word. She put the glasses into her purse. "There, is that better?"

"Much." Without them, she was even plainer. But he remembered, then; she was the girl who'd come out of the elevator when he'd gone into the building where Panache's offices were. She'd been wearing a sweater and her eyes were red, as if she'd been crying.

What was hard to understand was how such an ordinary broad could be working for an outfit like Panache.

But then she explained it. "I'm a phone girl, you see. That is, actually I'm an actress. I just work at Panache on the side. But because I handle the phones, I know everything about how the system works."

That put it together. In fact, he now realized she must have answered the phone when he'd called there. And the actress part would explain the high drama she managed to get into everything she said. She'd probably make excusing herself to go to the bathroom sound as if she was about to give birth.

"You say the diskettes have other information?" he asked. "Besides the names?"

"Yes. On each client."

"Like what?"

"Address, age, business connection, preferences."

"Preferences?"

"Whether he likes blondes or brunettes, which of our girls he may already have been with, and anything else it might be helpful to know about him."

"Such as?"

"Such as if he likes to take a girl to dinner first, if he likes overnighters, things like that. And if there's anything unusual, whether it's about what he likes to do or something we ought to know about him. These things are in a kind of shorthand we use. Symbols."

"How will I know what they mean?"

"I was about to tell you. BJ is obvious, of course. And then there's D. That's for diver."

"As in muff?" This was bizarre.

"Right."

She didn't seem the least bit self-conscious about telling him this stuff. If anything, she seemed to be enjoying it. He realized that was probably because she saw this as part of the role she was playing, whatever that might be. Mata Hari? Angie Dickinson in the old "Police Woman" TV series? Monica was a piece of work.

"LP is also obvious," she said.

He kept his face straight. "Long-playing?"

"Hardly."

"What else?"

"PSL. That means Martha's permanent shit list."

"How does somebody get on that?"

"Bad manners. He gets drunk, or rough, tries to force the girl to do things she doesn't want to do. There could be any number of reasons. Anybody who's PSL, we don't book."

"Are there other symbols?"

"No, that's about it."

"Okay, let's have the diskettes." He held out his hand. "I'm really grateful to you. This will be a lot of help."

She went through her looking-over-the-shoulder routine once

again, then opened her purse and took out an envelope, which she passed to him.

He looked inside and saw two gray diskettes. "This is it?"

"Everything's on them."

"Good." He put the envelope into a pocket of his windbreaker.

"I can only pray you solve this, Lieutenant—Ben."

"Yeah. Now let me ask you something. What made you decide to do this?" Besides the drama in it, he said to himself.

She tilted her head, holding him in a soulful gaze. "My love for Caroline, for one thing."

"Uh-huh. And what else?"

"Fear. That something like what happened to her might happen again. You see, I care a great deal about the girls who work for us. We're like sisters. I couldn't bear to lose another one."

He waited.

"The other reason was because I heard them talking—Martha and Patrick. They didn't give a damn about her or anyone else, except themselves."

"What did they say?"

"That what they had to worry about now was damage control. Can you imagine that? Poor Caroline wasn't even buried yet, and all they were concerned about was damage control."

He shook his head, to let her know he was in sympathy.

"She went to her lawyer about it, and that was one of the things he told her."

"Who's her lawyer?"

"Abe Rakoff. He's a partner with Cohen, Dietrich and Rakoff."

Ben had never heard of him—or the firm, either. "What else did he say to her, do you know?"

"She told him she'd spoken to the police and he had a fit. He told her to hide everything and tell the police nothing. There's a secret compartment in the fireplace. They think it's very James Bond. You just touch the underside of the mantel and a door swings open."

"Did he say anything more?"

"Just that we shouldn't take any new clients for awhile. Martha was miffed about that."

"But she went along?"

"Yes. After she discussed it with Patrick, she gave us the word."

"And that was it?"

"Yes."

"Good girl, Monica. You'd make a great detective."

She smiled radiantly. The response reminded him of a mongrel bitch he'd known when he was a kid. You patted the dog on the head

133

and she'd roll over on her back with her paws in the air. If you patted Monica, you'd probably get the same reaction.

She turned serious. "I felt I owed it to Caroline to do this. Caroline and all the others."

"You did right. But there's one other thing I need."

"What is it?"

"The names of your girls."

Her eyes flickered. "Why do you need those?"

He knew why she was hesitating. "Because I have the same concern you do. I wouldn't want anything to happen to any of the others. And don't worry, I'm not connected with Vice. I won't do anything that could hurt them."

She spoke slowly. "Do I have your promise on that—your word of honor?"

He wasn't sure who she was doing now. Kathleen Turner, maybe. Or Angelica Huston. "You have my word of honor."

"Then I'm willing to help. It will take me a little time, though, to get you the names of the girls."

Okay, so she was going to stall. But he'd get the names, one way or another. "Let me ask you this. How'd you like to work for me? Under cover, of course."

Her eyebrows lifted. "You mean it?"

"I certainly do." He could see the reaction it was getting. She was probably seeing her name on the marquee: MONICA DARRIN IN *THE DETECTIVE'S HELPER*. A smash hit.

The soulful expression was back. "I'd die for the chance."

"You don't have to go that far. But are you saying you'd do it?"

"Yes. *Yes.*"

"Great. So here's what I want you to do. Call me whenever you can. Just let me know about anything you can pick up. If I'm not in, leave word. I'll call you back at home." He got a card out of his wallet and handed it to her. "Write down your home number for me."

She took a ballpoint from her purse and wrote on the card, then passed it back.

He put the card back into his wallet. "How many phone girls are there?"

"Three. Billie, Francesca, and me. We rotate, so there are always two of us on. But the night Caroline was killed Billie was sick, so I was alone.

"Martha doesn't take calls?"

"Only if a client asks for her."

"And some of them do?"

"Just the ones who think it's a big deal, going directly to the owner. As if they're getting special treatment."

"What does Patrick do?"

"He does some of the booking, too, especially for groups. He's good at that, sizing up a party and deciding who to send. And also he advises Martha on just about everything to do with the business."

"Does he own a piece of it?"

"Probably. I don't really know."

"Okay, so how do you do the booking?"

"Each of us has a box sheet on the desk with the names of the girls who're working that night. It's got columns, with a girl's name at the top of the column. Each box in the column has an hour of the evening printed in it. Let's say we book Ashley with somebody for two hours at the Hilton at eight. We put down the guy's name in her column, in the eight-o'clock box. Along with the name of the hotel and an arrow going to ten o'clock."

"I see."

"Then we let the others know Ashley's booked. That's so we don't book the same girl for two dates at the same time. And if we have another date for Ashley later on, we give her an hour to get there, even if it's right nearby."

"Give her time to get herself together."

"Exactly. Of course, we tell the clients our young ladies date only one gentleman an evening."

"Which isn't true."

"Are you kidding? Martha says the rule is, Keep 'em jumping and humping."

"How many girls do you have working, on an average night?"

"A dozen, maybe more."

"And what's the tab?"

"It depends. That two-hour date I gave you for an example? That's our shortest. For an ordinary girl, it would cost five hundred."

"Five hundred, and she's ordinary?"

"Uh-huh. But ordinary at Panache is beautiful. It's just that some are even more beautiful than others . . . or better for other reasons. Those are our specials, and they get more money. They're the girls who are really outstanding."

"Such as Caroline."

"Yes."

"What was the rate for her?"

"For that night, it was twelve hundred. And that was just for dinner and back to the hotel. If it had been an overnighter, it would have been more."

"What was the split?"

"Seven to her, five to Panache."

"Roughly sixty-forty. That standard, do you know?"

"With us it is. I'll say that much for Martha, she's fair to the girls. That's why the best people want to work for us."

"What about the tip?"

"The girl keeps it."

"So Panache's gross is how much, in a typical week—do you know that?"

"I'm not supposed to, but I do. It's around fifty thousand, but sometimes more."

Interesting, he thought. Fifty grand a week, and the expenses were peanuts. Despite Bellamy's telling him how she was an upstanding taxpayer, she'd be gigging the IRS for plenty.

He smiled at her. "Monica, I appreciate this a lot. You've really been terrific."

She drank the last of her wine, her eyes holding on him over the rim of the glass. When she put the glass down, she said, "And you've given me a new purpose, Ben. How can I ever thank you?"

"By giving me more of the same kind of help. It'll be a wonderful tribute to Caroline." That was laying it on pretty thick, but what the hell—it seemed to be the kind of thing she wanted to hear.

He paid the check and they walked out together. On the street, he hailed a cab and held the door open for her.

As she got into the taxi, she presented her cheek to be kissed. Ben gave it a peck, and when she was inside, he slammed the door.

Ingrid Bergman in *Casablanca,* he thought. And I'm Bogart.

The cab roared off.

# 29

Ben drove to 1 Police Plaza, where he got a uniformed female clerk to put the diskettes into an IBM one at a time so he could see what he had. When the data from the first one came onto the screen, he felt a rush. It was just as Monica had promised, and then some. Probably the most exclusive john list in New York, maybe in the United States.

The names were organized alphabetically, each entry stating where the guy worked and what his position was, plus the address of the company or organization. In some instances, his home address was listed as well. Also whether he was married, and other personal information on him. That part varied, probably representing whatever the girls had been able to pick up—clubs he belonged to, where he'd gone to college, and so on. Under that came the symbols. And under that were the names of girls, with a date and a place beside each name.

He stared at the screen, his excitement rising as the desk clerk scrolled the entries. One of these men might lead him to Caroline Patterson's killer. One of them might *be* the killer. Aloud he said, "Hot shit."

The clerk rolled her eyes at him. "Does that mean you're pleased, Lieutenant? Or do you have to go to the bathroom?"

He looked at her, seeing her for the first time. She probably weighed as much as he did, and like him, she had a mustache. Only hers was daintier.

"Anybody ever tell you you're adorable?" he asked.

"Often. You want a printout?"

While she ran it off, he called Flynn and told him to locate Spadone and Weisskopf, have them get to the Sixth as soon as possible.

He put the phone down, and when the clerk handed him the sheets of paper along with the diskettes, he gave her a quick kiss and ran. That's two in one day, he thought. Some sex life.

It took twenty minutes to wrestle the Ford through the traffic on his way back to the precinct house, nosing in and out of holes in the stream of cars, trucks, and taxis, wondering how cabbies could take it. If you drove in this mess all day long for a few years, you'd be ready for a frontal lobotomy.

When he walked into the squad room, Spadone and Weisskopf hadn't arrived yet. Flynn was on the phone, and the only other detective in the place was Carlos Rodriguez.

A black man was sitting in the chair beside Rodriguez's desk. He was burly, wearing a pink shirt open at the throat. A thick white bandage covered the bridge of his nose.

Ben walked past them and went to the Xerox to make copies of the printout.

"Why don't you use your brain?" Carlos asked the guy. "You got a brain, don't you Tyrone?"

"Course I got a brain, man," Tyrone said. "Don't gimme none a that shit. If I could tell you, I'd tell you."

"That so? Then lemme ask you. You know what's gonna happen

if you *don't* tell me? You go to a hard place, man. Back to Attica. This time, the DA gonna see you pull twenty, with a recommendation to the parole board you do the whole trip. No good time, no nothing."

Tyrone did not seem impressed. He sat back in his chair and picked his teeth with a fingernail.

Carlos leaned close. "Twenty years a long time, man. Only thing your dick gonna know is punks. You get out, it's over for you. But you tell me, we fix it you get only one, maybe two at the most. In a different joint, too, where they don't even know you. Maybe Elmira; it's nice there."

"Yeah? You the one ain't got a brain. I tell you and it don't matter where I go. I don't do one or two, not even one or two *minutes*. You know why? 'Cause soon as I go in there, I'm dead. See? So you take your deal, stick it up your spic ass."

"Okay, Tyrone. You want it like that? Maybe what we do is, we put the word out you told us where you get the stuff, *then* you go to Attica. How long you last then, man? One or two *seconds?*"

This time the black man made no reply.

"So come on," Carlos said. "You tell me, I pass you to Narcotics and we forget about the other shit—assault on a police officer, resisting arrest, illegal possession, all of it. Never happened. So how about it? I'm givin' you a break, man. I'm givin' you your *life.*"

Tyrone looked at him. "Sheeit."

Ben gathered his copies and went on into his office as Rodriguez and Tyrone continued their chat. Police work wasn't police work anymore, he thought. It was handeling in a fucking bazaar.

He closed the door behind him and sat down at his desk. The place was a mess. It was a small room to begin with, light from the overhead fluorescent bars casting a sickly glow on the green cinderblock walls, a little more coming through the frosted glass of the window. The bulletin board on the opposite wall was covered with notices and flyers and scribbled notes, a lot of it months old. He'd been meaning to sort the stuff out, but he'd probably do better to burn it, start over. Against another wall was a filing cabinet, gray metal like the desk. The top of the cabinet was heaped with black loose-leaf notebooks and more paper. Two straight-backed chairs stood on what little floor space remained open.

But the worst eyesore was his desk. It was overflowing with paper: DD5's, the daily reports detectives loathed having to fill out, memos, departmental directives, old newspaper clippings, ancient phone messages, and, atop the mess, as if holding it down, a coffee mug with an inch of sludge in the bottom.

There were also scribbled notes in his handwriting, some of them nearly indecipherable, even to him. The note taking was a habit he'd had from the time he'd moved up to detective/third, jotting down thoughts however haphazardly. Going back over them sometimes triggered an idea, gave him a direction to try he might otherwise have forgotten about. He'd want to sort those out, as well. When he got the time.

He pushed the pile aside to make room for the copies he'd made of the computer printout, and as he did, he noticed that one of the phone messages was from Patty. This one was recent; the penciled notation said she'd called an hour ago. As he looked at it, he felt a mix of emotions: guilt, but also a sense of relief. At least she hadn't written him off. He reached for the phone.

She answered on the second ring.

"Hi," Ben said. "It's me."

"Hi." Her voice sounded neutral: not cold, but not very warm, either. "How's it going?"

"Okay. Sorry I haven't been in touch sooner."

"It's all right. I understand. You're on that murder, right? The one in the Plaza?"

"Yeah. You see that on TV?"

"No, but one of the other girls in the club did. She told me about it. Must have been awful."

"I miss you," he said.

Her tone changed immediately. "Oh, Ben, I miss you, too. I know you . . . can't help it. It's just that—"

"Hey, I understand." There was a lot more he wanted to say, but saying it over the phone would be difficult. Impossible, in fact. "I'll try to get over there tonight. Pick you up at the club, take you home."

"I'd like that."

"See you then, honey." He was tempted to add "I love you," but he couldn't get the words out. Nevertheless, when he hung up, he felt a hell of a lot better.

There was a knock at the door and Flynn opened it. "Lou, Joe Spadone and Art Weisskopf are here."

"Good. Bring 'em in. And get another chair, will you? I want you in on this, too."

Flynn cocked his head. "You sound like things are lookin' up."

Ben thought of Patty again, and then glanced at the diskettes and the printout. "They are, Ed. They are."

139

# 30

Tolliver had made copies for each of the detectives. As he passed out the Xeroxed sheets, he related how he'd gotten the diskettes and explained how the entries were set up. Telling the men the information was sensitive wasn't necessary—all three whistled and made remarks as they read through the pages, recognizing names of a number of individuals and nearly all the organizations.

There were senior executives with blue-chip companies ranging from General Motors to IBM, most of them from the New York area, but many from other major cities, as well as lawyers, CPAs, doctors, and public officials. Among the latter were a federal judge, three congressmen, and two senators. There were editors from the *Times* and the *Post* and various magazines, and guys from all three TV networks, as well as others who were with cable networks and local stations. The names of many foreign diplomats were there, including members of a number of delegations to the UN.

There were also two high-ranking officers of the police department.

"For Christ's sake," Spadone said. "Look at this. Hi Donnelly is a regular." Donnelly was an NYPD inspector. "Not only that, it says he's got himself an LP."

"That's a typo," Weisskopf said. "It should say he *is* a large prick."

"He can afford broads like these?" Spadone said. "Inspectors' pay must've went up."

"It's on the pad," Art said. "You know, like you get a free sandwich, Joe, somebody important gets complimentary head. Makes you want to work harder for promotions, right?"

"Hey, here's Justin Frank," Flynn said. "The guy on CBS? He's the one who's always bellyaching about the city's declining morality. What a fucking hypocrite."

Spadone glanced at the entry. "What he means is, it's not declining fast enough. He's doing what he can to help."

Flynn peered at the other cops. "You know, something just went through my head."

"That was air, Ed," Spadone said. "Just close your mouth and it'll stop."

"No, wait," Flynn said. "Think a minute, what we got here. This

140

stuff ever fell in the wrong hands, not people like us, you know what it could be worth? Millions."

Weisskopf looked at him. "Whattaya mean, not people like us? We don't like money?"

"Yeah, what is it, Ed?" Spadone said. "You want to give up your share?"

"We could buy an island in the Pacific," Art said. "Like Brando. Stock it with about a hundred broads."

"None of 'em older than twenty," Spadone said. "After that, they're over the hill."

"Or maybe we go to Monaco," Weisskopf went on. "There's more action there. Casinos, discos, and we could live on a yacht."

Tolliver held up a hand. "If you guardians of the people don't mind, I'd like to suggest we do some work."

Spadone cleared his throat. "Sure, Lou. We were just kidding around."

"Yeah, I'm sure you were."

Weisskopf grinned. "Everybody's got a dream."

"Mine is we close this case," Ben said. "I want us to start by questioning the guys who saw Caroline Patterson. We'll run down the list, decide who interviews each one of them. And just to start things off, there's one on here belongs to me."

"Who's that, Lou?"

"His name's Barry Conklin. Head of the Rockford Company on Wall Street. Let's go down through the printout, starting at the top."

# *31*

When the meeting ended, Spadone, Weisskopf, and Tolliver each had a list of men who had done business with Panache. Ben ordered the pair from Midtown North to question the ones assigned to them as quickly as possible, reporting progress to him or to Ed Flynn as they went along.

As soon as the others had left his office, Ben called Jack Strickland, a detective sergeant who worked in the Fraud Bureau, headquartered at 100 Centre Street. Strickland had been in Ben's class at the Police Academy. Over the following years, they had seen each other only occasionally, and while Ben had remained single, Strickland had acquired a wife, four kids, a house in Levittown, a mortgage, and a potbelly.

"You married yet?" It was always the first question Strickland asked.

Ben gave him his usual reply. "What, with all this free pussy chasing me around?"

"Yeah," Strickland said, "I didn't think you would be."

"In fact, I had to hire a guy as my assistant, just so I could keep up with it."

Strickland sighed. "Lucky prick. Or should I say, lucky famous prick."

"Oh, shit. You, too? What happened, you see it on TV, about the Patterson case?"

"Lois did. She wanted to know how come you were getting to be a big deal and I was still a schnook."

"I hope you told her the truth, Jack."

"Of course I did. I explained how you had to be an ass-sucker to move up in the department."

Ben sensed the sergeant was only half-kidding.

"What can I do for you, Ben?"

"I need information on a Wall Street company called Rockford. You know the firm?"

"Oh yeah. We got a file on them you couldn't lift. What do you want to know?"

"Mostly about their chairman, a guy named Barry Conklin. You have stuff on him?"

"Sure. When do you want to come down?"

"Now, if you can give me some time."

"Well, let's see. I got a meeting with the mayor and the PC, and then lunch with the governor, but I can cancel those. Come ahead."

Ben thanked him and hung up. He told Flynn where he could be reached and left the precinct house.

This time, he tried going crosstown and then down the FDR Drive, but that route was no faster than any other he'd taken. In fact, because of some construction work on the Drive and even heavier traffic than usual, it took him a little over thirty minutes to reach the Criminal Justice building.

The Fraud Bureau was housed in offices that were spacious and comfortable, compared to what Ben was used to. The pace was different, too. Strickland was in shirt sleeves, sitting at a desk that was one of several in a large open area. At the desk next to his, a woman was doing her nails, and at the one on the other side, a guy was on the phone, talking about the Giants' upcoming game with the Redskins.

Strickland got coffee for them, and when Ben was seated beside the desk, Strickland placed a thickly packed file jacket in front of him.

"Anything you want to know is in there," Strickland said. "And if you have questions, just ask."

Ben looked at the file. Reading its contents would take hours. "What does this Rockford outfit do, exactly?"

"They call themselves investment bankers. But actually they specialize in IPOs."

"In what?"

"Initial public offerings. When a company wants to offer stock for the first time, Rockford underwrites it."

"They put up the money?"

"Right. But what's unusual with them is, they offer shares to the public when the company is just getting started. Sometimes even before. Most investment bankers don't do that. What they usually do is, they put venture capital in a young company to help it grow. Some of the money's their own, and some of it they get from private investors. Then later on, when the company's got a track record, they take it public and make a bundle."

"So why doesn't Rockford do the same thing?"

"The guy who runs it figured out a better scam."

"Barry Conklin."

"Right. The way Conklin sees it, why not let the public do most of the financing, right from the beginning?"

"I don't get it," Ben said. "How does he convince people to buy shares if the company hasn't even gotten started?"

Strickland grinned. "By telling them they'll get rich, of course. See, it goes like this. Let's say there are some guys working in a hot industry, like health care, or computer technology. And let's say they got a terrific new idea or maybe a product they can patent, and they want to start a company. But what they don't have is the money to do it with. So they go to Rockford for financing. Conklin puts up the dough. Only a little of it is his. Most of the capital comes from the IPO."

"So he gets most of the money by selling shares in a company that may not even exist yet?"

"Now you got it. And before that, before the stock is offered, Conklin makes a deal with the founders that calls for him to get the biggest piece of the pie. Usually around sixty percent. Then if the company hits, he's got himself a bonanza."

"How does he talk them into giving him that much of a cut?"

"Simple. They're so fucking glad to have somebody back them, they think he's Santa Claus."

"In other words, he's mostly using other people's money to finance the new company, but he winds up owning more than half of it."

"Right."

"While Joe Sap who buys stock gets screwed."

"Often. But not always. That is, somebody who buys shares will never see anything like the gains Conklin can make, but sometimes he does all right. Then other times, the venture falls on its ass, and the investor's left with certificates he can use to paper his bathroom."

"Which one happens more often?"

"What do you think? So far the bathroom is way ahead. But Conklin? Even if the company goes in the toilet, he got his money back selling the IPO."

"What about the guys who started the company?" Ben asked. "If it takes off, they do okay, too, right?"

"Wrong. They get the shaft. And they don't even know it until it's all done. At first, they're so happy to get the start-up money, they think they got a good deal. Conklin convinces them he's taking all the risks. It's only after the company's successful that they realize the shareholders are getting, say, thirty-five percent of the earnings, Conklin's getting sixty percent, and they get what's left over. What's more, Conklin has the equity of his stock. So if the company just happens to turn into a real smash, like Technomedical Corporation, for instance, Conklin makes another killing."

"How, by selling his shares?"

"Sure. He might get fifty or a hundred times what he put in. Or maybe he arranges for an acquisition by a major company and makes even more."

"Cute."

"Isn't it? God only knows what the guy's net worth is, but it has to run to a couple hundred million. It's buried in so many dummy corporations and trusts, the IRS runs up their own asshole trying to figure it out."

"What else do you know about him? What's his background?"

Strickland sat back and put one foot against the edge of his desk. "Grew up in Queens; father was an accountant. The family never had a lot of money, but they were comfortable. Barry was bright, and a hustler from the time he was in grammar school. Went to Cornell, and when he got out, he went straight to Wall Street. Started with Merrill Lynch, then moved to Lowell Barnes. There was talk about him being involved with insider trading, but the government never had enough for an indictment. Due to an unfortunate accident."

144

"What kind of an accident?"

"There was a guy in a law firm that handled mergers and acquisitions. The story was that he was feeding information to Conklin, and the federal prosecutor was preparing a case. But then the guy fell out the window of his office, on the forty-second floor."

"That *was* unfortunate."

"Wasn't it? But by that time, Conklin had made himself maybe thirty million bucks. From Lowell Barnes, he went to Rockford, which was an old white-shoe firm that was in trouble. When he got there, it was on the brink of bankruptcy. The partners were all old, which was one weakness, and the other was they were gentlemen. It was like throwing a shark in a school of goldfish."

"So he took it over?"

"In just under a year. Then he put his system to work and turned the place into a bucket shop, selling IPOs."

"And it's legal, the way he does it?"

"Yeah, but just barely. And lately, he's made a couple mistakes, on account of he's got an ego bigger than this building."

"You guys working up a case?"

"Right. It's a race between us and the feds."

"Think you'll get him?"

"Who knows? He's been accused a dozen times, but nothing stuck."

Ben gestured toward the desk. "That's some file."

"Oh yeah. We would dearly love to nail the bastard. But so far, he's been a moving target."

"You know anything about his personal life?"

"Some. He's married, with a new wife. Left his old one, a girl he met at Cornell, and two kids. Lives in an apartment here in town, also has a house in East Hampton. The company owns a jet, which flies him to places like Miami, San Juan, Atlantic City, sometimes Vegas."

"High roller?"

"Yeah, but no sucker. He just likes the flash. And the attention, people kissing his ass. Very vain about his appearance. He was a jock in college and stays in perfect shape. Loves the ladies. Which is probably what brings you down here, right?"

"How'd you guess?"

"It's the result of my superior training as a police officer. You think maybe he iced that broad in the Plaza?"

"It's like with your case, Jack—who knows? We can only hope so."

"I don't. We want that peckerhead ourselves."

# 32

The southern end of Manhattan is where the Dutch first settled in 1625, calling their community New Amsterdam. The island is quite narrow at that point, so that if you stand near the Trinity Church cemetery on Broadway, you can look in one direction and see the East River only a few blocks away, and then turn around and find the Hudson even closer.

Many of the streets are no more than a few yards wide. They are also winding and irregular, not laid out in an orderly fashion the way they are from Houston Street all the way up to where the Harlem River curves around past Baker Field and Inwood Hill Park, dividing Manhattan from the Bronx. But in this small area is the greatest concentration of economic power in America. The pirates here make Morgan and Blackbeard look like pikers.

Tolliver knew better than to drive into the district. The traffic was even worse than in other parts of the city, and when you arrived, you could forget about finding a place to park, with or without a police placard. So as much as he hated it, he took the subway. At least it was fast; he got off at the Wall Street stop less than ten minutes after leaving the Criminal Justice building.

When he came up from the station, he crossed Broadway and walked east on Wall. The offices were letting out, and the sidewalks were so jammed that many of the pedestrians spilled out into the street. Taxis and trucks crawled among them, irate drivers shouting and blowing horns. The pollution was worse, too, the air heavy with exhaust fumes and carrying a pervasive stink from the foul waters of the harbor.

The address Ben wanted was two blocks down. As he passed the New York Stock Exchange, he looked up at the building's massive facade and sensed the strength behind the carved stone figures, the six huge Ionic columns, each one hewn from a single shaft of granite. The volume of trading that went on in the place was mind-boggling. According to what he'd read in the newspapers, when anything less than 150 million shares changed hands, it was considered a slow day.

The Rockford building was also faced in stone, giving it an air of solidity. The lobby walls were clad in veined white marble, and the elevator doors were of lacquered brass. A directory said the executive offices were on the third floor. As Ben waited for an elevator, he thought of what Jack Strickland had told him about the company and its owner. To look at these surroundings, you'd think you were in the Bank of England. This guy Conklin must be some operator.

The reception room was paneled in rosewood, and the receptionist had gray hair. She was sitting at an antique desk that appeared only slightly older than she was. It occurred to Ben that she'd probably won this assignment on the basis that she exuded the same kind of timeless dependability as did her surroundings. He asked to see Mr. Conklin, showing the woman his shield, and she spoke briefly into a telephone. When she put it down, she said, "Mr. Conklin has left for the day."

"That his secretary you spoke to?"

The old lady had a genteel manner. "Yes, it was."

"Call her back, please. Tell her I want to talk with her."

She hesitated, then picked up the telephone once more. When she hung up this time, she said, "Miss Dowling will be right out. Please be seated."

Ben sat down on a sofa, beneath a portrait of a guy with mutton-chop whiskers and a massive belly. A moment later, a door opened, and another woman appeared, this one much younger, wearing a starched white blouse, horn-rims, and a frown. She looked at him with obvious distaste. "Lieutenant Tolliver?"

Ben stood up. "Yes, ma'am."

"I'm Sarah Dowling, Mr. Conklin's secretary. You wished to see me?"

"Yes, please. Can we go somewhere to talk?"

Miss Dowling was as starchy as her blouse. She glanced at the receptionist and apparently decided it would be better if the conversation was private. She turned back to the door and indicated that he was to follow.

Once inside, Ben found himself in a large open space with desks at which secretaries were typing and men were talking on telephones. The walls in here were also paneled in dark wood, and frescoes decorated the cream-colored vaulted ceiling. There were offices along the perimeter, and through the open doors he could see more men working the phones. Even though it was after five o'clock, the place seemed charged with energy. As he followed Miss Dowling down the wide corridor between the desks, he picked up snatches of what the men were saying into the telephones.

". . . just like I told you it would, Charley, the stock took off, and you weren't in it. Not very smart, Charley. So I'm . . ."

". . . and this one is dynamite. You know how genetic engineering is the wave of the future; it can't miss. Of course, we can't be . . ."

". . . there's only a small number of shares left. Barry's just letting a few friends in on it. That's why I knew you'd want to . . ."

"A sure thing? Nothing's a sure thing, Fred. Except someday we'll both be dead. But I'll say this, it's the nearest thing to it I ever . . ."

Her office was at the far end of the floor. He followed her through the door and she closed it behind him and told him to have a seat as she sat down at her desk. The furniture in here seemed to be all antiques, as well, and there were framed prints of harbor scenes on the walls.

She peered at him. "Now what is this all about, Lieutenant?"

"It's about a murder investigation."

Her jaw came down. "A *murder?*"

"Correct. It's important that I speak to your boss."

She recovered quickly. "Mr. Conklin has left for the day. I believe you were told that."

"Yes, I was. Where is he now?"

"I'm sorry, I don't know."

"Really? You strike me as a very efficient person, Miss Dowling."

The frown was back in place. "I assure you, I am."

"Okay, I was right. And that being the case, I'll bet you could come up with a couple of places where he might be."

"I don't think I—"

"So what I'll do is, I'll just wait while you make a few calls, on the off chance you might locate him."

She studied him for a moment. "Do you usually just barge in on people, unannounced?"

"Sometimes, when I'm working on a homicide. If you happen to reach Mr. Conklin, you might want to tell him the victim was a friend of his."

"Lieutenant, I really doubt very much that—"

He spoke softly. "A lady friend."

Her jaw came down again. It was turning out to be a reliable indicator of what she was thinking. Miss Dowling would be a soft touch in a game of seven-card stud.

"Tell you what," Ben said. "I'll just step outside for a few minutes. Then if you reach him, you can talk in private. Tell him it's about Caroline, and that I want to talk to him."

He got to his feet and smiled pleasantly. "Let me know what he says."

Without looking back, he opened the door and left her office, closing the door behind him.

Out here, the telephones were still going full blast. A few feet away,

148

a young guy in shirt sleeves was sitting at a desk, stabbing the buttons on the base of his phone with his index finger. While waiting for an answer, he held a three-by-five file card in his free hand and squinted at it.

As Ben watched, the guy said into the phone, "Hello, is this Edward Bartowitz? Oh, Berkowitz, sorry. This is Dan Parrick calling from the Rockford Company on Wall Street. We're the leading firm dealing in IPOs—Initial Public Offerings. Are you in the stock market, Ed? . . . Yeah, I know, but let me tell you, this is where the money is. Ground floor, you know? That's how the pros make the killings. Only reason I called you is this is an opportunity you ought to know about. The company is Biogenics. . . . Of course you never heard of it; it's new. Already there're only a few shares left. . . . Why you? Because we want to introduce you to our firm. With some of the companies we got started, investors made millions, Ed. You heard of Medicotech? Or Computergraphics? Zeracor? Guys who got in at the start got back thirty, forty times what they put in. . . . Of course there's no guarantee; you know that. What I'm giving you is *opportunity*. Tell you what. I'll put you down for five hundred shares, send you a prospectus. Then you'll see just how good this could be. Soon as you—"

The door opened, and Miss Dowling said, "Would you come in please, Lieutenant?"

When he went back inside, she remained standing. "I called Mr. Conklin's health club, on the off chance he might have stopped in after leaving here."

"Yes?"

"He said he'd be willing to give you a few minutes, but no more than that. He has a dinner engagement, later on."

"Sure. I appreciate your help. What's the name of the place?"

"The Manhattan Training Center. It's just a few blocks from here."

"Okay, how do I get there?"

She gave him directions, and as he left this time, he observed that Dan Parrick was already on another call.

"Let me tell you," Parrick said into the phone, "IPOs are where the money is. Ground floor, you know? That's how the pros . . ."

On the way back through the lobby, Ben realized what it was that had seemed so surprising. On the outside, Rockford was like a fine old safe: solid, dependable, in perfect condition. But then you swung open the door and saw what was crawling around inside. Even with the rotten air, it was a relief to get back onto the street.

149

# 33

The guy who greeted Ben said he was the club's director and to call him Joey. He was young and beefy, wearing sweatpants and a T-shirt with the Manhattan Training Center logo on it. He seemed impressed that Ben was a detective.

Joey was standing beside a counter with a register book lying open on the surface, and in the wall behind the counter were cubbyholes with bundles of shorts, socks, jocks, and more T-shirts in them. On the wall next to the cubbyholes was a panel with locker keys hanging from hooks.

Looking into the gym, Ben could see guys working with various types of equipment—Universal machines, barbells, treadmills, stationary bikes, punching bags, chinning bars. The men were all wearing the same outfits, T-shirts and shorts imprinted with the MTC logo. They seemed to fall into two categories, with very little in between. One bunch, by far the larger, had gray hair and paunches and moved slowly, their faces red, sweat dripping from their chins. They looked to Ben as if they were one heave away from a coronary.

The smaller group was comprised of young guys who appeared to be in good shape. A number of them obviously had been jocks at one time or another. They were also running sweat, but their bellies were flat and they moved quickly and with determination. One of them was doing squats with a bar that must have had at least two hundred pounds on it.

"Which one is Barry Conklin?" Ben asked.

Joey pointed to an area on the far side of the floor where several punching bags were mounted on platforms. "The guy in the center, the tall one on the speed bag."

Ben walked over there, making his way through the mass of grunting, heaving, panting men. It was hot in here, and the air was rank with sweat and body oil and linament. The smell was oddly pleasing to him. He smiled to himself as he realized that was because it was familiar, bringing back memories. When he was a kid, he'd boxed in the P.A.L. in the Bronx, and later as a teenager in the Golden Gloves. He'd gone all the way to the New York finals before a black middleweight from Brownsville had almost taken his head off with a left hook he never saw coming. He'd boxed in the Marine Corps, as well, in intercompany bouts, and even today he liked to mess around in the NYPD gym, when he got the chance.

Which wasn't often enough. He was in reasonably good condition, but he could be better. Lousy food and too much booze and erratic sleeping habits didn't make for the best training regimen.

The guy who'd been pointed out to him was big, taller than Ben and massive in the shoulders and chest, tapering down to a skinny waist and thick, taut legs—a true heavyweight. His face was unmarked, however, which meant that either he'd had only limited experience in the ring or else he was very good. His hair was black and on the long side, and he carried his squarish jaw thrust out aggressively. He was working with a six-ounce bag, rotating his fists rapidly, making the bag dance. His T-shirt and shorts were soaked.

Ben stood nearby, and although the guy didn't glance over at him, it was obvious he knew he had an audience. He picked up the pace, doubling up with each hand, first striking the bag straight on and then with the edge of the fist, then hitting it with the other hand the same way, so fast the thin red Everlast gloves were a blur and the sound was like the beating of a parade drum. Finally, he gave the bag one very hard shot and stepped back, looking over at his visitor with a smug expression on his face.

Ben's tone was pleasant. "You look as if you've had the gloves on a few times."

The big man picked a towel off a nearby rack and mopped his face with it as he stepped over to where Ben was standing. "Yeah, I boxed in college. You're the cop, right? You went to my office looking for me?"

Ben took out his wallet and held it open for the guy to see. "That's right. Lieutenant Ben Tolliver, Sixth Precinct. And you're Barry Conklin, is that correct?"

"Correct. My secretary told me you're investigating a homicide."

"Yes. A woman named Caroline Patterson. She was murdered in the Plaza Hotel on October fourteenth."

"So?"

"So she was a friend of yours. Only she called herself by her professional name when you knew her. Caroline Clark."

Conklin smiled, rubbing his arms now with the towel. "You've got it wrong, Lieutenant. I don't know any Caroline Patterson. Don't know any Caroline Clark, either."

"Is that so? I think you did. You got together with her a number of times over the past few months. Seven times, in fact. Not counting October fourteenth."

The smile stayed in place, cocksure and lazy, as if Conklin was enjoying the exchange. "You must be confusing me with somebody else. Or maybe somebody was using my name."

"I don't think so. She was a call girl, and you booked her through an escort service called Panache. I can tell you which nights, which hotels, and how much you paid her each time."

Conklin tossed the towel aside. "That's all very interesting, Lieutenant. I suppose you've also got witnesses, right? People who'd swear they saw me with her in those places you're talking about?"

"No, but—"

The smile vanished. "Then what are you wasting my time for? You think you can go charging into my company and bother my people, and then come in here like some nickelshit Joe Friday, just because you happened to get hold of my name someplace? Who gave it to you, by the way? One of those fartbrains in the DA's office who's looking to make a big score? You got absolutely no way to connect me with this whoever she is—or was. So now do me a favor, will you? Get the fuck out."

A few men who'd been working out nearby heard some of it. They stopped what they were doing and moved closer.

Ben kept his voice down. "Where were you on the fourteenth, Mr. Conklin?"

"I worked late that night. Which my secretary would confirm. If necessary, which it isn't."

"I may ask her to do that."

"Fine. But I'm gonna talk to my lawyers about this. You've got no business making accusations without one shred of proof. Now I told you, get out of here. Or else."

"Or else what?"

The big man hunched his shoulders. "Or I might have to take you by the neck and throw you out."

A murmur rose from the onlookers.

"I wouldn't try anything like that if I were you," Ben said.

Conklin moved closer. "No? You gonna stop me, Lieutenant?"

Ben stood stock-still, wondering if this asshole would actually try to muscle him. As unprofessional as he knew he was to think it, he wished Conklin would make the attempt.

But Conklin was enjoying himself. He kept shooting little side glances at his admirers, grandstanding for them. He cocked his head. "What's the matter, Lieutenant, afraid you might get your ass kicked? Tell you what. You give that badge of yours to Joey to hold for you, and we'll put on the gloves. I always wondered whether a cop had any balls, without that thing."

The group had grown larger. Somebody called out, "Come on, let's see whatcha got."

"Some other time," Ben said. "I'm sure we'll be talking again."

The grin was back on Conklin's face, but now it was more of a sneer. "That's where you're wrong, dickhead. This is the only chance you get. And you know what? I think what you are is a yellow faggot."

Ben felt the heat come up into his cheeks, as snickering and more catcalls issued from the onlookers. One of them yelled, "Nail him, Barry."

For a brief moment, he was tempted to hang one on Conklin's oversized jaw. But then reason prevailed.

He stepped back. "See you again soon."

"Fuck you." Conklin struck a pose, jaw thrust out, arms akimbo.

Ben turned away, aware that everyone in the place was staring and smirking, delighted to see the cop back down. It was what he could expect in a situation like this, but that didn't mean he could accept it. On the one hand, civilians expected the police to go to the wall for them, die for them if necessary. Yet there was nothing they liked better than to see a cop humiliated.

He took a step toward the door, and as he did, he felt a hand grip his shoulder and spin him around.

Conklin was wearing the contemptuous grin again. Apparently, he'd misread Ben's reluctance. And he was having a great time showing off for the crowd. As what he must have thought would be the final gesture of dismissal, he snapped the back of his hand across Ben's nose.

The blow wasn't serious, just hard enough to make Tolliver's eyes water. But Conklin had struck a police officer, which was all the excuse Ben needed.

He took a half step forward, then drove his right fist up to the wrist in Conklin's belly, the punch traveling no more than eight inches.

The big man's eyes popped in surprise and pain, the wind going out of him as from an exploding truck tire. He bent forward, and as he did, Ben hooked his left into Conklin's ear, knocking him into one of the onlookers and sending the guy sprawling.

Conklin recovered in a split second and came up swinging. But embarrassment and anger had upset his judgment. He was flailing, teeth clenched, face red with anger.

Ben slipped underneath, then straightened to throw another left hook, a harder one this time, because he was coming up out of a crouch with all his heft behind it. The punch landed solidly on Conklin's temple, stopping him in his tracks just long enough for

153

Ben to nail him with a right cross that was even harder, square on the point of his jaw. This time, Conklin went over backward, his head striking the polished wood floor with a sickening thump, as if somebody had dropped a pumpkin.

For a moment, the big man was motionless. Then he slowly pulled himself up into a sitting position, shaking his head and gasping for air. But he made no attempt to regain his feet.

There was dead silence in the gym. Ben turned and walked quickly back to the front entrance. As he opened the door, he heard Joey sputtering, asking Conklin whether he was all right.

When he reached the sidewalk, he saw that the streetlights had been turned on. The temperature had dropped noticeably, and with the wind coming off the harbor, the air was much cooler than it had been a short time ago. As he walked toward the subway entrance, he remembered that he'd made an appointment to visit Spencer Patterson at his estate in Rye.

That would not be pleasant. And yet, as he strode along among the crowd of pedestrians, it occurred to him that he'd never felt better in his life.

# 34

Massive stone pillars flanked the gates. When Ben drove up, lights flashed on, holding the Ford in a harsh white glare. A metallic voice said, "State your name and purpose."

Ben took the leather folder from his back pocket and held it out the window so that his shield would show. "Lieutenant Tolliver, New York Police Department. I have an appointment with Mr. Patterson."

"Follow the drive to the main residence," the voice instructed. "Park in the area on the right, near the other cars."

The gates swung open, and when he'd passed through, he saw a reflection of them in his rearview mirror, closing behind him. The driveway wound through groves of maples and oaks, his headlights picking up the vivid colors of the leaves. It wasn't until he came over a rise that he caught so much as a glimpse of the house.

It was a great sprawling structure, ablaze with light. Built of gray limestone, the center section had wings extending from either end, all of it three stories high, with a steep slate roof inset with dormers. The drive was circular in front of the house, and to one side was an area in which a half dozen cars were parked. Ben pulled the Ford to a stop alongside a Mercedes roadster and got out.

A figure loomed nearby. "Lieutenant Tolliver?"

"Yes?"

"I'm Baxter, security. If you'll walk ahead of me, please. Go straight to the front door."

The guy was massive, attired in a gray suit and carrying a walkie-talkie in one hand, a Mac-10 in the other. Ben stepped past him and went up a flagstone walk that led to the house.

The entrance was also floodlighted, and he raised a hand to shield his eyes from the fierce glare. The heavy doors swung open, silhouetting a man against the interior of a spacious foyer.

This one spoke with a British accent. "Good evening, sir. My name is Willis. Mr. Patterson is expecting you. If you'll follow me, please."

As he walked into the house, Ben's eyes adjusted to the softer interior light. The foyer's walls were hung with life-sized portraits of somebody's ancestors, presumably Patterson's. For once, Ben was glad he'd put on his blazer and a tie.

They went through an archway and down a corridor, and then Willis stopped before a door and knocked on it. From inside, a voice said to come in. Willis opened the door and stepped aside, then followed Ben into the room.

This was the library. Floor-to-ceiling bookcases lined the walls, and at the far end of the room, logs crackled in a cavernous fireplace. Oriental rugs covered the parquet floor.

Two men and two women sat facing each other in deeply upholstered chairs near the fire. One of the men was Spencer Patterson. He rose and stepped forward to greet Tolliver.

Patterson seemed much the same as when Ben had seen him in the morgue at Bellevue: strong-willed, decisive, the man in charge. Tonight, he had on a black velvet smoking jacket and a white shirt open at the throat, but there was nothing casual about his manner. "Hello, Lieutenant. Come over here and meet these people."

Ben followed him to where the others were sitting. The second man got up from his chair as they approached.

Patterson introduced them.

"My assistant, Joan Phillips, and my daughter Samantha. This is my attorney, Gregory Adams. Lieutenant Tolliver, of the New York Police Department."

Both women were young and attractive, the assistant a brunette,

Samantha Patterson blond, as her sister had been. They nodded to him.

"Sit down, Lieutenant," Patterson said. He indicated a chair in a grouping some distance away from where the foursome was gathered. "Willis will get you a drink. We're discussing Caroline's estate."

"I'll wait somewhere else," Ben said. "If you want me to."

"No, right there is fine. I'll be with you shortly."

Tolliver sat down in the chair. He noticed the others all had glasses. "Vodka, please," he said to Willis. "On the rocks." The butler bowed and left the room.

Patterson took his seat and turned to Adams. "You were saying, Greg?"

"There should be another board member," Adams said. He was tall and urbane, gray-haired like his host, wearing a navy pinstripe and a foulard tie. He settled back down in his chair as he spoke. "Someone to replace Caroline. I'm sorry to bring it up at a time like this, Spencer. I know how you must feel. But it's something that should be attended to."

"What's the rush?" The question came from Samantha Patterson. To Ben, she bore an unmistakable resemblance to what her sister must have looked like when she was alive. She had on a conservative charcoal suit and her hair had been pulled back in a French knot. But the features were similar: short straight nose, wide mouth, blue eyes.

"It's not a matter of rushing," the lawyer responded. "It's just that things should move forward in an orderly fashion. We don't ever want to give the courts an opportunity to act against the family's wishes."

Samantha's blue eyes held the lawyer in a cool gaze. "How could they do that?"

Adams shrugged. "The legacy could be challenged at any time. Not only by a New York court, where I'm sure we'd have no trouble handling a problem, but by the federal government."

"It's the IRS," Patterson said. "The sons of bitches."

Willis returned with a squat crystal glass and a napkin on a silver tray. Ben took the drink and sipped vodka as the butler retreated.

"Let me explain," Adams said to Samantha. "As you know, the legacy was established as a charitable foundation before your mother died. Her money, including what she'd inherited from her father, went into it at that time. And of course, your own father has contributed to it since. Generously."

"We all know that," Samantha said. "So what's the problem?"

"There isn't one. A problem is what we're trying to avoid. With

156

this type of foundation, a charitable-lead trust, the income from the estate goes into the foundation for a specified period of time, in this case until your father passes away."

"For Christ's sake, Gregory," Patterson said. "You mean until I *die,* don't you? Say what you mean."

The lawyer was unruffled. "Certainly, Spencer." He returned his attention to Samantha. "As you also know, it was set up to be overseen by a board of four directors. With your poor dear sister gone, that leaves only you, your father, and me. A replacement should be appointed as soon as possible."

She still didn't seem satisfied. "But why? Is the IRS about to come roaring down on us? You set up the foundation, didn't you—drew up the papers?"

"Yes, of course I did. And no, the IRS is not about to come roaring down on us, as you put it. But at the same time, we don't want to give anyone so much as a hint that the main purpose of the foundation is to avoid paying taxes."

Patterson snorted. "You really think the IRS are that stupid? Of course that's what it was set up for." He turned to his daughter. "Let's be sure we all understand this. The foundation gives away money to various nonprofit organizations, the Metropolitan Museum, Princeton, and so on. Then after I die, the remaining principal goes tax-free to my heirs. Or heir, as it is now. The idea is to keep the government's grubby fists the hell out of it. They know that as well as we do."

It was interesting, Ben thought. Obviously, the lawyer believed there just might be trouble, and he was trying to head it off before it materialized. Okay, that was one of the reasons people hired lawyers. The curious part was that this group would discuss the subject at length before an outsider, and one who was a police officer to boot. As if he wasn't even there.

But the reason for that was easy to figure out, as well. As far as Spencer Patterson was concerned, cops were of no consequence—a commodity he could purchase like somebody else might buy cigars.

Adams remained the picture of calm. "All the more reason to appoint a replacement and go right on with the foundation's good works of charity."

"All right, then," Patterson said. "Let's appoint one. I nominate Joan here. She's eminently qualified, and knows all the ins and outs of my business." A brief smile crossed his stern features. "Most of them, anyway."

Ben noticed an almost imperceptible reaction by Samantha Patterson as she heard this. She opened her mouth, but before she could say anything, Joan Phillips spoke up for the first time since Ben had arrived.

Her tone was relaxed and pleasant. "Sorry, Spencer. I think this is much too important for us to treat it hastily." She looked at Adams. "Although I certainly understand your concern, Gregory. I know you're right; someone should be appointed and soon. But it doesn't have to be decided tonight, does it?"

"No, of course not. Just so long as it's not put off. We can act tomorrow or the next day."

"The next day would be fine," she said. "That way, we'll all have time to think about it."

"Very well." Adams glanced at Patterson and then at Samantha. "All right with everyone?"

"Sure, that's fine," Patterson said.

Samantha said nothing.

Ben took a good look at the Phillips woman. It seemed to him that she'd defused what could have been a touchy situation, smoothly and diplomatically. Now that he'd focused on her, he noticed a few things. One was that she was quite young to have so much poise—not even thirty, he would guess—and for Patterson to have put her in a position of considerable responsibility.

Another thing he noticed was that she was very attractive. Her dark hair came just to her shoulders, and her eyes were also dark, although he couldn't be sure of their color. Like Samantha, she was dressed in a no-nonsense business suit, so he couldn't tell much about her body except that it was slim. But the suit didn't hide the fact that she had good legs.

As Ben studied her, Phillips saw him looking and glanced away, but she also crossed her legs.

"All right, then," Patterson said. "That's decided. You people will excuse me, but I told the lieutenant I'd speak with him." He rose to his feet, picking up his glass from a table beside his chair. It was a short brandy snifter, and it was half full. He looked at the others. "Go on talking. Willis will freshen your drinks."

Ben stood up and Patterson beckoned to him. "This way, Lieutenant."

Samantha fixed Ben with that steady ice blue gaze. "Maybe you should talk here. There might be things all of us could tell him."

Patterson grunted. "No, that won't be necessary. We'll be only a few minutes."

There was a door to the right of the fireplace. Carrying his drink, Ben followed the tall man through it, leaving the others behind.

# 35

The room they entered was Patterson's study. As in the library, the ceiling was at least twelve feet high, and logs were blazing in a fireplace in here, as well. The walls were lined with gun racks and mounted trophies. On the far side of the room, facing the door, was a wide brassbound desk. A pair of club chairs and a sofa were grouped at right angles to the desk, and the floor was covered in rugs of zebra hide and bearskin.

Ben looked up at the trophies. There was a lion, a Cape buffalo, and several other horned species, including a deer and a mountain goat. He wondered what impelled people to kill animals and then hang their heads on the wall. Was it the desire to commemorate the experience? Or was it to convince anyone who saw them that the hunter was a brave adventurer? Or maybe the killer was merely confirming the fact that he was an arrogant schmuck who had no respect for other creatures.

Patterson was watching him, holding his brandy snifter and wearing what seemed to Ben a self-satisfied expression. "You like hunting, Lieutenant?"

"I've never done much of it."

"Wonderful sport. I've been all over the world, shot just about every kind of game there is."

"Must have been a lot of fun," Ben said. "For you."

"Oh yes. Here, let's sit down." He led the way to the grouping of chairs, and both men took seats.

"What's happening with your investigation?" Patterson asked.

"It's moving along, but not as fast as I'd like."

"Why is that?"

"We're shorthanded. I could use more help."

"I see. So I gather you don't have a suspect."

"At this point, no. We don't have one."

"That's too bad."

"I wish I could report better progress."

Patterson surprised him. "On the other hand, even if you were to apprehend the person responsible, it wouldn't bring my daughter back, would it?"

"No, it wouldn't."

"And in the meantime, the rest of us have to go on experiencing pain for what happened. The media exposure has been hideous, just as I knew it would be."

"I'm sorry. The reporters are vultures, but there's no way to control them."

"Frankly, it's infuriating. The investigation is hardly worth it. What I want now is to put an end to this troublesome business."

It was hard for Ben to believe what he was hearing. In all his years on the job, he'd never met anybody who'd lost a family member and had an attitude like this.

Patterson drank some of his brandy. "And whereas I certainly believe the person should be caught and punished, all that would result in is more hoopla."

Did this guy think he could decide whether the case was to be closed or would stay open? That he'd make up his mind, depending on how much play the newspapers and TV gave it? Jesus.

"Regardless of the publicity," Ben said, "our job is to find the perpetrator."

"I'm aware of that. But as you admit, you're not making much progress."

The hell with the political ramifications. "Mr. Patterson, do you know what your daughter's reason was for going to the Plaza that night?"

The aristocratic features were impassive. "No, Lieutenant, I don't. And neither do you. Whatever theories you might have, that's all they amount to. Conjecture, and nothing more."

Ben opened his mouth, but before he could reply, Patterson said, "I took the liberty of calling a few acquaintances, and I was assured that anything that might, ah, cast aspersions on my daughter's reputation would never come to light. If you need confirmation, I suggest you check with your superiors."

Tolliver again found himself surprised, and then angry. What Patterson was telling him was, the situation had already been taken care of, and the way the case would be handled had been decided. He'd gotten to someone—the DA, maybe—and now he was telling Ben to be a good little cop and run along. Don't make waves.

And that had to be why Patterson agreed to see him. It was part of what having this kind of power was all about: You not only used it, you let people know about it.

But Ben would be damned if he'd just roll over. "Mr. Patterson, you were going to think about who some of your daughter's friends were, men she'd been seeing. Did you do that?"

"No, Lieutenant, I didn't. The fact is, I don't know of anyone she might have had a relationship with. And now you'll excuse me, but there are other matters I want to discuss with my lawyer. Make yourself comfortable, finish your drink. Willis will show you out."

Patterson stood up. "Good night, Lieutenant."

He left the room, Ben staring after him.

Minutes later, there was a knock and a different door opened, this one behind the desk, and Willis came into the room. "If you'll come this way, please."

Ben put his glass down on a table, rose, and followed him back through the door.

This was another hallway, and like the first one, it also led to the entrance hall. When they reached the front door, Ben heard someone call his name. He looked around to see Samantha Patterson approaching him.

"I'd like to speak with you," she said. "If you have a moment."

"Yes, of course."

She turned to Willis. "I'll show the lieutenant out."

"Yes, Miss Patterson." The butler bowed and left them.

"Let's go outside," she said to Ben. "Where we won't be overheard."

As soon as they went through the door, Baxter reappeared, but when he saw Samantha Patterson, the security man went back into the shadows.

She and Ben walked to where he'd parked his car. A light coating of frost had formed on the hood.

"I know what you're going through," she said. "He's telling you to forget about it, isn't he? Not in so many words, but that's the gist of it, right?"

"More or less."

"And will you?"

What was this—was she another one who considered herself an inheritor of the earth? If so, she could kindly fuck off. "No," he said. "I won't."

"Good. Somehow I didn't think you were the type who'd just knuckle under to him."

"Were you and Caroline close?"

"Oh, yeah, we were, in a way. That is, I was always the kid sister, and in awe of her. But I loved her. And I looked up to her."

"Do you know what she was doing in the hotel, why she went there, before she was killed?"

"Yes, I do. She told me herself about what she'd gotten into. She thought it was a big joke."

"A joke?"

"At Daddy's expense. That she was putting one over on him.

161

Using her looks and her smarts to make a lot of money doing something outrageous. Something she thought would give him a heart attack if he knew about it."

"I gather he's pretty straitlaced."

"Straitlaced? The term is hypocritical, Lieutenant. You met his so-called assistant just now, didn't you?"

"Miss Phillips?"

"Uh-huh. I don't suppose I'd have to draw you a picture of what she assists him with."

"Oh?"

"Exactly."

"About your sister. Do you know anything more about her private life, the men she was seeing?"

"I would say that for the past six or eight months, the only men she was seeing were the ones she did business with."

"Anybody else you can think of, who might have a reason for wanting to hurt her?"

"No. I've thought about that, too. She always had lots of men friends, and some of them were quite serious about her. But there were no hard feelings. If there had been, somehow I think I would have heard about it."

"Will you keep on thinking, see if you can come up with an idea for me, or a direction?"

"Absolutely."

He got out his wallet and gave her a card. "Call me if there's anything at all you think I'd want to know about."

"I will. I promise."

"Good. Tell me something."

"Yes?"

"You don't seem to have the same problems with your father that your sister did."

"I don't. But my feelings toward him are exactly the same as hers were."

"But then why are you—"

"Patience. I have it, and she didn't. As I tell myself every day, he can't live forever."

"And when he's gone, everything goes to you."

"Everything except what I have to fight for with that bitch who's sitting in the library. Good night, Lieutenant."

The traffic wasn't bad at this time of night. Ben took the Hutch and then went down the West Side, arriving at the Sixth Precinct station house only forty minutes after leaving the house in Rye.

162

# 36

The pizza had everything on it: mushrooms, pepperoni, sausage, peppers, and some other stuff Flynn didn't recognize. He picked up a stringy slice and bit into it, finding it hot and delicious.

"Olives," Spadone said. "They forgot the fucking olives."

"They didn't forget," Weisskopf said. "They figured you'd wanna have something to bitch about."

They were in the squad room and it was late and this was the first time any of them had kicked back all day. Flynn and Joe Stone were the only members of the Sixth in the group. Stone was a detective third, dark-skinned and muscular, who liked to wear flashy clothes. Tonight he had on a dove-gray suit with narrow lapels and a pearlescent sheen, set off with a tie that looked something like a tropical sunrise.

Ed had been about to leave, go visit his girlfriend who was married to a musician, when Spadone and Weisskopf came in and they ordered the pizza. They were sitting around a desk now with the greasy carton of pizza and cans of beer on it, ties pulled down, shirt collars unbuttoned—all except Flynn, who was as impeccable as ever, even though he was red-eyed from the long hours and lack of sleep.

Spadone had a slice of pizza in one hand, a can of Budweiser in the other. He looked at Weisskopf. "Hey, Art. Irishman and a Jew are in a bar. Two broads come in and the Irishman says, 'Let's go fuck 'em.' The Jew says, 'Outta what?' "

Stone guffawed. He had a mouthful of pizza and bits of it spewed onto his tie. Won't hurt it any, Flynn thought. Colors'll blend right in.

Weisskopf's expression didn't change. He swallowed some beer and put the can down on the desk. "That's a riot, Joe. You wanna know a riddle? A guinea and a Polack are in a plane. They're at ten thousand feet and both of 'em jump out at the same time. Which one hits the ground first?"

Spadone eyed him, making no reply.

Weisskopf raised both hands, palms up. "Who gives a shit?"

It sent Stone into another fit of laughter, adding to the mess on his tie. Keeps up, he'll need a bath, Flynn thought.

Weisskopf lifted a slice of pizza out of the carton and took a bite. "Where's the lieutenant?" he asked. "He coming back?"

"Yeah, he'll be here," Flynn replied. "Went up to Westchester to see the victim's father."

"You think he knew, the father?"

"Ben says no."

"You believe it?"

"Sure I believe it. Guy like that, prob'ly the last thing'd enter his head."

Spadone wiped his mouth with a paper napkin. "Better'n what entered her head."

Stone spoke up. "I hear those broads get a grand a night."

"The fuck do you know about it?" Spadone said. "Most you ever paid for pussy was ten bucks in Saigon."

"That's with the discount," Weisskopf said. "After he married her."

All three of these guys had served in Vietnam. Flynn had noticed that it often came up in their conversation.

Stone grinned, his teeth gleaming in his black face. "Man, Suzy's was something else. I shoulda bought stock in the fuckin' place."

Weisskopf grunted. "What a shithouse. The Pearl was the best joint in that town."

"Yeah? I never went there."

"That's because they didn't let spades in," Spadone said. "Which was too bad for you, but it was to protect the rest of us, see? Nothin' personal."

Stone snorted. "Bullshit. You got it ass-backward. I heard it was a claphouse for honkies."

"Wrong. Like Art says, the Pearl was the best. The girls in there knew shit you never even heard of."

"You got that right," Weisskopf said. "You ever had the Chinese knot?"

Stone looked at him. "What is it?"

"Greatest thing I ever had in my life." Weisskopf said. "Broad has this long thin cord made outta silk. She ties knots in it, about an inch apart. Then she stuffs it up your ass."

Stone was listening intently, his mouth open. "When you come," Weisskopf went on, "she pulls the string out. Bip, bip, bip, the knots tickle your prostate. Christ, what a sensation. Tears come outta your eyes, the wax comes outta your ears, it's fantastic."

"Jesus," Stone said.

Spadone belched. "I'll tell you, though. I'd like to try one of the broads in this Panache outfit. For research, you know? See what all the fuss is about."

"So why don't you?" Art said. "Just put in for it. I'm sure the lieutenant would okay the expense."

Footsteps sounded on the stairs.

"I think that's him now," Flynn said.

# 37

When Ben walked into the precinct house, two cops were at the desk with a guy who looked as if somebody had tried to shave him with a lawn mower. There were cuts, bruises, and pieces of tape all over his face, and his shirtfront was red with blood. The cops were attempting to get a statement from him, but the guy was telling them they'd made a mistake. It was just a friendly argument, he said.

The desk sergeant had white hair and a stack of ribbons above his shield. He was studying the guy's appearance. "What he hit you with?"

"A tool."

"What kinda tool?"

"A hammer."

"It was a friendly argument, and he hit you with a hammer?"

"It wasn't nothing. Just glanced off."

"Why'd he hit you?"

"Beats me."

"Where were you when he hit you?"

"In his apartment."

"Where in his apartment?"

"The bedroom."

"Where was his wife?"

"Uh, she was in there, too."

As Ben made the turn to the stairs leading up to the detective squad room on the second floor, two more cops came in through the Tenth Street entrance, dragging a male who was cursing them in Spanish. His hands were cuffed behind his back. He tried to bite one of the cops on the arm, and the other cop smashed a fist into the man's mouth.

*"Chinga tu madre!"* he screamed.

Mexican, Ben thought. Puerto Ricans and Colombians didn't say fuck your mother—they had their own expressions. He went on up the stairs.

It was strange, but coming in here and seeing all the shit going on actually gave him a twinge of nostalgia. The other cases the squad was on, that was detective work. In contrast, the Patterson murder was mostly a political vise with his nuts caught in it. And with everybody from the DA's office to Spencer Patterson turning the crank.

Meantime, the killer was free as a bird, seemingly the least important factor in the entire situation. Probably sneering at the cops and their feeble efforts to track him.

He thought then of Barry Conklin. Above the law? A guy who had nothing to fear because he knew how to work the system better than other people? Ben would be calling on Mr. Conklin again, bet on it.

When he reached the squad room, he saw Flynn, Stone, Weisskopf, and Spadone sitting around the carcass of a pizza, shooting the shit and drinking beer. His stomach rumbled, reminding him that what little he'd had to eat today he'd caught on the fly.

The detectives turned and greeted him. Flynn said, "There's still some pizza here, Lou, if you want it. And a beer."

Ben pulled up a chair and sat down, reaching for a slice of the pizza and biting off half of it. The pie was only lukewarm, but he was so hungry he didn't notice. He looked at the others and spoke around a mouthful. "So what's going on?"

Spadone pulled a notebook out of his inside jacket pocket and opened it. "I interviewed four of the guys on my list, Lou. All of 'em admitted balling the Patterson girl."

"Okay, good. Run through what you came up with."

Spadone consulted his notes. "First one was a VP with Fidelity Insurance. Name's Francis Whartley. He saw her twice in the last month, both times in the Pierre. They had dinner at Quo Vadis the first night, and the other time at Giambelli's. She stayed with him till around one A.M. on each date. Night of the murder, he was in Chicago on business."

"You check it?"

"Yeah, I did. He was at the Blackstone. I talked to the manager and had him look at his records. He was there."

"What else about him?"

"Like the printout said, he's married, lives in Scarsdale, two kids. Now he's shit-scared his wife'll find out he screws around."

"Uh-huh. Next."

"An Englishman, Robert Cullerton. Works for Granada, the British TV company. Some of their shows they sell to American TV. He comes to New York a couple times a month, stays at the Regency. He's here now. Divorced, has a son goes to school in France. This guy really flipped over her. Sent her flowers, gave her presents, tried to get her to quit and go live with him."

"He told you that?"

"Yeah, no problem. He came in on the Concord the day after she was killed. Said he was heartbroken."

"How many times did he see her?"

Spadone looked at the notebook. "He wasn't sure, but the printout said eleven times. He liked to take her to the theater and restaurants, show her off."

Ben ate the last of the pizza and wiped his fingers with a paper napkin. "Who else?"

"A Saudi, Ibn Faroud. He's an OPEC representative. One pop, a month ago. Said she was a stupid pig. You can get better women off the street, he said."

"Sounds like a maybe."

"No. He was pissed at Panache after that and wouldn't call them again. Also the printout said PSL, so it wouldn't have done him no good if he had. The night Patterson died, he was with two broads from Unique. That's another service. It checked out; the guy that runs it put me in touch with both girls."

"You really get into your work," Weisskopf said.

Spadone shot him a look.

"You have the girls' names there?" Ben asked.

"Yes."

"All right, that's three. You had one more."

Spadone smiled. "You'll love this. Roger Pembroke."

"The actor?"

"Right."

"Christ, he must be seventy."

"Seventy-four. Said she made him feel thirty again. Kind of nice, huh?"

"I'm misty-eyed. What about him?"

"Nothing there, either. He's in a play, didn't leave the theater that night until around twelve."

The phone rang. Stone went to his desk and answered it.

Ben spoke to Weisskopf. "How about you, Art—what've you got?"

"Four strikeouts and a possible." Like Spadone, the detective kept a small pocket notebook. Opening it, he glanced at the first page.

"The possible is a guy named Arturo Strada. He's an art dealer, owns a store on Madison near Sixty-eighth. He was with Patterson four times."

"Hey, Lou?" It was Stone.

Ben turned to see him holding the phone, his hand over the mouthpiece.

"It's for you. A woman. She wouldn't give her name, says it's important."

"Okay, I'll take it inside." He got to his feet and picked up a can of Budweiser from the desk, carrying it with him into his office.

After closing the door, he popped the beer and swallowed a long draft. Then he sat down and picked up the phone. "Tolliver."

The voice was so soft it was barely audible, but he recognized it at once. "Lieutenant, it's me. Your assistant."

"Hi, what's up?"

"I have . . . what you wanted."

"Great, I'll come and get it. Where can I meet you?"

"There's a restaurant, The Blue Balloon, on Seventy-first Street. Near Second."

"When?"

"I'm off at one. I'll go right over from here."

"I'll be there." He hung up.

So Monica had come through with the names of the girls who worked for Panache. In some ways, that could be a better route than checking the johns. He looked at his watch. Ten of twelve, so he had about an hour here before going uptown.

Taking the beer with him, he went back into the squad room and rejoined the group of detectives.

# 38

"We've got a leak," Martha said. She was sitting at her desk, tapping the surface with a pencil.

Patrick dropped onto the sofa, affecting a casual pose. He was in blue tonight, the soft shades of his gabardine trousers and suede shirt matching perfectly. His smooth features were expressionless. "A leak in what?"

Sometimes his cool was reassuring, but at other times it gave her a pain in the ass. "In our security. I've had a number of calls from clients telling me the police went to see them, asking about Caroline. I said I didn't know anything about it, but I don't think they believed me. Where've you been, by the way?"

He studied the manicured nails of his right hand. "I had dinner at Le Veau d'Or with Peter Damroche. He's going to direct a new play, by William Blake. And he has personal problems."

She shook a cigarette out of the pack on her desk and lit it with a gold Dunhill, blowing out a stream of smoke. "They were really pissed, and I don't blame them. They think I gave the police their names."

"Which you denied, you said."

"Of course I denied it. I didn't give the cops anything, for Christ's sake. You know that."

"Who were they—the clients who called?"

She looked at scribbles she'd made on a pad. "Strada, Whartley, Barrett and Faroud."

His eyebrows raised a quarter of an inch. "Ibn Faroud?"

"Can you believe it? Caroline had one date with him, and the only reason I sent her was because he said he'd pay double for someone really outstanding."

"Yes, I recall. He wanted something bizarre, didn't he?"

"What he wanted was to give her a douche with a bottle of champagne before he stuck it in."

"In her, you mean."

"What'd you think I meant, in the bottle? She refused and he slapped her around. She said he looked like a monkey, hair all over him. Yelling at her in Arabic. She got dressed and beat it. Jesus, a champagne bottle."

"Shades of Fatty Arbuckle."

"What?"

"Nothing. Caroline did that several times, if you remember. As soon as somebody asked for anything unconventional, she had a fit."

"I know, but it still didn't give him the right to beat her up."

"I suppose not. Where do you think the leak might be?"

She took a deep drag on the cigarette and exhaled slowly. "Has to be one of the phone girls, doesn't it? Nobody else knows who she dated. Except you and me."

"Mmm, that's true. The question is, which one?"

"I've thought about that, too. Francesca you can forget about. She's been with me for years; there's nobody better. And besides, she's got two kids. She's not about to fuck this up."

"Which leaves Monica and Billie."

"Uh-huh. And they're both a little flaky. I didn't think so at first, when I hired them. But you never know somebody until you know them."

"May I quote you?"

She waved her cigarette impatiently. "Don't be a smartass, Patrick. This whole thing has been exhausting. Bad enough she was murdered, without the cops raising hell with the business."

"So which one?"

"I wish I knew. Monica's more emotional. Outwardly, at least."

"Yes, but Billie's by far the more ambitious. And sometimes I sense jealousy there."

"Really?"

"Oh, yes. The way she looks at you—your clothes, jewelry."

"I never realized that."

"It's quite obvious."

She stubbed out the cigarette in a crystal ashtray, the gold bracelets on her wrists jingling. "Then we should keep an eye on both of them. What's wrong with your friend, by the way?"

"Peter? I'm afraid he has it, poor boy."

"Oh, God. AIDS?"

"You have no idea how many friends I've lost over the past few years. Some of the most creative people in the world. As if an evil spirit were reaching out for them, one after another."

"Must be terrible."

"It is, I assure you. Ghastly, in fact."

He stood up, smoothing wrinkles from his trousers with a brush of his long, slim fingers. "I presume you heard I booked a party for some of our Oriental friends?"

"Oh yes. One of them called from The Four Seasons while you were out. They were just finishing dinner. So solly, just double-checking to be sure ladies all set. I told him everything was fine. Is it?"

He smiled. "Of course it is. They're staying at the Essex House. Wait till they see what I'm sending. Ashley, Debbie, Janice, and Sandra. Do you get it?"

"No—what is it?"

"Every one of them is six feet tall, or close to it. Even the thought of tall American girls makes Japs come in their kimonos. When they see those girls, they'll think they're in Shinto heaven."

Martha laughed. "I love it."

"Yes. But about the leak."

"What about it?"

"I believe that could be a serious problem."

170

"Jesus, Patrick. You think I don't know that? Why do you suppose I'm worried?"

"We need to find out who it is. And then take care of it."

"How?"

"Leave that to me. And now if you'll excuse me, I want to look over the other bookings." He turned and left her office.

The intercom buzzed, and Martha picked up the phone. "Yes?"

"It's George Whitacre," Francesca said. "He wants to talk to you."

Martha put the phone down and keyed the name into the IBM. An instant later, data flashed onto the screen, telling her that George Whitacre owned an insurance company in Great Neck. Lived in Sands Point. Winter home in Hobe Sound. Married, three children. Went to Brown. Member of the Union League Club. Preferred busty blondes. Heavy tipper.

Her eyes on the monitor, she picked up the phone and punched the lighted button. "George, dear, how are you? I'm so pleased you called. You must be psychic; I've been thinking about you. We have someone new, and she's very special."

# 39

The Blue Balloon was jammed. People were standing four deep at the bar, all of them young. Except for one or two guys who were merely trying to look young, get some of the action. Despite the crowd, Ben picked out Monica right away. She had on the trench coat again, standing at the end of the bar holding a drink, the only person wearing dark glasses. He pushed his way through to her.

She didn't look at him, but instead stared straight ahead, hardly moving her lips when she spoke. "I thought we'd be lost in the crowd here," she said. "Less conspicuous."

"Sure. What're you drinking?"

"White wine spritzer."

He waved to one of the bartenders, and when he got the guy's attention ordered another spritzer for Monica, a beer for himself. The noise level in here was enough to shatter your eardrums.

"I think they suspect something," Monica said.

"Who suspects what?"

"Martha and Patrick. They were huddled together in her office, but I was too busy with the phone to hear what was going on. I know a couple of clients called to complain, though. They said the police had talked to them about Caroline."

"Uh-huh. But I take it business hasn't slowed down any?"

"It did a little, because some of the clients saw the news about the murder and the word got around from our girls who she was. That she was working for us, I mean. But now we're back to normal. Except we're still not taking any new clients."

"And the girls—how are they doing?"

"They're getting over it, too. They're still talking about it, but they're not so scared now. They think it was a freak kind of thing."

"Any of them taking special precautions?"

"I heard one or two bought Mace. Carry it with them. But most of them just say they're going to be extra careful."

Their drinks arrived. Ben said, "Cheers," and drank half his beer, then topped off his glass with what remained in the bottle.

Monica sipped the fresh spritzer. "Ben?"

"Yeah?"

"Here's the list. Of our girls." She slipped him an envelope. Her voice had become softer, the words barely understandable under the flood of sound in the bar. "You realize what I've done, don't you?"

"What's that?"

"I've put my life in your hands."

Melanie Griffith, he thought.

She continued to look straight ahead. "I hope you realize that. If they ever find out I'm helping you, I'm dead."

He put the envelope into his jacket pocket. "They won't hear it from me. And none of my men know, so take it easy. As long as you watch your step, you'll be fine."

"If you say so."

"I say so. You pick up anything else?"

"No, but I had an idea."

"What was it?"

"There's one girl Caroline was pretty friendly with. She might be able to help you."

"What's her name?"

"Melissa Martin. She's on the list."

"Thanks, I'll talk to her."

"For God's sake, don't let her find out how you got her name."

"No, of course not. Stop worrying."

"She's a model. Her agency's Fredrique."

"Okay, I'll get in touch with her." Ben finished his beer and

172

dropped some bills onto the bar. "You've been a terrific help. Remember, if you get anything more, or any other ideas, call me. Okay?"

She turned toward him then, and placed her hand on his. *"Vaya con Dios."*

Now she was Maria Cortez, and he was Clint Eastwood, about to ride out of Las Pietras and hunt down the bad guys.

"Good night, Monica."

He turned and pushed his way back through the noisy crowd.

# 40

W hen she came out onto the tiny stage, spots picked her up, bathing her in brilliant light that reflected from the sequins in her hair and on her harem costume, and especially from her eyes. Even from where he was sitting, at a table to one side and six or seven rows back, Ben could see how bright her eyes were.

The crowd in the club was putting out a steady stream of chatter, glasses clinking. Waitresses in slave-girl outfits moved among the tables, and in the spot beams, a haze of smoke drifted. But then Patty began to move, and the noise subsided until the only sound you heard was the music.

Ben had never been in an Arab country, but he was pretty sure what the musicians were producing was authentic. They were wearing burnooses and sitting cross-legged on the stage behind her, playing drums, an oboe, some sort of mandolin-type stringed instrument, and a tambourine. Except for the oboe player, they sang a kind of chant as they played. No one in the audience was watching them. Every eye in the place was fixed on Patty.

Her body gleamed under a thin coating of oil. She wasn't a big girl, but the musculature was amazing. Not like a weight lifter, one of those broads you saw on TV who looked like Schwarzenegger in drag, but with a control that enabled her to make every muscle dance.

They were dancing now, in her arms and her thighs and her belly. Her legs were spread slightly; her hands were at shoulder level. The muscles jumped and rippled, seeming to flow in one direction and then another. She kept it up for several minutes, building tension in

173

the room, hypnotizing the audience with the gleaming, twitching flesh.

Then she jumped. Straight up, whirling in a full 360, clapping her hands and landing in a crouch. Startled, the crowd gasped, then chuckled, and there was scattered applause. At that point, she began to move sinuously about the stage, covering it in long, exaggerated strides, head back, chest thrust out, back arched, and all the while with those incredible muscles writhing in synch with the music. Her steps grew quicker, and Ben knew it was meant to represent a chase, with Patty as the quarry. He knew it because she'd told him so, but whether the crowd understood that, he wasn't sure.

Not that it mattered. It was three o'clock in the morning and people were sitting here half-smashed, their jaws hanging open, guys wondering what it would be like with her, wishing they could find out, while their women hoped the men would be aroused enough to get it up when they finally staggered into bed.

Patty went into the third phase of her dance then, the one she said meant foreplay. In this one, she stayed in one place, and not only did the muscles move, but her hands stroked them with a suggestiveness that was inflaming, even to Ben.

Especially to Ben. He was the only guy in the joint who *knew* what it was like with her, that it was every bit as good as all the others thought it would be, and maybe even better. He wasn't sure whether knowing that made watching her more or less erotic than if he hadn't known it, but it didn't matter; he'd produced an erection he could hang his hat on.

Her fingers touched hidden clasps in her costume, and the bra and the transparent harem pants fell away. By the time she went into the last phase, the audience was bug-eyed, the men with desire and the women with what Ben supposed was jealousy, although there could have been some admiration in there, as well.

The lighting was different now, filters changing the spots from one color to another, soft blue to yellow and then gold deepening to orange, each one warmer than the one preceding it, until she was drenched in fiery red, as hot as the wriggling, twisting gyrations her body was going through. She was thrusting her pelvis, tossing her hair, her eyes closed, mouth open, moving faster and faster, the drums pounding in a rhythmic frenzy, and you didn't need much imagination to understand what that was supposed to represent.

When the climactic moment arrived, the music reached a shrieking crescendo, one long wailing gliss that was like a scream from deep inside a woman's throat, and Patty shuddered, muscles tense and trembling.

She held it, and held it, and suddenly there was silence, and the stage went to black.

For a long moment, the room was dead quiet. And then it rocked with thunderous applause. When the lights came up seconds later, the stage was bare.

The applause and calls for an encore went on for a full minute, but Ben knew she wouldn't return. She'd explained to him once, when he'd asked her why, that she never forgot the hoary maxim: Leave your audience wanting more. In fact, she wouldn't even come out for a bow. He thought that was taking things a little further than necessary, but who was he to argue?

"Another one, Ben?"

He looked up to see a waitress standing over him, her breasts squeezed into half-moons by a skimpy bodice. "Sure, and bring a glass of champagne, too. Please."

She picked up his empty and moved away. The noise level was back up to what it had been before Patty's performance, and people were starting to leave.

There was a drumroll from somewhere and a spot again hit the stage. A young guy in a tuxedo came on, but no one so much as glanced his way. He was fat and red-faced and the spot was reflecting from tiny droplets of sweat on his forehead and his upper lip. "Hello, hello," he said into the mike, a phony smile splitting his face. "I can tell you're a great audience because you all look so intelligent, so *with* it."

What possessed such people? Ben wondered. For every one who made it, there had to be a hundred characters like this guy, stumbling around the club circuit, never even a featured act, just a fill-in between performers the patrons came to see, about as exciting as Muzak.

The waitress was back with Ben's order. She put the glasses on the table and he said she could give him a check.

"Forget it," she said. "You know we won't take your money. Guido says to tell you you're always welcome."

He'd been expecting that, and he wouldn't argue. Instead, he dropped a ten-dollar bill onto her tray. "Thanks. But a tip's okay, isn't it?"

She smiled. "Always, honey, always." She tucked the bill into her cleavage, which was some trick, considering the skimpiness of her costume. When she moved off among the tables, he admired her rear end.

"My wife likes to talk while she's having sex," the comic said. "So she calls me up."

Ben wondered where he'd heard it. Rodney Dangerfield, probably. This guy might have had better nights, but it was unlikely.

"Hi." Patty gave him a quick kiss on the cheek and sat down. "This for me?"

"Sure."

"Thanks, you're a dear." She held up the glass and touched his with it. "I love champagne." There seemed to be nothing remaining of the annoyance she'd shown when he left her apartment. But maybe that was because she was feeling great at having put on a good show. She did four a night and now she was finished and she had to feel good about closing on a high note.

As she drank, her gaze moved around the room and then back to him. "How was I?"

He smiled. She was wearing a bulky sweater and jeans, no makeup, and her dark hair was tied up in a knot on top of her head. None of the customers would have guessed she was the same girl who'd been firing their emotions only a short time before. "You were great. Same as you always are."

Her eyes were searching his face. "Really? Tell me the truth."

It was funny. She'd given a hell of a performance, driven the audience batshit, and here she was begging him for reassurance. Was insecurity part of being a professional entertainer? Of course it was. "You were sensational. Better than that, even. I thought I was in Cairo or someplace."

Her face lit up in a little-girl smile and she sipped her champagne. "Cairo, my ass. That dance is strictly from Hoboken."

"Come on. It's authentic, isn't it?"

"You kidding me? It's not even real belly dancing. I just made it up over the past couple of years, swiping a little from here, a little from there."

"You fooled me."

"Everybody, probably."

"Then so long as no Arabs come around, you're okay."

"Think they care? They're like any other guys. All they want is their money's worth."

"You sure gave it to 'em."

"The Hoboken part's true. Did you know that?"

"I don't think so."

"My Uncle Nick runs a joint there. He gave me my start, let me dance on the bar."

"That was kind of him. Wonder you lived through it."

"You don't know Nick. Anybody touched me, he'd break their kneecaps. Also he's connected."

"I'm sure he'd appreciate your telling that to a cop."

"Hey, it's in another town, right?"

"And besides, the wench is dead."

"What? Oh, I know. I read that someplace, too. How's the rest of it go?"

"I don't remember." He did, but he didn't think telling her would be appropriate, under the circumstances.

"The crowd was really into it, weren't they?" She kept wanting to talk about her performance, still high from her dancing and from the audience reaction.

"Yeah, they were. Everybody was. Including me."

She smiled again. "Were you?"

"Sure. If I'd stood up, I could've been arrested for indecent exposure."

She laughed and gave his arm a playful punch.

"Might even've been thrown out of the department."

"Then you could go to work for Uncle Nick. He's a good guy, looked after me from the time my father died."

Ben was drinking vodka on the rocks. It seemed to have no more effect than water. He swallowed some of it. "That so?"

"Yeah. Everybody likes Nick Lavelli. And respects him, too."

"That your real name, Lavelli?"

"Uh-huh."

"See that? You fooled me again. I thought it was Lamont."

"Cut it out. You knew that was just a stage name. I changed it when I came to New York."

"I did that, too."

She looked at him. "Really? From what?"

"Tortellini."

She rolled her eyes. "Jesus, Ben. That was awful."

He nodded toward the stage. "No worse than that guy."

Joe Flopsweat was finishing up, carrying the mike off with him, waving to the audience and giving them his phony grin. But the patrons weren't responding. There were only about eight people left in the room, including Patty and Ben.

It was time for them to make an exit, as well. He wanted to take her home while the dance was still fresh in his mind.

# 41

I f you want to know about a man's personal life, follow him at night.

Bobbie stood outside the club for nearly an hour, wondering why Tolliver would go to such a place. Was this the detective's idea of relaxation at the end of a long, hard day? Sitting around over drinks in some skin joint? Probably it was. The smartest cops rarely possessed the intelligence of their namesakes in the K-9 Corps.

It was cold out here, the wind whipping dead leaves and scraps of paper along the nearly deserted street. She turned up the collar of her raincoat and glanced at her watch. Maybe she should pack it in, leave the lieutenant to enjoy the booze and the belly dancers. She could track him again, another time. Stepping off the curb, she waited for a cab. At this time of night, there weren't many around.

From behind her came the sound of laughter, and glancing over her shoulder, she saw several people emerge from the door of the club. One of them was Tolliver, and when she looked at him, she had her answer. The detective had his arm around a girl, holding her close to him.

Bobbie was wearing a slouch hat. She tugged it down over her forehead and hunched deeper into her coat, then turned and walked back onto the sidewalk, timing her steps so that she could get a good look at the girl when the couple went by. They paid no attention to her as they passed, the girl snuggling against Tolliver's shoulder and giggling.

She really was quite pretty. Small and dark, with large wide-set eyes and black hair. She had on a coat, but even so Bobbie could see that she had a good body. And her legs were beautiful.

So what was going on here? Tolliver had come to this dump by himself and left with the girl, which offered several possibilities. One was that she was a pickup, but you could forget that; she was too good-looking. Unless she was a hooker. But that wouldn't fly, either. The girls who operated out of bars were bums, and looked it. The most likely story was that she worked here. And not as a waitress—not with those legs. She was a dancer, bet on it.

Bobbie looked back and saw them getting into a dingy gray Ford sedan. The headlights went on, and then the car pulled away from the curb.

She resumed walking. As she turned the corner, she spotted a cab coming toward her. Again she stepped off the sidewalk, and hailed the taxi. The vehicle swerved over to where she was standing and came to a stop.

As Bobbie climbed into the cab, she smiled to herself. This little excursion had paid off, after all.

## 42

In the morning, Ben checked with the Fredrique agency on where Melissa Martin was working that day. He was told the model was shooting at a studio on West Twenty-fifth Street, run by a photographer named Bob Wolfe. He got into the Ford and drove there.

The street was choked with trucks that were illegally standing on both sides, leaving only a narrow passageway between them. He had to turn the corner onto Seventh Avenue before he could find a place to leave the Ford. Walking back to the address, he found himself between rows of grimy buildings that had housed light industry since the 1920s—companies that made sewing machines and shelf brackets and lighting fixtures, and others that wholesaled commodities ranging from textiles to chemicals.

There were a number of studios in the area now, because space here was relatively cheap. If you were Francesco Scavullo or Richard Avedon, you could afford a town house on the Upper East Side, but if you weren't, you located your studio in buildings like these.

Wolfe was on the eleventh floor. When Ben stepped off the elevator, he pressed a buzzer and showed his credentials to a pair of eyes that looked out at him through a slot in the wall. He waited until the reinforced steel door swung open, and a male voice told him to come in.

When he stepped inside, a young guy with a close-cropped beard said, "Hi, I'm Howard Gimple, Bob's assistant." He pushed the door shut and bolted it.

"I'm looking for Melissa Martin," Ben said. "I want to ask her a couple of questions."

"Yeah, she's here now. But can you wait a few minutes? We're right in the middle of shooting."

"Go ahead," Ben said. "I don't want to get in your way."

He followed Gimple to the setup, a section of corral in front of a photographic backdrop of snowcapped mountains. A model was perched on the fence rail, dressed in a shirt and whipcord pants and cowboy boots, her honey blond hair tumbling to her shoulders. Despite the outfit, she looked as if she'd never been west of the Palisades.

Wolfe was crouched over a tripod-mounted camera. As Ben watched, the photographer called out instructions to the girl as to how he wanted her to turn her head, or hold her chin, or smile, all the while shooting rapidly. The camera was rigged to a bank of strobes, so that each time he hit the trigger, there was a boom and a flash of light flooded the studio. After he'd made a couple of dozen exposures, he told the girl to take a break and change her shirt, and then he came over to where Ben was standing.

Wolfe was more of an outdoors type himself than his model was, with a rugged, seamy face and a thatch of brown hair, wearing khakis and with a light meter hanging from a lanyard around his neck. His assistant introduced them, and when Ben repeated his reason for the visit, Wolfe said, "Fine, but please don't take more than a few minutes."

While the photographer and Gimple fussed with the set and laid out freshly loaded magazines, a makeup woman touched up the blonde's face. When she'd finished, Ben drew the girl aside.

"I'd like to talk to you," he said.

"Yeah? Who are you?"

"My name is Ben Tolliver. I'm a detective with the police department."

She stiffened.

"Relax. All I want to do is ask you some questions about a friend of yours."

"Who's that?"

"Caroline Clark. Whose real name was Patterson."

Her eyes were a pale blue, and the expression in them wasn't cordial. "I don't know any—"

Ben raised a hand. "Look. Let's not waste each other's time. I know about Panache, and about how you spend your evenings. As far as I'm concerned, that's your business. Mine is to find out who killed Caroline."

"How do I know you're telling me the truth?"

"Think about it. If this was some kind of a vice bust, I'd just take you in. All I'm asking for is your help. And your name goes no further than the two of us."

"Suppose I refuse?"

He shrugged. "Then I look for another source. I guess whether you help or not depends on how you felt about her."

There was a rack of clothing across from where they were standing. She stepped over to it, apparently thinking about what he'd said. Ben followed.

She remained hesitant. "How much do you know about her?"

"Some. I know she was working. And I know about her background. I've talked with her father and her sister, and some of her other friends."

She was quiet for a moment, and then she turned back to him, seeming to have made a decision. "Okay, I'll tell you what I can."

"Good."

"The thing about Caroline was, it was different with her."

"Different how?"

"She liked to say she was doing it because her father cut her off, but that was bullshit, in my opinion."

"Why is that?"

"Because she could have bent a little, and he would have given her anything she wanted. Also there were plenty of guys who would have set her up."

"Then why?"

"Two reasons, mainly. For one, she figured she was sticking it to the old man. Has anybody told you she hated him?"

"Yeah, a few people have said that."

"They tell you why?"

"I gather it was because of the way he dominated his family."

"That's putting it mildly, Lieutenant. He was Mr. High-and-Mighty to the world, but he treated them like shit. He always had mistresses, and he never made any bones about it. Caroline told me he used to parade them around, even in front of her mother. He's got one now he calls his assistant."

"Joan Phillips."

"Right. A four-barreled bitch who's angling to become the next Mrs. Patterson."

"That explains a few things."

"Sure. Working as a hooker was Caroline's way of getting back at him."

"Yeah, I see."

"But don't kid yourself; another reason was that she really got a kick out of what she was doing. To the rest of us, it's a way to make as much as we can, while we can. But for her, it was like doing something dangerous just because it was thrilling. Like being a burglar, or performing in a high-wire act. Can you understand that?"

"Sure I can."

She began unbuttoning her shirt. "What else can I tell you?"

"What drew you two together?"

"I got to know her a little, and we liked each other. So I taught her the business."

"Didn't Martha do that?"

"Are you kidding? That old bag plays a game. She wants her young ladies to seem like amateurs. It adds to the crap the johns buy from her."

"Because they think they're seducing the girl?"

She pulled off the shirt and tossed it over the rack. She wasn't wearing a bra. "In a way, yes. But there's a lot of stuff a girl should know. About how to handle different guys, things to do with them."

It was hard for Ben to keep his eyes on her face. "She have any problems, that you know about? Enemies, or people who might have had it in for her, for whatever reason?"

She took her time picking out another shirt and putting it on. "Not that she ever mentioned to me. And besides, maybe it was somebody she didn't know."

"Okay. But think about it, will you?" He got out one of his cards and handed it to her. "If you come up with anything that could help, give me a call."

She tucked the card into a pocket of her pants. "Okay, I'll do that." There was a glint in her eye that might have been amusement. "Or maybe you could give me a call sometime. Say, when you get your Christmas bonus."

He grinned. "Thanks for your help."

"Don't mention it. To anyone."


Back down on the street, he stopped at a public telephone and called the squad room in the Sixth to check in. Joe Stone answered, and Ben asked for Ed Flynn.

When Ed came on the line, he said, "Lou, I been trying to reach you. We just got a call from Midtown North. Another homicide. White female in a house on Fifty-seventh Street."

"So?"

"She was a hooker. And the body was painted."

"Give me the address and get Spadone and Weisskopf up there."

He scribbled the information into his notebook and ran to where he'd parked the Ford.

# 43

When he arrived at the house, a young uniformed cop was standing on the landing outside the front door. As Ben went up the steps, he clipped his wallet to the collar of his windbreaker, letting it hang open so that his shield and ID would show. The kid logged him in.

"Where is it?" Ben asked.

The cop hooked a thumb over his shoulder. "There's a bedroom on the ground floor, Lieutenant. At the back of the house. She's in there."

Inside, CSU detectives were everywhere, as they had been in the Plaza. Technicians were dusting for prints and shooting photographs while others collected fiber samples. The interior of this place was different, however; the rooms were stuffed to overflowing. Statuary was crammed in along with the furniture, and every inch of the walls was hung with paintings in gilt frames. It looked like a museum that had run out of space.

Spadone emerged from a hallway. "Hya, Lou. We just got here. It's back this way."

Ben followed him down the hallway to a bedroom. Phil Monahan was standing near the door, talking to Weisskopf. More cops were inside the room, where flash cameras were producing bursts of light. Monahan and Weisskopf greeted him, and Ben nodded in return. They stepped aside and he went past them into the room.

The first thing that hit him was the stink. It was a cloying, heavy odor, the unmistakable stench of putrifying human flesh. No matter how many times he'd smelled it, the experience always triggered a gag reflex, and he had to fight an urge to puke. He waited a few seconds for his olfactory senses to become numbed, and then he approached the source.

The body of a young woman was spread-eagled upright on the posts at the foot of an elaborately carved bed. Each wrist was handcuffed to a finial at the top of a post, and each ankle was tied to the bottom, so that her arms and legs were wide apart. She was naked, and her body had been painted in the motif of the U.S. flag. Her left shoulder and breast and part of her belly were done up as a blue field with white stars, while the rest of her was covered in red and white stripes. Her face was also a flag, in miniature, with the blue field and the stars covering her left eye and half her forehead, the red and white stripes extending over her nose and her cheeks and jaw.

The cause of death was no mystery. The bone handle of a knife protruded from her vagina, and a dark stain covered a large area of the Oriental rug beneath her. The knife handle was black with dried blood.

Ben stepped closer and studied her face. It was thin, almost gaunt, which made the cheekbones seem overly prominent. Her hair was a dull brown and hung in lank strands. The eyes were partly open, pupils dilated and glazed. Her mouth was slack. Experience told him she'd died peacefully, not in pain, and that was odd.

He grasped her right knee and moved it from side to side, gently. Rigor mortis had left her long ago. Some red paint had come off on his fingers. He got out a handkerchief and wiped them clean.

The ME was standing nearby, writing in a notebook. He was the same one who'd covered the Patterson homicide, Robert Kurtz. The doctor looked up and said hello, then went back to making his notes while Ben continued to look at the body.

The brilliant hues of red, white, and blue were startling. In contrast with Patterson, this painting seemed to have been more carefully thought out. As if the guy had planned the idea ahead of time, and then had gone to a lot of trouble to bring it off.

"Aren't you going to salute?"

He turned to see Monahan standing nearby, a cynical smile on his freckled face. Like Weisskopf and Spadone, the Midtown North squad commander was wearing a neatly pressed suit. Except for the shields clipped to their breast pockets, all three might have been part of the lunchtime business crowd walking by out on the sidewalk. "How'd it come in?" Ben asked.

Monahan inclined his head toward the wall on his left. "Neighbor complained about the smell. We used DB45's when we got here, but it didn't do much good."

"Had to be the same guy," Spadone said. "Nobody knew about the paint job on Patterson, so it wasn't a copycat."

Ben looked at the knife handle. Simply shoving it into her vaginal tract would have done some damage, but not that much. The killer had to have twisted the blade one way and then another.

Kurtz saw what Ben was looking at and confirmed his suspicion. "He practically gave her a hysterectomy, Lieutenant." The ME pointed to the stain on the rug. "She lost most of her blood."

"When?"

"Five or six days ago, I'd say. Maybe longer."

Ben peered at her eyes, at the slack features of her face. "You sure she bled to death? Couldn't he have cut her after she was dead?"

"It's possible, but I don't think that's what happened," Kurtz said. "You're wondering why there's no sign of a struggle, right?"

"It crossed my mind."

"My hunch is she was drugged, either by the killer or maybe she OD'd. Then when she was out of it, he worked on her with the knife. I'll know when I do the post. She was a user, though. Take a look."

Ben moved closer, but all he could make out on the underside of her arms was the coat of paint.

"Back of her knees," Kurtz said.

Ben squatted beside her right leg. By moving it a little and turning his head, he could see there was no paint behind the knee, and small red puncture wounds were visible in the flesh. He stood up and again wiped his fingers with the handkerchief.

Monahan was watching, his arms folded. "Also she's got a coke nose."

That was something Ben had missed. He'd been so involved with the slack expression and the condition of her eyes, he'd gone right by it. But now despite the paint, he made out the way the bridge of her nose was slightly depressed, pulling the nostrils up. Eventually, if she'd lived and kept on snorting, she'd have looked like Miss Piggy.

"The CSU got her fingerprints," Monahan said. "I told them to send a set to Albany, see if we can get a make. Hope that was all right with you. Also I let Brennan and Shanley know." Shanley was Monahan's zone commander, like Brennan a captain.

Ben was careful to keep his face expressionless. He was aware that Weisskopf and Spadone were looking on, waiting for his reaction. "Sure. Thanks for the help."

He wondered whether Shanley had also been stung by Galupo's order to take the case away from Midtown North. Probably he had. So what Monahan was doing was making sure the brass were aware that Lieutenant Philip Monahan was not only being cooperative but was acting with initiative, providing aid where it was needed.

Which was a smoke screen for his real purpose: to have everybody including the chief of detectives conclude that Monahan would have handled the case just fine, without that asshole from the Sixth sticking his nose in, thank you. He'd probably even enlisted Shanley's support for getting the word to the PC, as well.

Ben turned to Weisskopf and Spadone. "Whose house is this?"

Weisskopf answered. "Guy named Julio Mendez."

"Colombian?"

"Right."

"Where is he?"

"Rikers."

"What?"

"Narcotics charge," Art said. "He's a mid-level guy in the cartel, goes back and forth to Bogotá. Or he did, until he was busted. Also he's a suspect in two homicides in Brooklyn."

"How long's he been at Rikers?"

"Three weeks."

"Any sign of a break-in here?"

"We didn't see any," Spadone said.

Which meant they hadn't looked for it specifically. "Double-check," Ben said. "Now."

As the two detectives left the room, Monahan said, "You need any more help from me?"

The question was almost funny. With a second homicide, almost surely by the same perpetrator, Ben could have kept fifty detectives busy—especially with this new angle of the house belonging to some Colombian hard-on in the drug trade.

"No," Ben said. "But thanks for lending a hand."

"Don't mention it." Monahan touched an index finger to his forehead in a mock salute. "See you later." He waved to the ME. "So long, Doc."

When the other detective had gone, Ben turned to the body once more. As he stared at the lifeless form, he let his mind drift, not forcing thoughts, but letting them come to him spontaneously.

The girl was a junkie. Was she a whore, as well? Probably. Looking around the bedroom, he saw nothing that might have belonged to her: no clothing, no jewelry, no bag, no purse, no makeup kit—nothing. This room was as overfurnished as the others he'd seen in the house, crammed with antique furniture and art objects, but there wasn't a single item he could tie to the victim.

What did that mean? Had the guy learned from the first murder? In that one, he'd left all of Patterson's personal possessions behind, even her ID. In this one, he'd apparently left nothing. He hadn't used makeup to decorate her body, either, but special paint. Probably the kind used in the theater. No doubt he'd brought it with him, all part of the plan.

What about the handcuffs and the rope? Most likely the killer had supplied those, as well. The cuffs were Smith & Wesson, standard police issue, and available in gun shops. You didn't need a permit to buy a pair. Without touching them, Ben could see tiny scratches in the chrome, indicating they'd had a fair amount of use. The rope was nylon, the kind people used on boats because it was strong but

186

pliable, never became stiff. It had been painted over along with her legs, red and white.

One of the CSU detectives came into the room, a guy Ben had worked with on other cases. He was older, heavyset, and ponderous, not far from retirement. His name was Dick Brady.

"Hello, Ben," Brady said. "Didn't see you come in."

"How's it going, Dick?"

"All right, I guess. I wasn't on the one in the Plaza, but the guys tell me a lot of the MO was the same. A hooker, all painted up."

"How do you know she was a hooker?"

Brady shrugged. "I seen a lot of dead whores. Take away the paint and this one is just about routine. On junk, in an S&M setup. The johns who go for this shit're nutballs, of course. Every once in a while, one of them gets carried away. Goes for the big kick, right?"

"Could be." Ben had seen them himself, a number of times. But he'd never seen anything like the decorations on Patterson and this one.

"If you and the doc are finished, we'll get samples of the paint," Brady said. "Also we'll take the cuffs and the rope to the lab. And the knife."

Art Weisskopf returned to the bedroom. "Nothing was forced, Lou. All the doors and the windows were locked."

"How'd the responding officers get in?"

"Forced the back door."

"No alarm?"

"No. I suppose Mr. Mendez wouldn't want cops paying a visit, no matter what was going on."

"Yeah, you're right." Ben turned back to Brady. "I want to have a look at that knife, before you take it."

"Sure." The CSU detective pulled a tissue out of his jacket pocket and handed it to Ben. "You can do the honors."

"Thanks a lot."

With Kurtz and the other detectives watching, Ben draped the tissue over the handle of the knife and grasped it with his thumb and forefinger. The knife came out easily, with no more than a gentle tug. The blade was six inches long. Like the handle, it was covered in blood, but the material on this part was still viscous.

As bad as the body smelled, the odor that now escaped from the oozing flesh had a foulness all its own. Ben clamped his jaws together and stepped away from the corpse, holding the knife carefully. He turned it from side to side, examining it, as the others moved closer.

"Krautsticker," Brady said.

Ben glanced at him questioningly.

"Made in Germany. You want, I'll take a look."

Ben passed the knife to him.

Brady held the knife in one hand, and with the other dug into one of his pockets, coming up with a folded sheet of clear plastic. He shook it out and laid it on the surface of a nearby table, then placed the knife on it and drew away the tissue.

Bending over the knife, he studied it for a moment. "This is a real good one." He pointed to the handle. "See there? That's the trigger button, and the one just below is the safety. Hard to see, with the blood all crusted over."

Ben and the others peered at the knife. Spadone had returned to the room and joined the group.

"It's a Solingen," Brady said. "You look close, you can see the Gemini twins on the blade there, that's their trademark. Nobody makes steel any better than this. And the handle's real bone, not plastic."

"Worth a couple C's in Harlem," Spadone said. "Almost as much as what they'd pay for a gun."

"Harder to find, though," Weisskopf said. "You can get switch-blades, but mostly they're cheap shit from Hong Kong or Taiwan."

"Send it back to me," Ben said to Brady, "just as soon as the lab's through with it."

"Will do."

Tolliver addressed Weisskopf and Spadone. "Get a statement from the neighbor, the one that turned in the complaint. Also do a house-to-house. Find out if anybody saw anything."

When the pair had again left the room, Ben said to Brady, "Be sure you get photographs in the morgue, when the paint's cleaned off."

"Sure. I'll have prints to you by tomorrow."

Kurtz spoke up. "You finished with the body, Lieutenant? If you are, we'll pack it up. The ambulance crew is here."

Ben turned and looked once more at the outlandish figure hanging from the bedposts. For an instant he thought of some of the so-called new art you saw in the Village. Mapplethorpe or some other one of those dipshits would have loved this scene.

"Yeah," he said at last. "She's all yours."

# 44

Stein was seeing his last patient of the day. Ben sat in the small waiting room and leafed through an old issue of *People* until the doctor led him back into his study.

An electric coffeepot was standing amidst the clutter on one of the tables. Stein poured mugs for both of them and handed one to Ben. "Looks as if your man is turning out to be quite an artist."

"No doubt, is there, it's the same guy?"

"Not in my mind. Is there in yours?"

"No. But this angle of the Colombian drug operator comes out of left field. Hard to tie that into what I've been able to turn up on Caroline Patterson."

"Possible there was a connection, though, don't you think? You wouldn't have expected her to become a call girl, either."

"True enough."

"But as far as that part is concerned, I really can't help you very much. Whether one or both of those women were involved in drug trafficking is a matter for police investigation. It's certainly out of my bailiwick. What I can tell you is that in my judgment, the killer was the same man, motivated by the same psychosis that led him to murder the Patterson woman."

"And not just a drug hit?"

"What do you think?"

". . . I suppose you're right. No doper would go through the trouble of painting her up that way after he killed her. Unless he was sending word to somebody. But even then, all he had to do was take her out."

"Exactly. And yet she was done up even more elaborately than the earlier one."

"Yeah, but it's hard for me to connect Patterson with this woman. This was a junkie whore working rough trade."

"Not hard if you look at it from the killer's perspective."

"Meaning?"

Stein stepped over to his desk and set his coffee mug down on it. He picked up an envelope, opening it and taking out a sheaf of color prints. They were the crime-scene photographs Ben had sent to him earlier in the day. The doctor spread them out on the desk. "Meaning he's telling us more about himself."

"Like what? We already know he hates women. So what about this new paint job—doing her up like the flag. What does that mean, he's pissed off at America, too?"

Stein smiled. "I don't think so. In fact, I doubt there's any significance to the design itself. There may be, of course, but I'd be surprised if there was."

As much as he respected the psychiatrist and valued his opinions, the guy also could be exasperating. Ben stepped to the desk and looked down at the pictures. "Okay, Doc—so what's he saying?"

"That what he hates isn't women per se."

"What is it, then?"

The owlish eyes fixed on Tolliver, holding him in an unblinking gaze. "What this man hates is whores."

# 45

"You can't be serious," Holland said.

They were sitting in his office, Ben in the visitor's chair, the ADA at his desk. Holland's trial preparation assistant was also in the room, putting papers into drawers in a filing cabinet.

"Can't I?" Ben said.

Holland toyed with a letter opener, lounging back in his chair and peering at Ben with a half-amused, half-bored expression. "Of course not. Just because another young woman turns up dead in Manhattan, that doesn't mean there's a connection between the two cases. I'll grant you this business of the paint is an odd coincidence, but even that was only vaguely similar, according to what you've told me. True?"

Ben forced himself to take a breath and let it out before answering. If there was one thing he couldn't stand, it was being condescended to, especially by a self-inflated prick like this one. "I don't think it could be called a coincidence. The circumstances are just too unusual."

"Are they really? I'm sure you'll agree there's nothing the least bit out of the ordinary about a dead hooker. Prostitutes get themselves killed all the time. Usually by pimps, or because a drug deal went wrong. Isn't that so? Whereupon the citizens have the usual reaction to the news. They yawn."

The TPA closed one file drawer and opened another. She was beamy, with a heavy ass to go along with her thick legs, and wore her dark hair piled up on top of her head. It was apparent to Ben that she was in here to snoop, listen to the conversation. He wished Holland would tell her to beat it.

"What I really want to know," the ADA said, "is how you're getting along in the Patterson case."

Ben kept his manner patient, outwardly at least. "We're checking johns. Guys known to use prostitutes."

"Good lord, that must include half the men in New York." He smiled at his wit. "Although I never could understand the attraction, myself. Whores are pitiful creatures, actually. How are you going about it?"

"We've got names, most of them supplied by Vice." Which was the truth, if not the whole truth. Ben was wary of revealing the source he'd developed inside Panache.

"How many?"

"Several hundred."

"And you have how many men to check them out, including yourself?"

Holland knew fucking well how many men Ben had in his alleged task force. He probably also knew Tolliver had been stonewalled when he'd tried to have more detectives assigned.

"There are three of us," Ben said. "Including me. And that's another reason investigating this new homicide could be helpful to us."

Holland frowned. "I'm afraid I don't follow your logic, Lieutenant. You're already shorthanded. How could having to work on still another case be helpful, as you put it?"

"Because I believe it's the same case. Which is a good reason to put more people on it. Also this latest killing starts to show a pattern. It gives us more to go on, including what may be a good lead. The man who owns the house is a Colombian drug dealer named Mendez. He's in jail, on Rikers Island."

"On what charge?"

"Narcotics, two counts of murder."

"How long has he been on Rikers?"

"Three weeks."

"So he was there when this homicide took place?"

"Yes."

Holland put the pen down on his desk. "Really, Lieutenant."

But Ben pressed on. "I think there's a possibility one of his people was using the house. The guy could have called in the girl and killed her, then painted the body."

The ADA's eyebrows lifted. "And you think he may be the same man who killed the Patterson girl?"

"Yes, I do."

"Well. I hesitate to second-guess police procedures. But I'll remind you of something. As we both know very well, one of the reasons I was chosen by the district attorney to handle the Patterson homicide was the sensitive nature of the case. It was the same reason you were assigned to it, Lieutenant . . . albeit on a different plane. Does it occur to you that there may be larger implications in what you're proposing?"

"Such as?"

"Such as, Caroline Patterson was murdered. That was sensational enough, without the media and the public learning what, in fact, the daughter of one of New York's most prominent citizens was doing that night in the Plaza. Whoever killed her smeared some makeup on the body after she was dead. Fortunately, even that aspect of the case hasn't become public, and if handled with tact, it never will."

"So?"

"So now we have another dead woman. This one's body was found in the house of a drug dealer who's already in jail facing murder charges. You don't know the identity of the woman, or even whether she was a prostitute. You merely think so. You do have evidence that she was a drug addict, although as yet there is no autopsy report to confirm that suspicion. The only connection you're able to make between the two cases is that in this new one, the woman's body was painted. But even that connection is extremely tenuous, because you say this time the killer used body paint, in a carefully contrived design that was totally different from what was done to Patterson. Correct, so far?"

Grudgingly, Ben admitted that it was.

"And what do you think would happen, Lieutenant, if the media were to learn the police thought it was all part of the same case? I'm sure you know, but permit me to point it out, anyway."

He drew his hand through the air, as if scanning a headline. "Another homicide by Patterson murderer." The hand moved again. "Cops believe Patterson a hooker, victim of a serial killer." And again. "Patterson murder tied to Colombian drug executions."

The ADA sat forward in his chair and fixed his gaze on Tolliver. "Lieutenant, I believe you'd better rethink this situation very carefully. I must also advise you, I'm going to discuss it with my bureau chief. I suggest you inform your superiors, as well. And now if you'll excuse me, I have a great deal of work to do."

Ben stood up, feeling the heat surge from his neck up into his cheeks. "See you later, counselor."

He turned and walked to the door. As he passed her, Holland's assistant shot him a smug glance. She was just as ugly from this angle as from behind. He slammed the door and went through the vestibule, heading for the elevators.

# 46

The trip to Rikers Island took forty-five minutes. A light rain was falling, and that made traffic on the FDR Drive even slower than usual. Ben went over the Queensboro Bridge, and then followed Queens Boulevard to the Brooklyn-Queens Expressway, driving north until he reached the causeway stretching out into the river next to La Guardia Airport.

As he drove across the narrow road that was the only connection between the 687-acre island and the mainland, he thought about how much the prison had changed during his years on the force. When he joined the NYPD, the inmate population had been about four thousand. Today, nearly twenty years later, it was almost four times as large, and the facility was bursting at the seams.

During that time, growth in the number of corrections officers had kept pace, swelling to more than eleven thousand. But overcrowding of prisoners had made the job of maintaining order almost impossible. Fights with knives, shanks, and other homemade weapons were common, and inmates killed each other—and occasionally a corrections officer as well—with regularity. The place was always on the verge of a riot.

Ben had phoned ahead, and when he reached the Otis Bantum Center, he was taken directly into a small room used for police interrogation of inmates. He sat down at a wooden table, and minutes later, the man he'd come here to see was led into the room by a pair of COs. One of the officers then left the room, while the other stood against the wall with an eye on the inmate.

Even in prison denims, Julio Mendez managed to look stylish. He wore the shirt with the top three buttons open, revealing tufts of hair on his chest. Ben guessed his age as about thirty-five. He seemed to be in good shape, with a flat belly and skinny hips. His face was clean shaven, and his black hair was a mass of tight black waves. When he smiled, light from the overhead fluorescents reflected from a gold tooth in the front of his upper jaw.

He smiled now as he sat down at the table across from Tolliver. "So, Detective. You come to get me outta this fucking place?"

"I came to ask you some questions," Ben said.

The smile became a sneer. "I don't answer no more questions. You wanna ask questions, my lawyer's gotta be here."

"There was a homicide," Ben said. "In your house."

Mendez cocked his head to one side as he studied his visitor. "The fuck you talking about?"

"A young woman was murdered. In your house on Fifty-seventh Street, about a week ago. Her body was just discovered."

The Colombian's black eyes narrowed. "You shittin' me?"

Ben had brought along an envelope. He opened it and drew out an eight-by-ten head shot that had been taken in the morgue, after the paint had been removed from the woman's body. He held the print up so that Mendez could see it. "You recognize her?"

Mendez squinted at the photograph, and then his gaze moved back to Ben. "I don't know that broad. I never saw her."

"You sure?"

"Yeah, I'm sure."

"Then what was she doing there?"

His swarthy features tensed. "Hey, what is this? You scumbags tryin' to set me up? You say I killed somebody even when I'm in a fucking jail? Okay, I confess. The COs took me outta here, put me in a boat. Then we took a taxi to my house. They stood around while I killed the broad, then we had a couple drinks and come back here. Okay?"

"Relax," Ben said. "Nobody thinks you killed her. But whoever did wasn't doing you any favors, either. They did her in your house."

Mendez blew air out between his lips in an expression of contempt.

"What they wanted," Ben said, "was to give you even more trouble than you've already got."

"Bullshit. You think I'm stupid or something? How could I have any more trouble than I got now?"

"It's possible, believe me."

"So what do you want?"

Ben held up the print once more. "Take another look, Julio. You sure you don't know her? Maybe she reminds you of somebody, even if you don't know her name?"

Mendez peered hard at the photo. He shook his head. "No. I swear to God, I don't know that broad."

"All right, then let me ask you this. We know you didn't do it, but it could be that whoever did wanted to get at you. So they killed her and left her in your house. Can you think who might have done that?"

Mendez looked blank for a moment, and then his face lit up in a grin, the gold tooth flashing. "Hey, you know something, Detective? You're a fucking clown. You think I'm gonna sit here, tell you about a bunch of people because you say some broad got killed in my house? That's funny, you know that? The cops must keep you around so you can tell jokes, huh? I 'preciate it, though. You come all the way over here on a shitty day like today so you can make me laugh. That's very nice, I 'preciate it. So thanks a lot, and now get the fuck outta here. I'm busy, see? I gotta call my broker, find out how the market did today."

Mendez stood up and turned to the CO. *"Hey, puerco. Se a cabao la fiesta."*

The man's face remained expressionless. Apparently, he didn't mind being called a pig by an inmate who had decided the party was over. Money had the same effect anywhere, in or out of jail.

The CO looked at Ben. "Okay, Lieutenant? You finished?"

"Yeah, I am. *Buenas suerte, Julio.*"

"Fuck you, Detective." Mendez hitched up his pants with his wrists and swaggered toward the door.

# 47

When Ben got back to the Sixth Precinct station house, he was surprised to see a swarm of reporters milling around the Charles Street entrance. As soon as they spotted him, the photographers began snapping pictures, and two of the TV guys taped him as he approached the door. The others yelled questions.

"Hey, Lieutenant—what ties this new one to Patterson?"

"Were they killed by the same assailant?"

"Were they both mixed up with Julio Mendez?"

"Is there a drug connection?"

He clamped his mouth shut and pushed through, ignoring their yapping. A uniformed cop was standing at the door to keep them out, and Ben knew there would be another cop outside the Tenth Street door, on the other side of the block. Refusing to let the media enter the precinct house would be on orders of the commanding officer of the Sixth, and it would result in complaints to the NYPD public-relations office. Which was somebody else's problem, not Tolliver's. For now he was only grateful that he didn't have to put up with the questioning.

Inside, the station house was relatively quiet. Two cops were holding a drunk by the arms while the desk sergeant attempted to get information from him. Whenever one of the cops let go, the drunk would sag and they'd have to grab him to keep him from falling to the floor. Ben trotted up the stairs to the squad room.

Flynn was at his desk, talking on the phone, and Petrusky and Rodriguez were at theirs, both of them typing with their index fingers and frowning from the effort. Joe Stone and two other detectives were also working in the room.

When he saw Ben, Flynn said something hastily into the phone and hung up.

"How's it going?" Ben asked.

"Okay, Lou." Flynn inclined his head toward Tolliver's office. "Brennan's in there. He came in about a half hour ago, looking for you. I told him you went over to Rikers, and he said he'd wait. I think he's reading the DD-5's."

"All right," Ben said. "What brought on that mob of reporters?"

"I suppose somebody made you coming out of the house on Fifty-seventh Street. They love the idea there's a connection between the two homicides, gives them a bigger story."

"What else is doing? Where are Weisskopf and Spadone?"

"Haven't heard from either one. But Albany got us an ID on this latest victim. Name was Lisa Miller. There's a sheet on her, one arrest for prostitution, little over a year ago."

"And that's all? Nothing after that?"

"No, that was it."

"They give you a home address?"

"Yeah, it's on West Sixty-eighth Street. I called the super. She moved in there a few months back. There's another girl living with her. I put it all on your desk."

"Okay, good."

"Also the DA's office called, on François the painter. They said they'll present to a grand jury."

Ben snorted. "An indictment wouldn't mean shit—a trial is what counts, and on that one, it'd be a joke."

"That's what I think, too."

"Who's on the case?"

"The ADA's a guy named Steve Perlman."

"Never heard of him."

"Carlos and Frank both been down there to give him statements. They tell me he's pretty good. I spoke to him myself this morning, on the phone. He said when they had the conference, François's lawyer laughed at them. Claimed the woman's death was an unfortunate accident and asked what evidence did the DA have it wasn't."

"Good question, huh?"

"Unfortunately, yes."

"Anything else?"

"Usual shit, nothing important."

"Okay, I'll go talk to Brennan."

When Ben opened the door to his office, he saw the zone commander sitting at the desk, leafing through DD-5 reports, as Flynn had said he would be.

Brennan looked up. "Afternoon, Lieutenant."

"Hello, Cap. How you doing?"

The older man leaned back in the chair. He was as rumpled as ever, his tie askew, the blue suit looking as if he'd slept in it. "That's what I came to ask you. I hear you been over to Rikers."

"Yeah, I wanted to talk to this Julio Mendez, the guy who owns the house on Fifty-seventh Street. But I didn't get very far with him. He thought I was trying to con him."

"That's what I came to talk to you about. This second homicide."

"Sure. You want some lemonade?" Ben kept a bottle of Popov in the bottom drawer of his desk. He reached for the drawer, but Brennan stopped him, holding up a meaty hand.

"I got a better idea," the captain said. "Let's go over to Grady's."

"Fine with me." Ben picked up the note Flynn had left for him containing information on the Miller woman and put it into the inside pocket of his windbreaker. There was also a stack of phone messages. They could wait until he got back.

Brennan stood up, and as he did, Ben reached for the telephone. "I want to make one call first."

"Go ahead." Brennan stretched, putting Ben in mind of a bear, the kind you saw in the circus, which despite its size and weight could do everything a man could do—even dance—but he was still a bear.

Getting out his pocket notebook, Ben flipped through the pages. When he found the number, he punched the buttons on the phone.

"Thank you for calling Panache," a female voice said. "How may I serve you?"

The voice was silky smooth, but it wasn't familiar. "Monica there?" Ben asked.

"Who's calling, please?"

"Personal friend."

"I'm sorry, but Monica no longer works here."

His antennae went up. "Since when?"

"A few days ago. Can I give her a message, in case she calls in?"

"No thanks." He hung up.

Brennan moved toward the door. "All set, Lieutenant?"

"After you, Cap."

"Which way'd you come in?"

"Charles Street."

"So you saw all those buzzards."

"Yeah."

"We'll go out the other door."

# 48

Grady's was a hangout for cops and hardhats. Just a block away from the Sixth, it was a place where you could put down bets on any sporting event you could think of, even Irish football. You could also get a blowjob if you wanted one; there were usually a couple of hookers around.

Grady himself tended bar and was always in the joint. It was easy for him to get to work, because he lived upstairs. Ben had heard the saloon keeper was a fence, and that certain cops passed him information in return for running a tab they never had to settle, but he didn't know whether it was true. Probably it was.

Grady was there now, a throwback to another era, with his handlebar mustache and black hair parted in the middle, wearing a small bow tie and a striped shirt with an apron over it. When Tolliver and Brennan climbed onto stools, Grady put both hands flat on the bar. "Gentlemen," he said. "What's it gonna be?"

"Bushmills," Brennan said. "Beer chaser."

"A beer for me," Ben said.

The zone commander glanced sideways at him. "You on a diet?"

"I got a lot to do. If I drink too much, it puts me to sleep."

"Me, too," Brennan said. "That's why I drink too much."

Ben looked around. There was sawdust on the floor and brass spittoons stood inside the footrails, and the air was musty with the odors of stale beer and cigar smoke. Pictures of old-time fighters hung on the walls, among them a number of Ben's childhood heroes, guys like Archie Moore and Rocky Graziano and Ray Robinson, and going way back, Billy Petrolle, the Fargo Express. The place was nearly deserted; only a few other customers were at the bar, arguing about mistakes the Giants had made against the Eagles on Sunday.

Except for hookers, you never saw women in here, although one time a few years ago a group of militant females had protested to Grady that he discriminated against them, and they demanded equal rights. Grady told them he didn't give a shit, they could come in any fucking time they wanted. Cunts were always welcome, he said.

Ben again thought of Monica. What had happened to her? If she'd decided to quit Panache, why hadn't she let him know? Or was it something more than that?

Grady put their drinks in front of them, and moved away. Ben raised his glass. "Prost."

"Luck," Brennan said. He knocked back the shot of Irish and chased it with the beer.

Ben drank some of his, still thinking of Monica. He could have kicked himself for not having tried to call her sooner.

The captain nodded to Grady for a refill. As the saloon keeper went about pouring more whiskey and another beer, Brennan said, "I got bad news, Ben."

"What is it?"

Brennan's gaze was straight ahead, fixed on the image of the two men in the back bar mirror. "The chief says Midtown North will handle this other homicide."

"What?"

"Yeah. He says there appears to be no connection between the two cases, and the PC decided it wouldn't do to get the citizens all riled up. You saw yourself how all them reporters was sniffing around. This'll help defuse that kind of stuff. Monahan's squad is already on it."

"Jesus Christ."

"He won't help you either, at least directly."

Ben thought back to his discussion with Brian Holland. "When did this come down?"

"Today. I wanted to tell you face-to-face."

"Thanks."

Grady set a pair of fresh glasses in front of Brennan.

"I know how you feel," the captain said.

"You do?"

"Yeah, I do. You don't think so, but it's the truth. See, there was a time when I was just like you, Lieutenant. Full of piss and vinegar. I figured the brass was all old farts who didn't know what the fuck they were doing. Not like me—I knew everything."

Ben made no comment.

"Then after a while I found out how things work. I learned you got two choices in the department. You can buck the tide, or you can swim with it. You buck it, you wind up on the bottom of the harbor. You follow me?"

"Uh-huh."

Brennan drank the Bushmills, then some of his beer. "My old man was a cop, I ever tell you that?"

Only every time we're in a bar together, Ben thought. "Yeah, you did."

"It was the same in his day, from what he used to tell me. Even though the department's changed a lot. Now you got all these spades and dagos, you never saw that when I come on the job. At least not in the upper ranks. What're you, by the way?"

The question caught him by surprise. "Kind of a crossbreed, I guess. Some Irish, some German. I don't know what else." He did know; his mother had told him one of her ancestors was English, but that was something he wouldn't mention.

Brennan nodded. "Mostly Irish, huh? Figures. Irish make the best cops, always have. Wouldn't be a department without us. In my old man's day, it was *all* Irish, practically. Today there're these factions. But that's not the problem."

Ben knew what was coming next.

"You want to know where the trouble started, why the cops can't control crime in New York? Goes all the way to the Supreme Court. *Miranda, Rosario,* all that shit. Everything to protect the fucking criminal. Every time a cop goes into a situation, he's got to think, one wrong move and my career is down the toilet. Two nights ago, there's this Rican in the Four-two. You hear about it?"

"What happened?"

"He snatches a purse off an old lady and she tries to stop him, so he knocks her down and kicks her in the head. Young cop chases the guy, corners him. The Rican sticks a hand in his back pocket; the cop shoots him. So what's next?"

"The cop is up on charges."

"Exactly." Brennan finished his beer and nodded to Grady again.

What the hell, Ben thought. He drained his glass. "I'll have one, too," he told Grady.

"With an Irish?" the saloon keeper asked.

"Sure, why not."

"The sheet on the Rican is longer than he is," Brennan went on. "Burglary, felonious assault, armed robbery."

"Ever convicted?"

"Once. He did three in Attica. But this night, all he's got in that pocket is a comb. No weapon."

"So why didn't the cops lend him one?"

"Too many people around. About fifty more PRs, all of them screaming police brutality."

Grady set them up again, and Ben downed the shot of Bushmills, feeling it warm his gut.

"That cop did the city a favor," Brennan said. "But you wait and see, they'll nail his ass to the wall."

Ben nodded, knowing the captain was right. When he swallowed some beer, it tasted mild, after the whiskey.

"Let me ask you something," Brennan said. "You got any enemies in the department, would you say?"

Ben shrugged. "None I can think of, offhand. But there could be a few guys I pissed off, one time or another. Why?"

"Galupo didn't come right out, but I sensed maybe somebody's got it in for you."

"The ADA on Patterson, maybe. Brian Holland?"

"No, not him. He passed the word you were a good investigator."

"Galupo tell you that?"

"Yeah, he did. And anyhow, Holland can afford to be magnanimous."

"Why's that?"

"They just gave him the Park Avenue rape. That's a real plum, that one."

Ben knew the case. Two black teenagers had slipped into an apartment house on Park Avenue by tricking the doorman. They did a push-in on an older woman, the wife of a prominent surgeon. She was alone in the apartment; it was the maid's day off. They beat her and took turns raping her, then left her to die in a pool of blood on the living room floor while they looted the apartment. When the doctor returned home, he thought at first she was dead, but then he found a slight pulse. He called an ambulance and they rushed her to Lenox Hill.

After months in intensive care, a miracle occurred. The woman had lost the sight in one eye, and it was questionable whether she'd ever walk again, but she'd retained most of her mental capacity. She was taken to the Twentieth Precinct station house on Eighty-second

Street, where the Manhattan Sex Crimes Unit is located, and she identified the teenagers in a lineup. Later, the doorman also picked them out. The media were having a field day with the story, and the black community was up in arms, howling frame-up.

"What I hear, the case is a lock," Brennan said. "And with all the publicity, the trial's gonna make Holland a hero. He plays it right, he could go anywhere from there."

"Good for him," Ben said. "Meantime, the department's doing everything it can to see Patterson never gets closed."

"Remember what I told you, Lieutenant. Don't buck the tide."

"So what's this about my having enemies?"

"I don't know. But somebody wants to put the screws to you."

Ben thought of Monahan, but decided not to push it. "What happens with Spadone and Weisskopf—they go back to Midtown North?"

"No. You get to keep them as long as you want."

"Lucky me."

"That's better, Lieutenant. Always look on the bright side."

# 49

B en glanced through the stack of phone messages. Most of them were of no consequence, calls from reporters and would-be tipsters. One caught his attention, however. It was from Mrs. B. Conklin, who requested that he return the call. He reached for the phone and tried the number.

A maid answered. Ben gave her his name, and Barry Conklin's wife came on the line seconds later.

Her voice was low and husky. "Lieutenant Tolliver?"

"Yes, ma'am. You called me?"

"I understand you met my husband recently. In his athletic club?" What the hell was this? "That's right, I did."

"I have some information for you. If it could be confidential that we talked. Is that possible? That it could be kept confidential?"

"Certainly. What is it you wanted to tell me?"

"I can't talk about it over the phone. I wouldn't want anybody to know about this, including my husband."

Then I hope you have the maid well trained, he thought. "Can you at least give me an idea of the subject, Mrs. Conklin?"

"I told you, not over the phone. Could you meet me somewhere?"

"Of course. You have a place in mind?"

"How about the King Cole room in the St. Regis? Say at five o'clock?"

"I'll be there." He hung up, wondering.

It was too late now for him to chase some of his ideas, after having been told about Galupo's decision.

And yet . . .

He flipped through the Rolodex until he found the number for the Midtown North detective squad, and then called it. He told the officer who answered he wanted to talk with Lieutenant Monahan.

When the squad leader came onto the line, his tone was conciliatory. "Hey, I'm sorry about your case."

I'll bet you are, Ben thought. "No problem, Phil. First it gets kicked my way, then yours."

"You still think the two of these things are connected?"

"Don't you?"

"I'm not so sure. Maybe, maybe not. Except for the paint, what else is there?"

"Both hookers, for one thing."

"Yeah, but some difference, huh?"

"You have a point there. I understand Albany made an ID?"

"Right."

"And she's got a roommate?"

"Also right."

"You talk to her yet, the roommate?"

"Two of our guys are over there now. Carter and Knight."

"You mind if I stop by and have a look?"

There was a moment's pause. "I'd say that's up to you. But you're sticking your neck out, aren't you? I mean, what the Chief decided was—"

"I have the knife," Ben said. "The lab sent it back to me. Only reason I'd be stopping by the apartment would be to give it to your detectives, okay?"

They both knew it was thin, but at least it was some sort of excuse. And if Tolliver kept hands off after that, why not?

"Yeah," Monahan said at last. "I guess that would be okay."

Ben found a parking space near the address Flynn had given him. The neighborhood was run-down and ratty, nothing like the same street on the east side of Central Park. There was no doorman in front of the building, and no one in the lobby but a fat guy sitting in a chair, chewing a toothpick and reading *El Diario*. He had on black pants and a T-shirt that said GO METS on the front of it.

"You the super?" Ben asked.

The guy looked him over. "Tha's right. Who you wanna see?"

Ben showed him his shield. "Lisa Miller have an apartment here?"

He got up slowly, rolling the toothpick around in his mouth. "Seven B. There two other cops already up there."

"They tell you Miss Miller is dead?"

"Yeah, they told me. What happen, she OD?"

"She was murdered."

The toothpick stopped moving. "Murdered?"

"The other cops—what'd they say to you?"

"They just said she died and they wanna know where is her apartment."

"What's your name?"

"Tomas Esperanza."

"You live here in the building?"

"Yeah, my apartment's in the basement."

"You know what Miss Miller did for a living?"

His eyes narrowed. "Hey, man—I don't want no trouble."

"Then answer the question."

"I don't know nothing."

"You knew she used, right? You said so. Asked me if she OD'd."

He chewed on the toothpick, nervously. "Wadda you want from me?"

"Answers. You answer my questions, I leave you alone. You don't, I toss your place for narcotics."

Tomas's jaw dropped, and the toothpick fell out of his mouth. He tried to tough it a little. "You got a warrant?"

"First I find the drugs," Ben said. "Then I get the warrant."

He wilted. "Okay. I knew she was a *puta.*"

"And she had a roommate, right?"

"Yeah. Beth."

"Beth?"

"I don't know her last name."

"She up there now?"

"Yes."

"The girls ever do business here, have men over?"

"I never seen any."

"You know if Miss Miller had a pimp, or a boyfriend?"

"No. She didn't."

"No? There was nobody?"

"She was a bull dyke, man. Beth was her girlfren'."

"Beth work, too?"

"No. She stayed home. Never went out."

"She a user?"

"I don't know."

"You don't?"

Tomas's eyes shifted.

"Maybe sometimes you got stuff for her, huh? Maybe you made a little deal with her? Did a little trade?"

"Hey, man—"

"Be sure you stick around, Tomas. I might want to talk with you some more."

There were two elevator doors. Ben pressed the button and waited as one of the cars slowly made its way down, the floor numbers clicking in a small window above the button. Cigarette butts were sticking out of a can of sand on the floor, and the wall had graffiti scrawled on it. Tomas must not work too hard, Ben thought. And the owners must not visit too often.

# 50

The girl looked about sixteen, slim as a boy except where her small breasts pushed out the front of her shirt. She had blue eyes and pale hair that hung in limp strands. Her eyes were puffy and her nose was red from what Ben supposed was crying, but when he looked closer, he decided it was from coke.

Bo Carter was questioning her, sitting in a chair while she curled catlike on a couch, barefoot and wearing cutoff jeans. Carter was a veteran detective Ben had known for a long time. He was sharply dressed, in a blue-gray suit and a muted tie. While Carter spoke, the girl slowly rocked to and fro, as if she was going in and out of focus. The room was shabbily furnished, littered with magazines and empty soda cans. Light came from windows at the end of the room and from a lamp beside the couch.

Ben sat nearby, keeping his mouth shut. Carter wasn't getting much out of her, not because she resisted answering his questions so much as that she seemed to have trouble understanding them. Carter's partner was nosing around somewhere else in the apartment. After a few minutes, Ben got up and left the room, going into the kitchen.

The air in here stank of rotting food. Clumps of it were clinging to dishes and plastic cartons on the table, covered with gray-green mold. More dirty dishes sat in the sink, and the contents of a garbage can had overflowed onto the floor. Ben opened the windows, and fresh air wafted into the room.

As he stepped back from the windows, he saw a metal lockbox lying open on the counter, a screwdriver and a pair of pliers nearby. The interior of the box looked like the inside of a pharmacy, filled with vials of capsules and pills of various colors and sizes. Some of the vials were uncapped, and their contents had spilled into the box and onto the counter. There was also an open plastic bag with a small amount of cocaine in it. He noticed that the lid of the box was bent, as if it had been forced open.

"Hey, Ben."

He turned to see Tom Knight enter the kitchen. The detective was tall and lean, and with his tan tweed sports jacket and suede vest, he looked like one of the characters you saw in the magazine section of the Sunday *Times*. The department was turning into a fashion show.

"Hello, Tom."

"I thought you were off this."

"I am. Just stopped by to deliver something. How's it going?"

Knight shrugged. "Kind of a nothing case, right? Somebody offed a hooker. So what else is new?" He thrust his jaw in the direction of the living room. "You saw the kid?"

"Yeah. I take it she's not giving you a whole lot."

"Stoned out of her fucking mind."

Ben glanced at the lockbox. "No wonder."

"Some stash, huh?"

"Yeah, it is. You come up with anything worthwhile?"

"No. Nothing but a pile of bills and some letters from the vic's mother."

"No address book?"

"Nope. I really went through the place, too. What was it you brought?"

"Come on, I'll show you." He turned and went back into the living room, Knight following.

Carter glanced up as they approached. He rolled his eyes. "The young lady's having a little trouble concentrating."

Or staying awake, Ben thought. After seeing the drugstore on the kitchen counter, he could only guess what was flowing through her veins. "Let me talk to her," he said to Carter.

"Be my guest."

206

Ben sat down in a chair near the couch and leaned forward, forearms resting on his knees. "How do you feel, Beth?"

The blue eyes were glassy. Even when looking in his direction, they didn't seem to see him. "Not too good."

"You coming down?"

There was no answer for a few seconds, and then the blond head bobbed once.

"I'm sorry about Lisa."

No response.

"The stuff in the kitchen, in the lockbox? That was hers, wasn't it? You broke open the box, because she wouldn't share with you. Isn't that right?"

Another pause. She began rocking back and forth again. Then she said, "Lisa was selfish."

"Sure. She wouldn't even let you go out, would she?"

"No."

"Just kept you shut up in here, huh? Must have been terrible."

"Yeah."

"When Lisa left, last time, where'd she go?"

"I don't know." She indicated Carter with a slow movement of her head. "I told him, I don't know."

"Was it to see a man?"

"Yeah, but I don't know who."

"She went out a lot, probably. That right?"

"Uh-huh."

"But she never took you with her."

"Nope."

"You know any of the men she was seeing?"

"No."

Ever hear her mention any of their names?"

"No. I told him, no."

"How about Julio Mendez?"

"No. I told him that, too."

"Did Lisa work alone, or for a service?"

"I don't know."

"Yes you do. Tell me."

"She used to."

"Used to what?"

"Work for one."

"Which one? What was the name of it?"

"I don't remember."

He let her sit there for a while, slowly rocking.

"Beth?"

"Yes?"

"You want a little hit? Make you feel better?"

The blue marbles fixed on him again. "Yeah."

"Okay. You think hard, tell me that name. The name of the service she used to work for. Then I'll ask our friends here to let you have something. All right?"

She was quiet for several seconds. Then she licked her lips. "Panache. That was the name of it. Panache."

"Good."

"She was gonna introduce me."

"But she never did?"

"No."

He reached into the pocket of his windbreaker and took out a slim bundle. He opened it, revealing the switchblade that had been used to kill Lisa Miller. The knife was clean now, its bone handle yellow and brown and black, the chrome-plated butt and the curved handle guards gleaming in the light from the lamp.

He thumbed the button and the blade snapped out, locking into place with a sharp click, too fast for the eye to follow.

"You ever seen this, Beth?"

"Yes."

"Where?"

"It was Lisa's."

"She carry it with her?"

"Yes."

"You ever see her use it?"

"I . . . no."

Ben pushed one of the handle guards, releasing the lock, and retracted the blade into the handle. He slid the safety on and handed the knife and the plastic wrapping to Carter, continuing to look at the girl.

"Did she own a pair of handcuffs?"

"Yes."

"Where are they?"

"I don't know. She took them with her."

"She always take them when she went out?"

"I don't know. I think so."

"How about a length of nylon rope?"

"Yeah, she had rope. You said you'd give me something."

"Sure. But first our friends here will want to ask you a few more questions. All right?"

"You said you would. You said you'd tell them."

"Okay. I'll go get the box while they talk to you. Deal?"

208

"Yeah, all right."

Bo Carter said, "Beth, you sure you never heard the name Julio Mendez?"

The girl shook her head wearily, and as Carter pressed her, repeating the question, Ben rose from his chair and went back into the kitchen.

He stood at the counter, thinking about what he'd learned. Lisa Miller was a hooker. At one time, she'd been on the street, according to her rap sheet. After that, she'd apparently moved up in the world, catching on with Panache. And then she'd gone in another direction, working rough trade.

Why?

The answer was obvious. It was lying all over the counter in front of him.

And if she'd no longer been with Panache, and didn't have a pimp, she must have kept her own book.

Which Knight hadn't been able to find.

Had she taken it with her, on that last date? Had her killer found it, along with her other things?

Unlikely. Hookers almost never carried a john book with them. Too valuable to lose, and also possibly incriminating in case of a bust. So where was it?

Someplace secure, of course. Someplace where she could keep it locked up.

He reached into the metal box and lifted out the bag of coke, then rummaged around among the vials and tubes and boxes, the red and yellow and blue capsules, the white pills.

And found it.

The book was small, a ring binder with a vinyl cover. Riffling through the alphabetized pages, he guessed there were forty or fifty names. Under *M,* there were three: Meacham, McEvans, Malamed. No Mendez. He slipped the book into his jacket pocket.

Scooping up the pills that were scattered over the counter, he dropped them back into the box. Then he put the bag of white powder back into it and carried the box into the living room.

The scene was unchanged. Carter was asking questions in a patient voice while Beth rocked slowly to and fro, seeming not to hear. Tom Knight was slumped in a nearby chair, looking bored.

Ben placed the box on the end table next to where the girl was sitting. "See you later," he said, and left the apartment.

# 51

When Ben arrived at the St. Regis, limos were double-parked out front. He pulled up behind a white stretch and blew his horn, but the driver paid no attention. Ben leaned on it, blasting the horn until a doorman ambled over and peered at the Ford with disdain.

The guy was dressed like a palace guard in an Errol Flynn movie, complete with a plumed hat. He even looked like Alan Hale. Ben showed him the tin. "Police officer. Tell the driver to move."

"We need this space for guests," Alan Hale said.

Ben was already fifteen minutes late. "Move the fucking limo or I bash in his ass end."

"All right, all right. Keep your shirt on." The doorman walked at the same slow pace to the driver's window of the limo and another conversation ensued. Ben blew the horn again and the limo finally crept away.

He pulled into the vacated space, still one car from the curb, and dropped the police plate onto the dash before getting out. As he locked his car, the doorman returned, pointing to a black Mercedes the Ford was now blocking. The Mercedes was sitting directly beneath a sign that said NO PARKING. "Hey, Officer," the doorman said, "how's he gonna get out?"

"He's not," Ben said, and went into the hotel.

The King Cole room took its name from a vast mural that ran almost the length of the room. Ben needn't have sweated it; the maître d' told him Mrs. Conklin had not yet arrived, and showed him to a table. When Ben sat down, a waiter asked what he'd like to drink. He started to order a vodka but thought better of it. "Water," he said.

The mural had been painted by Maxfield Parrish and was famous. It depicted King Cole sitting in the center of his court with a sly look on his face, while on either side of him his pages gave him knowing glances, their expressions ranging from amusement to annoyance. The people closest to the king appeared to have been gassed, which in fact they had. The gag, of course, was that his majesty had broken wind. For decades, New Yorkers had been asking rubes from out of town what they thought was going on in the mural, chuckling at their own sophistication as they revealed the answer.

The mural had always struck Ben as going to a lot of trouble and expense over a simple-minded fart joke.

Mrs. Conklin showed up at the same time the waiter arrived with Ben's water. As she sat down, she said she'd have a Beefeater martini straight up, with an olive. The man bowed and moved off.

Turning her attention to Ben, she gave him a dazzling smile. "Hope I didn't keep you waiting too long, Lieutenant?"

"No problem," he said. "I just got here myself."

"Good." She wasn't what he'd expected. Stunning, which wasn't so much of a surprise, but seemingly refined, which was. Her features were classic, clean-lined with delicate bone structure and a wide mouth that was all the more alluring without makeup. She was wearing a light blue jacket and a gray skirt, and a small red hat was perched on her raven hair. The only jewelry he could see was a link bracelet of Florentine gold. He put her age at thirty, give or take a year.

She opened her handbag and took out a package of Winstons. The bag was black alligator and made him think of another one he'd seen, in the Plaza Hotel. She extended the pack. "Care for a cigarette?"

"No, thanks."

"Mind if I smoke?"

"No, go right ahead."

She put one in her mouth and fished a small gold lighter out of the bag, but before she could light it, another waiter appeared as if by magic, striking a match and holding it to the end of her cigarette. She blew out a stream of smoke and the man did his act in reverse.

"I've been trying to stop," she said. "But obviously not succeeding. It's really a dreadful habit. Did you ever smoke?"

"For a while, when I was younger."

"But then you quit. You must have great willpower." Her voice was lovely, even lower than it had sounded on the phone. He wondered whether smoking had contributed to its timbre and hoped not, for her sake.

"Was it hard for you? To quit?"

"No, not very." In fact, it had been easy. He'd spent days in a field hospital near Da Nang, tubes stuck in his arms and up his nose, out of his head most of the time but aware that the doctors were continuing to dig bits of jagged metal from his legs and his buttocks. When at last he'd come around and learned they'd be shipping him to a base hospital in Japan, he was no longer addicted to nicotine.

The only thing he'd smoked in the years since was an occasional joint, and he couldn't remember when the last time had been. Yes he could. It was with a girl in his pad on Bank Street. It was her name he couldn't remember.

The waiter returned with Mrs. Conklin's martini. When he left them, she raised her glass and treated Ben to another smile. "Cheers."

He returned the salute and drank.

"Is that vodka you're having?"

He put his glass down, shaking his head. "Water."

"Oh my, Lieutenant. Surely you have some vices?"

He smiled. "Surely I do."

"But drinking isn't one of them, either?"

He thought of what he'd put away earlier, in Grady's saloon. "Sometimes it is." Her gaze locked with his for a moment, and he felt a current pass between them. Her eyes were a soft gray. You had better, he told himself, keep your mind on your business.

She sipped her drink, watching him. "I'm glad we could get together. As I told you, I have some information I think will interest you."

"What is it?"

"My husband intends to do you harm."

"What makes you think so?"

"He's discussed it with his lawyer. He wants to bring a suit against the police department, and another one against you personally."

"On what grounds, that I spanked him?"

"He claims it was an unprovoked assault. He's got some flunky who was in the club when you knocked him around. Someone he's coerced into agreeing to testify. He says he's lining up more witnesses, as well, that a number of people saw you hit him."

"That's true enough, I did. But he hit me first. All I did was defend myself. Regulations still permit that, as far as I know."

"According to him, you attacked him."

"His lawyer believe that?"

"I doubt it. His lawyer knows him."

"But he does as he's told."

"Everybody around him does."

"Except you."

"Except me." She laughed, the sound as pleasant as when she spoke.

"Why are you telling me this?"

"Because you can help me."

"To do what?"

"Prove that he uses whores."

"Why should I do that?"

She stubbed out her cigarette in an ashtray. "Because there are other things I can tell you, as well, which makes it a fair exchange. You see, he's a rotten bastard." She said it as if she was describing her husband's hairstyle.

"I take it your marriage has a few problems?"

"A few."

"How long you been married?"

"Three years. I'm not his first wife."

"Tell me about it, starting with you."

She drained her glass, and there was the waiter again. Ben nodded to him to bring her a fresh drink. She got out another cigarette, and the waiter lit it before he moved away.

She exhaled smoke. The fingers holding the cigarette were slender and suntanned, the nails gleaming with red polish. "The beginning was when I came to New York, seven years ago. From Cincinnati. I'd done some modeling there, and a photographer sent some pictures of me to Eileen Ford. She had me come in, and the next thing I knew, I was on the cover of *Cosmo* in a Scavullo photograph. I thought I was pretty hot stuff."

Ben thought of Melissa Martin. Obviously Mrs. Conklin played in a different league. "Every girl's dream."

"Sure. I was getting five hundred an hour and I was booked out the window. And not just studio stuff, either. I went on locations from Bermuda to Rome, and my day rate was two thousand plus expenses. But then I got married, to an actor. The first clue that I'd made a mistake was at our wedding, at Stonehenge, in Connecticut. While the reception was going on, I caught him with his pants down, as they say. In our suite."

"Another woman."

"That would have been easier to take. It was his best man."

"What did you do?"

"Pretended it didn't happen. That I was mistaken. That it was my fault. Can you understand that?"

"I think so."

The waiter returned with another martini, and she waited until he'd picked up the empty and left them before she went on.

"I was foolish enough to think I could change him, but of course I couldn't. I tried for a while, and then I went to Mexico for a divorce. When I came back, some friends invited me to a party, and there was Barry. Looking for a trophy. I fit the bill."

Ben smiled. "He ask you for a resumé?"

She sipped the fresh drink. "Not Barry, he's a sight buyer. I looked good, I dressed well, I had class. I could also talk about most sub-

213

jects, and people liked me. Therefore I was suitable for a wife. He gave me a huge rush, and I was so grateful after my first disaster, I let myself stumble into another one that was even worse."

"You said he was married before?"

"To his college sweetheart. He married her because her father had made a lot of money in the fur business and adored his daughter. Barry figured the old man would bankroll him, which he did. When he died, he left his money to her. Barry screwed her out of her inheritance, and then he dumped her."

"They have kids?"

"Boy and a girl. He dumped them, too. Didn't fit his image. Or what he'd decided his image should be."

"And then he married you."

"At first, I thought it was wonderful. He bought me nice clothes and jewelry and took me everywhere."

"Showing you off."

"Yes. But after a while I began to realize what I was to him."

"A possession."

"Exactly. Something to use, the way he used everything else. When I objected, he told me he could get himself a better piece of ass just by picking up the telephone. After that, I kept my ears open and heard him doing it. He'd arrange to meet them in hotels, but he wasn't very discreet. Almost as if he wanted me to know, to show me who was in charge. We fought about it, and he beat me up."

"So why not divorce him, too?"

"Because I am the most naïve woman in New York. Which I'm sure you've already decided."

"I haven't, but why do you say so?"

"Before we were married, I signed a prenuptial agreement."

"You *what?*"

"You see? I told you, didn't I?"

"But why?"

"I didn't know what it was. He gave me a big stack of papers. Said they had to do with insurance, and also some property he wanted to put in my name."

"And you didn't read them."

"I read the first few, and they were what he said they were. Or at least they seemed to be. There were pages and pages of legal gobbledygook. So I just signed them."

He was quiet for a moment.

She looked at him over the rim of her glass. "I wasn't exaggerating, was I? Have you ever heard of anything so dumb?"

"You weren't dumb; you trusted him. You were decent, and he took advantage of you."

Her gaze was holding on him. He couldn't remember knowing a woman with gray eyes.

"What about witnesses?" he asked.

"There weren't any. But now the papers all have witnesses' signatures, and they're notarized."

"So you're hoping you can find a way to break the agreement. Starting with proof of your husband's moral turpitude."

"You sound like my lawyer."

"He thinks there's a chance?"

"He smells money."

"Of course." A lawyer is a lawyer is a lawyer.

She finished her martini, and as he started to ask whether she wanted another, she said, "No more, thanks. Two is my limit."

"You said you kept your ears open, heard what was going on."

"Yes. After the beating, I wouldn't let him near me. So he's been talking to his lawyer about getting rid of me, too. Meanwhile, he just picks up the phone, as he puts it."

"And who does he call?"

"A service called Panache. The owner is a woman named Martha Bellamy. She and Barry are buddies. She sends him girls all the time."

"Do you know any of their names?"

"Some. One is called Caroline. Barry was furious because she turned him off after a few dates, refused to see him again."

"And the others?"

"There's a Candice, and a Jennifer and a Melissa. And others. None of them ever seems to use a last name. Of course, all I picked up were the conversations he had on the phone in his study. I'm sure there were many more calls from his office."

"Did you make notes on what you heard?"

"Better than that." She opened her bag again and took out a manila envelope. "These are tapes of the calls he made from home. After I listened in the first few times, I had his phone bugged. Some of the conversations are with his lawyer; some are with Panache. And there's other stuff in there, too, about his business deals. I don't know why you're investigating him this time, but I have a hunch some of this could be helpful to you. At the very least, I think you'll find listening to them worthwhile."

"I'm sure of it."

"Will you help me?"

"As much as I can. Meantime, what's going to happen? You said he's planning to get rid of you."

"Don't worry about me, Lieutenant. As you can see, this time I'm a step ahead. I've put some money aside, and I have a place of my own that he doesn't know about. My lawyer thinks we can beat him."

"Good luck."

"Thank you." She dropped cigarettes and lighter into her purse, and for a moment the gray eyes held him once more. "My name is Barbara."

"I'm Ben."

She smiled. "Bye, Ben. Call me."

And then she was gone.

He called a waiter over and asked for the check. The waiter told him the lady had taken care of it. He got up from the table and glanced once more at the flatulent king as he left the room.

Out on the street, a smartly dressed man carrying an attaché case was standing beside the blocked Mercedes, his face red with anger. Ben stepped past him and unlocked the door of the Ford.

The man followed him, saying, "Is this your car?"

"Yes it is." He got in behind the wheel.

The man's face grew redder. "What do you mean by blocking me in like this? You think because you're a cop you own the city? I'm a taxpayer and I resent it."

Ben shut the door and started his engine.

The man rapped his knuckles against the glass.

Ben rolled down the window and said, "Sir, you were parked illegally."

"You think that gives you a right? What's your badge number?"

"It's twenty-three skidoo," Ben said, and drove away.

# 52

The tapes contained three hours of Barrett Conklin's telephone calls. Ben listened to them on a portable SONY in his office, hearing Conklin confirm his wife's opinion: he was a rotten bastard. As promised, some conversations involved hiring girls from Panache, and some were with his lawyer about his plans for ridding himself of Mrs. Conklin.

But there were many other calls as well, to people whose identities were not always revealed, and on subjects that were not always clear. What was clear was that the chairman of the Rockford Company was a master manipulator whose main pleasure in life was screwing anybody he could, literally and figuratively.

Ben made notes as he listened, jotting down names and places, stopping now and then to check what was on the tapes with the printout of Panache's customer records. When he finished, he put the tapes back into the envelope. Although he might not understand all of what he had heard, he knew someone who would. In the morning, he'd send this stuff down to Jack Strickland, the detective in the Fraud Bureau. To Strickland, it would be like gold, Ben was sure of it.

Dinner was a lukewarm cheeseburger and a beer. He ate without enthusiasm, then dropped the empty carton and can into his wastebasket and cleared his desk.

Laying out the list of Panache's customers, he opened Lisa Miller's john book and ran down the names to see whether any of them matched. As he'd expected, more than half the names turned up in both places. Lisa apparently had built her business on guys she'd met through Panache. Best of all, four of the names in her book were of men who had also been with Caroline Patterson. But none of them was Barry Conklin.

He sat back in his chair, thinking about it. There were questions he wished he could ask Monica—but where the hell was she? Once again he got out her number and reached for the phone.

This time, he had an answer on the first ring. "Hello?" The voice was male, and sounded young.

"Monica there? Lieutenant Tolliver calling, Police Department."

"No. You haven't found her?"

"What? Who's this?"

"Derek Williams. I'm her friend, the one who reported her missing."

"When did you do that?"

"Yesterday. Are you with Missing Persons?"

"No, I wanted to talk to her about something else."

"I called yesterday morning. She's been gone almost a week now."

"You live with Miss Darrin?"

"We share the apartment, yes."

"When did you first find her gone?"

"I got home from work Tuesday night and she never showed up."

Ben made notes. "Where's work?"

"The Embassy Theater, on Forty-fifth Street."

"What do you do there?"

"I'm an usher."

"What time did you get home?"

"Little after twelve."

"That the usual?"

"Yes."

"And Monica?"

"She works nights for a telephone-answering service. Most of the time she's home by two, but sometimes she gets stuck, when her relief doesn't show up."

"Go on."

"But the next morning when I woke up, she still wasn't here. When I didn't hear from her, I was worried."

"You call the place she works?"

"No. I don't know their number. See, it's a confidential service. For celebrities? People like that. Monica said she had to keep it a secret."

"Then what?"

"Then I went to work, and when I got home that night, she still wasn't here. The next morning, I thought maybe she went to see her family, without telling me. So I called them, but they hadn't heard from her, either. Then I called Missing Persons."

"Monica tell you she was having any problems?"

"No. I mean, nothing out of the ordinary. She's been trying to get parts in the theater, or TV, and not doing very well. But no real problems."

"Anything else? She say anything about the job?"

"No, she never talks about it."

"Okay. I want you to think about anything that might be an idea where she went. Anything at all. Then call me. It's Lieutenant Tolliver, Sixth Precinct. Got that?"

"Yes sir."

Ben gave him the number.

"Lieutenant?"

"Yes?"

"You think something's happened to her?"

"I don't know."

"Jesus. This city—"

"Yeah. This city." He hung up.

She had warned him, and he'd sloughed her off. Don't worry about it, Monica.

Shit. Where was she now?

218

But slow down. Maybe *nothing* had happened. Maybe she'd just had enough of Derek and the job and skipped.

And maybe she hadn't.

He couldn't push it with Bellamy—not yet, anyway. If he did, he'd be telling her Monica had been a pipeline. Better to give it a day or two more, see whether she showed up.

He rubbed his eyes, then went back to the list of names, comparing them with the johns in Lisa's book. An hour later, he quit, fighting to stay awake.

What a bitch this had turned out to be. The Patterson case was one nobody gave a shit about—not the police, not the DA, not even Caroline Patterson's family. The media had almost forgotten about it, as well; there were other homicides to cover, other people dying.

Lately, there were times when he'd begun to doubt the department, and himself. He knew one reason was that he was experiencing what all cops go through: a feeling deeper than frustration—a fear that his efforts were in vain, that the problems were too many, the war unwinnable. For every bad guy you put away, there were a thousand more, sneering at you while they robbed, beat, raped, killed. With that came a growing conviction that you'd wasted your life, that it was too late to find a new direction.

The other doubt, concerning the department, was just as debilitating. This force you'd always believed in, this power, this ironclad protector of the people, had revealed itself to be like any other human institution. It had its share of corruption and incompetence, indifference and stupidity, fueled by greed and political ambition. No wonder so many cops ate the gun.

He rubbed his eyes again, wishing he could get some sleep.

There was a knock on his door, and Ed Flynn stuck his head in. "Lou, George Keller's on the phone, from the Two-eight. He says they got a dead hooker on One Hundred Twenty-first Street. She had your card in her shoe."

# 53

B rian Holland was in an expansive mood. Wearing a new tuxedo
Dunhill's had finished for him only a few days before, he strode
through the lobby of his apartment building to the waiting limousine, responding to the doorman's salute with a jaunty wave.

As he crossed the sidewalk, the chauffeur came to attention and
opened the door for him. Brian got into the car and settled back on
the seat, thinking that things were turning out well, after all. But
then, he'd always known they would.

For one thing, that absurd Patterson case had more or less blown
itself out. He could thank the NYPD for that. With their typical
bumbling, the investigation was going nowhere—which was the
cops' fault, not his. No one could point a finger at Brian Holland
over that. His reputation—and his political career—wouldn't be
stained by it. He'd even sent word to the Manhattan chief of detectives that he appreciated their efforts, saying he thought the lieutenant heading the task force was doing a fine job, under the
circumstances. It was a nice touch.

The truth, of course, was something else. Tolliver was an idiot who
could have made plenty of trouble, if he hadn't been pulled up short.
Linking Patterson to the murder of the other whore would have
ignited a firestorm, with the media going crazy, and Spencer Patterson infuriated. If there was one thing Brian did not need at this point,
it was for the wrath of one of New York's political powers to come
down on his head.

Now, thank God, he was on to bigger and better things. Getting
the Park Avenue rape was a marvelous stroke of good fortune. The
case was due to go to the grand jury this coming week, and an
indictment was certain.

This time, lurid coverage by TV and the newspapers was doing
him a favor. People were outraged by the vicious attack on the
physician's wife, as well they should be. The teenagers who had
beaten and raped her had been nothing more than savages. Only the
blacks were supporting them—and that was because the perpetrators
were also black, not because anyone with half a brain could think
they were innocent.

The cops on this one were excellent. Seasoned detectives with the
Manhattan Sex Crimes unit, they had both videotaped the boys'

confessions and gotten written statements from them. They'd also recovered one of the weapons, a homemade jimmy that had been ground down from a crowbar. It had been used to smash the woman's face in. There were photographs, too, before and after shots of the victim that were shocking to look at.

Robbery, assault, rape, attempted murder, every charge backed by indisputable proof, and all of it providing a wonderful opportunity for Brian to show off his courtroom skills before a huge audience. The case was better than good—it was perfect. And it was a long way from dealing with murdered whores no decent person could give a damn about.

Best of all, credit for its successful prosecution would go to Brian alone. There was a whole battery of ADAs working on it, but he was the senior prosecutor on the case. He would conduct the courtroom examinations; he would answer questions from the media. As far as the world was concerned, the white knight responsible for seeing that the evildoers got what they deserved would be Brian Holland. And no one else.

The limousine pulled to a stop in front of Stephanie's apartment house and Brian went in to fetch her, a spring in his step. Her place was only a few blocks from his, and the dance wasn't far, either—at the Waldorf. But Brian had hired the car because no one walked in New York if they could help it, especially at night. And also because there was no telling who might be at the entrance of the hotel when he and Stephanie arrived. It wouldn't do for them to go by cab; taxis were what you rode in for business, never on social occasions.

She was bubbling over when she answered the door. And looking quite beautiful, he thought. Her sandy blond hair was swept up and held in place by a pearl-studded barrette, the ends cascading down the back of her neck. She had on a red chiffon gown that was cut low to show off her ample breasts, and more pearls graced her throat.

They made, he mused, a stunning couple.

The event tonight was the Children's Ball, a charity gala held annually and always well attended. The mayor would be there, and the Manhattan DA, and a number of city council members, as well as people from television and the newspapers. Not merely reporters, but the executives who owned and ran the communications business.

Plus partners in leading law firms, and the heads of major corporations—New York's movers and shakers. Accompanied by their wives, they'd be amiable and relaxed as Brian moved deftly among them, making sure he met those he didn't know, and that he renewed acquaintances with those he did. Spencer Patterson would be there, as well—this was an ideal time to meet him.

221

It was also an ideal time for him to consolidate his relationship with Stephanie. Tucked away in the watch pocket under his cummerbund was a two-karat solitaire from Tiffany's. The stone was large enough to be impressive, but modest enough not to be gauche. She'd be thrilled, and that was another thing he was sure of.

When the chauffeur pulled the limo out into the stream of traffic, Brian took Stephanie's hand in his. "I can promise you," he said, "this will be an evening to remember."

# 54

The entire block was closed off, from Lenox Avenue on the east end to Adam Clayton Powell Boulevard on the west. Police barricades had been set up, and uniformed officers were preventing civilians from entering, either in vehicles or on foot. Ben identified himself, and a cop moved a blue-painted sawhorse aside so he could drive through. "Down the block on the right-hand side," the cop said. "You can't miss it."

Which was true; patrol cars and an ambulance were parked in the middle of the street, and the police had rigged portable floodlights to illuminate a vacant lot. On the opposite side of the street, residents of the squalid apartment houses were standing on the sidewalk and sitting on their front steps, gawking at the activity. Boom boxes were blasting rock and R&B, a dissonant clash of Prince and Aretha Franklin.

Ben pulled the Ford in among the other vehicles. As he got out of the car, he saw cops and technicians milling about some thirty feet in from the sidewalk, their forms casting long shadows in the garish light. Clipping the leather billfold containing his shield and ID to the collar of his windbreaker, he approached the group.

As in any similar open space in the city's poorer neighborhoods, the lot was strewn with litter. There were bricks and bottles and cans and chunks of plaster and heaps of garbage and the skeleton of a stripped car and pieces of rotting wood and a rusted bathtub, all of it making the scene strangely surrealistic. Ben picked his way through the debris until he reached the cluster of cops.

One of them looked up as he approached and moved slowly toward him. Tall and somber, with black skin and prematurely gray

222

hair, George Keller walked with a slouch, hands thrust into the pockets of his raincoat. Ben had known him almost as long as he'd been on the job. They'd never worked as partners, but at one time both had been in patrol cars out of Midtown South. Now Keller was also a detective, second grade.

Ben said hello, and Keller returned the greeting with a nod. He pulled a card out of his pocket. "Looks like you lost a contact."

Ben took the card, holding it up to the light and seeing his name and phone number on it. "You gonna need this, George?"

"No, it's all yours. The lady's over here."

He put the card into his pocket and followed Keller to where the men were gathered around an object on the ground. When he stepped closer, he saw the body of a young black woman, lying on her back. Her throat had been cut, so deeply it was nearly severed, only a few threads of tissue still connecting her head to her neck. She lay sprawled across a low mound of rubble, her legs long and slender, her thighs encased in skintight red spandex shorts. Her blouse was also red, but that was because it had been drenched in her blood. Some of the cloth on the sleeves was still white. He felt a twinge as he recognized her.

Even in death, her face seemed beautiful to him. With its delicate cheekbones and generous mouth, it was a model's face. Just as her slim body and graceful movements would have suited her to walk the runways of couturiers' salons, instead of the streets.

But that was sentimentalism, wasn't it? It occurred to him that he didn't know her last name.

"She familiar?" Keller asked.

"Oh yeah, I knew her. Name's Shirley. At least that was her street name. She used to give me things now and then."

"You know anything else about her?"

"Came from Georgia, I think. Also she hung out with a girl named Louise. And that's about it. I don't know who her pimp was."

"We'll send her prints to NYSID," Keller said. "She'll have a rap sheet like the phone book."

"Yeah. I'll ask around. Maybe one of the other girls knows something."

"Uh-huh."

"You find anything besides my card?"

"No. Only reason we found that was, it was stuck to the inside of her shoe."

"That's where she kept her money," Ben said. "Sometimes I gave her a few bucks for information, and that's where she put it."

"Wasn't none when we got here. Wasn't nothing on her but the card."

"Who found her?"

"Don't know. Somebody called nine-one-one, said there was a body."

"Yeah, well. Anything I can do, give me a call."

Keller's dark face was impassive. "Sure, Ben."

Ben sensed what the detective was thinking. This had to be degrading, having the white lieutenant come up here to see the dead black chick lying among the other bits of refuse. Both men understood that the entire incident would provide no more than a mild diversion for the neighborhood, something to hold people's interest only until the ambulance drove away with the corpse. If a whore's life was worth nothing in New York, a black whore's life was worth less.

Ben took a last look at Shirley. Then he turned and made his way back through the rubble to where his car was parked. He knew, as did Keller and every other man in the lot, that this was almost surely the end of it. She could have been murdered by her pimp, or by a john, or by another hooker—the possibilities were endless. But the chances were, the cops would never learn the truth.

Instead, they'd get an ID from Albany and if possible contact her family in Georgia. If the family would pay for it, the body would be embalmed and shipped home for burial. If not, it would go to Potter's Field on Long Island.

Meantime, the case would stay on the Two-eight's books forever; a homicide was never closed unless the case was solved. In Ben's own precinct, there were whole drawers full of files on open homicides, some of them going back fifty and sixty years. The perpetrators were surely dead themselves by now, but the case files would live on— yellowing scraps of paper, garish photographs of broken bodies.

When he reached the end of the street, a cop again moved a barricade to let him pass, and he drove onto Adam Clayton Powell Boulevard and turned left. At this time of night, he'd make good time going back down to the Village. But first he wanted to call Flynn. There was a phone booth down the block, in front of a store that sold fried-chicken takeout. He pulled over to the curb and got out of the car, digging into the pocket of his corduroys for change.

# 55

As Brian had promised, the evening was memorable. The ball was held in the Empire Room, which had been lavishly decorated with silver and red bunting and huge bouquets of fall flowers. The orchestra played melodies from many of Broadway's biggest hits, tunes from "My Fair Lady" and "South Pacific" and "Hello Dolly," among others. The crowd glittered, the men in black tie, the women in colorful gowns and sparkling with jewelry.

Brian danced often, maneuvering Stephanie so that during breaks in the music he'd be in a position to engage important people in ostensibly impromptu conversations. One of his Princeton classmates introduced him to Ethan Fedorko, a top-level CBS executive whose reputation as a programming genius was growing rapidly, and Fedorko in turn introduced him to Mark Wingate, the commentator slated to take over when Dan Rather was finally put out to pasture.

As Brian chatted with Wingate, he casually mentioned that he'd be heading the prosecution team in the Park Avenue rape case, noting with satisfaction how impressed Wingate seemed. Stephanie stood nearby, goggle-eyed that a well-known TV personality was not merely interested in what Brian had to say, but clearly fascinated.

And small wonder. Brian was brilliant, if he did say so himself. He told Wingate his main concern, overriding all others in importance, was to see that the black teenagers received a fair trial.

Wingate nodded sagely. "You're right, of course. That's vital. Not only for their sake, but for society's."

"Absolutely," Brian said. "No matter how strongly feelings may run against them, it's my duty to do everything in my power to protect their rights."

"Commendable. Very commendable. Particularly when all most prosecutors seem to care about is getting a conviction."

"That's not how I view my responsibilities," Brian said. "What I want to see is justice done."

"Of course. What was your name again?"

"Holland. Brian Holland." He said it slowly, making sure the commentator got it. Later on, when the case went to trial, Wingate would feel he knew the leader of the DA's team on a personal basis and respect him for his fairness. Like most journalists, whether they were in electronic or print media, the commentator was obviously a knee-jerk liberal, more concerned with the rights of defendants than with those of their victims.

"Many people believe they may not even be guilty," Wingate said. Brian handled it deftly. "Especially in the black community. But of course the Reverend Dan Marydale gets everybody stirred up, convinces them every time a black man goes to trial, it's a white conspiracy."

"True, but I must say I feel just as deeply as you do that a fair trial is the number-one priority."

"It certainly is," Brian said, thinking, You pompous asshole. There isn't the faintest doubt those niggers are guilty. But even if they weren't, I'd still get a conviction. The city is frightened to death of black criminals, and especially black rapists who prey on white women. When this is over, I'll be a hero. And you, Mr. Wingate, will help to make me famous.

"Brian!"

He turned to see the DA himself approaching, looking slightly befuddled, as usual, his halo of white hair framing his bald head, and with his lumbering wife in tow.

Brian smiled broadly. "Hello, sir. Good evening, ma'am. You both know Mark Wingate, I'm sure. And Stephanie, of course."

Having the old man recognize him so warmly at a social function was another feather in his already heavily laden cap. Wingate would be even more sure to remember him now, the bright young prosecutor who not only considered defendants' rights to be of great importance, but who was held in high esteem by the Manhattan district attorney personally. Even as he exchanged pleasantries, Brian's gaze picked out others he wanted to speak with, powerful people on whom he might someday call for help in advancing his career.

After a few minutes of perfunctory chatter, he heard the orchestra strike up "Begin the Beguine." The song was a favorite of Brian's, even if the composer had been a Yale man. Excusing himself, he swept Stephanie out onto the floor, expertly moving her toward a federal judge he knew slightly. The judge was talking with Spencer Patterson, thus providing a perfect opportunity for yet another key introduction.

As they whirled to the strains of the music, Brian felt immensely pleased with himself. When the evening ended, he'd take Stephanie back to her place and spend the night there. He could imagine the look on her face when he slipped the ring out of his pocket and presented it.

# 56

E d Flynn answered Ben's call, telling Tolliver Art Weisskopf had been in, looking for him.

It was hard to hear, with the Harlem street noise reverberating in the small semi-enclosed glass phone booth. "What's up?" Ben asked. "He get something?"

"I don't know," Flynn said. "He seemed kind of reluctant to talk about it, so I didn't push him."

"Where is he now?"

"Grady's. Said he'd be back in a half hour."

"Spadone with him?"

"No, haven't heard from him."

Ben said he was on his way to the precinct, and to tell Weisskopf to wait for him.

"Who was it, up there?" Flynn asked.

"A girl who used to give me information," Ben said. "Somebody cut her throat and dumped her. I'll see you as soon as I get back." He hung up.

As he started to step away from the booth, he felt a hard object prod the small of his back. A voice said, "Don' move, motherfucker. Or you be a dead honkie."

Ben froze, his hands at waist level.

"Keep on lookin' straight ahead," the voice said. "Put your hands up on the wall there, one on each side the phone."

Ben did as ordered, and out of the corner of his left eye, he saw a black hand reach in and strip him of his watch. He tensed, and the hard object jabbed him.

"I told you, don' move. I ain't gone tell you again. Next time, I just blow a hole in your white ass."

The hand patted him down, starting with his chest and sides and stopping at one trouser pocket to relieve him of some bills, and at the other to take his keys.

"This your car here, honkie? This piece a shit? I was you, I be ashamed to drive it."

The hand continued its exploration, and Ben felt a tug as it removed his wallet from his back pocket.

"Well now, lookit here. You the *po*lice? Ain't that a fuckin' joke.

Now I got me a badge. I gone be the baddest dude goin'. Hey—where's your gun?"

Once again, the hand patted him, this time under his armpits and on his rump. "Goddamn, man. Don' you know the law say you suppose to carry all the time? What you do, leave it in some pussy's bed? Kinda cop are you, man? I oughta re*port* you. Now you stay there, hear? Don' move or I blow your ass clean away. Later, motherfucker."

Ben felt another jab in the small of his back, and then the pressure was gone. There was the clack of heels on the sidewalk, going away from him in the direction of the Ford.

He whirled and dropped into a crouch, snaking the Smith out of the ankle holster inside his left shin and cocking it, holding the pistol in both hands and bringing it up to eye level, his legs wide apart in a combat stance, all of it in one swift motion.

The black man was bulky, wearing a dark jacket and a black cap, carrying a Tec-9 in his right hand.

"Hold it!" Ben shouted. "Stop right there!"

The man spun around, the heavy automatic already wildly spraying bullets as he turned. The sound of the shots was startlingly loud.

Ben put one in the guy's belly and saw him double over, then fired two more double-action. The .38 slugs punched into him, sending him reeling backward against the car. He tried to raise the gun and Ben took careful aim and shot him again.

The man collapsed against the right-front wheel of the Ford, blood pumping from the holes in his body. He slid down until he lay half on the sidewalk, half in the gutter, his hands and feet twitching.

Stepping over to him, Ben bent down and retrieved his wallet from the inside pocket of the man's jacket. As he straightened up, he saw that a crowd was gathering, black faces glowering at the white man standing over the bloody form on the sidewalk.

There were mutterings from the onlookers, and then angry shouts.

"Goddamn, he shot him!"

"You see it? You see what the motherfucker done?"

"Shot him!"

Ben held up his open wallet so that his shield would show, at the same time waving the Smith. "Police officer," he called out. "Don't come any closer."

"Fuckin' murderer," somebody yelled.

"Kill the white bastard."

They edged toward him, teeth bared, eyes gleaming with hatred. Mostly they were young men, some of them little more than kids, a few women among them as well.

228

Ben shoved his wallet back into his pocket and leveled the pistol. How many rounds did he have left—one? Two? Whatever, it wouldn't be enough. He was aware that a couple of youths had slipped around the Ford; it would only be a matter of time before they rushed him.

Bending down again, he picked up the gunman's Tec-9 from the sidewalk. He knew the piece had a 36-round magazine—there had to be at least a dozen cartridges still in the clip. Stuffing the Smith into his waistband, he held the automatic in both hands.

The crowd moved closer, at its center a young guy with a fade haircut, wearing a Knicks jacket and white sneakers. One hand was in his jacket pocket. "Yo, motherfucker," he snarled. "You good as dead."

"Kill him, Hobart," somebody shouted. "Shoot him!"

*Shoot* him? The kid had a gun? Ben trained the Tec-9 on him. "Hobart!" Ben yelled. "Put your hands on your head, or you get it next."

The youth spat. "Fuck you, whitey." But as he looked at Ben's eyes and then at the muzzle of the heavy automatic, he slowly raised his hands.

There were more shouts from the crowd, and then Ben heard another sound in the distance, barely discernible at first, but rapidly growing louder, the *who-ee-whoo-ee* of an approaching police siren.

The patrol car screeched to a stop inches behind the Ford, its roof lights flashing, but even then the crowd did not back off. Two cops, one black, one white, jumped out of the car and ran up to the people on the sidewalk. The black officer had been driving. He was carrying a nightstick, his partner a pump shotgun.

Seeing the youth with his hands atop his head, the driver shouted, "You! Stay where you are. Rest of you get the hell out of here!" He brandished the nightstick. "Go on, damn it, break it up. Out of here, now!"

Hobart suddenly dropped his hands and turned to run.

The cop's response was instantaneous. He slammed his stick against the side of the young man's head, the sound like the crack of a bat connecting with a fastball. Hobart's head jerked from the impact and he fell to the sidewalk, his face split open from his ear to his eye, blood pouring from the gash.

The second cop pushed the muzzle of the riot gun into the kid's face and then searched him, pulling a chrome-plated revolver from a pocket of his jacket. "You're under arrest, you dumb shit! You have the right to remain silent . . ."

The crowd drew back now, muttering, as the driver threatened them with the nightstick. "Go on," the cop yelled. "Get out! Hear? Break it up!"

They didn't disperse, but simply backed away, clustering around the front of the fried chicken takeout and the other stores along the street, all eyes on the scene at the curb.

Ben stood where he was, next to the body of the man he'd shot. Blood had soaked the dark jacket and was dripping into the gutter. The man's head was propped against the car's front wheel and his eyes remained open, as if he were staring back at the crowd.

Seconds later more sirens sounded, but Ben held the Tec-9 out front until the additional cops swarmed onto the sidewalk.

# 57

"I have a headache," Stephanie said.

Brian looked at her. Like all women, she could be a pain in the ass at times, and this evidently was going to be one of them. "I'll see if I can get you an aspirin."

"I don't want an aspirin; I want to go home. My period started this afternoon, and I've got cramps, as well as the headache."

Christ. One of the most important events of the season, and this fool decides to menstruate. He kept his tone even, not letting his irritation show. "It isn't even twelve o'clock, Steffie. As long as we're here, couldn't you just sort of hold on for a while?"

She set her mouth in a show of petulance. "I really don't feel well, Brian."

For an instant, he thought of bundling her into the limo and having the driver take her home, but then he realized that wouldn't do. People might think there was trouble between them, that they'd had a spat or something. Shit.

They were standing in the middle of the dance floor and her face had taken on that stubborn look it wore when she'd made a decision. It put him in mind of a spoiled child, which was exactly what Stephanie had been all her life and to a great extent still was.

He sighed, and made a last attempt. "This evening really is very important to me, you know."

"I have a headache, Brian. And cramps."

Even under these circumstances, he maintained steely control, managing a small, tight smile. "All right, darling. Let's get your things."

They made their way through the beautifully dressed throngs, couples dancing to the strains of "I Get a Kick Out of You," another of Brian's Cole Porter favorites. As he collected Stephanie's wrap and steered her through the lobby, he tried to console himself by reflecting on the contacts he'd made tonight, the people he'd spoken with and impressed.

As for how he could expect the remainder of the night to turn out, Robert Burns had been right: "The best laid schemes o' mice and men/Gang aft a-gley." Or as they'd parodied the line at Princeton, "The best planned lays . . ."

They arrived at Stephanie's apartment house only minutes later, and Brian had the driver wait while he took her inside and escorted her in the elevator up to her floor. As she put her key into the lock, he gave her a brief kiss and a pat on the arm, trying not to let his annoyance show. Annoyance? Hell, he was furious.

But he continued to hold his emotions in check. "Night, darling. Hope you feel better tomorrow."

"Will you call me?"

"Hm? Oh, yes. Of course."

She went inside and closed the door, and Brian took the elevator back down.

Minutes after that, he was in his own apartment. He turned on the lights and went to the bar, where he poured himself a glass of scotch, no ice or water, and gulped half of it. Then he took off his tuxedo jacket and his tie and threw them aside, slumping into a chair and drinking more of the whiskey, his mood growing steadily darker.

Goddamn it. He'd expected this to be a night of triumph, and instead . . .

But hadn't it been? The way he'd registered with Mark Wingate was alone worth the entire affair. To say nothing of the other introductions, the other contacts he'd made with influential people.

It was only the part with Stephanie that hadn't turned out the way he'd wanted it to. He reached under his cummerbund and took the ring from his watch pocket. Getting to his feet, he stepped over to his desk and opened a drawer, tossing the ring into it and slamming the drawer shut.

Frustration was eating at him. It always bothered him when something he'd made preparations for went off the track, and he'd been counting on spending the night in her bed. Maybe he ought to go into the other room and masturbate. That would at least get rid of the tension, if only for a short time. As he stood there, debating, his gaze fell on the leather-bound book in which he kept telephone numbers.

Should he? Even though whores were despicable creatures, they did serve a certain useful purpose when the situation demanded. And besides, when one had sufficient money, the quality of what was available was really quite high. In fact, you could buy not only beauty but enthusiasm, as well.

On the other hand, they could give you terrible problems. Not only did you open yourself up to the possibility of blackmail but, far worse, there was the danger of contracting disease. Brian had a deep fear of venereal infection. Yet that hazard could also be avoided, if you were careful, took precautions.

He struggled with the question for a long time, as conflicting emotions tugged at him, filling his mind with both desire and guilt. Trying to decide what to do, he chewed his lip until it was sore.

In the end, he sat down at the desk and drained the last of the scotch from his glass, then leafed through the book for the number he wanted. When he found it, he reached for the phone.

As soon as he heard the first ring, he was aware that his black mood had disappeared, and that the questions that had seemed so difficult a few minutes ago had been easily resolved. Now there was only a sense of excitement.

And anticipation.

# 58

Over three hours passed before Ben could leave the headquarters of the Two-eight. There were forms to fill out, and a detailed report of the shooting to be written. He made the report as succinct as possible, taking care to state only facts, putting down nothing that a zealous trial lawyer could later call opinion or claim was evidence of bias. He made no reference to the reason he'd gone to Harlem in the middle of the night, although of course he had informed the precinct commander of his purpose.

He also waited while the cops got a statement from Hobart, the self-appointed leader of the mob that had formed after the shots were fired. Hobart's head had been stitched up in the emergency room at Mount Sinai, and then the police had brought him to the precinct house. He was being held on a weapons charge, but the more important reason for arresting him was that he had been a witness to the gun battle, and the cops wanted that statement.

After considerable prodding, Hobart gave a generally accurate account of what had happened: a black man wearing a dark jacket and a cap had held a gun on another man who was making a phone call and robbed him. The man who was robbed was white. He identified himself as a cop and told the robber to stop. There was shooting by both men. The man in the cap was killed. Hobart had been in front of the fried-chicken takeout at the time and had seen all of it.

A clerk typed up the statement and Hobart signed it. As it turned out, Hobart's name was Delano Brown, but he used Hobart because he thought it sounded better.

The cops also got a make on the dead man. He was Terrance Bennett, alias nine other names, and he was on parole from Stormville, where he'd done six for armed robbery, second trip. The police had been looking for him in connection with a number of other robberies, as well as for several incidents of parole violation. In two of the robberies, gypsy cabdrivers had been shot to death.

After finishing the paperwork, Ben called Ed Flynn and filled him in, then phoned Captain Michael Brennan at his home in Brooklyn Heights, rolling the zone commander out of bed to apprise him of what had happened. Brennan said he'd see Ben at the Sixth in a few hours.

The commander of the Two-eight was a uniformed black captain named Banks. He took Ben into his office and told him to sit down, then poured two paper cups full of gin. Ben knocked his back in one long gulp, and the captain immediately refilled the cup.

"How you feeling?" Banks asked.

"Lousy," Ben said.

"First time?"

"No."

"But it still ain't easy, is it?"

Ben swallowed more gin, taking it slower this time, grateful for the warming, numbing effect. "No," he said. "It's not."

Banks slouched in his chair. His attitude was casual, but he was watching Ben closely. "You know, you did the city a favor, taking out that piece a dogshit. If you didn't, it'd be you in a rubber bag, 'stead of him."

"Yeah, I guess so."

"Only way to look at it," the captain said.

Of course it was. But the experience of killing another human being, seeing him lying in a gutter, his lifeblood running out of the

233

holes in his body, was sickening. It didn't matter that the man was a professional criminal, almost surely a murderer, and that what the captain had said was true. Ben had killed him, and the knowledge of it, the shock of realization, was only now coming into focus. He felt like throwing up.

"Course, you're gonna catch a lot of shit. You know that, too, don't you?"

Ben nodded.

"Folks up here don't care who he was, what he done. Only thing counts, he was black. And you're a white cop. The TV, the newspapers, they'll play it big. And that fat motherfucker Dan Marydale, he'll be in it up to his ass. He loves shit like this. He'll get the people crazy. Some of 'em are too fuckin' dumb to see what he is, and with the others, it don't matter; they just want to yell how they get beat on by whitey. You have to know all that up front. 'Fore it comes down on you."

"Thanks, Cap," Ben said.

"Yeah. Have another drink, Lieutenant." Before Ben could refuse, Banks leaned forward and topped off his cup once more. "And then go get some sleep. You're on that other thing, right? Big shot's daughter hookin' in the Plaza and got killed?"

Ben's eyebrows lifted, and Banks smiled, seeing the reaction.

"How'd you know that?" Ben asked.

"What, that she was hookin'?"

"Yes."

"Hell, man, anybody with half a brain could figure it. But on top a that, people talked about it. You makin' progress?"

"Not much."

"Uh-huh. How long you gonna be on it?"

Ben knew what he meant; at some point, Brennan and Galupo would decide the trail was cold, and that there were more pressing matters to occupy Tolliver's time. No matter how many detectives there were in the NYPD, it was never enough. Unless Ben got an unexpected break, the Patterson case eventually would be quietly pushed aside, relegated to a file that would gather dust and begin to molder, just one more open homicide in the annals of New York crime. Weisskopf and Spadone would resume their assignments at Midtown North, and Ben would go back to running his precinct squad. Caroline Patterson would be forgotten.

"I don't know," Ben said.

"You got much help?"

"Two detectives."

*"Two?* That's all?"

"Yes."

Banks chuckled softly. "Tells you somethin', don't it?"

"I guess it does." Ben downed the gin. This last one seemed almost smooth. "Say, Captain?"

"Yeah?"

"The girl whose body was found tonight. Shirley?"

"What about her?"

"If her family can't afford to bring her home, I'd like to kick in something toward that."

Banks's face was expressionless. "Yeah. George Keller'll handle it. He's up in the squad room. You can see him 'fore you go."

# 59

Waiting for the girl to arrive was harder than Brian had thought it would be. He hung his tuxedo jacket and tie in a closet in his bedroom and put on a yellow silk paisley robe, studying himself in the mirror and deciding he looked rather sophisticated. A little like Cole Porter, in fact, according to pictures he'd seen of the composer. Some of Porter's melodies were still echoing in his head, reminders of the music the orchestra had played at the Waldorf.

Going back into the living room, he poured himself another drink before turning on the TV and sitting down to watch.

He switched channels a few times, finding nothing much on but a rash of old movies, some of them so ancient they were in black and white. In one of them, Jane Russell was cavorting about, and the sight of her enormous tits aroused him to an even greater extent. He tried to concentrate on the movie but couldn't; he kept trying to imagine what the girl he was waiting for would be like. Fantasizing a little, he saw himself opening the front door and finding Jane Russell standing there.

Brian didn't know why he'd finally decided to call for a girl, especially after the way he'd agonized over it, his emotions tearing at him. It would have been a lot simpler to masturbate, as well as a great deal cheaper. And he wouldn't be taking chances. Yet it wasn't the first time he'd gone through this. So why had he?

For one thing, there was his disappointment at not spending the night with Stephanie. But it was more than that, he realized. He was angry with her for cutting short an evening that was so obviously of great importance to him, for acting like a stubborn cow, insisting that he take her home because she'd gotten the curse.

That was certainly the right word for it, wasn't it? In fact, it had a much broader application than merely to describe one of women's less attractive bodily functions. You could use it as a label for their entire sex. What was the line in "My Fair Lady," the old Lerner and Loewe musical, when Professor Higgins mused over the very question Brian was struggling with now?

Ah, "Why Can't a Woman Be More Like a Man?" That was it. But Lerner had it wrong. Or Shaw did. Or both of them. The fundamental question was, Why do we need women at all?

Because at times they meet certain sexual requirements. And because they're decorative. And because they can be useful for social purposes, and for running a household—taking care of shopping and paying bills and supervising the staff, if you had one.

Brian would have a staff, as soon as he was married. Starting with a housekeeper, and then in time, as he grew richer through what he'd inherit from his parents, adding a maid and a cook. And perhaps a chauffeur. He was already the beneficiary of a trust fund established by his grandfather that would keep him quite comfortable whether he worked or not, and when his parents died, he'd really be well-off.

Which was necessary nowadays, if one aspired to a political career, as he did. Otherwise, forget it. He couldn't imagine living on the meager salaries paid to holders of public office. If it hadn't been for his private income, he'd have joined one of New York's great old white-shoe firms as soon as he finished law school, you could bet on that.

If he had, he'd surely be a partner by now. But that sort of life had its drawbacks, as well. Unless you were a renowned criminal lawyer—which Brian would never even consider; defending Mafia scum and other such miscreants was a distasteful prospect—you worked in anonymity, known only to clients and associates.

No, politics was where the action was, and the rewards. He'd be famous in time, he was sure of it—a wealthy philanthropist who served society as an elected official, noble, selfless, thinking only of how he could improve the daily life of his constituents.

While he bettered his own life by seizing the highest and most desirable prize of all: *power.*

He'd be like a Kennedy, in that respect. Or a Rockefeller. Rich, famous, and *powerful.* First, there would be the polishing of his reputation through his brilliant record as a prosecutor. And after that would come his first run for office. The House, perhaps. Maybe

236

even the Senate? God, it could give you a hard-on, just thinking about it.

Which brought him back to the subject of the girl. Where in hell was she, anyway? Maybe he ought to call again, just to be sure she—"

The buzzer sounded.

He got out of his chair and turned off the television set, then went to the bar and put his glass down. Outwardly calm, he moved deliberately as he went into the foyer, but he was aware that his heart was beating rapidly. He paused before the mirror for a quick look at himself and was reassured. Except for the damnable thinning of the hair over his forehead, he really was quite handsome. He smoothed the paisley robe and opened the door.

She was beautiful.

Tall and lissome, with auburn hair brushed casually to one side, wearing a gray coat and gloves, carrying a black leather tote bag. Her features were neatly sculptured, her eyes large and hazel brown. And her full mouth was curved in a warm smile. "Hi," she said. "I'm Brenda."

He moved aside, returning the smile and feeling a surge of sexual desire. "Come on in. Let me take your coat."

She stepped into the foyer, and he shut and locked the front door. When he'd put her things into the closet, he led her into the living room, keeping up a stream of chatter about the weather and the traffic and other meaningless subjects, simply to have something to say that would obscure his nervousness. No, not nervousness, he decided—*excitement.*

Stopping at the bar, he asked whether she'd like a drink. She was standing with her back to him, looking out the bank of windows that faced south, taking in the spectacular blaze of lights that illuminated Manhattan at all hours of the night. She said she'd have a little one, and that whatever he was having would be fine.

He poured two short glasses of Scotch, adding ice this time, and as he did, he glanced over at her surreptitiously, studying her figure. She had on a clingy green dress that showed off her rear end and her legs, and from what he could see, they were perfect. She was wearing stockings, not panty hose, and black patent leather pumps that accentuated her elegantly turned calves. Just looking at her was giving him an erection.

He brought their drinks over to where she was standing and handed her a glass, casually slipping an arm around her waist and joining her in looking out at the magic carpet of lights. She smiled at him and they touched glasses and drank.

237

"I'm so glad you called," she said. Her voice was soft and pleasant, and he thought he detected a Midwest accent, but he wasn't sure. "I am, too," he said. "Come and sit down."

He guided her to a deeply upholstered sofa that faced the same bank of windows, then went to the cabinet housing his CD player. The music he selected consisted of melodies built on exotic rhythms, starting with "Night Drums" and building toward the most erotic composition he knew, Ravel's *Bolero*. When the first pulsations issued from the quadraphonic speakers, he turned down the lights and joined her on the sofa.

They talked for a long time, getting to know each other, just as if this was a normal date. She told him she was an assistant marketing director at the U.S. subsidiary of Boujou, a French cosmetics company, and that she'd come to New York only two years ago from Madison, Wisconsin, where she'd grown up and gone to the state university. She'd earned an MBA and had joined the company immediately after finishing graduate school and moving to Manhattan.

Brian told her he was also in business, investment banking, but that his work was dull and boring and he'd much rather talk about her. It must be wonderful, he said, working for an international company in such a glamorous industry.

She responded well to that, going on animatedly about how they planned an average of six major shade promotions annually, supporting each one with an advertising budget of at least 5 million dollars. It was all directly linked to the fashion business, with new styles and new colors heavily influencing the themes of the promotions.

They used two advertising agencies, she said, dividing assignments between them and playing one against the other, keeping both in a state of competitive frenzy. Part of her job was helping to manage the campaigns as they were developed, giving the agencies direction. It was very stimulating and very gratifying, just what she'd dreamed working in New York would be like.

Going on dates like this was something a model friend had introduced her to, she explained, but she rarely did it—only when she was sure it would be with someone very special and very nice, such as tonight.

Which had to be bullshit, he thought, but hearing it pleased him nevertheless. While they talked, which consisted almost entirely of Brenda speaking and Brian listening, he held her hand and sipped his whiskey, one part of his mind imagining what was to unfold a little later on.

This was actually much better, in many ways, than a real date with

238

someone new. He didn't have to sit here and wonder whether it would end up with him getting what he wanted; that was never even an issue. It had all been resolved with his phone call to the service.

Instead, he could enjoy her company and admire her beauty, aware that she'd take off the clingy green dress whenever he felt like having her do so. In fact, knowing she understood unequivocally that she was there to please him, to serve him in any sexual act he might desire, was itself thrilling to contemplate. It added still another wonderfully spicy dimension.

Brian freshened their drinks, and when she sipped hers, she looked at him over the rim of her glass.

Her voice was throaty. "You know, you're really a very attractive man. I think I'm quite lucky that you asked me here tonight."

It was as if she'd stroked him physically. He was immediately hard as a rock, wanting her. It didn't matter whether what she'd said was a practiced speech, whether she was sincere or didn't mean a word of it. He didn't stop to consider any of those possibilities. She'd *said* it, and hearing the words come out of that lush mouth was inflaming to him.

She leaned toward him and brushed his lips with hers. He could smell her, a mixed fragrance of perfume and musk, the essence of female.

"Would you mind," she asked softly, "if I took off my dress? Just being here with you is getting me excited. You don't mind, do you? I really want you very much."

His pulse was pounding, and he could feel it in his chest and his temples and most of all throbbing in his crotch. "I don't mind," he said. He could also hear the hoarseness in his voice, making it sound as if the words were coming from a throat other than his own. "I don't mind at all. Go ahead, take it off."

She stood up, and slowly undid the buttons on the front of the dress, her eyes never leaving his. Then she drew the dress up over her head and tossed it onto a nearby chair.

The music of *Bolero* was in full stride now, driving toward a climax, increasing in volume and intensity. Brian sat transfixed, mouth partly open, heart hammering, his gaze slowly leaving the girl's face and moving down her body, seeing the full breasts supported by a lacy, ivory-colored bra, the smoothly rounded hips with tiny bikini pants of the same ivory shade. She was also wearing a black garter belt that reminded him of the Parisian beauties depicted by Toulouse-Lautrec in his marvelous paintings.

As he watched, her hands slowly unfastened the bra and pulled it away, freeing those glorious breasts and revealing large dusky nipples. She took a deep breath, heightening the effect, and then slipped off the panties, stepping out of them but leaving on her garter belt and the black pumps.

She held out her arms and Brian stood up, his erection like a wooden club pushing out the front of his robe as he went to her and enfolded her in his embrace. He kissed her hungrily, her mouth opening and her tongue caressing his, hot and wet.

"Please take me," she whispered. "I'm so excited now, I can't stand it. Please. I don't want to come until you're inside me."

He gripped her wrist and led her into the bedroom, his head whirling as he pushed her down onto the bed and tore away his clothes.

# 60

Art Weisskopf was in the bunk room, dead to the world. He was curled up in a ball with a blanket pulled over him, dressed except for his jacket and shoes, snoring loudly. When Ben tapped his shoulder, he awoke with a start, then rolled off the bunk and stumbled into the squad room. His eyes were red, and a dark stubble covered his narrow jaw.

Ben shoved a mug of coffee toward him. Weisskopf held the mug in both hands, blinking and yawning as he leaned against one of the metal desks. Joe Stone and his partner, Dan Harrigan, were the only other detectives in the room. Both were trying to appear wide awake, but it had been obvious to Ben when he returned to the precinct house that they'd been catnapping. He said nothing about it; he was so tired himself he could barely stand, running on memory and nerves.

Looking out the windows facing Charles Street, he saw that the night was turning gray. It would be dawn soon. "Where's Flynn?" he asked.

Stone answered: "Seeing that broad, the one who's married to a musician? He'll be back before long."

"What makes you think so?"

"Her old man'll be coming home, when the joint he plays in closes. She'll get Ed out of there before that."

Ben turned to Weisskopf. "Flynn said you had something?"

Art sipped coffee. "I don't know, Lou. Maybe. Can we talk in your office?"

Once they were inside, Ben closed the door and waved the detective to a chair.

Weisskopf dropped into the seat and scratched among the whiskers on his jaw. He smelled of sweat and sour booze. "I hear you had a rough time uptown."

"Rough enough."

Art shook his head. "Fucking animals. You all right?"

"Yeah, I'm okay."

"Who was the guy?"

"A second tripper the parole board put back on the street. Been out since July, got mixed up in a bunch of robberies the Two-eight knows about. In two of them, gypsy cabbies were shot."

"Jesus."

"What've you got?"

"Wait a minute, I'll show you. Stuff's in my locker."

He put his coffee mug down on Ben's desk and left the office, returning a few moments later with a paper bag. He sat down and opened the bag, taking out a pair of handcuffs and placing them on Ben's desk.

"Remember these?"

Ben looked at the cuffs. "From the Miller homicide on Fifty-seventh Street? Mendez's house?"

"Right. The lab sent them back here. Said there were no prints on them. No latents, nothing. I was gonna get them up to Midtown North, but I got to thinking. You know you can buy a pair like these in any gun store, no questions asked. So it's more or less impossible to trace them. But they've got serial numbers on them, right? Take a look."

Ben picked up the cuffs. Stamped into the metal on one of them was the number B107934, just above the maker's name, Smith & Wesson, Springfield, Mass. USA.

"Okay. So?"

"So I thought what the hell, at least I could give it a shot. I called Smith and they told me what I expected. Nobody bothers to record the numbers, because there's no reason to. The dealers just sell them and that's that. But then I thought, what about Smith's numbers? They must keep records, right? So I asked them about it, and I found out they do keep them, but all the numbers tell you is what batch went to what distributor, see? Except—"

Ben finished it for him. "The cops."

"Right." Weisskopf picked up the cuffs once more, holding them so that one dangled. "The company says this pair was part of a shipment sold to the New York Police Department just ten years ago this past April. Now, there's still no way to trace them to an individual cop, because the department doesn't record the numbers, either. But one thing we do know is that where they went from the factory was the NYPD."

Ben took the cuffs from him and looked at them more closely. As he'd noticed earlier, there were myriad tiny scratches in the metal, indicating years of wear. Whoever had owned them hadn't just thrown them into a corner somewhere and forgotten about them. He'd *used* them.

Ben hadn't thought much about it before this, but he now realized what the markings were telling him. If Lisa Miller had been in New York for only a year or so, she couldn't have given the handcuffs that much of a beating. For a long time, they'd belonged to somebody else, and the chances were pretty good that the somebody had been a police officer.

Weisskopf was watching him. The detective's eyes were still red-rimmed, but there was no suggestion of sleepiness in them now. "Well?"

Ben dropped the cuffs onto his desk. "Okay, so they probably first belonged to a cop. In fact, they almost certainly belonged to a cop. But so what? Maybe he lost them, or they were stolen, six months after he went on the job. Or maybe he died and his widow gave them away. Maybe they belonged to ten other people, before Miller got hold of them. Like you say, there's no way of knowing."

Weisskopf drank more of his coffee and then rubbed his jaw again. He put his mug down. "You're right, Lou. But maybe, just maybe, that's not the way it was. Maybe they did belong to a cop, and then when he moved up in rank, he didn't carry them anymore. Instead, he used them for something else. So then he gave them to somebody he often used them on. Somebody like Lisa Miller."

"Yeah," Ben said. "Maybe. And maybe if the cow ate cement, it'd shit bricks."

Weisskopf grinned. "You sound like one of those guinea philosophers. First time I heard that was from Spadone."

"Uh-huh. But it says a lot about your theory. Too many maybes."

"I suppose so. But if we get something else, it'll be interesting to see if there's a fit."

"True. If we get something else."

Weisskopf dropped the cuffs back into the bag and stood up. He stretched, and yawned once more. "You don't mind, Lou, I'm going back in the bunk room."

"No, go ahead."

"You look as if you could use some shut-eye yourself."

"Maybe a little later," Ben said.

Weisskopf left the office, taking with him his coffee mug and the paper bag containing the handcuffs.

When he was alone, Ben got a pad and a ballpoint out of a drawer, preparing to make notes. Then he closed his eyes for a moment, to rest them.

And was instantly asleep.

# 61

M artha got up at noon, taking an hour to do her exercises and bathe. She was feeling much better about life in general, now that things had quieted down and business was more or less back to normal. Last night had been outstanding; Panache had sent girls on twenty-six dates. At an average of a thousand dollars each, that made for a highly respectable gross—well above what she usually could expect.

After her bath, she dressed in beige silk lounging pajamas and went into the kitchen to see how brunch was coming along. She'd had the room redone only a few months ago, and the work had turned out spectacularly well. The kitchen had been somewhat old-fashioned when she bought the place, but now the area was one of the apartment's best features, and one of her favorite rooms. With its dramatic skylight and marble countertops and floor, and the hand-painted Portuguese tiles, the kitchen gave her a sense of luxurious well-being just to walk into it.

Chang was busy at the center work station, wearing a starched white jacket, chopping chives with a huge knife. He looked up as she entered and smiled broadly. "Morning, Missy."

"Hello, Chang. How's it doing?"

"Very fine. Mr. Patrick come soon, yes?"

"Yes. You can make Bloodies as soon as he gets here."

The diminutive servant bowed. "Already made, Missy. In fridge, nice and spicy."

"Wonderful."

"You like to try?"

"No, I'll wait for Patrick." If she had one now, she'd have another when he arrived, and that wouldn't do. One Bloody at lunch was all she permitted herself, *ever.* You didn't keep a figure like hers with anything less than iron discipline. A cigarette would be okay, however. Turning, she went back down the hallway and into the living room.

This was the centerpiece of the apartment. It was by far the largest area, a full two stories high, with towering windows that extended all the way to the ceiling, facing west. The room was done entirely in white: white walls, white carpet, white furniture. Even the concert grand was white.

At first, Lawrence, her decorator, hadn't understood, even implying that such a scheme would be in questionable taste. You know, he said, that's the sort of thing an Ivana Trump would do, or someone like *that.* But then Martha had explained the reason: she wanted white for its total neutrality, in order for her art collection to have maximum impact. The rest of the room would provide only background—comfortable, of course, but merely a neutral field—against which her Picasso and the Miró and the Rothenberg and all the rest of her treasures would stand out brilliantly.

And then predictably, when the room was finished, Lawrence practically had an orgasm over it. Probably *did* have, in fact. He kept walking back and forth, ogling the paintings and the statuary and clasping and unclasping his hands, making little cooing sounds, like some oversized cockatoo. After that, of course, it became *his* room, as if he'd had the idea for it right from the beginning.

Martha sat down on a Barcelona chair upholstered in white leather and took a cigarette from the box on the coffee table. Like everything else in here, the box was special, hand-carved from okapi bone. She lit the cigarette with her Dupont and exhaled a blue cloud. Smoking was bad enough—she rationalized by reminding herself it was one of her few vices—but the amount she smoked was truly terrible. For her to go through three packs a day was nothing.

She crossed her legs and looked up at the wall opposite the windows, where much of her best stuff was hanging. Gauguin's *Native Women with Flowers* was there, and the Picasso, which had been painted during the Spaniard's Blue Period. There was also a Rousseau she especially loved, a strange jungly scene in which a monkey sat on a tree limb, blithely unaware of the yellow and black python reaching for him from above. Just being here, enjoying the incredible atmosphere created by the art, was intensely pleasurable to her.

Which was why she'd put so much of her money into the objects in the room. It drove her accountant crazy, because even though

244

every bit of it was insured and appreciated in value as dependably as night fell, it was risky, he said. Art was too much like fashion—it could go in or out, you never knew. How much better to have most of your investments in blue-chip stocks.

"So what would I do then, Jules," she'd asked him, "hang IBM certificates on the fucking wall?"

But that was an accountant for you. When they buried Jules, his tombstone would have only numbers on it.

The buzzer sounded and she stubbed out the cigarette in a Waterford ashtray. The houseman came down the hall, wiping his hands on a towel, but Martha rose from her chair and waved him off. "I'll get it, Chang. That has to be Patrick. You handle the Bloodies."

When she opened the door, the first thing she saw was an immense bouquet of red roses. Patrick Wickersham thrust his head around them and said, "I thought these would go well in the living room."

That was the thing about him. No matter how much his affectations and his air of superiority might rankle her from time to time, he did have taste, and he was always thoughtful. "How beautiful," she exclaimed, and offered her cheek to be kissed.

When they were settled in the living room, with the roses nestling in a crystal vase, Chang brought their drinks. He bowed out again, saying, "Brunch ready fifteen minutes."

Patrick raised his glass. "Cheers," he said, and drank. He was in forest green today, a loden jacket and slacks of his customary gabardine, a white cashmere turtleneck giving him a sporty look.

"Cheers, Patrick. That was some busy night, wasn't it? Did you check the receipts?"

He smiled. "Twenty-seven thousand two hundred and fifty-five dollars."

"God, that must be a record."

"Oh, I'm sure. For a weeknight, at least. And fully a third of it from new clients. Which means if we hadn't relaxed and started taking them again, we would have brought in nine thousand less."

"Then it's a good thing we did."

"Decidedly. I'm also pleased at the way a number of the new girls have turned out. Apparently, some of them are showing real promise."

"So I gather. I had a bunch of thank-you calls last night, which is always nice. And only one complaint."

"Oh? Who from?"

"The tongue."

"Art Mayer?"

245

"Yes. I sent him Sheila and he called in a huff after she left him. He was all pissed off, said she was very uncooperative."

"Good Lord. I thought all the girls loved being with him. All he wants is to go down on them. They should pay him, if you want my opinion."

"He's developed a new interest. I spoke to her after he called and complained, reached her at home. She said he's discovered sixty-nine and she wouldn't go for it. Said he had a suspicious-looking sore on his dick."

"A chancre?"

"How in the hell would I know what it was? I didn't see it; Sheila just told me about it. Said it was all raw and red."

"Sounds ghastly."

"Yes, but you know Sheila. She thought she was in for a picnic, just have a glass of champagne and smoke a joint while he ate her pussy. Instead, he sprang that on her. She refused when she saw this thing, whatever it was."

"Mmm. She might have been exaggerating."

"Sure. Maybe he just caught his pecker in his fly. Or maybe there wasn't anything, I don't know. Some of these kids are pretty flaky, no matter how careful I try to be when I hire them."

"Don't berate yourself on that count. Frankly, I'm dazzled by your ability to pick talent. You would have made a great casting director."

"Uh-huh. While I lived in the Village and made a pisspot salary."

"All right, then, a producer?"

"That's better. I could have been, you know. When I retired from the stage, I thought about it."

"Our gain, dear. And speaking of flaky girls, I'm sure you heard what happened to Lisa Miller."

"Yes, and I wasn't a bit surprised. Anybody who's crazy enough to work rough trade deserves what she gets."

"Made a ton of money, though. From what I heard."

"Lot of good it did her. Or will do her now, I should say. Anyway, most of it went up her nose. There's no room for a dog like that at Panache. Incidentally, the new phone girl is working out well."

"Andrea? I think she's terrific. Only one problem, though. She's too pretty. You wait and see; first thing you know, she'll be pestering you to send her on dates."

"She already has."

"And?"

"And maybe. I told her when I hired her I might give her a chance.

Meantime, she can be patient, stay on the phones for awhile. She's a big improvement over Monica."

"Isn't she, though?"

"By the way, about Monica."

"I'll take care of it."

"How?"

"Don't ask."

"All right, I won't." She sipped her drink, thinking it was eerie how he could bring her up short from time to time. In that respect, he was like the python in the Rousseau painting: beautiful to look at, calm to the point of serenity. So that you sometimes forgot what he was capable of.

Until he showed you.

Patrick finished his Bloody and set the glass down on the coffee table. "But while we're on the subject of our former employee, I'll bet you didn't see this morning's *Times,* did you?"

"No, why?"

"There's a story about her friend, the cop." He reached into the inside pocket of his jacket and brought out a newspaper clipping, handing it to her. "I thought you'd be interested."

Martha scanned the piece quickly, then went back to the top and read it again, slowly this time. The headline said:

## DETECTIVE KILLS ROBBER
## IN HARLEM SHOOT-OUT

The article was only a few paragraphs long, and written in the newspaper's dry, "just the facts, ma'am" style. But even so, the event it described must have been horrendous. A white cop in Harlem in the early-morning hours, dueling a black ex-convict armed with an automatic weapon and blowing him away, and then being rescued by more cops just as a mob was about to swarm over him. It gave you the creeps to read it, even though Tolliver was no friend.

She looked up to see Patrick watching her, sprawled in the deep white club chair with an amused expression on his face.

"I would call it good news," he said.

"What?"

"For us. Not as good as if it had been the other way around and the robber had killed *him,* but a nice break, anyway."

"You mean because this will keep him preoccupied?"

"My dear, preoccupied is hardly the word for it. You mustn't be misled by this nice polite little story in the *Times,* you know. That's the way they report everything. If you want a more realistic perspective, watch the way television treats it, or the *Post.*"

"I suppose that's true."

"I assure you, it's quite true. I had the television on in my bedroom, while I was dressing. There was an interview with that messenger of God, the Reverend Dan Marydale."

"Is he the fat nigger who's always running off at the mouth?"

"The very same. He said he'd spoken personally with a dozen witnesses, and they all told him the poor fellow Tolliver shot was unarmed, and the police planted the gun on him after he was killed."

"So why did Tolliver shoot him?"

"It was a setup, according to the reverend. The cops were trying to trap this innocent man in a drug bust, and he was merely running away, because he knew he hadn't done anything wrong."

Martha smirked. "How sad."

"Isn't it? But if this Tolliver was no threat to us earlier, I assure you he's even less of one now. When the media get through with him, he'll be investigating bums in the subway."

Chang reappeared, bowing and sneaking an admiring glance at Patrick. "Brunch served, Missy."

They went into the dining room, and when they were seated, the houseboy served them crab soufflé and a salad of asparagus tips marinade. He also offered wine, a Chassagne Montrachet, which she declined, but that Patrick drank with obvious enjoyment, declaring it superb.

It ought to be, Martha thought. Fucking stuff cost me eighty dollars a bottle.

"Frankly," Patrick said, "I think this makes a new beginning."

"Of what?"

"Us. And Panache. As far as I'm concerned, the opportunity is practically unlimited."

"We're doing okay, for the moment, anyway."

He smiled. "Sometimes I think you're afraid of success, Martha."

She spoke around a mouthful of soufflé. It was wonderful, seasoned exactly the way she liked it, with cayenne and a hint of curry. "I'm just conservative, that's all."

"But think about it. What this incident with Caroline and Monica and all has demonstrated is that no matter how threatening a situation may seem, it can always be handled. So why should we rest on our laurels? Instead of sitting here congratulating ourselves on what we made last night, why not think of expansion? After all, who knows how high is up?"

248

"Expansion how?"

He sipped wine and looked at the glass appreciatively. "This really is an outstanding Burgundy."

"Uh-huh. Expansion how?"

"Remember what I was saying about your extraordinary ability to pick talent? Why should we restrict our operation to the relatively few girls we have now?"

"Because what we have now is all we can manage and still keep Panache's standards up, that's why."

"But are you sure of that?"

"Of course I'm sure. Don't kid yourself, Patrick. What we've got here is a nice business, I'll grant you. But it's a *service* business, right?"

"Of course it is, but—"

"So the key to it is quality. If the quality of our service stays high, we make money. If it falls off, we're shit out of luck with nobody to thank but ourselves."

"Martha, I—"

"You know what it reminds me of? A high-class restaurant. You remember when La Caravelle was one of the best places in New York? Maybe *the* best? And then they figured what the hell, we've got it made. So the food slipped and the service slipped and before they knew it, they were fucked."

His tone was patient, as always, but she knew him well enough to sense his irritation. "We're not in the restaurant business."

"What's the difference? It's still based on service, and the quality of the product. Only what we serve is pussy."

"Perhaps you're right. But will you listen to what I'm trying to suggest?"

"Yes, go ahead." She'd finished her soufflé and wanted more, but if she had another helping, she'd have to skip dessert. "What is it?"

"I was thinking that instead of just the one place, we'd have two. You'd manage one, and I the other. Of course you'd be the principal owner, just as you are how. And you'd pick the girls—that goes without saying."

She stared at him. "Go into competition with ourselves? Are you out of your fucking mind?"

"I assure you, I'm not. At the present time, Panache is unquestionably the tops in New York. We have the best girls, the best reputation."

"Isn't that what I just said?"

"And yet despite that, you know as well as I do that many of our most loyal customers still call other services on occasion."

249

There was an ivory cigarette box on the table. She took a cigarette from the box and lit it, even though Patrick hadn't finished eating and she knew the smoke annoyed him. "That's because they're boys, Patrick. And boys always want something different from what they've got. If a boy was fucking Julia Roberts, he'd be thinking, wouldn't it be great if I was fucking Kelly Emberg?"

"I'm quite aware of that. In fact, you're confirming my point. If they want something different, or think they do, why shouldn't *we* give it to them, instead of someone else?"

Chang was back. "All finish?"

Both replied that they were, and as the houseboy cleared the table, Martha thought about Patrick's proposal. There was a lot of truth in what he was saying, not only about the opportunity but also about her reluctance to take chances.

And yet, wasn't that what had gotten her as far as she'd come? Being sure she always had her business under tight control, trying to anticipate every contingency? And despite that very caution, hadn't Caroline's murder been a total shock, as if somebody had dropped a bomb, right out of the blue?

It was easy for Patrick to sit here and make all these shrewd observations, barely disguising the fact that he thought he was a lot smarter than she was, that he always knew better. She studied his smooth features, the perfectly groomed dark hair, not a strand out of place. Maybe she should rethink a lot of things.

Chang bowed. "Dessert?"

Patrick twirled the stem of his wineglass. "Not for me, thank you. But I will have a touch more of this Montrachet."

"I'll have dessert," Martha said.

The houseboy left them, returning moments later. He served her fresh pear halves in a cognac sauce and poured more wine for Patrick.

By the time she'd taken her second bite, she'd figured it out, seen the direction she should take. She glanced at Patrick, and the image of Rousseau's python returned to her mind once more.

He was brilliant, and he had excellent judgment. He was also ambitious, cruel and amoral. Everything he did was weighed by one measure: Would it be good for Patrick?

In a word, he was dangerous.

And like the python, he had to be dealt with. Before he dealt with her.

# 62

There was a toothbrush in Ben's locker, and shaving gear. He used the toothbrush first, and then worked up a faceful of lather. Seeing his image in the mirror startled him, as he suddenly realized how haggard he'd become, how much his appearance had changed since he'd gone on the case. Later today, he'd go to his apartment and shower and trim his mustache and put on clean clothes, but for now brushing his teeth and scraping the whiskers off his jaw would have to do.

As he shaved, he thought about what he'd gone through the night before and his hand tensed. A drop of crimson appeared on his chin, bright against the white lather, and he cursed as he saw it. After rinsing his face, he stuck a scrap of toilet paper on the cut and then put his shirt back on, wishing he'd kept a fresh one in his locker.

At that point, Ed Flynn came into the bunk room and poured himself a mug of coffee from the battered electric pot. "Hya doing, Ben—feel better?"

"Sure, I'm fine."

Flynn set his mug down and picked up another. "Want some coffee?"

"Yeah, thanks. What's going on?"

"Captain's here, waiting for you. And there's a whole shitload of reporters."

"Oh, Christ."

"This guy Marydale had a press conference and said the guy who robbed you was unarmed. Said the cops planted the gun."

Ben took the mug of coffee from Flynn and sipped it. "So now the media want to stir it up some more by getting a response out of me, right?"

"Worse. Marydale's organized a demonstration, and guess where?"

"Shit, don't tell me."

"You got it. He's supposed to get here any minute. One of the guys from the *Post* said he called them himself. And there're all kinds of TV cameras down there. Plus a whole bunch of black people yelling and chanting. If it was up to Brennan, he'd drop grenades out the window."

Ben went down the hall past his office and into the squad room.

251

Seven or eight detectives were there, half of them working at their desks but several others standing at the windows and looking down onto Charles Street. As he approached them, Ben could hear the crowd clamoring from below.

Looking down, he saw a group of reporters and TV cameramen, and fanning out beyond them a mass of civilians, mostly black but with a number of white people, as well. The demonstrators were yelling and shouting, and as Flynn had said, many of them were sounding a chant, but Ben couldn't make out what the words were.

The whites in the crowd looked like typical Village radicals, the men with long hair and beards and dressed in ragged clothes, the women wearing sacklike dresses. The gathering reminded him of the mob that had given the cops so much trouble in Tompkins Square Park not long ago.

As he watched, more people ran up to join the crowd, shaking their fists and yelling as they came. Cops from the station house were trying to keep order, but from the looks of things, they'd most likely have to call for reinforcements.

Flynn pushed in alongside Ben, peering down at the source of the hubbub. "Some mess, huh?"

"It could be, if they can't control it," Ben said.

"Fucking media," a third voice said.

Ben turned to see Captain Brennan standing behind him, feet spread apart, massive arms folded, the physical stance clearly revealing his mental attitude.

"Hello, Cap."

"Morning. You were asleep when I got here, so I let you snooze. I figured you could use it."

"I was bushed last night," Ben admitted.

"Let's go in your office," Brennan said.

Ben followed him, telling Flynn to let them know if and when the Reverend Marydale showed up.

Inside the office, with the door shut, the zone commander sat opposite the desk while Tolliver took his customary seat. The clamor from the street was just as loud in here.

"So you almost got to be a statistic," Brennan said.

"I guess."

"You would have been number eleven for the year."

"That's nice. That I wasn't."

Brennan was watching him, his broad face impassive but the eyes narrowed. "You all right, Lieutenant?"

"Yeah, I'm okay."

"Taking it easy for a while will do you good."

252

"I was thinking," Ben said. "Maybe you could bend that a little." There was no change in the big Irishman's stoic expression. "Not a chance. Regulations say you work here until the DA's office presents it to a grand jury; you know that. It's strictly routine, nothing more. But that's the way it has to go."

"Uh-huh."

Brennan inclined his head toward the noise coming from the window. "Also this one's got race overtones. That bunch out there is just the beginning. The chief already had a call from the PC, who had a call from the mayor. You know the pressure the both of them are under. So you sit tight until it's heard."

Ben felt frustration building, but before he could respond, Brennan raised a meaty hand.

"The way to look at it," the captain said, "is that it's only procedure. You know the department's behind you. It's just that this is tricky business because of the politics."

Despite the few hours sleep he'd managed to get, Ben was exhausted and his nerves were raw. He leaned forward, fists clenched. "*Fuck* the politics! All I've heard since I got the Patterson case was this bullshit about politics. Last night, I'm making a phone call, and some dickhead ex-con puts a gun on me and robs me. Sure I shot him, after I told him to stop and he shot at me. Now you're telling me there's politics? Jesus Christ, the streets don't belong to the people anymore, you realize that? Any cocksucker with a gun figures he can do whatever he wants and the cops are afraid to stop him. Politics? The mayor and the PC can shove the politics up their ass!"

Brennan studied him for several seconds. When he spoke, his tone was mild. "You through, Lieutenant?"

Ben exhaled slowly. "Yeah, I'm through."

"Then relax."

He opened his hands and sat back, aware that the commotion outside had grown louder.

"I'll try to see all of it is speeded up," Brennan said. "But we have to go through it, show the public the department don't take the loss of a life lightly."

"I understand that. But I—"

There was a loud knock at the door, and Flynn opened it, thrusting his head into the office. "He's here. Marydale. Excuse me, but you said to let you know."

Ben got to his feet.

"If you're thinking about going down there, forget it," Brennan said. "That's just what those vultures want."

"I think the TV's gonna carry it live," Flynn said.

253

"There's a set in the bunk room," Ben said to Brennan. "We can watch it there."

When the three men reached the room, a crowd was already standing around the ancient set. The others made way for the ranking detectives, Ben and Brennan moving close to the screen. The set was small and the reception poor, but at least you could get what was going on.

A reporter was interviewing the Reverend Dan Marydale. The black clergyman was a familiar figure on New York television, a self-appointed champion of black causes who smelled a news opportunity the way a hound smelled a bitch in heat. He'd learned his game by studying Al Sharpton, acknowledged master of the technique.

"Reverend Marydale," the reporter was saying, "what is your view of this situation?" He shoved a mike toward the black man's mouth.

Marydale never spoke in public; he shouted. "My view is what you got here is murder. The man got shot last night 'cause he was black and the *po*lice tried to bust him on a phony drug rap. After they shot him, they didn't find no drugs, so they put a gun with him and say he threatened them."

"What about the statement from the man who was arrested? We're told he was an eyewitness, and that he told the police there was only one officer, who the deceased had tried to rob."

"That's a *lie!* Only reason the man gave that statement was because the cops beat him into it. I got other witnesses say that never happened. Saw the whole thing and it was a setup."

"Who are these witnesses?"

The question was obviously a plant, Ben thought.

"I got one of 'em right here," Marydale yelled. His hair had been straightened and hung to his shoulders in oily strands. When he moved his head, the hair swung in a way that reminded Ben of the fringes on a lamp shade.

Marydale pointed to a black man standing beside him. "This the witness. Michael Brown. He saw the *po*lice shoot the man down like a dog and then put a gun alongside of him, while the man's blood was runnin' out of him! Ain't that right, Mr. Brown?"

Michael Brown was wearing a shiny blue suit and a flashy tie, apparently having dressed for this occasion. He smiled broadly as the camera pushed in on him. "That's right," he said.

"You hear that?" Marydale howled. "There's a man saw what happened with his own eyes. He ain't afraid to speak up, tell the truth."

The commentator said, "What about the police contention that

254

the decedent, Tyrone Bennett, was an ex-convict wanted in connection with other robberies?"

"Man, what you expect they gonna say? And no matter what they claim Mr. Bennett done, that don't give 'em the right to shoot him down and plant a gun on him."

"Is it true the black community is united in protesting this latest incident involving police violence?"

"You damn right it's true! There gonna be a candlelight rally tonight at the African-American United Church on Lenox Avenue, and we expecting everybody gonna be there. Including his honor the mayor!"

"Reverend Marydale, last night's shooting took place in Harlem. Why have you and your followers gathered here today at the headquarters of the Sixth Precinct, in Greenwich Village?"

"Because this where the killer is. Lieutenant Ben Tolliver the one who shot Tyrone Bennett last night. He went all the way up to Harlem and killed a black man for no reason. What we want now is for this white lieutenant to come on out here and tell the people of New York why he done it. Face up to it like a man!"

"We're told the case will automatically be presented to a grand jury. Would you comment on that?"

"Course it's gonna go to the grand jury. This cop committed murder, man. He got to be put on trial, got to be prosecuted under the law!"

"Isn't that up to the grand jury to decide?"

Marydale's eyes popped in anger. "Hey, man—you jivin' me? You tryin' to downplay a *murder*?"

"Thank you, Reverend Marydale. We're reporting to you live from Sixth Precinct police headquarters, where an angry crowd has gathered—"

Someone turned off the set. Joe Stone, the only black detective in the squad, said, "That fat fuck."

Carlos Rodriguez was standing near Stone. "Hey, Joe," Carlos said, "you goin' to that rally? Sing a couple hymns?"

Stone looked at him. "Up yours, spic."

Ben poured himself another mug of coffee and went back to his office, Brennan trailing. The other detectives drifted into the squad room, some of them settling down at their desks, others gathering in clusters to talk. There was still some noise out on the street, but the crowd was nowhere near as raucous as it had been earlier. Now that the television interview had concluded, there wasn't much reason for people to hang around.

Brennan closed the door but remained standing. "Wait'll they're gone, and then get out of here, go home and get some rest. I'll be in touch tomorrow, tell you what's going on."

Ben felt as if what he was experiencing wasn't real, as if all this was happening to someone else, and he was merely a bystander. The anger he'd felt earlier had disappeared, and in its place was an emptiness, the cold ashes of burnout. He heard himself say, "Okay, Cap. I'll do that."

Brennan had that watchful look on his face again, his features calm except for the narrowing of his eyes. "Don't let this get to you, Lieutenant. You come up with any dumb ideas, you call me, understand?"

Ben understood. He'd seen cops fall apart himself often enough. He nodded.

Brennan opened the door. As he went out of the office, he looked back. "There's an old Irish saying. When you got troubles, don't have a drink. Have a hundred." He left, closing the door behind him.

# 63

He went to Patty's place, pounding on the door to awaken her. After peering out through the peephole, she opened the door and let him in. She had on a robe and her hair was in curlers. Her eyes widened as she looked at him, and when he walked in, she shut the door behind him and led him into the bedroom.

"Get undressed," she said. "I'll run a bath."

He pulled off his windbreaker and tossed it over a chair. "I'd rather take a shower."

Her tone was firm. "Don't argue. It'll be ready in a couple of minutes. You don't just *look* like shit, Lieutenant."

For once, he was too tired to argue. He took everything off, depositing the rank clothing in a heap on the chair. The holster carrying his Smith, he put on her dresser. When she called him from the bathroom, he went in and stepped into the tub, the water so hot that when he sat down he thought his balls were scalded.

He stayed in for a long time, dozing while she added more hot water and scrubbed his skin with a soapy washcloth. By the time he got out, he felt as if he were made of rubber. Once back in the bedroom, he collapsed onto the bed and she pulled the covers over him.

As tired as he was, he slept fitfully, pursued in his dreams by a black man with a heavy automatic. Ben ran and ran, but each time he turned a corner, the man was there waiting for him, grinning as he raised the gun.

In the middle of the afternoon he awoke, feeling groggy and stiff. He went into the bathroom and urinated, then splashed water on his face. He could hear Patty moving around in the kitchen, but he didn't go in. Instead, he stumbled back into bed. This time, he slept like the dead.

"Ben?"

"Mm?"

"Ben—you awake?"

He opened his eyes and blinked. The room was in semidarkness. Patty was sitting on the bed, looking down at him. She wore one of his shirts and apparently nothing else. He reached for her, but she held him off.

"I made some dinner for you."

He looked at his watch, but he was unable to read it. "What time is it?"

"Seven o'clock. There are clean clothes on the chair. Put something on and come on in."

He did as he'd been told, aware as he pulled on a pair of pants and a fresh shirt that a heavenly aroma was coming from the other room. Following his nose, he went into the tiny kitchen.

She'd put out a tablecloth, and her best china. Candles were flickering, tall white ones in a silver holder. He sat down, and she placed a huge bowl of pasta in front of him. "Go ahead and start," she said. "Don't wait for me."

He could always eat, in fact was hungry most of the time. This evening, he could have eaten his shoe. The pasta was vermicelli, in a fiery red sauce of tomatoes, peppers, garlic, and black olives, hot enough to bring tears to his eyes. Patty sprinkled Parmesan onto the steaming food and then sat down opposite him. Her own portion was less than a third the size of his.

She'd made hot garlic bread as well, and a salad of lettuce and sliced raw mushrooms in olive oil and vinegar. To drink, there was Chianti she poured from a straw-covered bottle.

For the next several minutes, Ben said nothing. There was a time to talk, and a time to eat. For someone whose stomach was as empty as his had been, this was a time to eat.

It wasn't until he was more than halfway through the meal that he began to relax. Patty watched him, as usual consuming only an occasional forkful of her own dinner, along with small sips of the

257

wine. He could see she was pleased by the way he was devouring his food.

She nibbled on a bit of garlic bread. "You like it?"

He answered around a mouthful. "Terrific. I love pasta—must be part guinea."

"It's a Sicilian dish. You know what it's called?"

He shook his head, his jaws working.

"*Puttanesca.* Whore's pasta."

He twirled strands on his fork and stuffed them into his mouth. "Do I have to join the union?"

"They call it that because in the old country when a prostitute worked all night, she'd be hungry in the morning. She'd want something spicy to wake her up."

"A civilized custom," Ben said. "But I prefer to eat it before sex, not after."

"Who said you're gonna get any of that—before *or* after?"

"I was hoping," he said.

"I'll think about it."

"When do you go to work?"

"Oh, I'll leave about nine. We do the first show at ten-thirty."

"You were great the other night."

The remark pleased her as well, he saw. "You think so, really?"

"I know so."

"You know so? How?"

"When you finished, every guy in the place had a hard-on. I looked, to make sure."

"Oh Ben, that's terrible. God." But she liked hearing that, too, despite her feigned protest.

He poured more wine for them. "This was fantastic. I'm beginning to feel human again."

"Good, I'm glad." She sipped some of the Chianti. "Ben? I saw all that awful business on the news. While you were asleep."

"The Reverend Marydale?"

"That, and a lot of other stuff, too. It must have been horrible for you. I'm sorry to bring it up, but I wanted to tell you I understand how you must feel."

"Gets people's attention," Ben said. "It's called manufacturing news. Marydale knows it, and so do the TV guys. But he also knows how to play them. It's like a quid pro quo. He puts out all that shit and they put him on the tube."

"Is it true, that you're suspended?"

"No, just restricted to working at the precinct house for a few days. It's only a technicality."

She chewed her lower lip. "I was wondering . . ."

"Yes?"

"If I took some time off, maybe we could go away someplace. Upstate, say, to that inn you told me about."

He was about to tell her to forget it, that in spite of the restriction, there was plenty he could be doing on the Patterson case, but he caught himself in time. "I don't know. The department may make me stay here, so I'm available for a hearing."

"But you will try? See if you can do it?"

"Sure." His hands were in plain view, so he crossed his feet under the table.

"I think it could be wonderful."

He frowned. "I'm not so sure."

She was startled. "Why not?"

"How could I have an opinion, unless I had a sample ahead of time?"

"You're a foxy bastard, aren't you?"

"You have to play the angles," he said.

She got up, unbuttoning the front of her shirt as she approached him.

Her skin was firm and smooth and he buried his face between her breasts.

"Ouch," she whispered. "You could use another shave."

"First things first." He stood up and brushed his lips against her open mouth.

She reached down and gripped him. "It's a deal," she said.

# 64

The lobby of the Park Lane was thronged with people: guests arriving, guests departing, guests coming back from shopping or business.

Bobbie loved the atmosphere, the hustle and bustle. And more than that, she loved the style of the place. It was different from her other favorite *luxe* hotels in New York, and for that matter different from any of the ones she knew in Europe. Not like the Plaza, just down the street, or the Grand in Rome, or the Plaza Athénée in Paris. This one was much brighter, more airy, less formal than the others. More like the Beverly Hills in L.A., for example.

And yet it was just as elegant in its own way as any of them. The crystal chandelier, the vast areas of white marble, the polished wood, and the exquisite bouquets of flowers, all contributed to the air of sophistication she found so stimulating.

The reservations clerk was a darkly handsome young man who spoke with a slight accent. He smiled as she approached the counter. "Good evening. May I help you?"

Bobbie returned the smile. She was wearing the new red coat she'd bought at Saks, and she was sure that with the contrast the coat made with her black hair and the white silk scarf at her throat, she looked especially attractive. "Good evening. I'm Mrs. Frank Wellington. You're holding a reservation for my husband and me."

"Yes, Mrs. Wellington. Just one moment, please." He riffled through his reservation index and came up with a card. "Here we are. Mr. and Mrs. Frank Wellington of Grosse Pointe, Michigan. How long will you be staying with us, Mrs. Wellington?"

"Through the weekend," Bobbie said.

The clerk made a note and placed a registration form and a pen in front of her.

As Bobbie filled out the form, she said, "I asked for one of your suites, overlooking the park?"

"Yes, ma'am, we have that for you. May I have a credit card, please?"

She opened her purse and took out a gold AmEx, handing it to him. "This is my husband's. He'll be coming in later tonight from Detroit."

"That's fine, ma'am. Thank you." The clerk ran the card through the machine in front of him, then returned it to her. "The bellman will take your luggage, Mrs. Wellington. Enjoy your stay."

"Thank you. I'm sure I will."

Five minutes later she was in the suite, a nice one overlooking Central Park, just as promised. She'd brought along one bag, her Mark Cross pigskin. The bellman placed it on a folding rack at the foot of one of the beds and fussed about, checking the closets and the bath while Bobbie stood at a window in the living room, looking down at the traffic whizzing along Central Park South.

The streetlights revealed that in the park beyond, most of the foliage had fallen from the trees. The weather had turned much colder; it was hard to realize it was November already. How had the autumn slipped by so quickly?

The bellman came back into the room. "Is there anything I can get you, ma'am?"

260

"No, that will be all, thank you." She handed him a ten-dollar bill and he left the suite.

There was a bouquet of flowers on the sideboard, yellow mums arranged in a bed of orange and red maple leaves. She admired them as she stood at the desk and picked up the telephone, calling a number so familiar that it wasn't necessary for her to look it up.

A drink would go well, she thought, wishing she'd brought a bottle with her. She wouldn't call room service; that had been a mistake last time. The fewer people who came into contact with her now, the fewer who would remember her later.

The female voice that answered the call was well modulated, low-pitched, and pleasant. "Good evening, this is Panache. How may we serve you?"

In the deepest tone she could manage, Bobbie said, "Hi, this is Frank Wellington calling. I'm at the Park Lane, and I'd like some company."

# 65

After Patty left the apartment, Ben put on his pants and a shirt. He took a thick manila envelope from the pocket of his windbreaker and carried it into the kitchen. She'd cleared the table and put the dishes into the dishwasher, which was now chugging and wheezing, and she'd also left a pot of fresh coffee on the stove. He poured himself a cup and got a pad and pencil out of a drawer. Then he sat down and opened the envelope, spreading its contents out on the table.

The first problem was to make sense of his notes. As he read through them, he began jotting down a fresh list of names, with Barry Conklin's at the top. Next to it he wrote that of Conklin's wife, Barbara. He would talk to her again, and he'd also check with Jack Strickland on the detective's reaction to the tapes Ben had sent him.

Next, he put down the names Martha Bellamy and Patrick Wickersham. The pair had been effective, so far, in their efforts to stonewall him. But he was sure there was more to be uncovered there. Monica hadn't simply vanished into thin air; somebody had given her a push. He jotted down her name, and beside it that of her boyfriend, Derek Williams. Rodney Burnaford came next; the broker wasn't nearly the friendly little boy next door he wanted Ben to think he was.

Below those names, he wrote Melissa Martin's, and then that of Joan Phillips, the woman Spencer Patterson referred to as his assistant. From what both Samantha Patterson and Martin had said, Phillips was somebody he should look into.

Ben sat back then, drinking coffee and thinking. Still another angle to pursue was the girls who worked for Panache, and whose names Monica had given him. Melissa Martin was the only one he'd contacted so far. He looked over the printout of Panache's customers, seeing where he'd checked off names in red pencil. Then he looked at the list of girls, starting to examine the matchups. After a moment, he threw down his pencil in disgust.

What he'd been doing for the past half hour wasn't merely sorting out ideas; he'd also inadvertently put his main problem into sharp focus. Ordinarily, if he was running a task force on a major homicide, he'd have dozens of detectives checking out leads, grinding it out with the painstaking attention to detail that was the basis of good police work.

Instead, he was sitting here now like the village idiot—alone, scorned, technically restricted, the subject of a storm of adverse publicity. And with more work to do than he could accomplish by himself in six months. If it had been doubtful earlier that the two guys he'd had working with him would stay on, it was all but certain now that they wouldn't. Weisskopf and Spadone were probably already back at Midtown North. Again he felt a sharp jab of anger.

You simple shit, he thought. When they put you on this thing, you should have told them to stuff it. If Brennan and Galupo didn't like it, fuck 'em—they could get themselves another boy.

Instead, he'd walked right into it. Of all the galling, frustrating experiences he'd had over the years on the job, this had to be the worst. He'd been deliberately used by the brass, hung with an impossible assignment strictly for PR purposes, just so the department could look good. And stumbling into the shooting in Harlem had compounded his problems, turned him into a pariah. He was Lieutenant Asshole, no question about it.

So now what? What would make the most sense for him to do next—besides retiring from the NYPD?

There was only one answer. Crack this fucking case. Show the bastards.

He went back to the pile of papers on the table. Among them was the small notebook he'd swiped from Lisa Miller's apartment, containing her john list. He opened the book and began to read.

# 66

In contrast to the well-organized Panache files, Lisa's book was a mess. Most of the scribbles were barely decipherable, consisting of no more than a first name and in some instances a phone number with a few arcane symbols. Some entries were smeared and blotted, and one page apparently had served as a coaster at some point; the wrinkled paper bore the outline of the bottom of a glass, and the ink had run. All that remained were illegible blue streaks.

What Ben had been hoping for was a match between the two lists. A john who had patronized both Lisa and Panache would certainly be worth checking, and one who had been entertained by Lisa as well as Caroline Patterson just might turn out to be a home run. But after the first run-through of Lisa's book, he felt sharp disappointment; the thing looked like some kid had used it to doodle in.

And yet messy or not, the book was all he had on the girl whose body had been turned into an outlandish replica of the American flag. Telling himself to be patient, he poured more coffee and made a fresh start on the book, studying each page with care, trying to make sense of the hieroglyphics. As he worked at it, he realized why the entries were in such abysmal shape: when Lisa had made them, she'd been stoned.

Nevertheless, he did manage to find several entries that matched. The names meant nothing to him, with one exception: a listing on Hiram Donnelly was in the Panache printout, and one of the entries in Lisa's book was Hiram D. There couldn't be many Hiram D.'s running around New York hiring whores; it had to be the same man. Donnelly was the police inspector whose name had caused such hilarity when Weisskopf and Spadone had run across it in the Panache list.

It was no joke now. Especially when Ben thought about Art Weisskopf's discovery that Lisa Miller's handcuffs had first been owned by the NYPD. He made notes of his own on Donnelly, realizing as he did that he would be juggling an extremely hot potato.

Glancing back over the notes reminded him he'd wanted to take another look at Rodney Burnaford, as well. The stockbroker's name was in the Panache list, but not in Lisa's book. Ben was about to go on to something else when it occurred to him that he might simply have overlooked the entry, or failed to decipher it. He went through the book again, page by page.

And found it.

Roddy B, it said. The entry was barely readable, but it was there. And as in the case of Hiram Donnelly, the name was too distinctive not to fit. He wondered whether there were others he'd missed, and decided there probably were. Going back into the book, he tried to find an entry for Barry Conklin, but came up empty. Shit. Running across that would have been too good to be true.

He worked on the book for another hour, and finally pushed his notes aside. After a while, you got punchy, he knew, failed to see things that might jump out at you when you were fresh. He'd go at it again later, or maybe in the morning. Stuffing the wad of notes and the printout and the rest of it back into the manila envelope, he got up and stretched. There was still a little coffee left in the pot. He was about to pour it into his cup when he had a better idea.

Patty kept her liquor in one of the lower kitchen cabinets. He opened the cabinet and got out a bottle of Jack Daniel's. Glasses were up above. He chose a squat oversized one and packed it with ice from the freezer. Then he poured amber fluid until the ice crackled and the whiskey was level with the top of the glass. He raised the drink and contemplated it for a moment, holding it so that the light from the overhead fixture was refracted by the booze.

First, however, he'd check in. He put the glass down and picked the telephone off the wall, punching the buttons with an index finger.

Flynn answered the call.

"Ed, it's me, Tolliver."

The sergeant sounded both relieved and anxious. "Lou! How you doing—you all right?"

"Of course I'm all right. What the hell did you think I'd be?"

"I dunno. Drunk maybe. If I was you, that's what I'd be."

Ben looked at the brimming glass on the table in front of him. "That's why you'll never make a great detective, Ed. What's going on?"

"Reporters. Up to our ass in 'em all day. You seen the TV?"

"No, but I heard about it. What else?"

"Brennan called, said I should tell you to take his advice. You know what he meant?"

Ben continued to study the glass of Jack Daniel's. As he did, one of the ice cubes came unstuck from another and rolled over. It was amazing, the little things you noticed, if you paid attention. "Yeah, I think so."

"He said he'd talk to you later. Also a Mrs. Conklin called."

"When was that?"

"This afternoon. Said to call her tomorrow, during the day."

When her husband isn't home, Ben thought. "Any others?"

"Yeah, but just ratshit."

"How's business?"

"One homicide, on Spring Street last night. Couple neighbors got bombed and had an argument. One guy stabbed the other with an ice pick."

"Any witnesses?"

"About a dozen. Happened in the street, in front of where they live."

"You get a statement?"

"Yup, on videotape and a written. But the guy's lawyer is already screaming coercion."

"Figures. Who caught it?"

"Carlos. He did a good job. After he read the guy *Miranda,* he got a statement from a witness on that, too. Also on the tape, we had the perp say he made the statement voluntarily."

"Good. It should stick."

"I hope."

"Weisskopf or Spadone been in?"

"Haven't seen 'em."

"All right, I'll talk to you tomorrow. Anything important comes up, you know where you can reach me."

"Okay. And Ben?"

"Yeah?"

"Get some, uh—relaxation, will you?"

"I plan to, Ed. I plan to." He hung up.

The glass on the table had begun to sweat. Moisture ran down its sides in tiny rivulets. When he put his hand around it, the glass was cold to his touch.

Ben remembered reading someplace a few lines by a Roman poet. They went something like:

> These things we hold dear
> A bath, fresh robes
> Food and wine and love
> And sleep

Ben had had his sleep and his bath, and his food and wine and love. Now he was sitting here in his fresh robes, about to have more wine. He raised the glass and took a long swallow of Mr. Daniel's Tennessee whiskey.

The poet had it right; nothing had changed much over the past couple thousand years.

He drank again, savoring the smooth, clean taste.

# 67

Bobbie's mouth was dry, and it was hard for her to breathe normally. It was odd, but at moments like this, when she was trembling with anticipation and excitement, the thought of her parents would suddenly pop into her mind. She would see them together, calm and composed, the very soul of propriety. Her mother would appear prim, her father staunch and confident. To look at them, no one would ever guess the truth of their relationship.

Bobbie had never had to guess. From the time she was a tiny child, she had watched them in secret, when they were unaware they were being observed. Sometimes late at night, she would awaken to the strange noises coming from down the hall, and then she'd sneak out of bed and tiptoe to their room, opening the door a crack so that she could see as well as hear them.

That was when her mother would have the face of a demon, sweat dripping from her sharp features and her body glistening in the lamplight. She would have pins and other sharp objects, including a small kitchen knife, and she would jab them into her husband's back and his buttocks while he groveled on the floor like a whipped dog, licking her feet and sobbing. Then Bobbie's mother would kick him until he rolled over onto his bloody back. Cursing him, she would squat over him and sit on his face while she spat obscenities.

Even now, the thought of what Bobbie had seen on those nighttime forays would fill her with a baffling mixture of emotions. She would be furious, and yet at the same time wildly aroused. But the memories were secrets she had never revealed to anyone—not even to the doctors they'd taken her to during her adolescence.

Those had been the worst years of her life. Knowing what she did, her father's hypocrisy had filled her with disgust. Outwardly the stern, upright churchgoer, a powerful and successful businessman, his public persona was nothing but a mask. She had resisted him, challenged his authority, held him in total contempt. And he had responded by treating her in the cruelest way he could: he ignored her.

But then once, when she'd defied him, he'd become enraged and struck her full in the face with his closed fist. The blow knocked Bobbie to the floor, leaving her dazed and with blood dribbling from her nose. To her astonishment, while she lay there, she'd had a deep, shuddering orgasm.

But damn it, why was she thinking about such events now? They were long past, things that seemed not to have happened to her but to someone else entirely. And the problems with her parents, she'd learned to handle years ago. Now the pair were simply a couple of old, stupid people who were nearing the end of their lives. Soon they would be dead, and she would forget them altogether.

The doorbell rang.

Bobbie jumped at the sound, even though she'd been expecting it, had been waiting for it for the past hour. She remained motionless for three beats, then went to the door of the suite and unlocked it, opening it just a crack.

In the same deep tones she'd used on the phone when she called Panache, she called out, "Who is it?"

"Melissa," the girl answered.

Bobbie opened the door, standing behind it and saying, "Come on in."

When she entered the foyer, Bobbie closed the door behind her and held the muzzle of the .38 S&W Police Special one inch from her nose.

The girl looked at the pistol and then at Bobbie. Her eyes bulged; her jaw dropped. For an instant, she seemed not to comprehend, but then her eyes grew even wider and the color drained from her face. *"You!"*

"Shut up," Bobbie said. "Or I'll blow your brains out. You understand?"

She nodded, her mouth quivering, the expression on her face now revealing abject terror.

Bobbie moved around behind her, continuing to hold the pistol close to the girl's head. "Walk straight ahead," Bobbie commanded. "Slowly."

When they reached the center of the living room, she said, "Stop. Now take off your clothes."

The girl was trembling, her shoulders shaking visibly. In a small, tight voice, she said, "Listen, couldn't we—"

Bobbie jabbed her in the back of the neck with the barrel of the revolver. "I said shut up," she hissed. "I won't tell you again, you stupid cunt. You open your mouth again and you're dead."

The trembling grew even more pronounced, but she kept silent.

"Go on—take off your clothes," Bobbie grated. "Drop the bag and take them off."

Her hand released the tote she'd been carrying, and it fell to the carpet. She unbuttoned her coat then, pulling it off.

Bobbie said, "Just drop everything on the floor. Get going."

The young woman did as she was ordered, methodically removing each article of clothing.

Watching her from behind as she stripped produced a wild emotional reaction in Bobbie, a mixture of rage and excitement. She felt her own pulse begin to hammer in her chest, her breath grow short as the pieces fell away, revealing the girl's smooth shoulders, her roundly curved buttocks and slim legs.

When she took off her hat, Melissa's shimmering strands of blond hair tumbled down her back. She went on undressing until she was down to her bikini pants, garter belt, stockings, and shoes.

Bobbie reached out and pulled a straight-backed chair away from the desk, positioning it near the girl. "Sit here," she ordered, "and take off the rest."

Her hands shaking, the young woman dropped onto the chair and pulled off her heels. Then she undid the garter belt, rolling down her stockings and dropping them onto the pile. Lastly, she squirmed out of her panties.

Bobbie remained behind her. "Stay there," she snapped. "And don't move."

Melissa was completely naked now, sitting bolt upright in the chair. Continuing to hold the gun on her, Bobbie again reached out to the desk, opening the center drawer and taking out the hypodermic needle she'd placed in it earlier.

She held the needle in her left hand and pointed it toward the ceiling, testing it by depressing the plunger slightly. A tiny jet squirted from the tip.

Then she stood still for a moment, struggling to control her anger and her excitement, willing her nerves to calm down. When her hand was steady, she moved closer.

The girl was obviously rigid with fear, every muscle tensed. Her head was tilted back slightly, as if expecting a blow. She was still trembling, but not enough, Bobbie decided, for it to be a problem.

268

The carotid artery was clearly defined in the side of her neck, a delicate blue vertical line that contrasted with her pale skin. Bobbie could see it pulsing just below the jaw, the rapid pumping of the girl's heart seeming to give the artery a life of its own.

Keeping the needle behind the young woman's field of vision, Bobbie brought the tip to within a hair's breadth of the blue line.

*Now.*

She plunged the needle into the artery and mashed the plunger with her thumb.

Melissa screamed. And twisted violently, struggling to rise from the chair and pawing at her neck. The movement dislodged the hypodermic and she staggered sideways, turning her head from sidetoside.

Bobbie stepped back and watched, her eyes bright, holding the needle in one hand, the pistol in the other.

The young woman cried out again, the sound this time trailing off to a low moan. She sank to the carpet and crouched there on her hands and knees, twisting her head to one side and then the other. Her mouth opened, and she collapsed facedown, froth bubbling from her lips. Her fingers and toes quivered, then jerked convulsively for a full minute.

And then she was still.

# *68*

In the morning, Ben woke up to the aroma of coffee perking and bacon frying, surprised that his head was clear after what he'd done to the bottle of Jack Daniel's. He showered and shaved and then ate an enormous breakfast of scrambled eggs and bacon, and English muffins dripping with butter and smeared with blackberry jam. He drank two cups of coffee, and afterward he and Patty went back to bed for an hour. By the time he got up again, he was feeling better than he had in weeks.

As he got dressed, she lay in bed, watching him.

"I never heard you come in," he said.

"Small wonder."

He buttoned his shirt, glancing at her in the mirror. "Sometimes a few drinks relaxes me."

"You mean embalms you."

"Whatever. I've been thinking."

"Yes?"

"Maybe you're right. A few days off wouldn't be such a bad idea. We could get out of here, take a trip to that place upstate."

"You mean it?"

"Sure."

"Hey, that would be just great. Maybe the day after tomorrow?"

"Or this afternoon?"

"Oh, I couldn't do that. I'd have to let Guido know, give him advance warning. He's always been so nice to me."

"That's because you pack the joint for him, not just because he thinks you have a cute ass."

"Don't be vulgar."

"Who's vulgar? I'm just telling it like it is. So let's split the difference. You tell him tonight, we leave tomorrow. How about it?"

"Maybe. I'll see how it goes."

"Okay, but I'm counting on you."

"Good."

He gave her a quick kiss, put on his windbreaker, and left the apartment.

When he arrived at the precinct house and walked into the squad room, Ed Flynn said, "Hey, Lou, I been trying to reach you."

"What's up?"

"Another woman was killed last night. In the Park Lane. And she was painted."

"Christ."

"Yeah. Joe Spadone called. He thought you'd want to know about it."

"What else did he tell you?"

"Just that a maid found the body and went crazy. Then somebody tipped off the media."

"Look out."

"And how. This'll make some story."

Ben did an about-face. "I'll see you later."

Flynn grabbed his arm. "You're not going up there?"

"The hell I'm not."

The sergeant tightened his grip. "Ben, listen to me. You'd be sticking your ass out a mile. If the media sees you, they could take that as proof the cops believe the same guy did all three."

"The reporters aren't stupid. They'll make the connection anyhow."

"Sure, but you'd be confirming it for them. And not only that, you're supposed to be restricted. The brass'll come down on you like a ton of shit. You could get busted, you know that?"

"Yeah, I do." He pulled his arm free, and headed for the stairs.

# 69

B en had thought nothing could top the first two in this case, but he was wrong.

The body was lying on the sofa in the living room of the suite. Only it didn't look like a body. What it looked like was a monstrous penis, nearly six feet long. The shaft was pink, and the head was bright red. Seeing it stopped him cold.

A CSU photographer was taking pictures, the flashes from his camera illuminating the room with intermittent bursts of light. Standing nearby, waiting for him to finish, was Dr. Robert Kurtz, the assistant medical examiner who had worked on the others.

To Ben, the scene was an outsized pornographic cartoon. He tried again to comprehend the kind of mind that could come up with an idea like this, to understand how its owner would spend the time and effort to create this three-dimensional obscenity, to say nothing of the breadth of his imagination.

Over time, you saw a lot of shocking things as a cop, evidence of what, in moments of rage or passion, human beings were capable of doing to one another. And then once in a while, you saw what madness could produce. First Patterson, then Miller, and now this.

Phil Monahan was there also, along with Art Weisskopf and Joe Spadone. All three nodded to him, their expressions wary, watching his reaction as he looked at the grotesque form on the sofa.

Ben stepped closer. The woman's nude limbs had been tightly bound to her sides, her knees and ankles also trussed. After that, a thick coat of pink paint had been applied to every square inch of skin from her shoulders to her toes, to make her body resemble an erect male member.

But the head was what brought off the effect. Something had been pulled over it, perhaps a nylon stocking, and then it had been painted a vivid crimson. None of her features was discernable; the head was simply a large red knob on the end of the pink shaft.

It was crude, and disgusting. But when you looked at it, you couldn't fail to understand what it represented.

Midtown North's squad commander moved in alongside. "I thought you were on vacation."

"Just passing by," Ben said.

Monahan inclined his head toward the thing on the sofa. "This guy gets more creative every time out."

"Or more crazy," Ben said.

Monahan's freckled face wore a smirk. "Maybe he was going for a place in *Guinness*. The world's biggest schvantz."

Dick Brady came out of the bedroom. "Morning, Ben."

"Hello, Dick. You ever see anything like this?"

The CSU detective shook his head. "No, never. We get this guy, the shrinks'll have a field day."

Ben turned to Monahan. "How did she die?"

"Don't know yet. We're waiting for somebody to take that cover off her head."

"I'll get it off," Brady said. He took an X-Acto knife from his equipment case and knelt beside the body. Weisskopf and Spadone moved in also, the group standing in a semicircle around the sofa.

Slowly and carefully, Brady slit the red-encrusted material, then drew it away from the woman's head.

Ben felt a tightening in the pit of his stomach as he recognized her. The blond hair was matted and her eyes were glazed, but there was no mistaking that face. He thought of what she'd looked like in Wolfe's studio, coolly teasing him as she changed her shirt. And then he thought of Shirley, lying on a pile of rubble in a vacant lot in Harlem with her throat cut.

"We'll get her prints," Brady said. "They'll go out for an ID right away."

"I know who she is," Ben said.

The others looked at him.

"Her name's Melissa Martin. She was a model. And a hooker."

"That figures," Monahan said. "What else do you know about her?"

"Not much." He wanted time to think it through.

But Monahan pressed him. "You got any ideas about what happened here?"

"No. Not right this minute."

Monahan turned to the ME. "So what killed her, Doc?"

Kurtz shrugged. "Hard to say, until we clean the goop off her and then do a post. Without the paint, I could see how the blood settled in the body. But this one wasn't strangled, and at the moment I don't

272

see any evidence of a wound. Don't hold me to it, but if I had to guess, I'd say poison."

"If it was, it must have been fast-acting," Monahan said. "Her face isn't twisted up, the way it would be if she'd died from strychnine or arsenic."

"That's true," Kurtz said. "It would've been a substance that had an instantaneous effect. Something that would shut down the central nervous system."

"Such as?"

"Sodium pentobarbital, maybe. Or cyclobarbital. A heavy dose of either would do it." The ME took a small flashlight from his pocket and, lifting one of the eyelids, directed the beam at her pupil.

From where he was standing, Ben could see that it was fully dilated, which would tend to confirm Kurtz's theory.

Ben turned to Spadone. "He leave anything behind?"

"Nothing we found so far. Apparently, he used makeup remover to clean up with, so there're probably no prints, either."

"It's like he learns from each one," Weisskopf said. "In the Plaza, he was sloppy. But then when he did the flag lady, he took everything with him but the knife. This is the cleanest one yet."

Ben glanced around the room. It was decorated in light tones, bleached oak and gold trim, the carpet a soft green. The effect should have been garish, but instead it put him in mind of what you'd see in a tony beach resort. And instead of being out of character in a grubby, high-powered city, the color scheme was somehow peaceful—an oasis in a stone desert.

Another of the CSU detectives was taping shut a small plastic bag. "Anything in the bedroom?" Ben asked him.

"We got some fibers in there, and a few more drops of makeup, but that was all." He nodded toward the body. "That looks like nylon rope he used to bind her up with. We'll run it through the lab."

Ben turned to Spadone. "You say there was nothing here that belonged to her?"

"Nothing," Spadone said. "He must have taken everything with him. Her clothes, purse, whatever."

"Who rented the room?"

"Registered to a Mr. and Mrs. Frank Wellington, from Grosse Pointe, Michigan."

"I called Wellington," Weisskopf said. "He looked in his wallet and his AmEx card was missing. He works for General Motors, and a couple days ago he came to New York, stayed in a company apartment. So he didn't use the card, he said. That's why he didn't notice it was gone until I called."

"You get a description of the guy who registered?" Ben asked.

"Not yet," Spadone said. "Both the desk clerk and the bellman who were on last night haven't come in yet."

"We'll question them as soon as they get here," Monahan said. He was making an effort to seem reasonable, but Ben could see he was pissed at having another detective messing around in this—especially when Ben now seemed to be second-guessing his procedures.

Weisskopf looked at Ben. "You happen to know if she worked for Panache, Lieutenant?"

Ben wasn't about to give them that. He shrugged.

"She might not have been with a service at all," Monahan said. "Plenty of these broads are solos."

Not so, Ben thought. Monahan didn't know as much about the business as he wanted you to think he did.

The others went on talking, but Ben tuned them out. He was looking at the girl's body, again feeling anger and frustration. In the whole mix, the cops and their politics, the media and their lust for a lurid story, she was the one thing nobody gave a damn about. Just one more dead whore.

He thought of what Shirley had said to him: "Turning tricks can be dangerous, man."

It was time to get out of here. He went to the door, raising his hand in a half wave as he left. "See you guys later."

The elevator arrived, and two white-clad members of an ambulance crew stepped out, carrying equipment cases and a folding gurney. Ben moved past them into the car.

As the elevator made its descent, he thought about what Monahan had asked him. Did he have any ideas? He did—one good one. How good? He'd know in a few minutes.

# 70

Ben got off the elevator on the second floor and took the stairs the rest of the way, in an effort to avoid reporters who might be hanging around the lobby. When he got there, he saw several standing near the cop who was stationed at the blocked-off elevator. He recognized one guy from the *Post* and another from WPIX-TV. None of them noticed him as he made his way into the hotel's management offices, flashing his shield and telling a clerk he was on police business.

Once inside, he approached a door marked MGR, knocked once, and went in. A heavyset man looked up from his desk as Ben again produced the gold shield and identified himself.

"You the manager?" Ben asked him.

"I'm one of them. My name is D'Allesandro." With his thatch of black hair and olive skin, he might have been Italian, or maybe Spanish. Ben detected a slight accent, but he couldn't quite place it. The people who ran luxury hotels in New York were all multilingual, because of the international nature of their clientele.

"I'm on the homicide investigation," Ben said. That would get Monahan further pissed off when he heard about it, which was just too bad.

D'Allesandro was visibly distraught. He shook his head. "Terrible," he said. "We do the best we can with security, but it's impossible to screen everybody who comes in. Our guests expect protection, but a lot of them, they get furious if we question them."

"Sure, I understand."

"The other detectives spoke with our security officers. You wish to see them also?"

"Not just now," Ben said. "I wanted to talk to you."

"Very well. Sit down, Lieutenant. You like a cup of coffee?"

"That sounds good." He dropped into a chair in front of the desk.

"How do you take it?"

"Black, please."

The manager picked up his phone and spoke into it. He was wearing a sand-colored jacket and a green tie; evidently whoever had decorated the Park Lane had decorated its staff, as well. When he put the phone down, he said, "I explained to the other police officers, the people who were on last night haven't come in yet."

"I know," Ben said.

"This murder, how ghastly. After the maid found the woman's body, I saw how it had been painted. Somebody who did such a thing must be crazy, no?"

"Yes, he must be. Can you show me the registration form for the room?"

"Of course." He opened a drawer in his desk. "I put it here for safekeeping. One of the officers looked at it this morning." He took out the form and placed it on the desk in front of Tolliver.

As Spadone had said, the guests had registered as Mr. and Mrs. Frank Wellington, of 127 Oak Place, Grosse Pointe, Michigan. The information had been printed in neat block letters. But the signature was what Ben was looking for.

In contrast to the printed information, the name had been signed in a loose scribble, with looping flourishes that made it barely legible. As if the signator had written it thousands of times, until it had taken on an individual and highly distinctive character. But despite the swirls and the run-together letters, he could make it out well enough. It said, *Mrs. F. J. Wellington.*

As he'd suspected it would. For a full minute, Ben stared at the scrawl. *Mrs.* Wellington. Spadone hadn't caught that.

As he studied the signature, the door of the office opened and a hotel waiter brought in a tray with a silver pot, cups and saucers, napkins, and a small plate of cookies. He placed them on the manager's desk and poured coffee into the cups. D'Allesandro nodded to him, and the man left the room.

Ben looked at the array in front of him and smiled. "I'm not used to such service."

"We like to be hospitable," D'Allesandro said. "The coffee is French roast, very strong."

Ben drank from his cup. The black liquid was as advertised; he was sure a spoon would stand straight up in it.

His host pointed to the cookies. "Please."

Ben ate one, politely, wishing he could wipe out the plate. He looked again at the registration form. "This says the credit card was American Express and belonged to Frank J. Wellington. But Mrs. Wellington made this out and signed it."

The manager shrugged. "That is not uncommon, for the wife to register. Sometimes when people arrive in New York, the husband has a business appointment. The wife checks them in."

"But with his credit card?"

"Also not unusual. He gives her his card to check in with, because he wants the bill to go to him. Maybe for expense account reasons, whatever."

"Okay, but look. The registration clerk needs a card for identification purposes, right? And for safety's sake, to keep someone from skipping out without paying their bill. True?"

"Yes, of course."

"So a wife could use her own card, but then when they check out, the husband could present his card and that's how the hotel would bill the charge."

The manager looked puzzled. "Yes, that often happens. But we see it done this way, as well. The wife using her husband's card."

"Then the clerk would think nothing of it?"

276

"No. As I say, it would not be unusual."

"Okay. Would you ask someone to make me a copy of this?"

"Yes, at once." He picked up the phone and spoke into it once more.

Ben sipped coffee and ate another cookie. They were almond wafers, still warm. Christ, but he was hungry.

A young woman attired in the same sand, white, and green scheme came into the office, and D'Allesandro handed her the registration form. She smiled at Ben and went out again.

The manager tapped the surface of his desk with a forefinger. He was sweating slightly, and a faint sheen was visible on his forehead and his nose. "How long will you people have to be here, Lieutenant? With this investigation?"

"Not much longer," Ben said. "They're getting ready to remove the body now." He saw D'Allesandro flinch as he said it.

"Could they take it out through the back entrance, on the Fifty-ninth Street side of the lobby? It's, that is . . ."

"Yes, of course. I understand how you feel. I'm sure the ambulance is already out there."

The manager took a handkerchief from his breast pocket and blotted his face with it. "A thing like this can have an extremely bad effect on business. Not just where it took place, but for everybody. It's devastating to the hotels."

Also devastating to the girl upstairs, Ben thought. But he said nothing. He drank the rest of his coffee and declined an offer of more.

The young woman returned to the office and gave D'Allesandro the registration form and the copy. He thanked her, and as she left, he took a manila envelope from a desk drawer and slipped the copy into it, handing it to Ben.

"You've been very helpful," Tolliver said. He tucked the envelope into a jacket pocket already stuffed with his notes. Getting to his feet, he shook the manager's hand, finding the palm sweaty. "Don't bother to see me out; I know the way." He turned and left the office.

In the lobby, the ambulance attendants emerged from the elevator and began wheeling the gurney toward the south end of the hotel. A green bag was trussed to the gurney, and two uniformed cops were leading the way. A small crowd of reporters tagged along like kids following an ice cream cart, throwing out questions to the cops, who ignored them.

Ben turned in the opposite direction, going out the front entrance onto Central Park South and heading toward Fifth Avenue. Walking around the block to where he'd left his car would take longer, but he wanted to avoid the gaggle of reporters.

He noticed that the sun had disappeared behind ominous gray clouds and the wind had freshened. As he zipped up his windbreaker, Ben was aware that the sense of excitement he'd felt earlier was growing stronger. It would have been good to wait for the clerk and the bellman to come in, to talk with them. But it wasn't necessary; he was sure of it. They'd tell him that the woman who registered last night was slim and good-looking, well dressed and with dark hair. Maybe wearing glasses.

He could almost picture her.

And he also knew which service had sent the girl to the Park Lane.

He didn't know the reason for the connection, but only that there was a connection. One thing tied all three dead hookers together.

Panache.

He strode along the sidewalk at a rapid pace, turning the corner as he went by the front of the Plaza. By the time he reached Fifty-ninth Street, he'd broken into a trot, brushing past the pedestrians as he hurried toward his car.

# 71

The apartment house was one of the big ones on the east side of Park Avenue in the eighties. A few blocks north of here the wide street with its beautifully planted gardens and immaculate buildings butted up against an Hispanic slum, but this area was one of the city's most fashionable. Tall and stately, the gray stone tower exuded confidence and tradition, the accoutrements of old money.

Even the doorman's uniform showed class. It was a conservative dark blue with brass buttons, nothing like the quasi-military kitsch you saw on doormen in front of the flashy new buildings along Third and Second avenues. As Ben approached the entrance, he wondered whether any of the building's other residents knew their neighbor was one of New York's leading madams.

The doorman glanced at him, taking in the windbreaker and worn corduroys. His tone was glacial. "May I help you?"

Ben flipped open his wallet, the tin seeming to make only a slight impression. "Let's step inside," he said, "where we can be a little more private."

The building featured an outer lobby, where people could wait for a taxi or for a chauffeur to bring a car around.

When they entered it, Ben said, "There's been an increase in crime in this neighborhood. I'm sure you're aware of that."

That thawed him out a little. "Oh yes. You couldn't help but be aware. It's terrible what goes on nowadays. The doctor's wife lives just a few blocks farther down Park. The one who was beaten and raped?"

"Yes. That's why I'm making a security check. Martha Bellamy is a resident here, isn't she?"

"Yes, in the penthouse. Has there been a problem?"

"We're just keeping a sharp eye," Ben said.

"That's good, Officer. It's reassuring."

"I'll be around for a while, checking things out."

"Very well."

The doorman went back outside, and Ben turned and walked into the main lobby. The area was in keeping with the building's exterior, with polished marble floors inlaid with strips of brass, a large chandelier hanging from the tall ceiling. Gilt-framed mirrors decorated the paneled walls.

When an elevator door opened, the car disgorged a pretty blond nurse pushing an old man in a wheelchair. The geezer was wrapped in a red plaid blanket and wearing a tweed cap. After they passed him, Ben stepped into the car and pushed the button marked PH.

When he reached the penthouse floor, he saw that there were two doors, an ornately paneled one directly ahead of him, and a plain one at the end of the area. He chose the plain one, assuming it was the service entrance.

The man who answered the buzzer was a tiny Oriental. He opened the door a crack, his bland features registering surprise as he looked up at his unexpected visitor.

Ben shoved his foot into the crack and held up his shield. "Police officer. Stand away from the door and keep your mouth shut."

The houseboy moved back, his slanted eyes wide as Tolliver stepped passed him and closed the door. With his starched white jacket and his diminutive body, he put Ben in mind of a miniature waiter. They were standing in a kitchen that added to the impression; it looked like what you'd see in a fancy restaurant, with the cooktop, stacked ovens, outsized refrigerator, and freezer all in stainless steel.

"What's your name?" Ben asked.

"Chang."

"Okay, Chang, where's Miss Bellamy?"

The houseboy pointed.

"I'm going in to have a talk with her," Ben said. "You stay here and be quiet. Understand?"

His reply was half nod, half bow.

Ben walked in the direction the tiny man had indicated. It was a hallway, with a large dining room on the left and an arched doorway leading into an open area at the end. He went through the archway into a huge two-story living room with a floor-to-ceiling bank of windows. His footsteps made no sound in the ankle-deep white carpeting as he entered the room.

Martha Bellamy and her assistant were standing at the windows, carrying on an animated discussion. At least, Bellamy was animated; Wickersham seemed totally relaxed. Bellamy was waving her arms. She had on peach-colored pajamas that set off her red hair, and she was talking loudly. They didn't notice Ben.

Bellamy thrust out her chin. "I don't care what you say, Patrick— I'm scared shitless. Melissa's one of our brightest girls. It's just impossible for me to believe she'd do something like this."

"There's always a first time," he said. "And if we haven't heard anything, why get excited?"

"Why? Why the fuck do you think? Caroline was murdered just down the street from there. Maybe the same thing—Christ, I can't even say it. But if she is okay, if she did do something like stay with the guy, she would have called in to let us know. Especially after what happened to Caroline. All the girls are being extra careful now. You know that."

"Of course I know it. I'm merely pointing out there's no reason to panic."

"You might not think so, Patrick. But I think we ought to call the police and report her missing."

Ben said, "You don't have to."

Bellamy let out a shriek as she spun around to face him. "You! What the hell are you doing in here?"

Ben walked toward them. "I came to talk about one of your girls."

Wickersham drew himself erect. His powder blue outfit seemed at odds with his stern expression. "How dare you barge in this way? Get out at once!"

"Don't go tinkle in your panties," Ben said. He turned to Bellamy. "You had a girl in the Park Lane last night, right? Melissa Martin?"

She gasped. "Oh, Jesus. What about her?"

"She was murdered," Ben said. "A maid discovered the body just a couple of hours ago."

It was as if he'd slugged her. She staggered back a step, then

280

stumbled over to a sofa and slumped down on it, burying her face in her hands and moaning.

Wickersham remained unruffled, gazing imperiously at Ben. "This is private property, Lieutenant. You have no right to be here."

Ben didn't bother to answer. He stayed where he was, waiting for Bellamy to get herself together. Looking around the room, he saw that everything was white: the furniture, the drapes, the carpet, even the piano. Everything but some statues and the pictures that covered the soaring walls. The paintings were of all shapes and sizes, a few with subjects you could recognize, but most of them looking as if a maniac had heaved buckets of paint at the canvas.

Bellamy pulled a tissue out of the pocket of her pajamas and blew her nose loudly. When she looked up, her eyes were red-rimmed, but her face was again set in the attitude of belligerence Ben remembered from their first meeting.

"What happened," she said, "to Melissa?"

"We don't know yet. We have to wait for a postmortem to tell us the exact cause of death."

Wickersham folded his arms. "How do we know it's Melissa? Has she been identified?"

"Oh, get off it, Patrick," Bellamy said. "Of course it's Melissa. Jesus Christ, how terrible. And the business. What will this do . . ." Her voice trailed off.

"How long had she been with you?"

"Maybe a year." She shook her head. "Nobody's safe. Nobody's safe in this fucking city. Why do we have a police force, if you can't protect people?"

Ben sat down in one of the white chairs. "What's unsafe is to work for Panache."

"What are you saying?"

"Caroline Patterson, Lisa Miller, Melissa Martin—they were all your girls. Including Miller, at one time."

Bellamy's tone dropped to a whisper. "My God."

"Who was Melissa seeing, in the Park Lane?"

"For heaven's sake, Martha," Wickersham said. "Are you going to let this cop push you around? He forces his way in here and tricks you into spilling your guts and you go along with it? At least call Abe. Or I will."

Abe? That would be Bellamy's lawyer, Ben thought. Abe Rakoff, of Cohen, Dietrich and Rakoff. Monica had told him that.

He spoke to Bellamy. "Sure. You can call your lawyer, if you want to. And then the whole thing goes public. Murdered call girls all worked for Panache. Madam questioned. John list subpoenaed. Ought to make a pretty hot story, huh?"

Wickersham moved toward her. "Martha, he's just trying—"

"Shut up, Patrick." Her eyes were fixed on Ben. "What happens if I cooperate—how far does it go?"

"Same deal I offered you before," Ben said. "Help us, and the police will keep the lid on. I can practically guarantee it."

Wickersham snorted contemptuously. "*Practically* guarantee it? What kind of double-talk is that?"

Bellamy ignored him, saying to Ben, "You give me your word you'll keep Panache's name—and *my* name—out of it?"

"It's stayed out so far, hasn't it? I give you my word I'll do my level best to keep it that way."

She ran a hand through her curly red mane. "His name was Frank Wellington."

Wickersham looked at the ceiling and shook his head.

"From Grosse Pointe, Michigan," Ben said.

Bellamy was startled. "How did you know that?"

"From the hotel register. Did you book the date yourself?"

"No, Francesca did. She's one of the phone girls. When Melissa didn't call in, I almost went crazy, worrying. I stayed at the office myself until just a couple of hours ago."

Ben looked at Wickersham. "How about you—were you there?"

"No. I was out ill."

He turned back to Bellamy. "When she didn't call, did you try to get in touch with her?"

"Yes, of course. I called her apartment several times during the night, but there was no answer. I also called the hotel room, but there was no answer there, either."

Ben sat back, looking up at the paintings on the wall above Bellamy's head. Some of them were downright weird. One was a portrait of a woman with both eyes on the same side of her nose. Another showed a tree with a clock draped over one of the limbs. And those were the ones you could figure out. Most of the others were of the heave-the-paint variety.

"This Frank Wellington," Ben said. "He ever do business with you before?"

Bellamy lit a cigarette and exhaled a stream of smoke. "No, he was new. I checked the entry when we didn't hear from Melissa."

"Uh-huh. You say Francesca booked the date?"

"Yes."

A white telephone stood on an end table near where Bellamy was sitting. Ben pointed to it. "Call her. Tell her I want to talk to her, that it's okay to answer my questions."

Bellamy hesitated. "What about—"

"Just tell her to give me straight answers."

She took another drag on the cigarette and mashed it out in an ashtray. Then she picked up the telephone and called a number. A moment later, she spoke into the phone briefly. A pause followed; evidently, she was getting some resistance at the other end.

"I can't tell you right now," Bellamy said into the phone. There was another pause, and then her voice took on a hard edge. "Francesca, I'll *tell* you *later*. Now goddamn it, answer the man's questions." Without waiting for a response, she passed the handset to Ben.

"Hello, Francesca," he said. "This is Lieutenant Tolliver."

The voice had none of the silkiness he'd heard whenever he'd called Panache. It was thin and cracked, as if its owner was on the verge of hysteria. "She's dead, isn't she? Tell me the truth."

As gently as he could, he said, "Yes, she's dead."

A low wail came through the receiver. "Oh, God."

"Francesca, it's terrible what happened. But I'm talking to you now because we need your help. Do you understand?"

". . . Yes."

"We have to find whoever was responsible. So we can punish him for what he did, and also to protect other girls, you see?"

She was sniffling. "Yes, I understand."

"Okay, now take your time, and think. Last night when the call came in, do you remember it?"

"Yes. His name was Frank Wellington."

"Can you tell me what he sounded like?"

"Just a guy. He sounded nice. I mean, I don't remember anything bad, or unusual. I would have noticed that."

"Martha said he was a new customer."

"That's right. He told me he was from Michigan, staying at the Park Lane."

"Go on."

"I asked if he'd called us before, and he said no. I asked for a reference, and he said he was a friend of Hi Donnelly."

Ben felt an almost physical jolt. "Say again?"

"He said he hadn't called before, but he knew Hi Donnelly. That's Inspector Donnelly of the police. So I thought he must be okay."

"Then what?"

"He asked for a girl. Said he wanted a blonde. So I described a

283

few, but he was fussy. Then when I told him about Melissa, he said she sounded exactly like what he was looking for."

"What else?"

"I asked him if he wanted to take her out. You know, to dinner or anything, and he said no, she should just come to his suite as soon as possible."

"And that was it?"

"No, I called him back to confirm. We always do that with a new client. See, supposedly it's to say the girl will be there soon, but actually it's to be sure he's where he says he is."

"Did you record all the things you're telling me now?"

"No, I didn't have time. We were very busy."

"Okay. Is there anything more you remember? Anything at all?"

"I don't think so. That was pretty much everything."

"Thanks, Francesca. You've been a big help." He hung up.

Martha Bellamy lit another cigarette. Glancing at her, Ben wondered whether she knew about the john saying he was a friend of Inspector Donnelly's. Instinctively, he decided not to mention it. It was something he had to think about before discussing it with anyone.

"Melissa have a boyfriend?"

"No, I'm pretty sure she didn't."

"She ever in any kind of trouble, do you know?"

"Not that I know of."

"All right." He got up from the chair. "I'll be talking to you again soon. Meantime, if there's anything you think of that could help, call me."

Bellamy extinguished her cigarette in the ashtray. "I'll show you out."

She rose from the sofa and Ben followed her out of the living room and into the front hall. It was a rotunda, with a circular stairway leading up to the second floor and a domed skylight in the ceiling.

At the door, she turned to him. She was almost as tall as he was, slim and slinky in the peach-colored pajamas. It wasn't hard to guess how she'd worked her way up in the business. "Remember your promise, Lieutenant."

"I told you, I'll do everything I can."

She touched the collar of his jacket with a slender forefinger. "Maybe when all this is over, we could get to know each other better. I have a feeling I could do you a lot of good."

"Maybe you could," he said. He opened the door and crossed to the elevator, pressing the button. The car arrived a moment later, and as he stepped into it and looked back, he saw her standing in the doorway, watching him.

When he got back to where he'd parked, he unlocked the car and climbed into the driver's seat. It had started to rain, fat gray drops that splashed on the windshield and ran down the glass in dirty streaks. He sat there for a time, not starting the engine, thinking about what he'd learned.

It would be good to talk to somebody, test his ideas. Brennan, for instance. And yet at this point, he couldn't bring himself to trust anybody in the upper levels of the NYPD. Hi Donnelly? What was the connection?

And another thing. This time, a woman had registered at the hotel, but a man had called Panache, asking for a girl. Was it a couple, after all?

Reaching into the pocket of his windbreaker, he got out the envelope containing his notes. Along with it was a crumpled slip reminding him to return Barbara Conklin's call. He put the slip aside and opened the envelope, taking out the printout of Panache's customers. He flipped through the pages until he came to Donnelly's name, then checked the girls the inspector had been with. Caroline's name was on the list, but Melissa's was not.

He looked at the telephone message, and that triggered another idea. Going back to the printout, he looked up the entry for Barry Conklin. It said that on April 14 of that year, Conklin had seen Melissa Martin in the St. Regis, the same hotel where Ben had drinks with Mrs. Conklin.

There had been no mention of Melissa, however, in the conversations Barbara Conklin had recorded. Conklin must have made the call from his office, or possibly he'd called from the hotel.

Ben stuffed the papers back into the envelope and returned it to his jacket pocket. The rain was coming down harder now. He started the Ford's engine and turned on his wipers, then drove across Park and turned onto the southbound side.

What he wanted was a telephone.

# 72

The Tuscany was a small, sleepy hotel on Thirty-ninth Street, off Madison Avenue. Barbara Conklin had suggested it, she said, because it was out of the way.

There was a restaurant on the ground floor, and a bar. Ben waited in the bar for a half hour, nursing a beer and thinking that if he didn't get something to eat soon, he'd fall down. It was late afternoon and there was no one in the place now except for Ben and the bartender and two guys who were discussing some kind of business deal.

The businessmen were sitting at a table drinking scotch and sounding a little drunk, which struck Ben as not the best condition to be in if you were doing any serious negotiating. But that was their problem, not his. From his seat at the bar, he could see it was still raining outside, gray sheets bouncing off the roofs of taxis crawling past the hotel.

When she came in, he had the same reaction as the first time he'd seen her, struck by her stylishness and the air of femininity she seemed to radiate. She was wearing a trench coat and a slouch hat, and when she saw him she smiled warmly, pulling off the hat and shaking out her black hair, greeting him in her low, husky voice.

He helped her onto the bar stool next to his and she rolled up the hat and stuffed it into a pocket of her trench coat. Ben told the bartender to bring her a Beefeater martini straight up, very dry and with an olive.

"I see you remembered, Lieutenant."

"That I did."

She nodded at the nearly empty glass of beer in front of him. "But you switched."

"Also right."

"You see? I remembered, too."

Women had a way of doing that, he thought. Turning some little thing into a kind of significant understanding the two of you were sharing.

"So how are you?" he asked.

She unbuttoned the coat and pulled it open, revealing a blue cashmere sweater. "Holding my own with Barry, if that's what you mean. And better than that, actually. I have something more for you."

286

"What is it?"

"It's about a scheme he's involved in. Do you know a company called Barclay Telecom?"

"I don't think so."

The bartender served her martini and she said, "Cheers," and sipped it before continuing.

"They make equipment for telephone companies. Switching and relaying devices and other stuff. They're very hot right now because they've developed a product that codifies customer information and automatically builds data bases. I learned that part by talking to my broker."

Ben wondered what this had to do with him. But he was conscious of her perfume, and aware that it was pleasant to be close to her while she talked.

She took a package of Winstons from her bag and lit one with a small gold lighter. "So what's happening is that several bigger companies want to acquire them, but Barclay says they won't sell, they intend to remain independent. What they don't know is that the Salzac group is planning a takeover."

"Salzac. Corporate raiders?"

"Right. They've been quietly buying up shares, and they're going to make a tender offer."

Ben finished his beer and signaled to the bartender to give him another. He turned back to her. "Okay, so?"

"So the brokerage Salzac is using is Coleman Baker."

"And your husband has a connection there."

"How did you know that?"

"I guessed."

"You guessed right. He's been paying an officer in Coleman Baker large amounts of money to keep him informed, all of it in cash. Very cloak-and-dagger. And now Barry's also buying Barclay stock, through several dummy accounts. He figures he'll make a killing when Salzac announces their offer."

"Insider trading and highly illegal."

"Exactly. And isn't that great? I mean, that I got wind of it? And not only that, but my clever little bug picked up several of his conversations." She went back into her purse and withdrew an envelope, triumphantly placing it on the bar in front of him. "There you are, Lieutenant. As they say on TV, I got the goods."

The bartender placed a fresh glass of draught beer alongside the envelope and moved away. Ben drank some of the beer. It was ice-cold and tasted fine, but it did little to appease his hunger. "That's great," he said to her, "for you. But it doesn't help me."

287

Her face fell. "Doesn't help you? You just said what he's doing is highly illegal."

"It is. Not only a violation of New York law but federal as well."

"Then what are you saying?"

"The trouble is, I'm working on a homicide investigation. What you're telling me about is securities fraud."

"But you're a police officer."

"Sure, but this isn't my bailiwick. All I can do is pass the information and the tapes to someone who works on cases like this. I'm sure he'll be very interested. Although I should point out to you the tapes would never be admissible as evidence, no matter what your husband says in them."

"Why not?"

"Because they were obtained illegally. He didn't know you were recording his calls."

She crushed out her cigarette in an ashtray and raised her glass, not sipping this time but gulping its contents. She put the empty glass down on the bar. "Shit!"

He observed that she was just as attractive when angry, maybe more so. "Hey, I'm sure the tip will be valuable, whether the tapes can be used or not. And if your husband is prosecuted on a charge like this, it would give your own chances for successful litigation a big boost. You tell your lawyer about it?"

"Yes, but not in the detail I gave you. I just said I thought Barry could be in trouble over a crooked stock deal. He said good, that would be further evidence of amoral practices."

"So, you see? And by the way, I gather you picked up more on his extracurricular activities?"

"With his whores? It's all on the tapes. But why is that different from the other stuff?"

"Because I don't need it for evidence. What it can give me is information."

"Then that means I've helped you, right? And that's good. I was sort of hoping you'd also find what I put together on the stock deal valuable. It may sound silly, but I felt I was doing it as much for you as for myself. Or to be perfectly honest, that I was doing it for both of us."

"For both of us?"

The gray eyes held on him. "Yes. And that was . . . exciting to me. You're a very attractive man, Ben."

Holy Christ, he thought. I'm having another wonderful day. Not just one, but two sexy broads letting me know all I'd have to do is ask.

288

What Barbara Conklin did next seemed innocent enough. But it had a very erotic effect on him. She placed her hand on his and squeezed, continuing to fix him with those large, soft eyes. He felt desire rush through him.

Her voice fell even lower. "It's a rainy afternoon, you know. And we just happen to be in a hotel."

A scene flashed through his mind. He was upstairs in a room with her, and he'd taken off her coat and the blue sweater and everything else and they were on the bed and he was fucking her brains out.

He came within an inch, maybe a millimeter, of taking her up on it. But then his brain kicked in.

*Cool it, you asshole. She's not so hard up she has to tree a cop. She may sound horny and bat her eyes at you, but you can be sure she's tougher than she looks. Whatever it is she wants, it's a lot more than a dance on your dick.*

He withdrew his hand and patted hers. "I have to get back downtown. Much as I'd like to stay here with you."

Something flickered in the gray eyes. Another show of anger? Whatever, it was gone in an instant.

He dug into his pants pocket for some bills and put them on the bar. Then he took her arm as she got off the stool. Carrying the envelope she'd brought him, he steered her out of the place.

The tycoons were still trying to outwit each other through an alcoholic blur, and as Ben and Barbara Conklin passed their table, the men abruptly suspended their talk and stared at her. One said something to the other out of the corner of his mouth, but Ben didn't hear what it was. He didn't have to; he knew what it was like to watch her walk.

Out on the street, the downpour was as steady and as dreary as it had been when he'd gone into the hotel. They stood under the awning outside the entrance.

"Drop you somewhere?" Ben asked.

She turned up the collar of her trench coat and retrieved the hat from her pocket, unrolling it and tugging it down on her head. "No thanks, I have a car."

There was a Mercedes at the curb, and as the chauffeur caught sight of them he jumped out, opening an umbrella and rushing to hold it over her. He guided her to the car, opening the rear door and standing there until she was inside and then closing the door after her. Just before the car pulled away, she leaned close to the window and gave Ben a little wave. This time, her smile wasn't quite as radiant.

On his way to the Village, Ben stopped at a delicatessen and bought a pastrami on rye. The meat was hot and greasy and he drove with one hand and held the sandwich with the other as he wolfed it. That was another thing about New York: it was where you got the best pastrami in the world. When he finished the sandwich, he regretted having bought only one.

As usual, there was no place to park the Ford; he had to leave it two blocks away and walk back to the precinct house in the rain. Barbara Conklin had said there was more in the tapes on her husband's whoring, and he was anxious to listen to them. It was possible that she'd done him a bigger favor than she'd thought.

Even bigger than the one she'd offered to do him.

# 73

Stein's voice was a metallic crackle in the telephone receiver. "You say the body was made up in the shape of a phallus?"

"Right. I couldn't believe it, and neither could any of the other cops."

"But you see how that fits in, don't you—how it's in line with what I was saying about confused sexual identity?"

"Yeah, I guess I can. And it would square with your theory about the guy hating whores."

"Yes. But this is something else again. I'm sure you've seen bodies mutilated so as to indicate a change in sex. Male genitals cut off, objects thrust into a female's vagina, and so on. To the uninformed observer, it would seem to be simply an act of defilement. But it's much more than that. Even if the killer has no conscious idea of why he's doing it."

"I understand."

"This man you were telling me about. Did you say his name was Conklin?"

"Right," Ben said. "Barry Conklin. He runs an investment firm on Wall Street."

"You said he hires prostitutes regularly. Would you know how frequently?"

"Not exactly. Just that he sees a lot of them. He calls a service for them from his home, and probably from his office, as well, but I don't really know how often."

"But from what you do know of it, would it seem to be compulsive with him?"

Trying to answer that would be getting Ben in over his head. And besides, a good deal of this had come to him secondhand. "I couldn't say. Most of what I know about it is what his wife has told me."

"Mmm. That's another thing I find curious. Have you thought about that? About their relationship, I mean? That it might not be what she says it is, but perhaps something else altogether?"

"Yeah," Ben said. "I have thought about it. It's one of the things I wanted to ask your opinion on."

"Yes. I'll want to think about it further, but from what you've said about them, they seem like more than just a strange couple. The husband's obsessive public displays of masculinity, the extreme aggressiveness, and so on—I would say he's someone who should be looked into very carefully. And the wife. She also sounds interesting."

"She is that, Doc. Believe me."

"She could be something quite different from what she wants you to think she is."

"I've already got a sense of it. She came on to me, when we were in that bar."

"Oh? But of course, there's nothing so unusual about that. Evidently she hates her husband, whether for the reasons she gave you or for some others she hasn't revealed. And for a rejected or embittered wife to make advances to someone else would hardly be surprising."

"No, it wouldn't. Still . . ."

"There's another idea I thought might be helpful to you."

"What is it?"

"Simply that the man you're looking for didn't suddenly turn into a monster. Whatever his problem might be, it's been festering for a very long time, I assure you. Undoubtedly since his childhood."

"Yeah, I realize that."

"So what I was going to suggest is that you give me the names of the people you have the most reason to suspect. This Conklin and anyone else. I'll see if I can't run a little background check on them."

"Background check?"

"Yes. Chances are your man was treated, or even hospitalized, at one or more times in his life. Such records are all held in confidence, as you know, but I have contacts. There are people I could call."

"That's quite an idea, Doc."

"It's a long shot. But it could be productive."

291

And it could also put Tolliver's tit in a wringer, if it ever came to light. "Let me think about that one. I'll call you in a day or so."

"Fine. Meantime, don't hesitate to get in touch if anything else occurs to you."

"I'll do that, too. And thanks." He hung up.

His desk was a mound of paper. He pushed some of it aside, thinking the day would soon arrive when cops would spend all their time filling out forms and typing reports. As it was, the NYPD had more people on desks than out where the action was. No wonder the bad guys were winning the war.

Ed Flynn had trailed him into the office. "Brennan called, Lou. He sounded pissed. I think somebody tipped him off you went to the Park Lane. He wants you to call him."

"Uh-huh. He say anything more about it?"

"No, that was it. But we had reporters around again this afternoon. They're going wild over the case."

"Why'd they come here? It's not ours."

"Like we expected, they tied all three homicides together. Screaming about crazed killer preying on young women, shit like that."

Ben took the tapes and his notes and the other junk out of his pockets and dumped all of it onto the desk. "Where's that little Sony, do you know?"

"I think Carlos has it."

"Okay. I'm gonna need help from him and Frank."

"Sure."

"Who else is on?"

"Joe Stone and Dan Harrigan. They're out working on some car heists."

"What's that all about?"

"A gang's been picking up expensive sports cars. It's a truck operation."

"A tow truck? How do they get away with that? Too visible, isn't it?"

"No, Joe says this is different. The way it works is, you order a car from them. Let's say a Porsche Nine-eleven. Runs about seventy-five from a dealer, but these guys'll get you one for half that. You put down ten on deposit, they guarantee delivery inside of a week."

"How do they use the truck?"

"It's got an enclosed cargo area, looks like a big delivery van. They drive around town at night, until they spot your Porsche. The truck pulls up alongside, and the doors open. A forklift comes out, goes underneath the car, picks it up, and brings it into the truck. The doors close; the truck drives away. Just like a frog catching a fly."

"I'll be damned."

"American ingenuity," Flynn said. "Whole thing takes about thirty seconds. They do it so gentle, they don't even set off the alarm."

"Sounds like a case for SLATS to me." SLATS was the Safe, Loft and Truck Squad, working out of Midtown South.

"Yeah, but Joe and Danny have done a lot of work on it."

"Yeah, all right. Let 'em stay with it, then."

"Sure. I was just gonna get some coffee. You want some?"

"Thanks, Ed. I could use it."

Ben sat down at his desk and sorted out the pile of material he'd brought back with him. Then he telephoned police headquarters and asked for Captain Brennan. He was told the captain was out, and Ben said to leave a message that he'd returned the call.

Gathering up the printout of Panache's customers and Lisa Miller's book, he went into the squad room and put them down on a metal table. He called Rodriguez and Petrusky over, and told them to check the material for johns who had done business with the murdered girls. They were to organize the names into groups, he explained. One would contain men who had been with only one of the victims, another would have the names of men who had seen two of them, and the third would consist of men who been with all three.

"We looking for anything else?" Carlos asked.

"Anything you can find that might give us a lead," Ben said. "Weisskopf and Spadone ran down some of those guys when they were here, but nothing turned out to be productive. And anyhow, that was when we had only one dead hooker, instead of the three we've got now. Maybe fresh eyes will see something."

Flynn returned, carrying two mugs of coffee. He handed one to Ben. "You need my help, I'll be around for a while."

"Thanks, Ed. You can pitch in with Carlos and Frank on this stuff. Anybody else wants me, I'm not here."

"Got it."

"Say, Carlos," Ben said, "you got that little tape recorder?"

"Sure, it's right on my desk." He stepped away, returning a moment later and handing the machine to Tolliver.

Petrusky got out a stack of yellow pads and some pencils, dropping them onto the table and pulling up a chair. He sat down, scratching his bald head and opening his shirt collar, and began looking through the printout. "What happens if we hit something, Lou—we get a reward?"

"Sure," Ben said. "You get Christmas off." Carrying the Sony and the mug of coffee, he went back into his office and closed the door.

He spent several hours with the recordings, playing some of them back three and four times while he made notes. What Barbara Conklin had told him appeared to be true: her husband stood to make a killing when the Salzac group made its tender offer for Barclay Telecom shares. With no more effort than a series of phone calls, he'd be in line for a profit of 10 or 15 million dollars, maybe more. Jack Strickland would be very pleased to get this stuff.

But for Ben's purposes, the tapes were a disappointment. If anything, Conklin seemed to have slackened off on his assignations. There were only a few calls to Panache, each time to arrange for a girl to come to his room at the St. Regis for a couple of hours. And each time, he'd asked Martha Bellamy to send him girls he hadn't seen before.

Ben again felt pangs of frustration. What he'd love to do would be to land on Conklin with proof that the guy had been connected to Melissa Martin as well as to Caroline Patterson and see whether he couldn't flush the truth out of him. But that would be stupid. Any wrong move on Tolliver's part would be like handing the bastard a gift.

At around ten o'clock, Flynn came back into the office, wearing his jacket this time. "I'm gonna cut out, Lou. You need anything before I go?"

"What's this, a short day?"

"I got a date. The lady gets crazy if I don't give her regular service."

"Must be nice to be loved."

"It's beautiful. Especially when she's married to somebody else, so I'm not responsible."

"Don't be so sure."

"See you in the morning," Flynn said. He left and closed the door.

An hour later, Ben went into the squad room to share a pizza and drink a beer with Rodriguez and Petrusky. He asked how it was going.

"Couple of two-out-of-threes," Carlos said. "But no three-baggers."

"I shoulda been born female," Petrusky said. "These broads make a fortune."

Carlos stuffed pizza into his mouth. "It ain't too late, Frank. I know a doctor could fix you up."

Afterward, Ben returned to his office to resume working on his notes, trying to fit the pieces together, cross-checking names and theories until his eyes blurred. Finally, he sat back and stretched, debating whether he should get out of here and go back to Patty's or maybe to his own place. He was too tired to do much more tonight, and bitter that he hadn't made the progress he'd hoped he would.

But there was still a lot of work to do. Somewhere in all the mess—the printout of Panache's customers, Lisa Miller's john book, the list of girls who worked for Panache, the unorganized reams of notes he'd made, the DD-5 reports from Spadone and Weisskopf during the short time he'd had the pair working for him—somewhere was the answer; he was sure of it. The question was how to dig it out.

He dozed off then, awakening with a start, cold and stiff.

The hell with it, he thought. If I don't get some sack time, I won't be worth a damn tomorrow.

He left his office and went into the bunk room, kicking off his shoes and rolling onto an unoccupied mattress. He pulled a blanket over himself, and seconds later fell into a deep sleep.

# 74

He was up at eight, stumbling to his locker for his razor and toothbrush. The ablutions helped to wake him up, although he could have used a hot shower and several more hours of sleep. He poured himself a mug of coffee, grateful that one of the detectives had made a fresh pot, and went back into his office.

As he'd hoped, the pile on his desk seemed less formidable than it had the night before. He sat down and looked at his notes, checking out what he'd written on a pad.

In some ways, the Melissa Martin homicide was similar to the Patterson killing. In both, two people had been involved, a male and a female. At the Plaza, a woman had registered, supposedly for her boss. She'd called Panache, arranged for the service to send a girl. Members of the hotel staff had seen her, but not the man. This time, a man had called for the girl.

In the Martin case, a woman had also registered, ostensibly for herself and her husband. In both instances, identification had been supplied in the form of lost or stolen credit cards. And both times, Panache had been given the names of other customers as references. One had been an executive based in Los Angeles, and that had turned out to be phony; the guy was clean. The other name was that of a high-ranking officer in the NYPD. The fact that the inspector actually had done business with Panache was something Ben would handle with extreme caution.

And what about the Miller murder? In that one, the killer's MO had been different, except for two factors: the painted body and Lisa's one-time connection with Panache. And where had those handcuffs come from? He wished now he'd thought to question Martha Bellamy about Miller.

He still hadn't found anything that would definitely tie in Barry Conklin as a suspect, but that didn't mean he wouldn't, if he kept at it.

And there were others he wanted to check out, as well.

Petrusky and Rodriguez also had spent a few hours in the bunk room. When Ben emerged from his office, he found that both detectives had gone back to work on the lists of johns, but they had little to show for their efforts. They hadn't found a single man who had been serviced by all three girls.

Stick with it anyway, he told them—there had to be a connection there someplace. Somebody had wanted to hurt the girls or Panache or both, and it was an odds-on bet that the somebody had been a customer.

Petrusky was bleary-eyed. He ran a hand over the stubble on his jaw. "You think maybe we could get some help, Ben?"

"Where from? Every other guy in the squad is loaded with work. So just do the best you can. Later on, Ed and I'll give you a hand."

The trouble was, if Ben didn't come up with something soon, he could forget doing any further work on the Patterson case. The brass had done everything possible to separate it from the other two homicides, for reasons of their own. Again he wondered where Inspector Donnelly might fit into all of this. Did Galupo know the answer to that, or did Brennan? If they did and were keeping it under wraps, it wouldn't be the first time a cop had been protected by the blue wall.

But the worst thing Ben could do would be to do nothing. He went back into his office and called Brian Holland, saying he had to see him, it was important.

The ADA sounded harried and impatient. He told Tolliver he was busy with an important case, but finally he agreed to give him a few minutes that afternoon. Ben said he'd be there and hung up. Next, he called the Fraud Bureau and told Jack Strickland he had something for him, saying he'd drop it off later in the day.

Ed Flynn showed up at eleven, his suit sharply pressed. He and

Ben went out for a hamburger at noon, and after that, Flynn returned to the station house while Ben drove down to his two-room apartment on Bank Street, carrying the tapes with him.

He showered and trimmed his mustache, then put on gray flannels and a fresh white shirt and a tie. His navy blazer came last.

Inspecting himself in the dresser mirror, he was surprised at how presentable he seemed. Tolliver reporting for duty, sir. Junior vice president in your fucking bank. Ugh.

As he was about to go out the door, he remembered to call Patty. After six rings, he gave up; she was probably at the gym or out for a walk. Either that or using her hair dryer. With that thing on, she wouldn't hear a bomb go off.

He left the apartment carrying the tapes, locking and double-locking the doors behind him out of habit, not because he owned anything worth stealing. Down on the street, he climbed into the Ford and drove over to Seventh Avenue, taking it down to Canal and then going southeast to Centre. At this time of day, it was a fairly easy trip; he made it in under fifteen minutes.

As he placed the police placard on the dash and got out of the car, he found himself sensing trouble. Maybe it was the result of having been a cop for so long, but whatever it was, he could smell it.

# 75

The halls of the Criminal Justice Building were thronged with wrongdoers, many accompanied by family members indistinguishable from the perpetrators. And cruising among them like sharks swimming through schools of lesser flesh-eaters were the deadliest predators of all, the lawyers.

Ben showed his ID to the guard and headed for the Fraud Bureau. It was a little early for his appointment with Holland; he'd drop in on Strickland first.

When he walked in, he found the sergeant in shirt sleeves, looking laid-back and relaxed, more like somebody working in a business office than a cop. Ben sat down in the visitor's chair.

"I hear you're catching a fair amount of shit these days," Strickland said. He had one foot up against the edge of his desk, a smile on his pale, narrow face.

"You might say that," Ben admitted.

"Is it true, about them trying to nail you on that thing in Harlem?" Stories had a way of getting around. "I don't know," Ben said. "There'll be a departmental hearing, sometime in the next couple of days."

Strickland shook his head. "Getting so a cop's got two battles on his hands. One with the scumballs on the street, the other with the bureaucracy."

How much experience Strickland might have had with street battles was debatable, but Ben wasn't here to swap war stories.

"By the way," Strickland said, "whatever happened with Barry Conklin? You were gonna question him, last time I talked to you."

"That's what I'm here to see you about," Ben said. He laid the envelope containing the tapes on the desk. "I brought you some recordings I think you'll find interesting."

"Recordings of what?"

"Telephone conversations between Conklin and a vice president of Coleman Baker. About how the Salzac group is secretly planning a hostile takeover of Barclay Telecom. Conklin's paying the broker for information while he buys all the Barclay stock he can get."

Strickland looked at the envelope, and then at Ben. "No shit?"

"Would I kid you, Jack?"

The sergeant sat up straight in his chair and opened the envelope, taking out the cassettes. "Where'd you get these, Ben?"

"From Mrs. Conklin."

Strickland's narrow face fell. "She recorded them?"

"Yeah, but don't look so disappointed. I know these aren't admissible, but they'll tell you where you can get stuff that will be. You wouldn't want me to hand you the case all wrapped up, would you?"

Strickland tapped a finger against one of the cassettes. "Hey, even listening to them could be a problem. You know how careful we have to be about disclosure."

"Cut the bullshit," Ben said. "Only two people know I gave you these. I'm one, and you're the other. I certainly don't plan to talk about it—do you?"

The sergeant shook his head as he stared at the cassettes. A hen worrying over her chicks. "I just wouldn't want to see something like this get fucked up."

"Then don't fuck it up," Ben said.

"I'm gonna have to talk to my boss about it, and he's gonna insist on knowing how I got the tapes."

Ben sighed. "Look, Jack. You came back from lunch and there was this envelope on your desk, right? You listened to the tapes, and

298

Lord Amighty. Okay? There'll be enough glory in this one to make everybody happy, including your boss."

"I suppose you're right, if it's handled carefully."

"Uh-huh."

Strickland's gaze narrowed. "Now let me ask you something. If you don't mind."

"Shoot."

"What's your angle? Or are you just being generous?"

"I don't have an angle. I'm merely outraged by the way Mr. Conklin flouts the law."

"Come on."

"However, I will admit that I wouldn't be too upset if Conklin fell into grief."

Strickland grinned. "That's more like it. He is a sleazy son of a bitch, isn't he?"

"And there is one thing you can do. Keep an eye out for anything that could help me, okay?"

"You still think Conklin could have been mixed up with that girl? Or girls?"

"Yeah, I do."

"Okay. We get anything, I'll let you know."

"Good."

Strickland looked at the tapes again. Probably thought if he stared at them hard enough, he'd find a secret message printed on the cover. "One more point," he said.

"Yes?"

"How come Mrs. Conklin gave you these? How'd you make contact with her?"

"It's my reputation as a stud," Ben said. "You know how women talk. When she heard about me, she tracked me down."

Strickland grinned again, but this time it was more of a leer. "You know, I'll bet that's not far from the truth."

Ben stood up. "Eat your heart out, Jack. But don't forget our deal."

"Hey, I won't. This could be a hell of a case. Really big."

"That's how careers are made," Ben said. "See you later."

# 76

B rian Holland made him wait. While Ben sat in the tiny vestibule outside the ADA's office, Holland's assistant asked whether he wanted coffee and then brought him a cup. He couldn't remember her name, but the beehive hairdo and the fat butt were familiar enough. Although the courtesy she was showing now seemed out of character. Maybe wearing a jacket and tie had earned him some respect.

When Holland finally called him in, the ADA didn't seem thrilled to see him. He didn't look as well organized as he had on Ben's last visit, either. His face wore a harassed expression, and the untidy stacks of paper on his desk reminded Ben of the mess in his own office. But at least the TPA wasn't floating around in here, eager to listen in on their discussion.

As Ben took a chair, Holland frowned. "Frankly, Lieutenant, I was surprised to hear from you. The word around here is you're going to be indicted for that shooting in Harlem the other night."

Ben's mouth fell open. *Indicted?* What the fuck was this?

A glint appeared in Holland's eye as he noticed the reaction. "You weren't aware of that, I gather?"

"I'm waiting for a departmental hearing," Ben said.

"Uh-huh. But don't be too startled by what the grand jury does, no matter what your department decides." He smiled.

He's enjoying this, Ben thought. The prick.

"And don't blame the DA's office," Holland went on. "The mayor's getting a lot of heat from various groups. I'm sure you know the Reverend Marydale has been rousing the rabble."

"I know there's been some pressure," Ben said.

"Some pressure? That's a marvelous example of understatement."

Ben's mind was whirling. Was this what had been going on behind his back—the NYPD knuckling under to political pressure? Was this why he hadn't heard from Brennan? He'd tried to return the captain's call, but after that there'd been silence from 1 Police Plaza. An indictment? Christ.

Holland glanced at his watch. "What is it you wanted to see me about? I'm a busy man."

"I wanted to bring you up-to-date on what's been happening on the case I'm working on."

The ADA's eyebrows lifted. "I must say, Tolliver, you're persistent. I would have thought your superiors would have explained your situation, but since they haven't, permit me."

Ben waited, controlling his irritation with an effort.

"First off," Holland said. "This business of the shooting is no joke. You killed a man. And according to dozens of witnesses, there was no reason to do so."

"There was plenty of reason," Ben snapped. "He was armed with—"

Holland raised a hand, cutting him off. "Please. I'm not trying the case, I'm simply telling you what's going on. From what I understand, you'll almost surely be indicted on a charge of second-degree murder, and the case will be vigorously prosecuted. Don't quote me on that—I'm doing you a favor by letting you know. And as far as the murders of those prostitutes is concerned, you're not even involved in it any longer."

"I'm still on the Patterson case," Ben said.

"Which, I understand, is just about dead. No leads, no new evidence. And despite the blathering by the media, not much interest from the public, either." He leaned forward. "Look, I'm trying to be patient, I really am. But what exactly brings you down here, anyway?"

Ben took a deep breath. "I think I'm very close to a major breakthrough." That was a rash exaggeration, but Ben was angry. He felt like hanging one on this superior jerkoff.

"What makes you think so?"

"All three of those girls worked for the same service—Panache. They sent Caroline Patterson to the Plaza. The second victim, Lisa Miller, was no longer with them when she was killed, but she had been at one time. And now this latest one in the Park Lane, Melissa Martin, was also booked by them. What's more, all three bodies were painted after the girls were killed."

Holland cocked his head. "And you think you're on to something? Two of the girls worked for this Panache, and the third one once did? And then after they were dead, somebody decorated them, or whatever? Let me ask you something, Lieutenant. You've worked on many homicide cases, haven't you?"

"Yes, I have."

"Then tell me. Just how unusual is it in a sex crime for the killer to mutilate or disfigure the body of his victim in some fashion or other?"

Ben exhaled. "It's not unusual. It's common."

"Of course it is. And the way these women were painted—was it the same in each case?"

"No, it wasn't. But—"

"But what? Don't you see that so far, all you're showing me is coincidence?"

Ben felt heat creeping up his neck and into his face. "Okay, but there are dozens of those slimeball outfits in New York. When three girls are murdered within a few weeks of each other and all three worked for the same service, that's got to be more than just a coincidence. And so does the paint."

"Then how about some concrete evidence?"

Ben should have backed off at that point, but he was too angry to be sensible. "I'll have it, and soon."

"Fine. But don't you think a meeting with me would be more productive if we met after you'd done all this brilliant work, instead of before?"

"I had a reason."

"Which was?"

"I didn't want to see the case put on the shelf and forgotten about. I wanted it to stay alive."

"Despite the fact that you're not even supposed to be investigating two of those homicides? It seems to me your own department has seen this more clearly than you have."

"What does that mean?"

"It means that high-ranking police officials understand the district attorney's problem. Which is that there is a horrendous logjam of felony cases in this city. Over two thousand homicides this year, and close to five thousand rapes. More than a hundred thousand robberies. Plus all the other types of crimes. Are you aware of that?"

"Of course I am."

"And did you also know that to try the people who committed those crimes, we have only a few hundred prosecutors?"

"Yes, I know that, too."

"Then tell me this. Do you honestly believe that except for the media anyone really cares very much about this trio of dead whores—three hookers who had some makeup splashed on them after they were killed?"

Ben knew when he was licked. Or at least when to fold his hand and hope for a better deal. He'd heard more or less the same "who gives a shit" speech from Brennan not long ago.

But Holland wasn't finished. "Even Patterson's own father was relieved not to have the family name dragged through the mud. In

302

fact, as I believe you're aware, helping to protect that name was one of the reasons I was asked to take the case in the first place."

Ben made no reply.

The ADA sat back in his chair. "Listen, Lieutenant. At the present time, I'm personally handling more than a dozen major felonies. In every one of them, we have an excellent chance of getting a conviction, but only because of meticulous preparation. On top of that, I've been assigned to prosecute one of the most important rape cases the city has ever tried."

"The doctor's wife."

"Correct. A trial not only New York but the entire country will be watching. People *care* about that woman. She's socially prominent, well educated, married to a distinguished physician. She's the mother of three grown children, all of them successful. And she's worked hard for a number of charities. For someone of her stature to be violated and so badly beaten she was left for dead was damn near unthinkable, even in this city."

"I'm familiar with the case," Ben said.

But Holland was rolling. "Her assault by those savages inflamed decent people everywhere. And now her courage has become a symbol. It's a sign that society is willing to take a stand for what's right. And to punish those who do wrong."

He's rehearsing, Ben thought. Trying out the charge he'll make to the jury.

"Contrast that," Holland said, "with this thing you're so worked up about. Three dead sluts. And if you had a perpetrator, do you think he'd go to prison? Hardly. Even some court-appointed hack would base his defense on the *McNaughton* rule. Your man would spend a few years in a nice comfortable facility, and then a panel of psychiatrists would declare him no threat to the public and he'd be right back among us."

A knock sounded at the door, and Miss Beehive opened it. "Sorry," she said to Holland, "but you're late for your meeting."

He nodded, rising from his chair. To Ben he said, "Be sure to keep me posted if you come up with anything solid."

Ben mumbled that he would and went to the door.

"Oh, and Tolliver?"

He turned, to see Holland adjusting his tie.

"Good luck on that shooting charge."

Ben went out and closed the door, taking the elevator down to the gloomy stone-clad lobby and leaving via the south entrance. As he went out of the building, he saw a black hooker just ahead of him, most likely leaving after a court appearance. From the rear, she

303

reminded him of Shirley, tall and slim, wearing an orange miniskirt and white boots.

When the girl reached the sidewalk, she stopped and glanced over the traffic moving past on Centre Street. The driver of one of the cars saw her and swerved over to the curb. He rolled down his window and she leaned on the sill.

As Ben walked by, he heard the girl say to the driver, "Hello, sugar. You lookin' for some fun?"

# 77

B y midnight, they'd checked and double-checked every name they had, going over and over them, trying to put together any combination that would give them a direction. Ben and Ed Flynn were working as one team and Frank Petrusky and Carlos Rodriguez the other. But all they had to show for their efforts were voluminous piles of paper filled with scribbles and check marks.

Ben looked at the heap on his desk and was aware that his back and his neck ached and it was hard to focus his eyes. Fatigue from lack of rest and tension was bad enough, but when you added to it the realization that you'd spent your time running in circles and accomplishing nothing, it was numbing.

He shoved his notes aside and picked up a folder containing reports of the interviews he and Weisskopf and Spadone had made earlier, when they were chasing johns who'd paid for the services of Caroline Patterson. He leafed through the reports for the twentieth or thirtieth time, and then tossed the folder down as well. There was nothing remarkable in any of them, just as there was nothing in the lists of names to suggest a lead or point to a guy who seemed more likely than the next one.

He sat back then, rubbing his eyes. When he looked up, he saw that Flynn was watching him, sitting quietly on the other side of the desk.

"You know what I think?" Ed asked.

"What?"

"I hate to say it, but it looks to me as if this isn't gonna work."

"Maybe."

"Don't get me wrong, Lou. I think going through this stuff was

304

positively the right thing to do. It could have given us a lead, no doubt about it. But."

"Yeah, I know. But. We're coming up empty."

"Trouble is, going through a bunch of names is one thing. But what we really need is to run down the johns themselves. How many were actually questioned, a dozen? That's nothing."

"Sure, Ed. You're right. But to do that, we need manpower, which we don't have. And which we're not about to get."

"I don't know why, but Patterson's the one puzzles me the most. Not that we've got answers on either of the other two. You ever wonder if maybe it was somebody she didn't know at all?"

"Yeah, of course I have." So had Melissa Martin. The picture of her changing her shirt in Wolfe's studio returned to his mind. She'd raised the same question. As he thought of her, another mental impression appeared. In this one, her body was covered with pink paint and her eyes were glazed, staring dully at nothing.

"If you look at it that way, it's altogether different," Flynn went on. "For instance, let's say the guy's a flat-out nut case. He rents a room, calls for a girl, and then when Patterson shows up, he kills her. Just for the thrill of it."

"In two of them, he didn't rent the room. A woman did."

"So maybe they both did it. That's happened, too, you know. There was that husband and wife in Flatbush, you remember that? Got their kicks torturing a girl together. Then the husband would screw the victim while the wife watched, and after that the old lady would go to work with a machete."

Ben thought of his discussions with Dr. Stein. "You know the old saying, Ed. Love is sharing."

"Hey, that could be what's going on here, too."

"Uh-huh, it could. But right now, I'm finding it a little hard to concentrate."

"Tell you the truth, so am I," Flynn said. He looked at his watch. "Too late to visit my friend. You feel like going to Grady's for a drink?"

"Good idea."

"Hey, Lou?" Petrusky was standing in the doorway. His collar was open, and there were half-moon sweat stains in the armpits of his shirt.

"Yeah, Frank?"

"Come take a look at this, will you? It's something Carlos noticed."

"Sure." Ben got up and walked with the rumpled detective into the squad room, Flynn following.

305

Rodriguez and Petrusky had been working on the table at one side of the room. Copies of their notes and the Panache john list were spread out on the surface, pieces of paper littering the floor, as well.

Carlos was hunched over the table, peering intently at the sheets in front of him. For once, he too looked disheveled. A dark shadow covered his chin, and his silver sport shirt was unbuttoned down the front, revealing a heavy gold chain with a St. Christopher's medal affixed to it. There were ink smudges on the collar of the shirt.

Ben put a hand on the detective's shoulder as he looked down at the material on the table. "What've you got, Carlos?"

"Maybe nothing," Rodriguez said. "But look. We been spending all our time checking names. We checked, double-checked. *Nada.* Then I thought, what about the *places* where the johns called the girls to? Most of the time, they were either to hotels or the guy's apartment. But not always. What got me started was, I noticed a couple guys had girls come right to their offices. For instance, there's one guy who's a bond broker downtown. Lot of times, he likes to get a relaxing blowjob in his office after lunch."

"Yeah, so?"

"So I went through that with Patterson and the other two. With the addresses, I mean."

"Working backward," Ben said.

"Right. I didn't get what I was looking for, exactly. There was no place where all three of them went. But look at this. In the printout, there's this address on East Seventy-fourth Street. I made a check next to it because Melissa Martin went there one night back in February. Guy's name was Edward Blake. He was a one-time customer for Panache."

"Okay, so what?"

"So then I noticed the same address for an earlier date, last December. Only that time, the john's name was James Tyrell. The girl they sent there then was somebody called Debbie, and Tyrell was another one-shot. Then just for the hell of it, I went through Lisa Miller's book, and guess what?"

"You found the address again."

"Yes. But the name she had down was Grant. So I thought, what is this? I go back over them again, and I see each time it's the same apartment—Fifteen C. Now don't tell me it's three horny guys living together."

"No," Ben said. "I won't tell you that."

Flynn was standing with them, staring down at the sheets of paper spread out on the table. "Maybe we should check the stuff out again."

306

It was late and Ben was tired and he'd been at this kind of work for too many years to get steamed up over what could be nothing more than a fluke. But at the same time, he knew it was the relentless sifting of details that often produced results.

He arched his back and stretched. "Yeah, okay. Carlos, you and Frank can give us a hand, and we'll go through the lists Ed and I have been working on. Stay where you are; I'll bring them out here."

There were several hundred additional entries to check out, but with all four of them sharing the effort, it didn't take long to go through the names.

The results were disappointing. When they finished, they'd failed to find another instance in which the East Seventy-fourth Street address showed up. And as Carlos had said, he'd only matched Miller and Martin with it, not Caroline Patterson.

The four men sat looking at each other. Flynn spoke first. "I think it's time we got that drink."

"Sure," Ben said. "Be with you in a minute. But first I want to make a call." He got up and went back into his office.

It was past one o'clock, close to quitting time for Panache, but he wanted to ask Martha Bellamy about that address. As Carlos had conjectured, maybe the whole thing was a big nothing. On the other hand, maybe Bellamy had never noticed the oddity, either. But the red-haired madam was too sharp, too canny not to pick up something like that. In any event, the fact that the address had popped up three times, but with the request for a girl coming from a different guy on each occasion, was strange. As it had Carlos, the discovery had made Ben more than a little curious. And the one person who probably could shed some light was Bellamy.

He reached for the phone.

"Good evening, this is Panache. May I help you?"

The phone girls all sounded alike. He took a chance. "Francesca?"

"No, Billie."

"This is Ben Tolliver. Let me speak to Martha."

"I'm sorry, she's not in. But I'll be happy to take care of you, Mr. Tolliver."

"It's personal," he said. "Has she left for the night?"

"I'm sorry, I can't give out that information."

"Then let me talk to Patrick."

"Mr. Wickersham isn't here, either."

Exasperated, Ben said, "Look, Billie—this is important. How long ago did they leave?"

There was a pause, and then the girl said, "They haven't been here at all tonight. But don't tell them I—"

"Did they call in?"

"I'm sorry, I really can't tell you any more than that."

He hung up. What was going on here? Panache was Martha Bellamy's flesh and blood, in more ways than one. He couldn't imagine her not coming in while the place was doing business, let alone not even making contact.

Looking through his notes, he found the number for her apartment and called it. There was no answer. After a time, he put the phone down, wondering.

Had they skipped? Taken a pile of money and run off to someplace like Liechtenstein or Monaco?

That was ridiculous. Martha Bellamy would sooner cut off her hand than leave the operation it had taken her years to build into the most successful call-girl business in New York, to say nothing of the obvious affection she had for that weird white museum she called home.

Flynn was standing in the doorway, jacket on, tie in place. "You ready, Ben?"

Ben looked up. "Change in plans, Ed. You go ahead. I've got a stop to make." He put on his blazer and left the office.

## 78

There was a different doorman on at night. Ben didn't want to have him call Bellamy's apartment. In the event she didn't answer, it would make it just that much harder for him to get in. Instead, he used the same ruse he had the last time he'd been here, displaying his shield and telling the man he was making a security check, just looking the building over as part of the city's crime-prevention procedures.

As before, he waited in the lobby for a chance to enter an elevator. It came when a taxi pulled to the curb in front of the apartment house. There were two passengers inside, a blond cupcake and a red-faced fat man who was boisterously drunk. The fat man apparently was a tenant; the doorman greeted him by name. As the blonde and the doorman struggled to get him out of the cab, he began to sing "Some Enchanted Evening" in a loud voice.

Ben stepped into an elevator car and pressed the button for the penthouse.

This time, he chose the main entrance. He hit the buzzer and waited, then pressed it again. No response. From there, he stepped to the service entrance and leaned on the buzzer for that one, but with the same result.

Each of the doors had two locks. If all of them were engaged, he could forget about slipping in. But he tried one in the service entrance anyway, taking a plastic credit card from his wallet and sliding it into the crack in the door, depressing the tongue of the lower lock.

The door swung open on the first try, as easily as that. Which told him the locks had not been properly secured; only one had been set, and with its snap function alone. The door had simply been slammed shut. He stepped into the apartment and quietly closed the door behind him.

Rule one on an entry like this was, Stop and listen. He did, for a full minute. All the lights were on in the huge kitchen, reflecting from the white walls and cabinets, the tiles and the marble floor and the stainless steel of the appliances and the sinks. But except for the hum of the refrigerator and the freezer, there was no sound in the place. In fact, so well insulated was it that he couldn't even hear traffic noise from the streets below.

If no one was here, why had the locks not been secured, and why were the lights on?

Instinctively, he crouched and pulled the Smith from its holster, straightening up and holding the snub-nosed revolver so that its muzzle pointed upward.

After a moment, he stepped into the hallway leading from the kitchen into the living room. To his left was the dining room, with its glass-topped table and gilded chairs. The ornate chandelier depending from the ceiling over the table was also ablaze. It appeared that every light in the apartment was on.

He passed through the archway at the end of the hall, looking from side to side as he entered the vast two-story living room. There was no one in here, either.

The wall opposite was the one with windows that stretched all the way to the ceiling. The drapes were open, and the view was spectacular. He was facing west, looking across Park Avenue, and despite the hour, lights gleamed from thousands of windows in other buildings. Beyond lay the black void of Central Park, and in the distance were more lights, a glittering carpet extending to the Hudson and across it into New Jersey.

Turning, he took in the white furniture and the white grand piano and the statuary and the soaring walls hung with dozens of paintings. Even knowing as little as he did of art, he was sure the collection was worth a fortune. But to his eye, the pictures still looked as if they were the result of a kid having a tantrum. And the statues weren't much better. Most of the figures were made of metal, either silver or blackened iron. No matter what the critics might say, he wouldn't give ten dollars for the entire mess, paintings and all.

He wondered whether the apartment had been constructed this way when Bellamy had bought it, and decided it probably hadn't. The building was an old co-op, and he was fairly certain you didn't find two-story living rooms in the penthouses of structures like this one. She must have spent a great deal of money to have the conversion done. But then, she could afford it.

Which posed another question: What else was there? These rooms were the only ones he'd seen, but there was the circular stairway in the rotunda leading up to another level. Up there was where he'd find Martha Bellamy's bedroom.

As he started out of the living room, he noticed an ashtray on one of the coffee tables. It was heavy crystal, shaped like a bowl, and lying in it was what remained of a cigarette. He bent over it for a closer look. The ash was about three inches long, attached to a white filter tip with an imprint of red lipstick on it.

A woman had lighted the cigarette, but then had put it into the ashtray and left it there, where it had smoldered down to the filter. What had distracted her?

He walked out into the front hall. There were two doors in the wall opposite the circular stairway. He opened the first one and found a closet with a number of women's coats hanging in it. The second door led into a powder room containing a vanity, sink, and toilet; its walls were covered in nubby white silk. From there, he went up the stairway, continuing to hold the pistol in his right hand. His feet made no sound in the deep white carpet.

In the hallway up here, there was a succession of doors on his left, another door on his right, and one more at the end of the passage. He tried the ones to his left, finding them to be linen closets and a storage area filled with luggage. Then he opened the door on the opposite side and looked into Martha Bellamy's bedroom.

This room was also done in white, and still more paintings lined the walls in here, except for one that was covered in floor-to-ceiling mirrors. On a raised platform at the far end was an enormous bed with bookcases and a stereo set into the headboard. Flanking end tables held lamps and a telephone, and a television set hung from above, over the foot of the bed. Near where Ben stood was a writing desk and a chair, and just beyond that a chaise lounge.

He noticed French doors midway along the outside wall. Opening them, he saw that they led out onto a large terrace enclosed in retractable glass panels. The furniture on the terrace was pale sand and white, and there were several ficus trees in stone pots. Closing the doors, he returned his attention to the bedroom.

The area was immaculate, with not so much as a single piece of furniture out of place, not an article of clothing or a magazine lying where someone might have dropped it. Except for some vases filled with flowers, it was as if the room had never been lived in.

On one of the bedside tables was a control panel. He touched one of the buttons on the panel. There was the barely audible whir of an electric motor, and the mirrored panels rotated, revealing closets running the entire length of the room. Inside were packed rows of feminine clothing. He touched the button again and the panels swung shut.

Just to the right of the bed was a door he supposed led into Bellamy's bath. He opened it. This room was also oversized, and also all in white. The material was mostly marble, but the effect was softened by many lush green plants that stood in pots and hung from overhead. There was a sunken tub in the center of the floor, looking to Ben like a miniature swimming pool.

Back in the bedroom, he glanced around once more before leaving it, thinking wryly that this room was larger than his entire apartment, to say nothing of the contrast in the way they were furnished.

But where was Bellamy? The closet containing luggage hadn't looked as if any pieces had been withdrawn from it; the suitcases and trunks were all neatly aligned.

And where was the little Oriental houseboy, Chang? Was he a live-in servant, or did he merely come in during the day? No—daytime help wouldn't suit Bellamy's style, nor would that fit her working schedule. She'd want him right here at all times, ready to carry out her orders.

He left the room and went down the hall, opening the door at the end. Beyond it was a back stairway. He went down the stairs and arrived at two more doors. He opened the first and found that it led into a small bedroom with a sitting area as well as a single bed.

This room was as neat and orderly as he'd found Bellamy's, each piece of furniture set just so. On the dresser was a photograph in a silver frame, a black and white of an old woman who might have been Chinese. At the far end of the room was a closet, and beside it a bathroom.

From there, he went back into the hallway and tried the second door. It opened into the kitchen. He'd come full circle.

Damn it, he'd been through every inch of the apartment and

hadn't found so much as a hint as to where Martha Bellamy might have gone. Except for the cigarette ash in the living room, which suggested that she might have been surprised by something or someone, or else had abruptly turned her attention elsewhere.

Or had suddenly left the place.

Ben felt a sense of growing apprehension. Call it yet another example of cop's instinct, or perhaps a natural distrust honed through years of dealing with duplicity and deceit and evil in every imaginable form, but he sensed that something was very wrong.

More than that. He *knew* it.

Looking over the cavernous kitchen once more, he noticed utensils and other objects on the work surface of the center island. Stepping closer, he saw that there was a knife and a vegetable parer, and several plates of uncooked food: pieces of chicken and sliced mushrooms, cloves of garlic, plum tomatoes, and chopped peppers. There was also an uncapped bottle of olive oil. Obviously someone— Chang, no doubt—had been working here, preparing a meal.

Just as the cigarette ash in the living room had, these items also suggested an interruption, an unexpected distraction. They—and the ash—were also the only things he'd seen that spoiled the neatness of the apartment. Who had come in here and surprised Chang and his employer?

And what had happened next?

As he wrestled with the questions, he moved around the kitchen, opening cabinets and cupboards above and beneath the tiled counters. Nothing inside any of them was unusual; he saw dishes and glasses in some, small appliances including a Cuisinart, a blender, and a knife sharpener in others. Under the cooktop were drawers containing pots and pans.

There was a second door near the one going into the hall. He opened it and peered into a pantry stocked with canned goods and packaged supplies. One wall was used for wine storage; the racks held perhaps a hundred bottles.

Going back to the center island, he tried to imagine where Chang had been when he was interrupted. Judging from the position of the knife, which lay on a butcher-block surface set into one part of the island, he probably had been facing the door through which Ben had come. Standing there for a moment, Ben pictured the tiny man looking up in surprise. But it still told him nothing.

He resumed poking about, the impression growing that the kitchen could easily handle the demands a restaurant would place on it. The refrigerator was across from the island. He opened it and inspected its contents: cream, butter, eggs, vegetables in a crisper, a

312

number of covered dishes, an assortment of condiments and sauces standing in the door racks. Lying on their sides on one of the shelves were six bottles of Taittinger champagne. He closed the door.

It was strange, but the feeling persisted that he'd stumbled onto something terrible. People didn't simply evaporate; apparently something had caused Martha Bellamy and the servant to drop everything and run out of here. But what?

And why had she been at home in the first place? From what he knew of her, it would have been totally unlike her to simply take the evening off, stay here and not go to her office. Or to go anywhere else, for that matter. He knew that when Panache was in action, so was she—overseeing the calls, taking the ones from important customers herself, deciding what girls to send where, handling unforseen developments, making sure the dates were fulfilled and the times logged. There was no way she'd stay away.

Or had she left here *before* the evening started? Had Chang begun preparing the meal for himself? It was hard to tell from the food lying on the work surface. When ready, the dish might have been enough to serve one person or two. He prodded a piece of chicken with his forefinger and found it still cold to the touch. Had it been frozen?

The freezer was almost identical in size and shape to the refrigerator. He opened the door and peered inside.

And found Chang.

# 79

The Casbah was going full blast. Colored spotlights played on the small stage while a troop of belly dancers gyrated, hips grinding and bumping, tits bouncing, the girls moving in sync with the frenzied rhythms of the drums and tambourines. In the audience, men ogled the dancers, glassy stares fixed on the undulating flesh. Clouds of tobacco smoke drifted through the spot beams as waitresses in harem pants moved among the tables, serving drinks. If not for the fact that nearly all the customers were American, the club might have been in Cairo or Marrakech, Tunis or Algiers.

Bobbie was sitting by herself at the bar, a barely touched scotch and water in front of her. She was dressed informally tonight, black slacks and a gray turtleneck sweater, a black leather jacket. Outwardly appearing bored, she took in all of it with eyes as watchful as a spider's.

The club's patrons, she thought, were grungy. Nearly all the men had women with them, and some of the women seemed to be as fascinated by the performance onstage as their escorts.

What was it that turned these guys on? Did the simulated sexual thrusting stir them up—reenergize jaded libidos? Or was it that they enjoyed fantasizing, wishing that later on they'd be humping one of the nubile creatures they were watching, instead of the wife or girlfriend they'd brought along?

Not that all the women in the crowd were dogs. Although most of them looked cheap and flashy, many were also young and well built. In fact, now that she noticed it, Bobbie estimated that on average they were at least twenty years younger than the men.

But it was the males who inspired a mixture of curiosity and contempt. Sitting there in their too sharply cut suits, overweight and jowly, obviously out of shape from lack of exercise and stuffing their faces with rich food and booze, they struck her as the type you'd see in Las Vegas or Atlantic City—owners of businesses that threw off more cash than they wanted to report to the IRS, good-time Charlies whose idea of la dolce vita was many drinks, a thick steak, a tour of joints like this one, and finally a piece of ass.

As she watched, she became aware of a presence alongside her. "Hey, honey," a male voice said. "Buy you a drink?"

She glanced at him, taking in the carefully styled head of greasy hair, the off-white sports jacket, the shirt collar open at the throat and spread wide to reveal a gold chain nestling in a patch of chest hairs.

His thick lips curled in a smile. "How about it?"

Her tone was flat. "No thanks." She swung her gaze back to the dancers, who had now reached what evidently was the high point of their act.

He moved closer, until he was near enough for her to smell a mixture of cologne, sweat, and cigar breath. "Don't be coy, baby," he said. "My friends call me Ray. What'll it be?"

Bobbie looked at him. "Get the fuck away from me."

The thick lips popped open, then twisted into a snarl. "Hey, listen, sweetheart—"

"I said get the fuck away," she snapped. "Or I start screaming rape."

"Jesus Christ, what got into—"

"Now! Move it!"

"All right, all right. I'm going." He receded into the mass of

314

drinkers at the bar, mumbling about the snotty bitches you could run into.

When she again looked at the stage, Bobbie felt a thrill as she realized the moment she'd come here for had arrived. The featured act was on, a beautiful young woman with a lush body that rippled like silk, glossy black hair framing a lovely face with large dark eyes and a wonderfully full, sulky mouth.

Bobbie picked up her glass and took a long swallow, experiencing a glow partly inspired by the whiskey but in larger part by the stunning figure on the stage.

A hush fell over the crowd, the music pulsed and surged, and the young woman began to dance.

# *80*

Inside the freezer, wisps of vapor curled like smoke. Chang was sitting in the bottom of the compartment, facing outward. He'd pulled himself into a ball, with his knees tucked under his chin and his arms wrapped tightly around his shins, as if somehow he could ward off the cold. His face had a bluish tinge, and his lips were drawn back over clenched teeth. His dark slanted eyes were covered by a light coating of frost.

Ben reached in and grasped one of the thin shoulders, finding it stiff to his touch. The tiny man had to have been in here for many hours. And he'd obviously been alive when he entered the freezer. The lower shelves had been removed and placed at the bottom to make room for him, and the shelves above his head were crammed with packages of meats and vegetables. From what Tolliver could see, there were no bruises or contusions, no signs that he'd been beaten or physically forced into the chamber that had turned him into a Popsicle.

Ben leaned down and shoved the pistol back into its holster. As he straightened up, he realized the sight of the small body was suggesting an idea that he couldn't quite make clear. He stepped away from the freezer, and then returned to it and closed the door. The ME and the CSU detectives would want to see the corpse exactly as he'd found it.

Whatever the notion in the back of his mind, it continued to nag

315

at him, as persistent as an insect bite. It was something to do with the frozen body. Chang's body was reminding him of something else. Something he'd seen in—

He had it. He turned and half-walked, half-ran down the hallway and back into the living room. Looking at the array of statues along the wall, he knew what had been picking at his subconscious.

Among the figures was one that was markedly different from the others. It wasn't abstract, as they were, barely recognizable as depicting the human form. Instead, this one was much more realistic. It was a silver sculpture of a nude woman, done life-size. The statue was standing against the wall with head lolling, arms spread wide, feet together—as if the subject had been crucified.

Which indeed it had.

Up close, Ben saw the spikes. One had been driven through each outstretched hand, a third through the feet, holding them—and the figure—to the wall. He touched the woman's side, and when he looked at his fingers, he saw they were smeared with silver paint. He reached out again, placing his fingertips under her chin, and looked into Martha Bellamy's face.

Everything was silver. Her eyeballs, her semiparted lips, the hair on her head, even her pubis. Every inch of her body gleamed like buffed metal. Whoever had done this must have sprayed the stuff on, Ben thought. And done it with skill and great care.

It was impossible for him to tell how she'd been killed. There was no evidence of strangulation, but there might be wounds that were obscured by the silver paint. Or like Melissa Martin, she could have died from poison. With the metallic coating, her face gave him no clue as to what agony she might have felt, what fear she'd experienced, when she met death.

It was as if the killer had made an effort, as his painting skills improved, to preserve his subject, make it look as good as possible. What had he thought that would result in—applause?

As Ben looked at Bellamy's face, a drop of blood oozed from one of her nostrils, bright red against the silver. It hung there for an instant, and then dropped into his palm in a small crimson splash. He stepped back, letting her head fall forward once more.

So the killer had taken the trouble to recompose her features before he'd begun to paint. But now Ben knew there would be a wound, perhaps in her back. Or maybe there would be evidence of a crushing blow to the rear of her skull. Whatever, the ME would find it.

Taking a handkerchief from his back pocket, Ben wiped the paint and the blood from his hand. There was a telephone on one of the end tables. Stepping over to it, he turned the handkerchief to expose a clean section and covered the handset with the cloth. Then he picked up the phone and called the detective squad at the Sixth Precinct station house.

Joe Stone answered the call. Ben explained where he was and what he'd found, then told Stone to call Captain Brennan and give him the information. He said he'd check in later, and hung up. Calling Brennan himself would have been simple enough, but with all the undercurrents that had developed with this case, the last thing he wanted to hear was the zone commander ordering him to back off.

So now what? Ben had all but forgotten why he'd come up here tonight in the first place. The question of what significance there might be in three johns all supposedly living at the same address seemed almost trivial at this point.

Or did it?

He dug the scrap of paper out his pocket and looked at it. The address was only a few blocks from here. It wasn't much to go on, in fact presented no strong suggestion of a lead. There was nothing more to it than the fact that it was odd.

But what else did he have?

He took one last look at the silver-hued corpse nailed to the wall and left the apartment.

# *81*

The movements of the belly dancers had been tame, compared to what was happening on the small stage now. The beautiful young woman had mesmerized the men in the audience with the early phases of her dance. But at this point she was teasing them, making them feel they were doing everything but actually mounting her as she writhed and twisted, her pelvis moving in and out, the wanton expression on her face telling them she was on the edge of orgasm.

So were they. Bobbie could see them staring, many with mouths open, looking as if they were about to come. She hated them for it.

But she hated the dancer more. Basically what the woman was performing was a lewd exhibition, like the ones you could see in live-sex clubs not only in New York but in many other cities, as well. Bobbie had once been in a dive in Chinatown that featured a woman with a pony.

So what was the difference, between this and any other kind of whoring? The men here tonight had paid for sex, and that was what the dancer was selling. She was getting money not just to fuck one or two or ten of these gaping pigs, but to peddle herself to all of them.

Did it matter whether they were actually sticking their cocks into her? Wasn't this practically the same thing—simply another way to get them off, no different from a handjob or a blowjob? And in some ways, wasn't it even worse, because it was so public? Like masturbating in Macy's window with a horde of panting slimeballs pressing their noses against the glass.

And how revolting that this slut on the stage was the woman of a police detective, a brave upholder of the law. Talk about hypocrisy!

But that was to be expected. The man was an ape, whose meddling had already caused much pain, and nearly irreparable damage. Now the time had arrived to put an end to it, to call finis before he could cause more. Now it would be his turn to know what suffering felt like.

The dancer was reaching the climax of her dance, which was itself the portrayal of a climax. Her head was thrown back, her body coated with sweat. As she flung herself about in her final thrashing, drops of moisture flew from her chin and her fingertips and her breasts, tiny showers sparkling in the harsh beams of the spotlights.

Suddenly, she became rigid. Back arched, head thrown back, her muscles twitched, her nipples quivered. She opened her mouth and a wailing cry sounded from deep in her throat. The pounding of the drums was deafening.

She held it. And held it.

And then the music stopped and the spotlights were extinguished and the entire interior of the club was in darkness. A moment later, the lights came up again, and now the dancer was gone.

The applause was thunderous. Many of the men at the tables were shouting for more—animals howling for another piece of meat. They kept it up for several minutes, but the young woman did not reappear.

Instead, a vapid-faced comic in a tuxedo came on, holding a hand mike and beginning a monologue to which no one paid the slightest attention.

Bobbie finished her drink and smiled to herself. So the dancer was through for the night. Or rather, she thought she was.

Actually, this was only the beginning.

# 82

The building was another older structure, of the kind real estate agents touted as prewar. On a side street, it was quiet and sedate, smaller than the one housing Bellamy's apartment but no less elegant.

This time, it was even more important for Ben to get inside without letting the doorman know why he was there. He was prepared to give the guy the usual story as he approached the doors leading into the small, well-furnished lobby, but as soon as he walked in, he saw that it wouldn't be necessary.

The doorman was sound asleep, sitting in a deeply upholstered chair, his cap tilted down over his face, his white-gloved hands folded over his ample belly. If Ben had been a tenant, the guy might have wound up getting fired. It certainly was what he deserved.

The elevator doors opened almost silently. Not that it mattered; the doorman was out of it, snoring steadily. Ben stepped into the car and pressed the button for the fifteenth floor.

As he rode up, he was again struck by mental images of what he'd seen in Bellamy's apartment—the Chinese houseboy frozen stiff, his mistress decorating the living room wall. Ben knew the impressions would stay with him for a very long time.

Apartment C was to the right at the end of the hall. He walked to the door and tried the buzzer.

No answer. He tried again and still got no response.

As were the doors of most apartments in New York, this one was equipped with two locks. He got out his plastic card and slipped it into the crack, but the tongue wouldn't budge. Whoever lived here had double-locked the door before leaving.

He stood there for a moment, considering his options. Maybe the doorman could help, after all—although he wouldn't be aware of it. Returning to the elevator, Ben descended into the lobby.

The doorman seemed not to have moved. Under the cap, the guy's face remained buried in the folds of his heavy blue uniform, and rasping snores continued to pour out of him in a steady cadence.

Ben looked around the small lobby for the door he knew would be there. He stepped to it and swung the door open. Inside was a space the size of a closet, containing the telephone system that connected the lobby to each of the apartments. There was also a cabinet on the wall, and that was what he was after.

Hanging in the cabinet were sets of keys, each hook identified by an apartment number. He took the keys from the one marked 15C and went back to the elevator.

On the way past the slumbering doorman, he shook his head. A good burglar could haul enough swag out of a joint like this to retire, while Field Marshall Dickhead went right on snoring.

Seconds later, Ben was again standing at the apartment door, and now each lock opened with a soft *snick*.

# *83*

B obbie stood in a dark doorway, a short distance from the entrance to the club. The wind had come up, lifting scraps of paper and dust from the sidewalk and whipping them about in miniature whirlwinds. She turned up the collar of her jacket and hunched her shoulders against the predawn chill.

Most of the Casbah's patrons had departed, the half-drunk sports lurching away with their women hanging on to them. A few walked to parked cars; others had taken taxis. Most of the crew had left as well; Bobbie watched the dancers and the waitresses go off in twos and threes, some with boyfriends, calling out good nights as they disappeared into shadows created by the pallid glow of the streetlamps.

After a time, she began to worry that she might have missed her, that she might not have spotted her among the other dancers. But that was unlikely. The last time Bobbie was here, when the girl had left the club with Tolliver, Bobbie had gotten a good look at her in street clothes. Still, maybe tonight she'd simply slipped away and Bobbie hadn't noticed.

The possibility was making her itchy. She didn't know where the young woman lived; knew only that she worked in this mangy nightclub. Damn it, Bobbie *had* to find her. She had to do this *tonight*. Before it went any further. Before anyone stumbled onto what was contained in the apartment house miles to the north of here, on Park Avenue, in another world.

Before anyone uncovered *any more of it*.

320

But suppose she *had* missed her. Then what? There was no way Bobbie could get any more information on her without asking questions that would leave a trail. And even if she could, there was no one to ask tonight. She'd have to wait an entire day—twenty-four hours—before coming back here again tomorrow night for another try.

And then what? Things were happening so fast it was almost impossible to keep up with them, to stay in control. And control was what Bobbie needed—*had to have*—to resolve this insane, hateful situation, to be rid of it forever.

The mere thought of being free was enough to send her spirits soaring. It was like contemplating something wonderful you were waiting for, something you wanted very much to happen. Like planning a trip to a beautiful place, where you longed to be. If only—

*There she was.*

How silly of Bobbie to think she could have missed her. Even wrapped in a trench coat and with a beret pulled down on her head, there was no mistaking that lithe form. The girl was actually quite small, when you saw her dressed. It was when she was naked—or nearly so, for her dance—that it was hard to gauge her size. And the reason for that was obvious as well, if you thought about it.

The answer was in her proportions. So perfectly was she put together, so ideally formed and joined and muscled, that you had no way of knowing whether she was large or small. And perhaps that was because you didn't care, but were only dazzled by the beauty of her body. During her pubescence, Bobbie had seen pictures of Michelangelo's *David* and had fallen in love with the dreamlike youth. Later, when she visited Florence for the first time, she was astonished to find the marble figure twice life-size. The dancer was like that, only in reverse. On the stage, she'd appeared to be much larger than in fact she was.

As Bobbie watched, the young woman stepped off the curb and waved to a passing cab, but the vehicle roared past. She stayed where she was, craning her neck in hopes of catching another.

It was time to make a move. Bobbie left the doorway and strode boldly along the sidewalk, her heels clicking sharply on the concrete. When she drew near the young woman, she stepped into the street and looked in the same direction, as if she was also hoping to flag a taxi.

For a minute or so, she remained silent, not so much as glancing in the smaller woman's direction. Then offhandedly she remarked, "Not so easy to get one, this time of night."

"No."

321

Okay, so a laconic reply was what you'd expect her to give a stranger.

"I'd walk," Bobbie said, "but I'm tired and my feet hurt. I live only a short way from here, but I'd rather take a cab."

Nothing.

Bobbie's stance was slouched, casual. But she was only inches away from her. "Maybe you'd care to share one?"

"No. I'd rather not."

Bobbie looked at her and smiled. "That's okay, I understand. Sorry, I didn't mean to be pushy."

That softened her, a little. "Nothing personal," she said.

"No. Nothing personal."

A cab came down the street, its roof light indicating it was unengaged. The dancer again raised her arm and waved.

"We'll take this one," Bobbie said.

Her face registered surprise. "I said—"

Bobbie hooked the woman's arm with her own, and with her free hand pressed the point of the knife against the trench coat, just below the dancer's breast. "I said we'll take this one. If you yell or try anything at all, I'll run this right through you."

The taxi drew to a stop and Bobbie kept the dancer between the vehicle and herself, holding the knife out of the driver's line of vision.

"Open the door," Bobbie said.

She did as ordered, and both women got into the cab.

The driver was hunched over the wheel, a dark form beyond the bullet-resistant plastic shield that separated him from his passengers.

Bobbie applied pressure to the knife, until the point was on the verge of lancing through the cloth of the young woman's coat. Reaching back with her other hand, she shut the door of the taxi.

"Give him your address," she said.

# 84

The apartment wasn't large, but it was handsomely furnished in a strong, masculine style. Ben moved slowly, turning on lights as he went. He held the Smith in his right hand, even though he felt sure he was alone here.

The living room made him think of what you'd see in a men's club.

The walls were dark green, and the woodwork, including the fire-place and the doors and the crown moldings around the ten-foot ceilings, was white. The furniture was mostly brown leather, a sofa and several club chairs, and there were paintings of racing yachts on the walls and over the mantel. A Persian rug covered the floor.

Against one wall stood a massive mahogany desk, and there were bookcases flanking the fireplace. He tried the drawers in the desk and found them locked.

To his left was a dining alcove containing a Queen Anne table and eight chairs. White painted cabinets were built into the corners of the alcove. Looking around the living room, he noticed a drop-leaf table with magazines stacked on it, along with a wooden box bound with brass corners. He went to the box and opened it. Inside was a matched pair of antique dueling pistols fitted in beds of red velvet, flintlocks with scrolled engravings and butts inset with pearl.

Closing the box, he saw that there were other antique weapons scattered about, as well: a dirk with a jeweled handle lying on one of the bookshelves, a cavalry sword hanging above the desk, a percussion rifle over one of the doors.

He went through the door with the rifle above it and found that it led into a bedroom that was similar in its masculine theme. More antique weapons and paintings of yachts hung on the green walls. The bed was a double, built of black wood that might have been ebony, and covered with a throw of lush brown fur. A dresser made of the same black wood stood at the far end of the room. At the other end was a smaller writing desk with bookcases over it, and a red leather chair. This desk was also locked.

Opening a closet door, he saw that it was packed with suits and sports jackets, the floor lined with perhaps two dozen pairs of shoes.

The bath was through a door to the right of the closet, more modern that the rest of the apartment, with a glass-enclosed shower and white fixtures that looked new. Another door nearby was locked.

Going back into the living room, he looked for an entrance to the kitchen, finding it in the dining alcove. The space was well organized but small, nothing like the huge room in Bellamy's apartment. He thought of what he'd found when he went there earlier, seeing in his mind's eye the tiny Oriental huddled in the freezer, and the bizarre silver figure splayed on the living room wall with spikes through the hands and feet, a drop of blood oozing from its nose.

He poked around in the kitchen for a time, opening cabinets and drawers and finding nothing of interest. He'd seen every room there was to see, and still he had no idea who the apartment's occupant was. But he was sure of one thing: No matter what the Panache records indicated, three men did not live here.

One did.

A thought occurred to him. There was a place he *hadn't* seen. What was on the other side of the locked door in the bedroom? He left the kitchen and went back to the door.

It was paneled, and secured by an old-fashioned box lock. There was no way to slip the tongue on one of these—without a key, you could forget about opening it. There weren't even screws visible in the lock; they'd be hidden on the inside. The only other way you could get through the door would be to take it off the hinges—or else smash your way in. Examining it, he saw that the hinges were set into the jamb, which left the smashing approach. He shook his head.

But maybe a key wasn't out of the question. Glancing about, he noticed drawers in a bedside table. He found a box of Kleenex in one, a deck of playing cards and a glass coaster in the other. Next he tried the drawers in the dresser, with no better luck. The top ones contained an assortment of scarves, handkerchiefs, and socks; the lower ones were packed with shirts, underwear, and sweaters.

Atop the dresser was a leather stud box. He opened it, revealing cuff links, tie tacks, collar stays, a gold ring with an onyx stone, a set of formal studs, and a small, worn leather case. He opened that.

Inside was a single key.

Taking the key to the door, he inserted it into the lock. It worked perfectly. He turned the knob and pushed the door open, and holding the pistol ahead of him went through the door.

The area he found himself in was dark. He fumbled along the wall for a light switch, found one, and flipped it on. What he saw next astonished him.

He was standing in another apartment. But this one was as different from the other as night from day. Whereas the first was severely masculine, with strong dark colors and heavy furniture, this one was soft and feminine, done in hues ranging from pink and orchid and gray to purple and violet. The furniture, too, unmistakably reflected a woman's taste. It was all gentle curves and rich textures, plump and sleek and sensual. He looked behind him, and then back to where he stood now.

Male and female.

Yin and yang.

What the hell was going on here?

324

# 85

"Lock the door," Bobbie commanded. They were in the small front hallway, and she was holding the knife so that any additional pressure would drive the point through the layers of cloth and into flesh. The young woman hesitated.

"Do it!"

Patty moved then, locking and double-locking the door. When she finished, she turned, her face white and her eyes wide but showing determination, nevertheless. Despite the knife point pressing against her, she thrust out her chin. "What do you want? Is it money? I'll give you everything I have if you'll just take it and get out."

Bobbie chuckled, looking at her. She really was quite beautiful, even without the makeup she'd worn in the club—*especially* without the makeup. Her eyes were large and set far apart. They were dark, almost black. And her mouth was lovely. Very full, so that it looked almost petulant, as Bobbie had thought while watching her dance. It was the kind of mouth you wanted to kiss when you looked at it, the kind you could imagine cries of pleasure coming from, under the right circumstances.

"Well, what about it?" she said. "Do you want money?"

"No," Bobbie replied. "I don't."

She was becoming emboldened. "Listen, my boyfriend's a cop, and he'll be here any minute. Now why don't you get smart? Take whatever you want and get out of here."

It was time she learned respect. Bobbie slowly brought the knife up from the girl's body to within an inch of her face. The blade was long and curved, gleaming in the lamplight. But there was still defiance in the young woman's gaze, in the set of her jaw.

Bobbie flicked her wrist and the knife point caught the corner of the girl's mouth, slicing it open.

So sudden was the move that for an instant she seemed not to realize what had happened. Then blood spurted from the cut. She cried out in pain, holding her fingers to her mouth, shock and fear registering in her dark eyes.

Bobbie's voice was icy. "Unless you do exactly as I tell you, I'll cut you again. Only next time, I'll cut your throat. Do you understand?"

Blood was running down the girl's fingers, dripping from the heel of her hand. She nodded.

"Good." Bobbie took a handkerchief from the pocket of her slacks and handed it to her.

As the girl pressed the cloth against the wound, Bobbie said, "Take off your clothes."

Her eyes grew wider. "What?"

The knife came up again. "You don't believe me, you stupid little bitch?"

The young woman held out her other hand. "No, please don't. I believe you." She fumbled with the buttons and snaps, struggling to get out of the trench coat and the dress under it, using only one hand as much as possible while the other held the handkerchief to her face. The white cloth showed a dark red stain that grew larger as she stripped down to bra and panties.

Bobbie gestured with the knife. "Go on, those too."

The girl unhooked the bra and dropped it onto the pile of clothing at her feet, then pulled the panties down and stepped out of them. Her eyes were fixed on her assailant, the corners filling with tears.

Standing close to her and seeing her naked was a thrill. The full, deep breasts, the flat belly and curved hips, and the finely turned legs were wonderful. She had the perfectly tuned body of an athlete—or a dancer.

Bobbie pointed with the knife to the heap on the floor. "Pick up your things and take them into your bedroom. I'll be right behind you, so don't get any dumb ideas."

She knelt and gathered the articles of clothing. The effort required both hands, and as the handkerchief fell away, blood flowed afresh from the flapping wound and ran down her chin. Holding her clothes in her arms, she led the way into the bedroom, the knife point inches from the small of her back.

When they reached the center of the room, Bobbie told her to stop, and to throw the pile aside. She complied, her hands trembling.

The room was small, but like the rest of the apartment, neat and orderly. The bed was against the wall on one side, and a small dresser and a chair were across from it. Illumination was from a single lamp on the dresser.

"Bring that chair over here," Bobbie ordered.

After she put it in place, Bobbie told her to sit on it, facing the door. "You said your boyfriend would be here any minute. Does he have a key?"

She seemed dazed, as she sat down on the chair. Blood continued to run from her wounded mouth, dripping onto her breast.

"Well, does he?"

Her voice was very small. "Yes."

326

There was a box of Kleenex on the bedside table. Bobbie stepped to the table and tossed the box to her. Then she sat down on the bed, holding the knife.

She looked at the naked girl and smiled. "Good. We'll wait for him."

# 86

B en walked slowly through the connecting apartment, his mind reeling.

Why this arrangement, and who lived here?

As he'd thought when he first saw the way the place was furnished, its occupant was a woman; the closets were filled with feminine apparel. But who was she?

And what was her relationship to the guy who lived in the other apartment—was she his girlfriend? Wife? Mistress?

Whatever, a hell of a lot of money had gone into decorating this one. It was done in a mix of Art Deco and antiques, many of them Oriental, the blend of colors reminding him of a display of orchids he'd once seen in a florist's shop near Washington Square.

But for all the opulence of the rooms, the bathroom was the most spectacular feature; it seemed nothing less than palatial. With its blond onyx and mirrored panels, a sunken tub with gold swans for faucets, a trick dome in the ceiling with a cherub-filled sky painted on it—this one was even more elaborate than the bath in Martha Bellamy's penthouse.

He went back through the bedroom and into the living room, taking it all in and wondering. And at the same time sensing that despite the beauty and the richness of the furnishings, the atmosphere in here was eerie.

He was about to return to the first apartment when he realized there was something else that was very odd about this one.

*There was no front entrance.*

At first, he thought he might be mistaken, that he'd either taken a wrong turn or simply overlooked it. But when he made another check of the rooms, he found it was true; the only way you could get in or out was via the door he'd come through. What the hell kind of a woman would put up with such a thing?

On a hunch, he went back to the door and inspected the lock. As he'd suspected, it could not be engaged from this side. Which meant the guy could lock her in here, keep her a prisoner in the apartment. It got weirder by the minute.

His curiosity growing, he went back through the door into the masculine bedroom and from there into the living room. If there was any place to find an answer to this riddle, chances were it would be in the huge old mahogany desk. There would be papers in it, and they'd at least reveal the name of the man who lived here. He tried the drawers again. Every one of them was securely locked.

Shit. Hunting for another key would be pointless; the only one he'd run across earlier was the key to the neighboring apartment. He was tempted to force the locks, but instinct told him he'd be wise not to leave evidence that he'd been here, let alone that he'd damaged the place. He had no warrant, and no matter how strange the arrangement of the double apartments might seem, or how curious it was that somebody had palmed off the idea of three men living here, there was no excuse for a cop rummaging around in private property.

Especially a cop who was supposed to be confined to desk duty, with the threat of a murder indictment hanging over his head. Get caught at this and Galupo would cut his balls off.

But wait a minute—he'd seen a desk in the other apartment, as well. Maybe that one wasn't as secure as the desk in here. Retracing his steps, he went back into the living room in the adjoining space.

The piece was antique French provincial, slim and delicate. The locks on these drawers also seemed fragile. He got out his pocket-knife and tried the center one, sliding the thin blade into the crack and finding the lock simple to jimmy. He opened the drawer.

It was full of papers, most of them receipts from department stores and boutiques that sold women's apparel. They were carbons, and he was unable to decipher the scribbled signature. Whoever she was, the woman spent a fortune on clothes.

*But who was she?*

He jimmied the drawer on the left side, and found it crammed with junk: postage stamps, notepaper, pens, pencils, scissors, an eraser, a stapler, paper clips, rubber bands, loose change. He closed the drawer, and opened the one on the opposite side.

This one contained more papers. On top of the pile was a report from SmithKline Beecham Clinical Laboratories.

The doctor's name was in a block in the upper-left-hand corner. He was Arthur Kolberg, whose offices were at 750 Park Avenue. The upper right-hand corner, where the patient's name would have been, was missing. It had been cut out, either with scissors or a razor blade.

328

Why?

He glanced through the report. As he realized what it was telling him, he went back to the top, and this time read it more slowly.

The report said Darkfield microscopy of serum issuing from a lesion indicated regional lymphodemopathy. A blood test had then revealed the presence of the spirochete *Treponema pallidum*.

The patient had tested positive for syphilis.

Ben looked through the other papers in the drawer. They were notes and prescriptions from Dr. Kolberg, and from them Ben pieced together a history.

Early this year, the patient had developed a genital sore, which the doctor had diagnosed as a chancre. The lab report confirmed it. In Dr. Kolberg's opinion, the period of incubation had been three to four weeks after sexual contact. He had prescribed massive doses of penicillin, and several months later, Kolberg had pronounced the patient cured. From each of these sheets of paper, the patient's name had been excised.

Ben straightened up, more curious now than ever. Maybe there were other places in this room he should examine also. He opened a commode and found it filled with liquor bottles. The drawer in an end table contained nothing but a book of matches and some cocktail napkins. It was tantalizing to stand here, instinct telling him he was close to something, but not knowing what it was.

There was also the problem that he'd been here for some time. At any moment, the occupants of this strange place could come walking through the front door. Frustrated or not, he should get the hell out. He'd actually closed the drawer in the end table and turned away when something registered on his conciousness.

It was the inscription on the matchbook cover. He opened the drawer again and picked up the matches. The cover was glossy black, with white letters that said:

*Come to the Casbah*

**THE HOTTEST NIGHTCLUB IN NEW YORK**

**Belly dancers! Music! No cover charge!**

Jesus Christ. Could this be only a coincidence? Or was it something more than that? He stared at the words, and a cold sense of unease gripped him.

There was a telephone on the desk. Even though she'd be in bed by now, he'd call her. And if it pissed her off to have him wake her up, so be it. At least it would put his mind at rest. He lifted the phone and called the number.

She wasn't asleep.

He knew that because she answered on the first ring. He'd heard the way she sounded when she was blown out of sleep often enough to know she'd been wide awake when the telephone rang.

"Sorry I didn't get to the club," he said.

"That's all right."

"Everything okay with you?"

". . . Yes."

He tensed. "You sure?"

"I'm . . . okay."

"Hey, Patty—what is it?"

"Are you coming down here?"

"Sure. I'll be there."

After a pause, she said, "How soon?"

"I don't know. Is it important?"

"Come soon."

"Listen, is there—"

There was a click, and then the sound of the dial tone. He slammed the phone down, and again looked at the matchbook cover with the name of the club imprinted on it.

Something was wrong. Very wrong. And in a way he didn't understand. Yet somehow all of this tied together; he was sure of it.

But how?

He left the apartment, locking the door behind him, and took the elevator back down to the lobby.

The doorman was still snoring. Ben stepped past him and hung the keys to the apartment back on their assigned hook in the cabinet. Then he went to the front entrance.

As he reached it, the doorman stretched and yawned. Ben glanced at him. The man pushed his cap farther down on his head and settled lower into his chair, making smacking noises with his lips.

*Good night, you schmuck.*

On the street, the night was still pitch-black, and the air was very cold. He climbed into the Ford and started the engine. The quickest route to the Village would be to go down Fifth Avenue and then cut across Fourteenth Street. He pulled the car into a U-turn and drove as fast as he could push it.

# 87

There were no open spaces in front of her building. Ben double-parked and, remembering his experience in Harlem, took the Beretta from the glove compartment before leaving the car.

Once inside the small apartment house, he ran up the stairs two at a time. When he reached her front door, he stood listening for a moment, hearing no sound from within.

Hey, calm down, he told himself. You probably let your nerves run away with you, got your balls in an uproar over nothing. Chances are, she's asleep by now. So don't scare her by waving the gun around.

He slid the pistol into his waistband and unlocked the door, opening it as quietly as possible. Then he stepped inside.

"That you, Ben?" It was Patty's voice.

"Yes, it's me." He closed the door.

"I'm in here." The voice was coming from the bedroom, and she sounded okay.

You jerk, he berated himself. What you need is a drink and some sleep. A lot of sleep. Which you're not going to get for a while. He walked through the living room and into the bedroom.

The sight of her hit him like an electric shock.

Patty was sitting in a chair in the center of the room, facing the door. She was naked, and there were smears of blood on her mouth and her chin and her breasts. Standing behind her and holding a knife to her neck was a woman with shoulder-length black hair.

"Stand still," the woman said. "Or she's dead."

The only light in the room was coming from the small lamp on the dresser. But it was enough for Ben to see that the edge of the blade was pressed against Patty's throat.

In a fraction of a second, he calculated his chances and put them at zero. Before he could so much as reach for the pistol, the knife would slice through her jugular, and once that happened, there'd be no way on earth he could save her.

He looked at the woman. Standing in the shadows created by the dim light, she was wearing a black leather jacket and a turtleneck sweater, and she was smiling. In the semidarkness, he was unable to see her face well, but there was something strangely familiar about

331

her. Even her voice reminded him of someone, but just who that was eluded him.

The woman spoke again, her tone cold and flat. "Do exactly as I say. If you make one wrong move, I'll kill her. You think I don't mean it? Watch."

Her other hand went to the top of Patty's head and seized a clump of hair. Holding the hair in a tight grip, she drew the knife in a horizontal line in the flesh of her victim's neck, just deep enough to cut the flesh, probably missing the artery by no more than a millimeter.

Patty gasped in pain, and the cut rapidly filled with blood. Her eyes were bulging with fear as the fresh wound sent a scarlet trickle down her neck. She began breathing heavily, her breasts heaving. She looked as if she might pass out.

"You see?" the woman said.

The crazy bitch is enjoying this, Ben thought. She didn't have to cut her—she did it for pleasure. "What do you want me to do?"

"Very slowly," the woman said, "take out your gun. Use just two fingers. Drop it on the floor in front of you."

Ben did as she ordered, the Beretta landing with a thump at his feet.

"Now kick it over to me."

He did that as well, sending the pistol skidding across the carpet.

Continuing to hold the knife against Patty's throat, the woman crouched and picked up the gun. When she straightened up, she used the thumb and forefinger of the hand holding the knife to pull back the slide and snap a round into the Beretta's chamber. Then she trained the pistol on him.

Her voice rose. "You fool. You ignorant, meddling clown. Too dense to figure it out, but just smart enough to cause trouble. No, not smart—stubborn. If you'd just left it alone, let it be forgotten the way everybody wanted it to be, you wouldn't be in this mess. And neither would your little whore of a girlfriend. But you couldn't leave it, could you? Poor, stupid Tolliver. Born dumb to die dumb."

As she spoke, her voice became more resonant, deeper in tone. It was no longer a woman's voice, but a man's—its sound a harsh, angry bark. "So now you both die. She dies, and so do you. All because you had to keep on rooting around like a pig in shit."

Christ. The voice was—no, it couldn't be. That was impossible. And yet—

"You'll be found together, Tolliver. And you know something? Nobody in the entire fucking world will care. You'll be just one more idiot cop who went off the deep end—a poor dumb turd who killed

332

his girlfriend and then himself. An embarrassment to the department. A one-day story on TV and that's the end of it."

There was no doubt now. Hearing that voice, Ben was positive.
Realization rolled over him like a wave of icy seawater. "I know you.
I know who you are."

"Do you, shithead?"

"Yes. I do."

Brian Holland snatched the black wig from his head and threw it
aside.

Without it, he was recognizable but grotesque, as if he were a
parody of himself. His face was done up in crimson lipstick and blue
eye shadow and mascara, and the thinning black hair and the broad
jaw made him look like a man, the garish makeup like a woman. His
freakish appearance was made worse by the way his mouth kept
twisting from a grin to a grimace and back again.

"Take a good look, you fucker," Holland rasped. "Because it's the
last one you get. First she goes, and then you." He raised the pistol,
and turned the muzzle toward Patty.

# *88*

*Stall,* Ben thought. Stall him and keep him talking and watch for a
chance. "It won't work, Holland. My squad knows as much as I do.
If I don't get you, they will."

The lipsticked mouth was grinning again. He swung the Beretta
back toward Tolliver. "Bullshit. Every cop has the same mentality
you do. The IQ of an amoeba."

"We also know why you did it."

Holland sneered. "You flatter yourself, as usual."

"Do I? You got syph, didn't you? Caught yourself a nice fat case
of syphilis from a whore when you were in your boy mode. You used
whores all the time, but when you called to have them come to your
apartment, you gave the service phony names, so they wouldn't
know who you really were. Probably paid that slug of a doorman to
go along with the gag. The whore would ask for Mr. Whatever, and
he'd send them right up to Fifteen C."

The grin faded. "What do you know about where I live?"

"I told you, we know a lot about you. We even know the name of your doctor. It's Kolberg, right? Isn't he the one who pumped you full of penicillin—over two million units at a time? He really turned your ass into a pincushion, didn't he?"

Holland frowned. "Where did you get that?"

It was Ben's turn to smile. "Routine detective work, Holland. What happened, by the way? You had a chancre, but where was it—on your dick? Or on your pussy?"

"Goddamn you."

Patty groaned in pain. She was slumped in the chair, her head lolling.

Keep him going, Ben thought. Keep him going. "And who gave it to you? Lisa Miller? Melissa Martin? Is that why you killed them? Must have driven you even crazier than you already were, running around in that pink cuckoo nest with a dress on while the bugs were eating a hole in your crotch."

His eyes had bright pinpoints in them. "I don't know which one infected me. So I made sure I took care of the one who did by getting both of them."

"But why Patterson?"

"A quirk of fate. I asked for the prettiest blonde Panache had, assuming they'd send me Melissa Martin. When Caroline Patterson came into that suite, I was surprised. And of course, I didn't know who she was, at the time. But then I thought it would be amusing to play a little game with her. So I did. I played several games, in fact. Not the least of which was to decorate her."

"Why did you do that?"

There was an odd expression on Holland's face, as if mentally he was somewhere else. "Why did I do it?"

"Yes, why did you paint her body? Why did you paint all of them?"

The expression became a sly smirk. "I was fulfilling a wish for them, of course. They wanted to be painted ladies, so I helped them attain their goal. Starting with Patterson." He threw his head back and laughed. Then just as suddenly, his face twisted into a grimace. "But there was another reason, as well. I wanted the world to know what they were. Filthy, revolting whores."

"Must have been a hell of a shock, when the first one turned out to be Spencer Patterson's daughter and then the DA assigned you to the case."

"Everyone encounters bad luck from time to time. It's the strong who can surmount it."

"Uh-huh. But why did you do Bellamy?"

"Bellamy? Then you found her?"

334

"Yes. I was there earlier tonight. Found Chang, too."

"One work of art, one frozen Chink."

"All because she was the madam who sent them to you?"

"Of course not, you oaf. When you kept stirring things up, I was afraid she might go back through her records and come up with the curious fact that she had several clients who all seemed to be living in the same place. That somehow it might lead to me."

"And I suppose you did Chang because he got in the way. Or saw you."

"Correct, for once." Again he stretched his scarlet mouth into the demented grin. "Not bad, Mr. Detective. One out of ten or so. That's better than you usually do, isn't it? But in all fairness, I'll also admit that I knew just about everything you were doing. Some of it you told me about, some of it you wrote up."

"My memos to Brennan."

"Exactly."

"Must have made it easy for you, working from inside. For stolen credit cards, or the handcuffs, or any other ID you needed, all you had to do was to go into the detectives' lockers down there, right? Even the keys to Julio Mendez's house were there. True?"

"Of course. These so-called detectives are as sloppy as you are. And as dumb. Leaving evidence lying around in open lockers. Stupidity must be characteristic of the breed."

Patty groaned again. She was glassy-eyed, and blood continued to ooze from the cuts at the corner of her mouth and her neck.

Maybe if I could inch toward him, Ben thought. A foot or so at a time. Get close enough and I'd have a chance to kick his gun hand. He kept his eyes locked on Holland's. "You know what I thought, when I found Bellamy and the houseboy?"

"What did you think?"

"That maybe her assistant had done it."

"Patrick? That simpering faggot. He was as surprised to see me as she was."

"He was there?"

"Oh, yes. But you didn't find him, did you?"

"No, I didn't."

"You know, it's a pity you won't have an opportunity to start all over again. As a uniformed rookie, so that you might learn the fundamentals. I think that's where you're really lacking. You don't seem to know the basics of police work."

"What did you do with him?"

The grin was back. "Did you notice how well equipped that

kitchen was? Overequipped, actually. Probably bigger than the ones in most restaurants. Another example of vulgar excess."

"So?"

"So, Mr. Detective, if you'd done your job properly, really looked the place over, you would have seen that it had every conceivable type of appliance. Including an electric meat grinder, a garbage-disposal unit, and a trash compacter. I put all three of them to work, and presto! No more Wickersham. He became yesterday's fruitcake. The little bit I couldn't get rid of, the stuff I took out of the compacter, I just dropped off in a garbage can on the street in front of a restaurant. Nobody would ever identify what was left as having been a human being at one time. But then, Patrick wouldn't qualify for such a description, anyway, do you think?"

"I think you made a lot of mistakes," Ben said. "By now, my men will be on their way to your apartment. Or should I say your apartments?"

Patty swayed to one side, as if she was about to topple from the chair. Holland dropped the knife to the floor and grabbed her shoulder, steadying her, while he kept the Beretta trained on Ben.

But he was sufficiently distracted for Tolliver to move a step closer.

Holland looked up, and his face grew distorted with rage. "Get back! Back, goddamn you! Do you thing I'm one of those stupid niggers you can handle like a trained monkey?"

Ben stepped backward, raising both hands, palms up. "Hey, take it easy. I'm not going anywhere."

"You're not? *You're not?* That's what you think, Lieutenant. First she goes, and then you, both by your gun!"

The hand holding Patty's shoulder wrenched her around to face him.

She looked at the pistol, and then at Holland. She was whimpering. "Please. Please don't."

He held the Beretta on her for a moment, his painted lips drawn back over clenched teeth.

Then he shot her.

The blast was deafening as the 9mm slug tore into her body with sledgehammer force, knocking her over backward in the chair, leaving her sprawled on the carpet, blood pumping from the hole in her chest.

In one swift motion, Ben scooped the Smith from its holster and got off a shot. But it was hurried, and he missed his target.

Holland fired again, and Ben felt the sting as the bullet singed his right cheek. He turned and dove through the doorway behind him, rolling to one side as he hit the floor, holding the pistol in front of him with both hands.

# 89

B en lay flat on his belly, struggling to catch his breath. He shouted, "Give it up, Holland! Throw your gun out the door and then come out with your hands in the air."

For answer, the Beretta roared twice more, the bullets tearing through the wall an inch above Tolliver's head.

Shit. With one gone, the Smith had five live left in the cylinder. Even after firing three shots, Holland still had twelve rounds—more than twice Ben's firepower. With his left hand, Ben patted down his pockets, hoping he'd find extra cartridges and knowing goddamn well he wouldn't.

*He killed her.*

The thought was numbing, almost too painful for him to grasp. The murdering bastard had shot her down as if she were vermin. Jesus Christ.

He yelled again: "Come out, Holland. It's over!"

This time, there was only silence in the bedroom. Moving as slowly and as cautiously as possible, Ben got to his knees, waited, and then stood up. Holding himself in profile beside the doorway, he strained his ears to pick up any telltale sound from within the room. There was nothing. Somewhere far off in the apartment house, people were shouting, and a woman screamed.

All you have to do is stand here, he told himself. If he tries to run for it, you can nail him. If he stays there, so what—the cops'll be here soon, and you can smoke him out. The neighbors will have called 911 by now. You should be hearing police sirens any second.

But fuck it. *He killed her.* And I'm going to blow his head off.

He thumbed back the hammer on the Smith, knowing the single-action would give him a little more accuracy. With the two-inch barrel, he needed every advantage he could give himself. He took a deep breath and, holding the pistol out front, leapt through the door.

Patty's body lay on the floor, faceup. There was no one else in the room.

The door to the bathroom was ajar. Tolliver ran in there, and saw that the window over the toilet was open. Jumping up onto the toilet seat, he poked his head out the window.

There was a drainpipe nearby, attached to the outside wall, and

337

Holland could have climbed down that. But when Ben looked down, he saw no trace of the man.

Several people had gathered on the sidewalk, some of them wearing bathrobes. They were probably tenants of the building or neighbors attracted by the sound of the shots, and they were looking up, their faces pale and openmouthed. A woman among them pointed upward and shrieked, and instinctively Ben pulled his head back as a shot rang out from above.

Holland was on the roof. Apparently, he'd climbed up the drainpipe, not down it. He figured I'd look down, Ben thought, give him a clean shot. He almost made it.

This apartment was on the top floor; there had to be a stairway somewhere, leading up to the roof. Ben ran back through the rooms and out into the hall.

There was a door at the far end marked KEEP CLOSED AT ALL TIMES. He went to it and pushed it open. Inside, a narrow stairway led up to another door, this one secured with a bar handle. Racing up the stairs, he opened the door a crack and looked out.

There was gray light now; from the east, pale streaks reached across the sky. But on the tarred surface of the roof, he could see steam rising, and that was all. His quarry was nowhere in sight.

Slipping out the door, he crouched low, holding the pistol ready. Holland had chosen a good escape route; these old houses all butted up against each other, and many had flat roofs like this one. You could run the length of the block, going from one building to the next with no problem. The only obstacles were low parapets, and there weren't many of those.

But there were plenty of places to hide. Along the surfaces were dark corners, and the small raised structures that housed stairways, and here and there pitched roofs rising from the flat parts. The question was, which direction had Holland taken?

Logic said it was where the greater number of adjoining buildings lay, most of the roofs obscured by shadows. Tolliver made his way through the gloom, swinging his gaze from side to side, not sure whether Holland had skipped or was lying in wait for him up here somewhere, maybe taking aim at this instant. He stepped over a parapet, thinking a slug could kill him without his ever knowing where it had come from.

The roof he was on now was a narrow strip, tarred like the one he'd just left, and ahead of him on this surface a peak with skylights in it rose another ten feet or so.

He took one step at a time, even though emotion was telling him to run as fast as he could, that if he didn't run, he'd never get the son

338

of a bitch. But he'd seen situations like this before, as had every other cop who'd been on the job for any length of time. Hurry, and you could catch a bellyful of lead.

He was halfway along the roof when he heard a shout from down on the street, a woman's voice. Stepping to the edge, he looked back to where the small knot of spectators had gathered outside Patty's building. He was some distance from them now, but he could see people pointing upward and could hear them yelling.

Suddenly, he realized what had happened. He'd been suckered into wandering from roof to roof like an idiot. And while he was up here following a false trail, Holland had climbed back down and returned to the apartment.

*Why?*

Because the man was crazy, and that was reason enough. Ben turned and sprinted, leaping over the parapet and racing back to the shed covering the stairway.

The door was locked. And the fucking thing was made of metal, security against the burglars who roamed every neighborhood in the city. In anger and frustration, he fired a shot at the lock. The slug merely scarred the steel plate, ricocheting with a high-pitched whine.

God *damn* it. Wasting one of the few rounds he had left was stupid. He looked around, hoping to come up with a way to force the door and finding none.

*The drainpipe.*

If Holland had gone down it, so would he. Running to the edge of the roof, he looked down. There was a gutter there, and the pipe was connected to that. He stuffed the revolver into his waistband and climbed over.

As soon as he put his hands on the gutter, he felt it wobble; probably the strain imposed by Holland's clambering had pulled the brackets loose. Praying they'd hold long enough for him to make the window, he clamped his legs around the vertical pipe and began to shinny down. He estimated the distance to the window to be eight or nine feet.

He was halfway there when the brackets let go further. The drainpipe bent, and he slid rapidly the rest of the way, trying to step on the window ledge but missing it, his foot skidding off the narrow wooden lip.

The window was closed. And undoubtedly locked. Hanging on to the rickety drainpipe with his hands, he drew back his leg and kicked a hole through one of the panes of glass in the window.

At that moment, the brackets holding the gutter to the edge of the roof tore out altogether, and both the gutter and the pipe Ben was

339

clinging to fell away from the building. He had no choice but to let go and try for the window; the alternative was to drop three stories onto a cement sidewalk. He twisted his body, legs flailing, and made a desperate lunge.

One hand caught the window ledge; the other grasped the munion where he'd kicked out the pane of glass. When his lower body slammed into the side of the building, he held on somehow, dangling by a tenuous grip.

Taking a deep breath, he pulled himself up until he could get one knee onto the ledge. Holding on to the munion with one hand, he yanked the revolver out of his waistband with the other and shattered several more panes. Then he jammed the gun back into his pants and hauled himself upward until he could kneel on the window ledge. He was dimly aware that the crowd down on the sidewalk had grown larger; he could hear people shouting.

He was also conscious of pain in his hands. Both palms were slippery with blood; he must have cut hell out of them on the shards of glass left in the window frame. Reaching in, he flipped back the lock and raised the sash.

As he stepped down onto the toilet seat, he saw that the door of the bathroom was closed. Holland had probably locked that, as well. Ben wiped his bloody hands on his pants legs and drew the Smith as he tried the doorknob. He'd guessed right; the door was locked.

Instinctively, he stepped to one side and crouched down, and that saved his life. Bullets crashed through the door, sending splinters flying and filling the air in the tiny room with dust and smoke.

He thought there were five shots, but he wasn't sure. Nor was he sure how many Holland had fired earlier. Four? Five? How many did the bastard have left?

And where the fuck were the cops?

He went to one knee, fighting for breath, his heart pounding, and yelled, "Give it up—there's no way out!"

That brought another shot. But only one; Holland also had to be counting.

The door was a mass of splintered wood. Looking up at it, Ben could see light from the bedroom coming through the holes. He waited for a minute, and then another, the brief passage of time seeming like hours. No sound was coming now from the other side of the door.

He tried again. "You're finished, Holland. You hear me?"

There was no response, but now his ears picked up the distant two-note wail of police sirens from out on the street.

It's about fucking time, he thought.

But Holland would hear the sound as well, and beat it out of here—if he hadn't already. The thought of his getting away was infuriating.

The hell with caution. Tolliver stood up and kicked the door open.

Holland was gone. There was only Patty's naked body, lying faceup on the floor. When Ben stepped into the room, he understood why Holland had come back here from the roof.

*He'd painted her.*

Not in the painstaking manner he'd done the others; there hadn't been time for that. Instead, he'd striped her with lipstick. Her face and breasts and belly and legs were covered with bright red streaks. There were wavy lines and zigzags and crosses and arrows, her body a map drawn by a madman. A circle had been drawn around the bullet wound in her chest.

Ben knelt beside her, feeling a surge of hot, mindless rage. But as he crouched there, he noticed a faint bubbling on Patty's lips.

Placing his head on her chest, he heard her heartbeat. It was faint and erratic, but it was there.

*Dear God—she was still alive.*

He looked at the bullet wound. The slug might have shattered her clavicle and then been deflected. Whatever, she had a chance.

But there was nothing he could do for her at this point—the cops would call an ambulance. What Ben wanted now was Holland. He turned and ran through the apartment once more, racing through the front door and down the hall to the stairs. Somewhere below, he could hear footsteps pounding.

# 90

When he reached the ground floor, Ben heard tires screeching and the police sirens winding down. At the same time, a door slammed at the rear of the building. There was a hallway leading in that direction. He turned the corner and ran to the door, yanking it open.

Like many old houses in the Village, this one had a small walled-in courtyard behind it. A sumac tree stood just outside the door, and the area was overgrown with weeds. The sun was up now, not yet visible from where he stood, but sending weak yellow rays across the neighboring houses. Ben stepped around the tree and saw Brian Holland climbing over the top of the wall.

Holding the Smith in both hands, he took aim and fired, and as his target disappeared, he castigated himself for throwing away still another round. At a range longer than his arm, the pistol wasn't worth a shit. He rammed the weapon back into his pants and ran for the wall.

It was about eight feet high, and he had to jump for a handhold at the top. When he swung a leg over it, he found himself looking into another courtyard, in the rear of a house facing onto the next street.

Holland was standing close to the house. He snapped off a shot that whistled within an inch of Ben's left ear, then turned and ran around the corner.

Four, Ben thought. He's got four left. I think. But if I'm going to make a mistake, it had better be on the high side. He dropped over the wall and ran in the direction Holland had taken.

Out on the street, there was scant traffic, a delivery truck and a couple of taxis. There were also a few pedestrians on the sidewalks, probably people on their way to early jobs. There was also a black hooker, apparently looking for one last trick before calling it a night.

But no Holland.

Ben's gaze swept the street and the sidewalk in both directions, but there was no sign of him. Had he flagged a cab? No—he wouldn't have stopped to try. By the time he got one, Ben would have been all over him.

So where was he?

Damn. Two blocks up there was a subway entrance, the Broadway Seventh Avenue line. That had to be where he'd gone—all Holland would have to do was jump onto a train and in minutes he'd be miles away.

Ben sprinted for the entrance, his lungs burning as he raced along the sidewalk. When he reached the steps, he bounded down them. People were coming up the stairs toward him, which meant a train had just arrived. In a few seconds, the train would pull out, and in all likelihood Holland would be on it.

Ben shoved his way through the departing passengers. When he reached a landing, he turned the corner, and looking down, he saw the turnstiles that led onto the platform.

A commotion of some kind was taking place there; he could see two men struggling. One of them was tall and burly, a skinhead dressed in a Knicks warm-up and jeans. The other was slim and dark-haired, wearing a black leather jacket, and with makeup on his face.

Ben ran down the steps toward them. He didn't know what had caused the altercation; they might simply have collided as Holland ran for the train.

The skinhead shouted, "Faggot cocksucker!" and swung his fist. Holland shot him twice in the face. The blasts from the Beretta sounded like explosions in the underground chamber. The big man went down in a bloody heap as people screamed and fell over each other in their efforts to get away from the shooting.

Ben leveled the Smith. "Holland—stop!"

The grotesque face turned in Tolliver's direction, and the Beretta came up and fired again.

The slug passed so close, Ben could feel the wind. Steadying his pistol hand with his left, he got off two shots. He knew the first was wide, but the second might have hit his target; he wasn't sure.

Holland climbed over the turnstile and scrambled for the train.

Ben ran the rest of the way down the stairs, stepping over the body that was lying on its back, a bloody pulp where the face had been. He leaped the turnstile and sprinted.

The train was pulling out.

Holland reached it, but too late. The doors were shut, and it was picking up speed. He ran alongside, hammering on the metal skin with the pistol.

And then the train was gone. For an instant, he seemed to freeze, then whirled and fired again.

The shot missed.

Now the question was, what did he have left?

None?

One?

Ben had lost count long ago. He held the snub-nosed revolver at eye level, praying the Baretta was dry. If it wasn't, it would be one against one: the 9mm against the .38, each man with one last chance.

Ben took a cautious step forward, aiming for Holland's chest because that would give him the largest target area. As he did, Holland raised the automatic and pulled the trigger.

Nothing.

And then Ben saw why: the Beretta's slide had kicked back and stayed open. The magazine was empty. He felt an enormous sense of relief.

For a moment, Holland appeared not to comprehend what had happened. He looked at the pistol, then threw it aside.

Ben's arms and shoulders were weak, and his legs were trembling slightly. His mouth was so dry it was hard to speak, and his voice was a croak. "That's all—we're going out of here. Step ahead of me. Slowly."

Holland's eyes swung back to fix on Ben, the expression in them still blank. But then his shoulders slumped as he seemed to realize it was over.

Ben gestured with the Smith. "Let's go. Now."

As Holland complied, Ben moved close behind him. They went back through the turnstile, and as they did, Tolliver noticed that a number of people had remained on the other side, gaping.

They passed the man Holland had shot, and Ben glanced down at the bloody form. The wrong place, he thought, at the wrong time.

His gaze went from there to the faces of the onlookers huddled against the wall, their eyes wide as they stared at Tolliver and his prisoner. As he looked at them, he saw the mouths of several people pop open. What were they—?

Holland whirled and swung the knife in a slashing arc.

Too late, Ben realized what had happened and cursed himself. He'd forgotten all about the goddamn knife; Holland must have picked it up when he'd returned to carry out his obscene ritual with Patty's body. Tolliver stumbled backward and the knife blade ripped through his blazer and sliced open his chest.

Holland was on him like a jungle cat, slamming Ben to the concrete floor and straddling him.

Tolliver grabbed the knife hand with his left and gripped it, and for an instant the two men were locked, motionless.

Ben stared up at the figure above him. The wild look in the eyes was exaggerated by the mascara and purple eye shadow; the scarlet lips were drawn back in a grimace.

Straining with the effort, Holland forced the point of the blade downward. "You're scum," he hissed.

Ben jammed the muzzle of the Smith into the painted mouth. "And you're dead." He pulled the trigger.

The top of Holland's head exploded. His body jerked upright from the impact, and then fell to one side.

Ben lay on his back, without the strength to pull himself up. His chest felt warm and wet, and he could hear people screaming and the clatter of feet approaching.

His gaze turned toward the stairs, and he saw two uniformed cops running toward him with pistols drawn. One of them crouched over him, holding a cocked .38 in Ben's face.

"My name is Tolliver," Ben said. "I'm a police officer."

# 91

In the emergency room of St. Vincent's Hospital, a crew of medics intubated Patty's trachea to keep her breathing, then slowed the bleeding from the hole in her chest with pressure dressings. Doctors administered antibiotics and started an IV of packed red cells, and after that took X-rays. From there she was wheeled into an operating room, where a team headed by Dr. Barton Wilkes, a surgeon who had dealt with more than his share of gunshot wounds, spent four hours attempting to repair the damage done by the 9mm slug that had passed through her body.

The projectile had struck the top of her right clavicle, which had deflected it upward and caused it to miss the scapula on that side by less than an inch before exiting her back. Her lung had collapsed, and the muscle and neural injuries were considerable; the round had ripped a cavity through the pectoralis major and the trapezius, as well as severing a number of nerves affecting her arm, shoulder and neck.

The surgeon cut away flesh that had been destroyed by the bullet, and then made an exhaustive effort to rejoin the ruptured muscles and blood vessels, and to mend the torn nerves. When he'd done all he could, he inserted a chest tube and closed the wound, and lastly sutured the cut in the corner of her mouth. The one in her neck was less serious; they cleaned and dressed it with antibiotics and a covering of gauze before sending her off to intensive care.

When Dr. Wilkes came out of the operating room, pulling the mask off his face, Ben was waiting for him. The surgeon was a tall man, and his green surgical gown was smeared red with blood. Random drops had also splattered his glasses and his cap.

Tolliver didn't look too good himself—his shirt was torn and draped loosely over his shoulders, and his chest was heavily bandaged where the people in the same emergency room had cleaned and taped the knife cut Holland had inflicted.

Wilkes frowned as Ben approached. "Who are you?"

Ben showed him his shield. "Lieutenant Tolliver, Sixth Precinct detective squad. I was with her when she was shot."

The doctor took off his gloves and walked into the scrubroom, Ben following. Wilkes tossed the gloves into a receptacle and arched his back, fatigue showing on his face, and then bent over a sink to wash his hands. Other men in the yellow-tiled room paid no attention to them.

Ben was almost afraid to ask. "How's she doing?"

"Too early to say," Wilkes replied. "I'll tell you this, though, she was damn lucky."

"That mean she'll make it?"

"Not necessarily. But I hope so. She's young, and she seemed to be in good shape. The luck was having that bullet deflect up instead of down. If it'd gone the other way, it would've hit her heart. And then forget it."

"Yeah." The sense of relief was like a cool breeze wafting over him.

Wilkes finished washing his hands and grabbed paper towels from a wall dispenser. "There's still a downside, even if she recovers. She'll have trouble raising her right arm, may never get full use again. And she won't be quite as pretty."

"The cut on her mouth?"

"That too. But she also lost a fair amount of tissue."

Ben understood what that meant; too many times he'd seen what a bullet could do to the human body.

Wilkes took off his glasses and washed them in the sink before putting them back on. Then he removed his cap and gown and threw them into the receptacle as well. His gray hair was matted with sweat.

He arched his back once more, rubbing it with both hands. "But the important thing is, she's alive. You know, it's a crazy thing about guns. People see these shows on TV, somebody gets shot, nothing to it. The guy falls down, no blood, and in the next scene he's running around with a Band-Aid. All bullshit."

"I know," Ben said.

"Yeah, I expect you do." He turned to leave. "Have a good day, Lieutenant."

"You too," Ben said. "And doc?"

"Yes?"

"Thanks."

Wilkes gave him a funny look and left the room.

In the days that followed, Lieutenant Ben Tolliver received an official commendation from the police commissioner in a ceremony at One Police Plaza. The media ran a rash of exposure stories with headlines such as MURDEROUS ASSISTANT DA LED SECRET LIFE, and then the case was shoved out of the spotlight by a series of killings in Queens. The trial of the two men who raped the doctor's wife came next, and the prosecutor, a bright young man named Howard Kessler, became a nationally known figure.

A grand jury declined to indict Tolliver in connection with the shooting in Harlem, which inspired another stream of protests by the Reverend Dan Marydale and his followers. After that the Sixth Precinct detective squad resumed normal operations, if working a steady stream of homicides, sex crimes, assaults, burglaries, muggings and assorted lesser felonies could be called normal.

Ben checked Missing Persons, but nothing further turned up on Monica Darrin, the Panache phone girl who'd been so eager to help him. Until one morning he received a letter written on violet stationery and postmarked Youngstown, Ohio, telling him the sender had decided a career in New York wasn't worth dying for. It was signed, With love, Your Assistant.

Patty spent the next two months in St. Vincent's, and four more after that at her uncle Nick's place in New Jersey. Ben visited when he could, each time feeling silly about lugging along a bouquet of flowers he'd bought from a florist on Seventh Avenue. It wasn't until June that she was strong enough to travel. And that was when he finally made good on the promise he'd given her more times than he could count.

Hickory Hill was a two-hundred-year-old inn near Lake Sacandaga in upstate New York. It took almost five hours to drive up there in the Ford, but Patty insisted the trip was no problem, probably because she was determined to let nothing prevent her from making it. Azaleas were out by then, and dogwood blossoms, and they passed through miles of country where the houses were set far apart on green meadows with trees and stone walls and cows grazing. To Ben it was like entering a different world.

The inn was lovely. It had spectacular gardens, and views of the lake, and in the distance you could see mountains looming on the western horizon. Their room featured a four-poster bed with a feather mattress that must have been a foot deep.

As the surgeon had foreseen, Patty was sensitive about the scars. She'd found she could hide the one on her face with makeup, and clothing obscured the larger marks on her chest and back. When she was alone with Ben, however, she was shy about having him see the shiny patches of skin on her body.

She was even more troubled by the fact that the wounds had left her slightly asymmetrical, with her right breast lower than her left. But she was determined to rebuild her damaged muscles by diligently following the program of exercises the doctors had laid out as part of her therapy. One of the routines involved squeezing a soft rubber

347

ball while holding it as high as possible, and she let out a triumphant yell the first time she managed to lift her arm above her head. Ben told her she was a little late to be learning the communist salute, and she transferred the ball to her other hand and threw it at him.

About the only thing he had to be careful of was not to put any weight on her upper body. Which not only presented no difficulty, but led to trying some interesting interpersonal attitudes they'd never experienced before.

As far as asymmetry was concerned, he never even noticed.